MURDER IN LISBON

MURDER IN LISBON

by

Sidney F. Davis
191 Via Perignon
Naples, Florida 34119
941 352 4626

ABOUT THE BOOK

As the flames of war engulf the Continent in 1940 refugees from the war torn countries flee to Lisbon, the melting pot of Europe.

A Pan American Captain is brutally murdered in Lisbon. His friend, Curtis Westbrook, senior Captain for Pan American, flies to Lisbon seeking clues about the murder, but he is soon caught up in the maelstrom of a dangerous and secret mission hatched by President Roosevelt in the desperate attempt to preserve the hopelessly divided French Resistance and the exiled Charles De Guille.

Westbrook flies the flying boat, the Yankee Clipper, from Lisbon to London at the height of the Battle of Britain with two very unusual passengers.

PREFACE

In late 1940, shortly after the death of her lover, F. Scott Fitzgerald, the columnist Sheila Graham flew on a Clipper from New York to Lisbon. The flames of war were beginning to engulf the Continent of Europe. Graham described Lisbon as a city that was "an international whirlpool into which were swept from every direction people of all nationalities, race, colour, and tongues, none wishing to stay, but all forced to remain long days, weeks, and sometimes months awaiting transportation."

CHAPTER 1
ACROSS THE ATLANTIC

June 11, 1940.

Although he'd read the report a hundred times since the California Clipper left New York, he still couldn't understand how such a horrible death could have happened to one of his closest friends.

A distraught Curtis Westbrook, the senior line-pilot for Pan American Airways System, sat on the edge of the bunk in the crew's quarters of the huge Boeing flying boat now approaching Lisbon Harbor for landing. His deep-set blue eyes scanned once again a report from the Lisbon Police sent to Pan American's headquarters in New York.

Finishing the report, he summarized what had happened to Phineas Holloran, Captain of the Yankee Clipper: Whoever had murdered him had first bound him, then stabbed him in the groin with a sharp instrument. After he had bled to death, the murderer threw his body into the river. When found, his body was bloated and disfigured from bites and sting marks inflicted by the creatures of the Tagus. Why in hell did they even have to mention that? The police say they have no clues or motive for the killing. Westbrook noticed the signature of "Joseph Gasparo" as the author of the report. His title, typed below his signature, was "Chief Inspector of the Lisbon Police Department." Westbrook made a mental note to call Gasparo for an appointment as soon as he got to the hotel.

Feeling a light bump and the deceleration of the aircraft as it landed on the choppy waters, Westbrook promised himself the answers would be found. He glanced at his watch and calculated it was 1600 local time.

Peering out the port hole several minutes after landing, Westbrook saw the mooring detail securing the Clipper to the pier. Standing up and stretching his tall frame, he ran his hand through his dark silver streaked wavy hair. After knotting his black tie and putting on his uniform coat, he tucked the police report into his inside coat pocket. Passing through the Control

Cabin, he retrieved his suitcase from the crew's closet, opened the cockpit door, and bid the flight deck crew goodby. Westbrook had been dispatched to Lisbon to bring the Yankee Clipper home.

As he deplaned, Westbrook remembered Holloran as a jovial Irishman, ready to share his love of flying in the company of friends; around strangers, however, he was guarded and shy. Based on what he had read in the police report he thought his murder unusually cruel and senseless. Phineas had no enemies. He was a great guy who minded his own business. Who the hell could've done this sort of thing?

Both of the huge seaplanes were moored about fifty yards apart at the modern Cabo Ruivo Airport, the water facility Pan American leased on the Tagus. It was the largest seaplane facility in the world.

Walking down the pier, Westbrook took in the cloudless sky and fragrant summer breezes mixing with the pungent, salty aromas of the waterfront. He thought briefly of Joanna and how she'd love Lisbon. He had to cancel a dinner date with her to make the flight. He patted the pocket of his uniform jacket, feeling the box containing the one-carat solitaire diamond engagement ring he had planned to give her at the canceled dinner. For some reason it made him feel better.

"It's good to see you, Curtis," Thomas Littleton, the Yankee Clipper's co-pilot said. "We're all glad Mr. Trippe sent you to take us back." He shook hands and patted Westbrook on the shoulder. "Terrible about Phineas. We all thought the world of him."

"Thanks. President Roosevelt called Trippe personally before I left New York. He's very upset about it too, even told the OSS here to offer assistance to the Lisbon Police in finding the murderer." He paused to look at the Yankee Clipper bobbing beside the pier. "What kind of load have we got tomorrow?"

"Only four passengers--two male Portuguese citizens and a German diplomat and his wife. Good deal of cargo though, including about $500,000 worth of gold bullion belonging to a prominent Jewish family in Lisbon. The consignee is a small firm in Philadelphia which is apparently owned by the brother of one of the family members. We're booked into the Aviz Hotel for the evening. Car's waiting to go any time you say."

"I'm ready. Breakfast in the hotel dining room tomorrow with the bridge crew at 0800. Once we're on board issue side arms to the flight deck crew. Also, I want as much biographical data you can get on the four passengers, particularly the Germans."

"Roger," Littleton replied. "I'll check with the Embassy as soon as we get to the hotel."

Westbrook shook hands with the remaining crew members, each of whom he knew, and then walked up the pier with Littleton to the two waiting sedans.

After checking into his hotel room Westbrook called and arranged an appointment with Inspector Gasparo, who seemed pleased that he called.

The twenty five minute taxi ride through the narrow, crooked streets of the ancient Rossario District with its summer flowers in gay profusion and children playing noisily everywhere refreshed Westbrook.

The Lisbon police headquarter was a large, nondescript cement block building built nearly a hundred years before.

Gasparo met him at the reception desk and led him back to his office. Slightly stooped, stocky and simian faced, he appeared to be in his early to mid-sixties and Westbrook sensed an alert intelligence.

"I'm glad I was able to arrange this meeting at your convenience, Captain Westbrook. We're so pleased Pan Am still flies here when so many other services have been disrupted by the war." Gasparo pointed to a chair which faced the front of his desk, cluttered with files. They sat down.

"Thank you, Inspector. I appreciate your seeing me on such short notice. This is my fifth or sixth visit to Lisbon, and I always enjoy coming back."

"Are you going to be flying those magnificent machines here on a regular basis now?"

"I hope so. I'm not `flying the line,' just yet. But we'll see." He paused as Gasparo lit a cigarette, carefully blowing his smoke away from the Captain. "You no doubt have family waiting on you for dinner, so I'll be as brief as I can."

"No, no, it's quite all right," Gasparo assured him. "Take all the time you need. I insist."

"Phineas Holloran was one of my best friends, Inspector. He was tough, but he was also a regular guy. None of his friends, including me, will ever buy the notion that he was up to something no good here in Lisbon. I hope you and your people come up with some answers--and quickly." Distraught, Westbrook buried his face in his hands. His eyes filled with tears.

"I can see how upset you are. Regrettably, though, we don't have all of the resources that the police in most big American cities have. But please be assured I won't rest until the killers have been apprehended. I cannot offer you more."

"Killers? Do you know for sure there was more than one?" Westbrook had regained his composure.

"Not really. Just a hunch. Captain Holloran was a big man who had been restrained for some time before his death. Someone like me is inclined to make certain assumptions in reconstructing the crime, but we simply don't know yet whether there were one or twenty-one assailants, and I'm very sorry if I gave you the impression I'm smarter than I really am." Gasparo gave Westbrook a tired smile.

Feeling frustrated and tired and ready to end the meeting to get some rest, Westbrook stood. "I appreciate your time this evening. Is there anything else you can tell me?"

Gasparo cocked his head. "I fear I've been mysterious, so let me be frank. I have no clues. If I did, I would certainly share them with you, at least to the extent our departmental policy would permit. I can tell you that I'm personally troubled by the fact that this doesn't appear to be a typical Lisbon murder. Too brutal and drawn out. Captain Holloran was probably tortured for several hours before his death. In this city most murders are usually committed in the heat of passion--quick, one bullet, one knife wound. And poof! It's all over." Gasparo extended his hand. "I hope you'll stay in touch."

* * * * *

The next morning the five members of the flight crew, each

4

dressed casually in sport shirts and slacks, were seated around a table in a corner of the colorfully decorated hotel restaurant. Rested, each man felt relaxed and confident about his upcoming duties on the way back to New York.

It was Westbrook's first opportunity to talk to the three other flight deck crew: Wesley Andrews, the navigator, "Dutch" Anderson, the flight engineer, and Hershel Jenkins the radio operator who answered to the nickname of "Sparks."

While two waiters in starched linen jackets hovered over the men, pouring thick, hot black coffee and proffering juice and croissants, Andrews began the early weather briefing. "The early forecast predicts unusually high head winds for a summer crossing, combined with heavy rain squalls that could reach as high as 20,000 feet. These intense cells may produce heavy turbulence, down drafts and lightning activity which may pose a serious risk to any aircraft in the area." He read from a teletype copy of the weather report, and the overtones of the pending weather weren't lost on the seasoned crew. The Clippers rarely flew over 1,000 feet westbound from Europe, which at that altitude would mean heavy sea spray and thick fog close to the surface of the ocean.

Feeling the mood of his crew turning somber as he finished his second cup of coffee, Westbrook said, "Wesley, ask for initial clearance to ten thousand feet. But I don't want the passengers wearing oxygen masks unless absolutely necessary, so try and get a final altitude clearance of six to eight."

"Right, Captain."

"Hull and engine report, Tommy."

"We hit a log taxiing in. There was some minor damage to the hull forward of the starboard sponson. Appears to be a very small crack in the sponson, but it didn't impact the fuel tanks. Not a grounding item," Littleton said.

"Give me a full report when the pre-flight is completed once we get to the airport."

"Aye, aye, sir."

"What did you come up with on the passengers?"

"Not much on the two Portuguese. They both work for a small munitions firm in Massachusetts."

"What about the two Germans? Nazis?"

"Yes. The diplomat, Herr Beck, is from an old German aristocracy and goes by `Count' Beck. He was awarded the Iron Cross First Class in the war for bravery against the British, but the story from the Embassy is that he and Hitler have an uneasy truce for now. While Beck is a member of the Nazi Party, he's still aristocracy, and Hitler just doesn't trust those people. Incidentally--the Count just happens to be Berlin's Ambassador to Portugal."

"Interesting, thanks. Any comments on the preliminary flight plan?" Westbrook asked. He had circulated it among the flight crew as they ate breakfast.

"Looks good, Captain," Littleton said. The others chimed in their approval as well.

"All right, gentlemen," Westbrook said, standing up from the dining table. "We depart at 1300 hours. Meet me at operations at 1100. From the sound of the forecast we're going to have a fairly rough trip, and I want everything in trim before we leave. Tommy, since we have a light passenger load please tell the stewards to reduce the usual galley inventory. Let's keep it light. We have a heavy cargo load and I want to buy all the range we can get."

Westbrook arrived an hour early for the 1100 crew meeting in order to get an advance weather briefing from the Pan Am meteorologist. Ominous clouds were already swirling over the Tagus, and the ground swells in the river were just under three feet, the highest for Clipper water operations. Sunlight was visible through the clouds, so he knew the tops couldn't be too high, but the forecast held no assurances.

The meteorologist shook his head pessimistically. "I'm not sure, Captain Westbrook. You might be better off waiting a day before leaving. It looks like these are going to be the worst storms in three years at least."

"The Count's raising hell," commented Sparks Jenkins, who had just joined them. "He's been saying that if we can't get him to New York by the thirteenth, he'll sue the airline _and_ us. He seems a little hysterical."

"Let's cut the crap," Westbrook said angrily. "If he doesn't get to New York on schedule, it'll be because I made the decision that the only alternative is that we all die tonight. I'd better talk to this guy--has he checked in yet?" The last thing Westbrook wanted or needed was a disgruntled passenger, even with a light passenger load, if the weather was going to be acting up.

"Yes, sir, he and his wife are at the scales now."

Westbrook went down two flights of stairs to the Pan American passenger check-in area located outdoors adjacent to the boarding pier. The only passenger activity was taking place around the large set of scales where the four passengers and their luggage were being weighed. Two porters were standing by the scales, chatting idly with little to do. Since the beginning of the war the modern facilities of Cabo Ruivo had gone largely unused except for Pan American's scheduled bi-weekly service. Great Britain had discontinued its daily Sunderland flying boat service from Southampton as soon as the war started in September, 1939. Occasionally, maritime reconnaissance seaplanes of the belligerents, as well as of the neutrals, would land for service but that was rare.

Westbrook didn't like confrontations with passengers. He had a fiery temper which he had managed to control only over time. Even so, he had long ago admitted to himself how difficult it was to relate to people who paid the price of a small house to fly across the Atlantic and back. He'd grown up on a small dirt farm owned by his uncle just outside of Tallahassee, Florida. He lived with the uncle because his father was a calvary sergeant in the regular army--away most of the time. His mother had been confined to a TB sanatorium in Arizona from which she never emerged. His uncle gave him what he needed emotionally, but had very little to offer him in the way of worldly goods.

His uncle used to take him into the pine forests along the Florida pan handle where he taught him to hunt and shoot all sorts of game. "Just remember to lead your target, Curtis," he would say softly as Westbrook began aiming. He learned to use a gun with unerring accuracy.

Westbrook's father's absences came to an abrupt halt on July 1, 1898. A volunteer in Colonel Theodore Roosevelt's First Volunteer Calvary Regiment, he charged a Spanish fortification on the top of a ridge in the eastern part of Cuba. During the ensuing action, the elder Westbrook lost his right leg from an enemy hand grenade, thrown while he was wiping out a three-man Spanish machine gun nest that was pouring murderous fire down the ridge, inflicting heavy casualties on the Americans. Colonel Roosevelt nominated him for the Congressional Medal of Honor, which was approved by Congress within six weeks.

The hero returned to Tallahassee in January, 1899, but was unable to cope with reality once the novelty of his fame wore off. He drank heavily and was of little help to his brother tending the farm, which was finally foreclosed in 1911. The family lived hand to mouth for the next three years. When he was fourteen Westbrook got a job at the old St. Joe logging camp outside of town. He worked there after school and during vacations. He grew lean and strong working as a lumber jack, saving what money he earned to help the family stay together until he finished high school in 1913.

He wore his cousins hand-me-downs to the small public school he attended. During his sophomore year his math teacher was impressed with his ability to handle math problems at the college level and loaned him a four book series entitled <u>Dave Darrin at Annapolis</u>. The series depicted the life of a super-midshipman at Annapolis in a series of romantic episodes. When his senior year rolled around Westbrook wrote, with his math teacher's help, the newly-elected President Wilson and requested a presidential appointment to the Naval Academy based on his father's Medal of Honor, and was accepted into the class of 1917. He soon learned that <u>Dave Darrin</u> was light years from the real thing, but Westbrook was desperate to escape the drudgery of poverty. He knew Annapolis was his only hope. His musings were interrupted by Beck's loud, angry voice.

Westbrook spotted Beck and the blond woman nervously clutching his arm. "I'm Captain Westbrook, in command of your flight this afternoon," he told them. "We hope to make your flight as comfortable as possible."

Beck was a short man with heavy jowls and a ruddy, mottled face from a lifetime of heavy drinking. "What's this I hear about waiting a day, Captain? We paid a king's ransom for this flight," he said in an agitated voice.

"It's a possibility. There is very rough weather predicted after we leave Horta. Have you met your fellow travelers?"

Beck gave Westbrook a studied look. "We very much prefer to stay to ourselves. Do you understand?"

"Yes," Westbrook said simply, "I do understand. And I want you to understand Mr. Beck, that I'm in command of the aircraft. I will make all decisions regarding its operation and the safety of its passengers and crew. That includes the possibility of delays due to weather."

Without saying a word, the German bowed slightly from the waist and turned his back on Westbrook.

Pleased with his performance, Westbrook entered the Clipper and went up the stairway to the Control Cabin just aft of the cockpit. The other crew members were there, seated around the navigator's table. Sitting down, Westbrook began the pre-departure briefing. The meeting lasted about an hour, and the crew could feel the wind rising as the Clipper strained at its moorings. Westbrook grew worried that the waves might be too high at the time of take-off.

When the briefing was over, Westbrook attempted to settle in the pilot's seat, but couldn't get comfortable. He looked out the cockpit window at the angry gray-green swells of the Tagus. He felt cramped, and as he stared out at turmoil in the water, he remembered standing next to Holloran in a bar. He remembered his smiling, cheerful friend, and also the fact that Holloran was stocky, but a good six inches shorter than he was. As he watched the spray of the Tagus plummet against the pier, he reached down and adjusted the pilot's seat to accommodate his body.

"What about the sponson damage, Tommy? Repaired?"

"Looks fine," Littleton said. "The repairmen here did a good job of patching."

"OK, good. Let's get started."

The four passengers were onboard, the cargo and luggage had been secured and Westbrook was anxious to get underway.

After the flight controls were unlocked and checked, the altimeter set, circuits tested and the propeller revolutions set in low pitch, Westbrook gave the order to start engines. Littleton primed the engines and depressed the starters of the two outboard engines first. Their propellers made a whirring noise as the electric starters slowly cranked them over. Next came the sound of the engines catching, coughing and belching small clouds of white smoke. The Clipper was ready to go. The final weather forecast confirmed Andrew's earlier report of heavy storm activity en route, but there was hope for some abatement about 400 miles east of New York. A final weather check after touchdown in the Azores for refueling would help Westbrook make his decision about going on.

"Lisbon tower, Pan American flight 9032 ready to taxi. Sea state and channel survey report please," Jenkins radioed. Before each Clipper departure Port Authority sailors, using harbor boats, visually surveyed the part of the channel used in take-off for possible debris which could damage the Clipper's hull.

"9032, tower. Sea state max for water operations. Captain's discretion. Harbor patrol reports no visible debris in the area."

"Well, we're OK," Westbrook said with relief.

He signaled the ground crew through the cockpit window to disengage the ground mooring lines from the cleats on the bow of the aircraft. Free from its moorings, the Clipper, carried by the current, moved quickly away.

The crew kept a lookout for rubble and surface traffic in the river, difficult to spot in the incoming fog. Seaplane pilots have a mortal fear of sailboats, which have the exclusive right of way over all motorized vessels on the water. While there was little likelihood of a sailboat being in the Tagus in that kind of weather, nothing could be taken for granted.

Westbrook eased the throttles forward on the two port engines, using asymmetrical thrust to make a gentle right turn out of the harbor into the straights of the river.

Once in the river, he turned the Clipper to a magnetic heading of 275 degrees. Hearing the swells slapping angrily against the hull of the Clipper, he closed the cockpit window, ran up the four engines, pushed hard on the rudder pedals and advanced the throttles to the full takeoff position, 43.5 inches of manifold pressure.

"I'll need your help on the rudders and the wheel, Tommy,"

Westbrook said. He worked the controls hard as the giant plane began moving up the river, bouncing hard on the swells until it gained sufficient speed to level its wings and escape the strong waves clinging to its hull.

Finally, the hull reached up on its step and broke the water with an enormous spray behind it. It was once again a graceful flying machine.

"Final departure clearance received from Lisbon Control, Captain," Sparks said. "Turn to heading 267 degrees magnetic. We're cleared to ten thousand feet as requested."

"Good," Westbrook said. In a half hour he would descend to six thousand feet where the air was more breathable.

Once the Clipper leveled off at its assigned altitude, Westbrook turned on the PA system. "Good afternoon, ladies, or perhaps I should say lady, and gentlemen. We're now flying on our assigned course and will land at Horta in about four and a half hours to refuel. Feel free to leave your seats and walk around if you like. Unfortunately, our weather forecast shows a lot of rain across our flight path, and perhaps some moderate turbulence later this evening, but this should be a minor inconvenience. As you may know, this airplane is constructed from aluminum and is able to withstand a lot of punishment, substantially more than we'll see later on." He hoped his voice didn't reveal his own uncertainty.

Except for a few pockets of buffeting down drafts, light chop and intermittent rain and lightning, the flight to Horta was uneventful. Littleton executed the approach and landing, touching down smoothly into the harbor. However, as they taxied in they noticed the weather was worsening. Large white-capped waves crashed against the shore of the harbor landing site.

Littleton picked up updated weather reports and studied them with concern while Westbrook checked for messages.

Passengers normally took the opportunity to de-plane in Horta and stretch their legs walking along the beach. But since the weather was bad, the stewards decided to set up an impromptu bar and buffet in the main cabin. The Becks remained in their suite, but accepted the head steward Eddie

Brighton's offer to deliver hors d'oeuvres and drinks to their compartment. The two Portuguese businessmen had the main cabin to themselves.

"Bit o'news 'ere, Sir," said a cockney ground crewman, shaking off his rain coat after servicing the Clipper. He was unshaven and dressed in cotton coveralls and a checkered shirt which were both soaked.

"And what might that be?" asked Westbrook, who was trying to finish his amended flight plan listing Bermuda as an alternate landing site.

"Appears a bunch of German submarines jumped a British convoy early tonight and sank the whole bloody lot. 'Eard about it listening to the BBC. Freighters, destroyers--the 'ole lot. This bloody war is so bad. I was at Ardennes during the Big War." The man gave a nervous laugh, revealing the fact that his two front teeth were missing.

There was a strange moment of silence. Then, the rain increased tremendously, sounding like a thousand dervishes dancing on the roof of the tin shack which housed the Pan Am operations facilities in Horta.

"No, it doesn't," a reflective Westbrook replied, his own memories harkening back to that vivid, hot summer day in late August, 1918.

After winning the Navy Cross for gallantry while flying a Macchi M-5 seaplane fighter on a combat mission over the Adriatic Sea near Porto Corsini, Italy, Westbrook was transferred to a land based fighter squadron in France where he quickly made the transition to the bi-wing Spad fighter. He was flying wing on a young Frenchman who was eager to kill the Boche. Instead, the Frenchman made the classic mistake of trying to outmaneuver an attacking German Fokker Tri-plane over Belgium with a tight wing over. The German had him in his gun sights at the top of the maneuver, and by choice, the coward shot at the French pilot, blowing his head away in a bloody mist which Westbrook could see from fifty yards away. The horrible image had stayed with him and his distaste for the Germans had never mellowed through the years.

The two pilots returned to the Clipper with new

meteorological charts. Their thin slickers offered little protection from the driving rain and they were soaked to the skin. There was still a hint of improving weather about four hundred miles east of New York, but that was nearly seventeen hundred miles away. A lot could happen before then, but Westbrook decided to give it a try. He thought he could change course south for Bermuda to avoid the storm. But he found things more complicated when he returned to the bridge. Wesley Andrews, his brow furrowed with concern, advised him that the point of no return would be reached about one hundred miles sooner than usual. At the point of no return the captain, depending on the winds, must continue on course, turn back to the last point of departure, head for a pre-selected alternate landing site, or risk a crash landing in the ocean. Still, Westbrook decided to continue west.

Littleton managed the taxi out, take off, and the climb out from Horta without incident, although evidence of the wind's volatility was apparent during the bumpy take off run.

When Littleton leveled off at six thousand feet, Westbrook turned on the wing landing lights to get a view of the water. Angry, gray swirling clouds, filled with water and dark winds were roiling skyward like phantoms of the night. "These thunderhead build-ups are incredible. Can we take up a more southerly heading, Wesley?"

Before Andrews could reply, there was a sudden, blinding lightning flash followed by a thunderous cascade of rain so thick neither pilot could see beyond the cockpit. Without warning, the giant Clipper, caught in a wind shear, shuddered as though in a seizure and fell sharply off on its left wing, nose down toward the Atlantic, engines screaming like mad demons. Littleton let out a cry filled with terror, his mouth contorted with fear. He was frozen on the controls. The altimeter needle was unwinding wildly, and the airspeed indicator was rapidly approaching the Clipper's "never exceed"--the theoretical breakup speed--of 184 knots.

"Pull up, Tom! Pull up!" Westbrook shouted as he lunged forward and grabbed his control wheel trying to pull it back, simultaneously turning it right in an effort to level the wings, and pushing full right rudder, all at the same time.

Westbrook slammed the throttles of the four powerful Wright Cyclone engines to maximum power, the mixture controls to "Full Rich", and the rpm levers to maximum revolutions. The Clipper vibrated throughout from the surge in thrust.

After several moments, through the miraculous disappearance of the fierce wind shear which created the predicament, the aircraft leveled off, its engines still screaming.

"One hundred feet, we almost crashed!" exclaimed a glassy eyed Littleton, his voice filled with fear as he read the altimeter. "If you hadn't asked for the higher altitude clearance, Captain, we'd all be dead!"

"Easy, easy. We're OK." Westbrook was very disturbed by the shrillness in Littleton's voice, but even more disturbed over the fact that he froze. He began reducing power settings and re-trimming the Clipper. But he admitted to himself that the sudden ferocity of the encounter was very unsettling. It's a game of inches, he thought, literally inches.

"That's salt water," Littleton said, slumped in his seat, his voice now no more than a loud whisper. He was pointing to the crusted spray on the windscreen, dissipating rapidly by the driving rain as the Clipper regained altitude. "I guess we flew through the tops of the waves."

"C'mon, Tommy, cut some slack. Ease up. Let's get this beauty trimmed up and back to altitude." Using the crew-only intercom Westbrook instructed Eddie Brighton to pass through the cabin and check on each of the passengers and survey the interior of the aircraft for possible structural damage from the near free fall. He was very relieved that the passenger complement was as small as it was. A large crowd, with one case of hysteria, could have meant pandemonium.

Westbrook then made another PA announcement, apologizing for the scare but also giving assurances that the flight deck crew felt the worst was over.

The winds were still stronger than forecast, and the rain was driving at a near gale force, forcing large rivulets of water through the seams of the wind screen, soaking the two pilots' trousers even further.

After several quick calculations by Andrews, and on his recommendation, Westbrook altered course sixteen degrees south of the current, assigned heading. Because of the wind direction, this alteration gave the Clipper a slightly better speed of advance over the water. However, Andrews said, "Captain, the Clipper still has only a marginal chance of reaching New York. Westbrook stared at him and knew he was right. Then he said, "Prepare dead reckoning plots to Bermuda, in case diversion is required." The point of no return had been reached, and Westbrook hedged his bet: split the course difference between New York and his alternate landing site, Bermuda, for three hours when the Clipper would be due north of Bermuda. If there was no slacking in the head winds after that time Westbrook would change course to due south and land in Bermuda. Clipper captains often relied on intuition more than anything to arrive at life and death decisions while hunting the wind, the ceaseless quest for favorable tail winds or the least unfavorable head winds.

After dining, the Becks retreated to their suite to read and play gin rummy, where the Count quaffed brandy. The two Portuguese, who stayed seated in the main cabin, alternatively slept and strategized over their new-found opportunities in America.

After flying for another hour and a half, Westbrook and the crew sensed a change in the weather.

"Wind seems to be dying down a little," Littleton said. The severest winds were behind the Clipper, but the rains continued. All the same, the entire bridge crew enjoyed a collective sense of relief.

About seven hundred miles east of New York, the radios began crackling--the static masking a voice filled with despair.

"Can't do much, Captain, it sounds like a distress signal, but no luck in homing in on it."

"Some poor devil floundering in this....."

Westbrook was suddenly interrupted by a much louder voice on the short wave: "Pan American Yankee Clipper, Pan American Yankee Clipper, this is HMS Pegasus, a Royal Navy destroyer escort, broadcasting in the blind. Do you read? Over."

The message was repeated before Sparks could respond.

"HMS Pegasus, this is Yankee Clipper, you're garbled, but we can read you. Over."

After a long pause there came a response. "Right, Clipper, this is Pegasus. We can give you our exact location, but we're about 650 nautical miles east of New York. We're the only survivor of a small convoy that was attacked by a German wolf pack early last night. We've been searching for survivors for nearly twelve hours and are running low on fuel. Going to have to depart shortly, but we're wondering if you could make a circle of the area with your landing lights on to give us one last try at saving some of our mates?"

The cockpit crew of the Clipper was stunned. Littleton began shaking his head in the negative, and started to protest, but Westbrook raised his hand to silence him.

In the weather conditions the Clipper was contending with, landing lights would create a strong reflection off the rain which could disorient the pilots. The heights of the waves would make it virtually impossible to locate rafts or lifeboats in the dark, let alone land the Clipper under such terrible conditions. It was nearly four hours until dawn.

Andrews did a rough calculation. "Based on their estimated position, Captain, the Pegasus is about an hour away. We'd have to alter course several degrees to the north to find her. Our most current weather report from the Continent is over two hours old. I tried to raise the weather station in the Azores about fifteen minutes ago with no luck. It's very dicey--we lose Bermuda as an alternate for one thing, and that's nothing to sneeze about."

"Hand me the mike," Westbrook said, biting his lip as he began to mull his very limited options. 'Pegasus, this is Captain Westbrook of the Yankee Clipper. We estimate we're about one hour's flying time to your position. Presently, we have zero visibility at six thousand feet. Unless you can report more favorable weather than we're having, I'd be risking the lives of my passengers and crew to divert to you. We're also approaching a critical fuel state. Unless we can find more favorable wind conditions, we cannot, repeat, cannot, offer any assistance.

Over."

After a slight pause, another voice, more crisp than the one before, responded. "Good evening, Captain Westbrook, this is Commander Stacey, Captain of <u>Pegasus</u>. We're presently showing overcast skies, only a light rain with a sea state of less than two. We were in that bloody mess you're in now all night, but it left us about 45 minutes ago. Winds here are out of the north-northwest at about fifteen knots, about twenty knots less than before. We know there were a number of survivors from the torpedoing because we've seen flares periodically, although we haven't been able to track down the sources fast enough. One pass by you, nothing more, might save a lot of lives. Over to you."

Westbrook paused, turned and looked at Littleton, who seemed to becoming more agitated. Andrew's face never moved a muscle. "Commander Stacey stand by while we solve some navigational problems and talk to the Company in New York, if we can raise them. In the meantime, give us your exact coordinates so we can plot a flight path. But please understand that at the present time I've neither permission nor the intention of coming to your assistance because of the risks to my passengers and crew. By the way, have you seen any U-boats since the attack? Over." If it was affirmative he would scrub all effort to assist <u>Pegasus</u>.

"Stacey here, thanks very much, Captain Westbrook. We'll be standing by. We had light Asdic contact about four hours ago. Appeared to be a partially submerged submarine, but we couldn't make a positive identification, and the target disappeared. Over and out."

"What do you think, Tommy?" Westbrook asked, testing his co-pilot, but approaching the ragged edge himself.

"I think it'd be a terrible gamble, Captain. From a logistical point of view, we're already in danger of not being able to make New York, or any alternate for that matter."

Westbrook listened to what Littleton had to say, and while he didn't like it, he suspected it was all too true. It still grated on him that Littleton didn't agree with him. <u>No damn balls</u>, he thought. <u>Not a damn one. How could Phineas stand him</u>?

"Company radio, this is Yankee Clipper, come in. Come in, over."

Sparks repeated the radio message three times, and there was only loud static in response.

"Try the wireless," Westbrook said.

Leaning as far forward as he could to look at the weather, he saw stars dancing in and out of the gray clouds. The rain was starting to slacken, but not much. Still, it was the prettiest sight he'd seen since before Horta.

"Wesley," Westbrook said with an added shot of confidence in his voice, "I think you might be able to get a star shot now."

"Roger, Captain. Keep those clouds moving away." With high expectations, Andrews retreated to the astral bubble on top of the Clipper's hull with his sextant in hand.

In spite of repeated efforts, the Clipper was unable to reach New York.

Littleton, who'd been sitting with his fists clutched in his lap, said, "Captain Westbrook, this is unreal. Why are we giving any thought to stopping in the middle of the Atlantic, in total darkness at the risk of some forced landing that may kill us all? With all due respect, Captain, I must disavow what you're about to do--particularly if you intend to try a landing--and warn you that I, in the interests of the safety and well being of this aircraft and all the people onboard, might have to replace..."

Before he could finish the sentence, Littleton felt the cold blue steel barrel of a Smith & Wesson .38 caliber pistol pressed, less than gently, against the nape of his neck.

"With all due respect to you, Mr. Littleton, you'd best get a hold of yourself. The Captain's in command here, and nothing I've seen or the other fellows here have seen, suggests otherwise." George Benson, the burly Chief Mechanic had just come to the bridge to give a damage report from the near spin into the sea. Nobody had noticed his arrival because of the darkness and the pre-occupation with what should be done, if anything, about Pegasus. His lighted Lucky Strike dangled from his lips, its ash red in the dark. He pushed the gun barrel further into Littleton's neck, then withdrew it, clicking the cylinder.

"Tom, what in hell's wrong with you?" asked an angry

Westbrook, turning in his seat to face Littleton. "You're supposed to be one of the best pilots on this whole damn airline. I don't believe--nor do I like--what I just heard. Pull yourself together!"

Littleton was in a cold sweat. His hands were trembling. He couldn't assist in any of his flight duties at the moment if he had to.

His hand went to his brow. "Captain, I don't know. Something's come over me, or feels like it." He clutched at his collar. "I'm sorry for the way I just acted. I didn't mean what I said. I just lost it."

Forcing a weak smile, and again mopping his sweat beaded brow, Littleton faced straight ahead, trying to resume his cockpit duties while Westbrook continued his instrument flight scan as he flew the aircraft.

Westbrook decided--for the moment--to further ignore the incident, but he was troubled by it. And he watched Littleton out of the corner of his eye. Brighton knocked on the door, and entered with a tray filled with mugs of freshly brewed coffee and sweet rolls.

"No discernible structural damage, Captain, just a lot of crap thrown around," Benson said as he picked up a sweet roll and left the bridge.

"Got a good shot, Captain. North Star," exclaimed an excited Andrews as he returned to the navigator's table. "Looks like there's some clearing out there. Tell you exactly where we are in just a few secs."

"We're getting a decline in head winds," Littleton said without emotion.

"Good," Westbrook replied. He wanted Littleton fully recovered because he suspected he was going to need his flying skills soon enough. Both men knew respites from bad weather over the Atlantic could be short, even in summertime. Weather was the constant, potentially mortal, foe of the airmen who flew the oceans.

"OK, Wesley, what if we alter course so we can make one run over the Pegasus? What kind of fuel reserves to New York are we talking about?"

After a few moments of intense calculations, Andrews said, "If the current head winds stay about where they are now, fifteen knots, we should have just less than an hour's reserve. But Captain, all bets are off if we pick up any more."

"What do you think, Tom?"

Moistening his lips with his tongue, Littleton said, "Given what Wesley says about reserves maybe we should go have a fast look and then be on our way."

Westbrook had already made up his mind, but he was comforted by Littleton's apparent turnaround, even though he sounded less than convincing.

"All right, Sparks, try to get the Company on the radio one more time and if you don't connect, try again every thirty minutes. Tommy, take the controls, I'll coordinate the run with Pegasus." Grimacing, Littleton took the large control wheel and placed his feet on the rudder pedals, hoping for the best.

"Estimate thirty-five minutes to Pegasus, Captain, but we need a position update," Andrews said, gingerly sipping his mug of hot coffee.

"Pegasus, Pegasus, this is Pan American Yankee Clipper. Over."

After what seemed to be an interminable amount of static, there came a reply, "Pan Am, this is Pegasus, please go ahead. Over." The voice was Commander Stacey's.

"Uh, right Pegasus, we're diverting toward you at the present time. We're prepared to conduct a twenty-five square mile search pattern for you, but we need coordinates and weather status, over."

The crew of Pegasus, weary and feeling alone beyond all measure, eagerly fed all the data that the Clipper crew needed as they finalized their approach to the search area.

"Better let the passengers know what we're up to," Westbrook said, switching to the public address system.

"Good evening, folks, this is the Captain. We've had a rather eventful evening, and I know the stewards have kept you fully informed of our situation. But something has come up rather suddenly which I wanted to personally tell you about.

"We've been in contact with a British warship which is the

only survivor of a mass sinking of British and Canadian merchant and war ships by German submarines early last night. We've been asked by the captain to make a one time sweep to determine whether there are any survivors. We here on the bridge have done a lot of soul searching, and more importantly, fuel and navigation calculations, to confirm or deny the wisdom of our decision. For humanitarian reasons we feel compelled to do this one-time fly over. It won't endanger you or the aircraft and will cause only a minimal delay in reaching New York. Your indulgence in this matter is greatly appreciated."

Westbrook had barely completed his announcement when there was a heavy pounding on the door to the bridge. It was a frightened Eddie Brighton.

"Eddie, what the hell's going on?" an exasperated Westbrook asked.

"It's Mr. Beck, he's gone crazy. He has a gun, Captain, and wants to see you right away!"

"I'll be right down!" Westbrook shouted. He quickly got out of his chair, retrieved his large leather flight bag from behind the navigator's table, unlocked it, and pulled out his .38 caliber pistol. He checked the cylinder. There were six bullets.

As soon as he reached the Lounge, Westbrook saw the red-faced Beck wild waving a pistol and sputtering some gibberish that he couldn't understand. He was dressed in a blue velveteen smoking jacket and black trousers, his pince-nez clamped firmly to the bridge of his nose.

"Herr Beck, remember me?, I'm Captain Westbrook, senior officer on board. What's the problem?"

"Stand back, Captain, or I'll shoot you. Sit down over there," Beck said, waving a Luger pistol towards one of the upholstered chairs.

Beck was very drunk. And very frightened. Westbrook followed his orders, carefully keeping the .38 out of view by tucking it under his leg as he sat down.

"Have you gone mad, Herr Beck, or is this some type of after dinner charade?" Westbrook asked, crossing his legs, trying to look as relaxed as possible. He was fighting time and he wanted this episode over as quickly as possible.

21

Beck's face flushed with red. "You're the madman, Herr Captain, risking the lives of everyone on this airplane to try and find survivors of sunken ships which you know are in the service of enemies of the Third Reich. America is a neutral country." Beck's speech was getting more slurred and spittle was flying from his mouth. "You cannot be permitted to carry out this folly. Unless I have your assurances that you'll abandon this nonsense immediately, I'll begin executing every American on this flight, beginning with your young steward and ending with you. Do I make myself clear?"

"Very clear indeed," Westbrook said. He suddenly realized he'd seriously underestimated Beck's resolve. "But I wish to make it clear that if there are any survivors still alive in the ocean, they're sailors from unarmed merchant ships who were sunk without warning by submarines from your country. We only plan to make one fly-over and then head directly to New York. We've no intention of engaging in any form of hostile activity. The Clipper is an unarmed civilian transport. If the tables were reversed we'd do the same for you. Please give me your pistol and we'll consider this matter closed." Westbrook extended his left hand and his right hand unlocked the safety on his Smith & Wesson.

Beck was not to be mollified. "Nein!" he shouted, as he began to look wildly around the cabin. Now, he seemed confused.

Beck's wife made a hasty retreat to the luxury suite and the two Portuguese passengers tried to look as though they were preoccupied, oblivious to the controversy.

Two thirds of the way down the spiral stair case, John Warner, the backup navigator sent by Littleton to see if Westbrook needed aid, spotted Westbrook sitting in the chair apparently doing nothing. Puzzled, he called to him, "Captain, we have contact with the Pegasus, and ..."

Startled, Beck wheeled around towards Warner, and fired two shots. The first shot hit Warner in the shoulder and spun him around, causing him to lose balance and fall backward down the stairs. The next shot missed and embedded in the forward bulkhead of the Lounge.

Beck then spun around, and fired blindly towards the seat that Westbrook had been sitting in, but Westbrook had dived behind one of the sofas.

Westbrook was furious. "You've shot one of my crewmen, Beck. Now, either put down your gun or I'll kill you. Every crewman is armed so you have no chance."

Beck fired his Luger at Westbrook. The bullet hit the upholstery, sending a puff of fiber and dust into the air. The two Portuguese passengers began cursing at Beck and Westbrook, further agitating Beck. His pince-nez slipped from his nose, and dangled from its ribbon affixed to his vest pocket.

"Captain, bridge," Littleton said anxiously over the public address system, not aware of what was transpiring in the Cabin. "Captain, we've got contact with <u>Pegasus</u>, and we're about fifteen minutes until closing. Can you advise from the cabin?"

Westbrook was worried that Littleton might panic if he couldn't get some kind of communication to him. Also, he saw Warner lying in a growing pool of his own blood. He badly needed assistance. But Westbrook knew he couldn't do anything until the confrontation with Beck was resolved. He decided to shoot him if he couldn't disarm him. He would give it one more try.

Westbrook dropped into the aisle next to his seat, exposed, but only if Beck looked directly his way. Beck now seemed to be totally confused, staring around the cabin with glazed eyes. One of the Portuguese passengers made a small waving gesture towards Beck, saying in broken English, "Senhor Beck, we are sympathetic towards what you are doing, but please stop now."

Ignoring the plea, Beck spun around once more, hunched over, and emptied his pistol onto the cabin floor. Then he dropped it. He threw himself into the aisle, sobbing uncontrollably as he drew into the fetal position. Westbrook, his pistol pointed at Beck, hammer cocked, cautiously walked over to him. He gently but firmly helped him to his feet and led him to the crew's cabin on the second deck. Westbrook helped him out of his jacket and hand-cuffed him to one of the crew's sleeping cots.

"Try and get some sleep. You'll feel much better after we

land. I'll send your wife up here to be with you in a few minutes." The sobbing Beck was struggling to regain his composure.

Westbrook rushed back to the bridge. Eddie Brighton had begun doctoring the injured Warner, who was sitting at the navigator's table, grimacing in pain. "Status report, Tommy."

"Damn rain cutting in again," Littleton said. "We should be about two minutes from Pegasus, Captain. They're reporting local rain squalls with one-to one-and-a-half miles visibility."

"OK, take her down to six hundred feet and hold her steady." The visibility was too poor to see anything more than whitecaps.

"We're right on, Captain, Andrews" said. "Best I can tell we've got about two foot...jeez! What the hell was that?"

Westbrook had seen the same thing from the cockpit, an image from an earlier time in his life. Another war.

The Clipper had just sped over a grey, whale-like form, barely discernible, but Westbrook knew what it was: a submarine, no doubt German.

"Six hundred feet, Captain." The turbulence was bouncing the Clipper around like a toy.

"Right, illuminate all lights, and standby. Pegasus, Clipper..." Westbrook didn't have time to finish his sentence before the Clipper roared over the small destroyer escort, which seemed to be floundering in the sea, all lights on, a searchlight pointed skyward.

Littleton was doing good work in holding the Clipper at altitude, as the external lights played havoc with his depth perception.

"Pegasus, Yankee Clipper. You apparently have a German submarine about one thousand yards off your port quarter. It's on the surface, but we couldn't see any running lights. It may be damaged, but we don't know for sure. Why the hell haven't you detected it?"

"Clipper, Pegasus. We stood down from general quarters about two hours ago, but we're going back to full battle conditions now. We think the bloody U-boat is in trouble. Could you possibly give us one more pass?"

Yankee Clipper was headed west, no survivors spotted.

Littleton shut off the outside lights. Andrews, his brow deeply furrowed, a half filled mug of cold coffee clutched in his left hand, was huddled over the charts and fuel tables, carefully measuring the options left. One thing everybody knew was that they were fast diminishing.

"Can't get another star shot just now, Captain. The weather's mucked up again."

"I know, I know. Why wasn't <u>Pegasus</u> more attentive? They're liable to get their collective asses blown out of the water."

"Yankee Clipper," the radio crackled. "This is Pan Am New York, calling in the blind, can you read?"

"Ignore them until I decide what the hell we're going to do here," Westbrook said. "Let's do a one-eighty and climb up to fifteen hundred feet. Don't turn on the lights again until I give you a `mark.' Don't dump any flares either, might start oil fires."

As the Clipper banked back towards the east, a light pink glow filtered throughout the cockpit, gradually growing in intensity. As the airplane leveled out on its new course, the entire flight crew froze in silent horror.

"Oh, no!" Littleton exclaimed.

The <u>Pegasus</u> was bathed in a wall of fire, distinguishable only as a twisted hulk of burning metal, painting the sea in a false dawn. The ship seemed to be dissolving.

Westbrook felt like something had knocked the wind out of him. The approaching scene came straight from Dante.

"Throttle back to eighty knots," he said softly. "Standby for the `mark.'"

As the Clipper approached the burning ship, Westbrook ordered the landing lights on. "All right, mark. Everybody keep a sharp eye out for survivors and the submarine."

"Saw 'em, Captain, must be twenty or thirty men. Some in life boats, but I didn't see many," Sparks said.

The fire below made an eerie glow on the underside of the Clipper's wings as it passed over the burning ship.

"Hold course for another two minutes. Leave the lights on and descend to five hundred," Westbrook ordered.

Almost by osmosis, it dawned on the crew what Westbrook

had in mind.

"It's madness, Captain. Sheer madness," said Littleton, who was still flying the Clipper, his arms aching from his long stint at the wheel. Westbrook ignored him.

"Winds out of the west at about fifteen to twenty knots, Captain, best I can tell," Andrews said, almost as on cue. "The waves look like they're cresting at about two feet, maybe a little more." No Clipper could land when waves were three feet or more. Marginal. A poorly executed landing would certainly result in the plane being crushed by the waves. It was all up to Westbrook.

"OK, Tommy, I've got the controls. Has anybody seen the submarine?" Westbrook inquired. All the responses were negative.

"Sparks, now you can contact the Company and tell them that we're going to make an open sea landing to pick up survivors from HMS <u>Pegasus</u>. Ask them if they can find out if there any Navy or Coast Guard ships in the area that can be dispatched out here in case we don't make it."

"Captain, Captain," Littleton said, "you're putting your whole career on the line. I'm not afraid of...."

Westbrook's knuckles turned ivory-white as he gripped his control wheel. "Then why don't you begin acting like you're not afraid," said an angry Westbrook. "It's time you got a hold of yourself. You're a critical part of this team, and I need you. But if you can't cut it, relieve yourself. I'm not prepared to let men die in the open sea because we weren't willing to take a calculated risk. Give me twenty degrees of flaps, put the mixtures full rich, 2100 rpms, and close the cowl flaps. If I hear anymore crap from you, you're going to join the Count, hand-cuffed to a cot in the crew's quarters."

Given the stress placed on the Clipper earlier, Westbrook took his control wheel and rotated it to check that he had full throw of the ailerons, then pumped his rudder pedals to insure they were fully functional. Satisfied, he turned into the wind and began reducing power. The die was cast.

CHAPTER 2
ACROSS THE ATLANTIC

"Anybody seen the submarine yet? It's fish-or-cut-bait time," Westbrook said as he finalized his approach to landing.

Westbrook was struggling with the control wheel and throttles as he fought to lose altitude against the updrafts and occasional high waves. He wondered to himself if he had gone crazy, or partially so at least.

That no further submarine sightings had been made reassured no one. Everyone knew one was out there--and close.

The Portuguese passengers had remained fairly docile after the Beck incident, but later, when Westbrook had announced his plan to land if at all possible and rescue survivors, they became hysterical.

"Senhor, we cannot swim! We cannot swim! Please don't do this! It is a violation of our rights as Portuguese citizens! We are neutral in this war. Please don't drag us into this!"

"Two hundred feet," Littleton said stoically as the Clipper began its final descent.

No longer confident of his co-pilot, Westbrook went down the final landing checklist himself. "OK, here we go, full flaps," he said pushing the flap handle to its full down position, as he began his final flare at fifty feet over the water. Pulling back on the wheel to raise the Clipper's nose to the landing attitude, Westbrook eased most of the power off, nursed it gently onto the air step just above the water, then pushed the wheel slightly forward, and closed the throttles. He was lucky. The Clipper settled nicely into an ocean trough, only wallowing slightly as its forward speed dissipated.

Its power gone, the Clipper began drifting toward the area where <u>Pegasus</u> had gone down. The intense oil fire was lighting up the water as if it were noon.

"It's an inferno," Westbrook said to Dutch Anderson, the flight engineer, who was busy securing non-essential switches on his panel. "Soon as you're finished set the sea and anchor watch to help look for survivors. Too deep to lower the anchor, so we'll have to keep an eye on the drift."

On instruction from Westbrook, who descended to the main cabin where Brighton had opened the entry doors, Littleton stayed in his co-pilot's seat. He was appalled by the carnage he could see from his side of the cockpit. Pieces of bodies, burned corpses, now grisly flotsam and jetsam, afloat in the mighty ocean.

The two stewards inflated the two large rubber life rafts stowed on the Clipper and shoved them out of the doors into the ocean, which appeared to be on fire, in hopes the survivors would be able to reach them. There was nothing else they could do.

Some of the more able survivors began swimming slowly towards the Clipper. The first few taken aboard, oil-soaked petty officers and seamen ranks, were exhausted, grateful, and angry. The senior officers of the ship, they said, had become preoccupied with the arrival of the Clipper and in their obsession with rescue, they had lost all sights on defensive behavior.

"What's the normal complement of a ship like <u>Pegasus</u>?" Westbrook asked one of the older petty officers, who was soaked in bunker oil, hunched on the cabin floor shivering. His teeth chattered when he answered.

"About sixty, sir. Including six officers, and four senior petty officers like me."

Westbrook was increasingly apprehensive about the U-boat. The Clipper was lit up like a New York skyline, so the survivors could find their way, most of them stupefied by the ferocious shock of the attack and the brutality of the open sea. Their water and oil soaked clothes impeded their ability to make much headway towards the Clipper.

"Do you have any idea how many men survived the attack?" Westbrook asked.

The old man wept profusely, partly from shock, partly from petroleum irritation, but mostly from the recognition of loss of friends and colleagues. He rocked back and forth from his squatting position in the aisle of the Lounge.

"No, sir, I don't. All my mates are gone. They was killed when the first torpedo hit. The captain, Lieutenant Commander

Stacey, was on the bridge with his Number One, when we was hit, but I ain't seen neither one since the attack."

"Captain Westbrook, please report to the bridge," a voice said over the PA system. It was George Benson, Chief Mechanic, so Westbrook took it as serious business. As he climbed the staircase to the bridge, the acrid odor of heavy fuel oil filled his nostrils.

When he returned to the bridge, Westbrook found Littleton slumped in his seat, staring vacantly.

"See anything yet?" Westbrook asked.

Littleton stammered, as though aroused from slumber, and said, "Captain, I'm...I'm, well, this whole thing is bizarre."

Westbrook shot a side glance at him, thinking he was totally out of his element.

"OK, Tommy," he sighed wearily. "We're both tired, but we're nearly there. Give me your best for the rest of the flight and then do what you think you have to do."

Littleton was visibly relieved. "Thanks, Captain. Let's get on with it."

A concerned George Benson, hunched over Dutch Anderson's instrument panel, looked up. "Captain, we need to get the hell out of here, and right now. We're having serious overheating problems with number two and three engines, and we sure as hell don't want to blow some jugs on takeoff. Also, those sailors I've talked to are certain that the German sub is still around."

The smell of bunker oil permeated the bridge of the Clipper. Along with the pitching waves, it had already caused nausea among the passengers and surviving sailors in the cabin. Mrs. Beck had long since retired to her suite, fearful of what awaited her husband in New York.

After receiving status reports from all crew members that every body and every thing was secure, Westbrook brought the Clipper around to its takeoff heading. After the aircraft had swung clockwise sixty degrees, he saw something. He immediately pulled the power off, and the Clipper's nose settled into the Atlantic, its momentum decelerating.

About sixty yards away, dead in the water with no lights,

was a submarine. Westbrook winced, as though in terrible pain. He had no doubts it was German. His worst fears had been realized and he felt it was over. The submarine could sink the Clipper and nobody would be the wiser. His mind began racing. Westbrook buzzed Brighton on the crew intercom. "Eddie, find the senior officer or non-com from Pegasus and get him up here on the double."

In a few moments Westbrook caught a glimpse of an oil soaked man approaching the bridge with Brighton. From the soiled uniform, it was impossible to distinguish his rank.

"This is Commander Stacey, Captain," said a smiling Brighton, proud of delivering the Captain of the Pegasus. Stacey appeared to be in shock. His eyes were dull and he had two lacerations on his left cheek and chin which had been bandaged by the Pan Am stewards. "Evening, Commander, let's get down to business. Here are my binoculars. Please look dead ahead."

"Bastards!" Stacey exclaimed. "We were sitting ducks...hold on! Hold on! There's something wrong here."

Stacey adjusted Westbrook's binoculars, bringing the U-boat into as sharp a focus as he could with the sea still choppy and his hands shaking. "Skipper, that bloody U-boat's in trouble! It's down slightly by the starboard bow, and her deck's awash. I don't think she can submerge. That's got to be the one that did us in."

"What do you think she might have in mind?"

"I really don't know. She knows you picked up British sailors, which very well gives her a reason for sinking us, but I'd gamble she won't. It'd be enough to bring the U.S. into the war. Couple that with the fact that she's wounded and has to be very careful to survive the long journey home, all suggests she'll do nothing. She's got a lot to sort out. I'd bet she's asking for instructions right now."

Westbrook was impressed with how quickly Stacey, still shaken from the agony of losing his ship with most of his men, could analyze the situation.

"Thank you, Commander, you've been a great help. Please return to the cabin. We'll be getting out of here shortly.

"Flash the Aldis lamp, Sparks. Tell them to stand clear of seaplane operations being conducted in international waters under orders from the United States Government."

Several moments after the message had been sent, Westbrook and Littleton, in their seats, cockpit windows open, saw the muzzle flash from the sub's .88 millimeter cannon. The shell could be heard from the bridge of the Clipper as it made a whooshing noise across its bow, exploding in the ocean less than twenty yards away.

After debating his options for several minutes, and concluding that he had none, Westbrook saw a green flashing light from the sub. Assuming that the green light had its international meaning for clearance, Westbrook cautiously applied power to finish the turn into the wind, put the throttles to maximum power and struggled with the wheel as the great airplane began pitching in the open sea, resisting the command to fly. Then suddenly, the Clipper surged onto the step and lifted gracefully into the air.

While the Clipper was on the water Andrews had been able to get some star shots and a fair estimate of the winds.

"What's the bad news, Wesley?" Westbrook asked, scanning the horizon as the Clipper roared westward, climbing to three thousand feet. His concerns now focused on the remaining fuel supply.

"Hold on a sec, Captain, I'm close. Believe it or not, I think we can make LaGuardia. The winds shifted with the passage of the front, and we actually have a light tail wind. If we lean the mixtures as much as we can, we should be on the money. Close, but we should make it."

Westbrook felt as if he'd been given a reprieve from the electric chair. He knew if he had to make another landing in the open sea to take on fuel, his career with Pan American was irretrievably lost; the Civil Aeronautics Authority would revoke his pilot's license without fail.

Westbrook was one of the best trans-oceanic pilots in the business, but he knew Beck and Littleton, especially, could mean trouble. Still, the saving of eighteen British sailors was satisfaction enough for him.

Beck could obviously be heavily discounted because he had become violent, wounding an American crewman. And he was drunk out of his mind in the process. Still, he was a high ranking diplomat of the Third Reich and could generate a lot of propaganda. He decided to take his chances with Beck. Beck had been way out of line, Nazi big-wig or not. Westbrook didn't believe the fellows who would direct the inquiry would be sympathetic to a Nazi hothead. Westbrook debated with himself over whether, at least technically, he had provoked a German warship on the high seas, possibly endangering America's neutral position in the war by violating the much publicized Neutrality Act.

Littleton could be another story. A seasoned pilot in the Pan Am system, he, like Westbrook, was a certified Master Ocean Pilot with thousands of hours of flying time. The only reason he was flying co-pilot on this trip was that Holloran had hand-picked him to back up what he thought might be his own somewhat rusty skills. Phineas had not been flying a regular line of time for some months, and wanted a steady hand to deal with the difficult and tricky landing and take off at Lisbon. Otherwise, Littleton occasionally flew the Clippers across the Atlantic to Europe, but most often flew the older Martin flying boats from Miami to South America. He wondered again why Phineas had picked him for the trip, and he needed to find out where Littleton really stood.

"OK, Tommy, we're leaned out about as much as we can. Feeling better?" Westbrook asked.

"Tired, Captain, really tired," Littleton responded with a wan smile. "This night has got to beat all, but I want you to know I'm proud of the way you acted and ashamed of the way I did. I wouldn't have had the courage to do what you did."

"It's a relative thing, Tom. I watched one of my best friends, an Englishmen, ram a German barrage balloon at the front very near the end of the war. The damn balloon was over our lines and could have been shot down by small arms fire." Westbrook's adrenalin had receded after the sub encounter, and he was tired. Recalling the story made him feel angry and sad. His voice was muted. "But, no, good old Henry had to give his life by ramming the damn thing in an SE-5. Went down in a ball of flames. I couldn't have done that in a hundred years for anybody. To me it was unnecessary, wasteful. Hell, the war was over.

"The problem is, you just forgot who's in command. Let me tell you up front I expect no favors at the board hearing which is sure to come."

Littleton's silence indicated the message that Westbrook expected to hear: "No commitment."

The pins and needles were tingling in both feet from having been in his seat for such a long time, so Westbrook gave the controls to Littleton and stifling a yawn, stood up, stretching as far as he could.

"Sparks, get me the Company on the radio. Ask for Charlie Sikes." Westbrook was standing near the navigator's table, a mug of fresh coffee in his hand.

After a pause, Sparks said, "Company's on the radio, Captain. Mr. Sikes."

Westbrook picked up the microphone and pressed the speaker button. "Evening Charlie, Curtis Westbrook. It's been a long journey."

"Curtis, what in the fuck is going on? Have you taken leave of your senses? Trippe's worried you crashed!"

Sikes, Pan Am's profane, veteran vice president for operations, loved Westbrook like a son. He had checked him out on every line he'd become qualified to fly, and news of his adventures of the evening had unnerved him. He had come into his office at 0400 after the duty radio operator at Pan Am operations woke him at home with a phone call to tell him Flight 9032 had failed to make several routine position reports.

"The worst is yet to come, Charlie. Herr Beck, the German Ambassador to Portugal, is in hand-cuffs in the crew's quarters. He was deep into the sauce, went berserk and shot our back up navigator after I announced that we were landing to pick up the British sailors. You better call the F.B.I. before we land."

There was a stunned silence on the New York side. "Jeez, Curtis, what haven't you done this evening?"

"Shit, Charlie, what the hell's the problem? We have some English sailors who wouldn't be around now if it hadn't been for us."

Westbrook didn't use much profanity, but with Sikes, it

always seemed to give him a comfort level that brought things into quick focus, and he needed to focus on the safety of his passengers and crew.

"Charlie, it's going to be as dark as the ace of spades when we touch down. Can you arrange to have some fire boats in the river with their lights on?"

"Fuel warning light on," Littleton said excitedly before Sikes could reply.

A new tension gripped the cockpit. There were no signs yet of the New York skyline.

"OK, Charlie, we've got low fuel state. Looks like we're about thirty minutes out. No sign of land yet. Should we switch to the tower or will you get the clearance?"

"Standby here," Sikes replied. "We'll get you set up for your approach, alert the tower and turn you over to them on final. How many gallons?"

"Twenty-five," Andrews replied tersely, distressed it was less than his earlier estimate.

"That ain't going to cut it, lads," Sikes said grimly.

"Yes it is, Charlie," Westbrook said. "We're leaned out so much we're practically running on air. We'll make it, but make sure the channel is clear. We won't have a second chance. Any sea fog?"

"Negative on the fog. Just got a sign the tower's standing by and approach control will call in a sec. I'll get the boats. See you guys soon."

Westbrook noticed a faint light on the horizon. "Looks like the skyline at about the eleven o'clock position," he said. He had to make a critical decision soon: land in the ocean again in the dark or stretch for the channel at LaGuardia, which meant lights but also the risk of fuel exhaustion and crashing in the middle of Manhattan. He took over the controls.

"Number one is starting to cough a little," Anderson said.

Westbrook eased the number one throttle forward to pump more fuel into the outboard engine on the left wing. The engine coughed again, then began to run more smoothly.

"Fifty miles to touchdown," Andrews said. "Twenty gallons remaining. The tail wind may save our butts yet." During normal operations the Clipper would still have in excess of one hundred gallons.

"Yankee Clipper, New York Control. Over."

Suddenly, the Clipper's two outboard engines sputtered and stopped.

"Feather one and four, Tommy!" Westbrook shouted as he advanced the throttles on the two remaining engines in an effort to maintain altitude.

Westbrook made his decision. "We have an emergency, New York. We need a straight in, and I mean straight in!" Westbrook said. He was now beginning to sweat as he fought loss of altitude. "We've lost number one and four engines and we need straight in to Rikers or we're going to have to ditch in the ocean. We're coming straight up the East River to avoid the buildings, but we're losing altitude."

"Uh, OK, 9032, you're cleared. Steer a magnetic heading of 265. Wind is following at 087 degrees, gusting slightly at four to seven knots. Fire boats are moving on station and we expect lighting momentarily. Please keep us advised if you need more assistance. Switch to tower frequency 111.0."

Littleton successfully feathered both of the dead engines, stopping the propellers from wind milling and creating additional, unwanted drag.

The Clipper was losing altitude and there was nothing that could be done about it. Westbrook flew up the East River, and by the time he reached the Upper East Side the aircraft was below the skyscrapers on his left. Normally, during landing operations, the Clippers flew up the Hudson River, west of the East River, to allow an easier and more comfortable turn to the final approach towards the Long Island Sound, but Westbrook didn't have the luxury for such a maneuver.

After flying for fifteen seconds past the northern tip of Roosevelt Island, Westbrook initiated a bank to the right, increasing it as sharply as he dared.

"All fuel gauges read empty, Captain," Littleton said, his voice without emotion.

"There's got to be some vapors in there," Westbrook said, only half kidding.

Descending through six hundred feet, still in a right bank, Rikers Channel came into view. Westbrook ordered full flaps and began to roll out of his bank to align the Clipper with the center of the Channel. He ordered the landing lights on, and, as if on cue, the fireboats turned their lights on, turning night into day on the water.

Westbrook advanced the throttles on the two inboard engines, and raised the Clipper's nose very slightly to compensate for the downwind landing. The stall warning buzzer went off, so he quickly lowered the nose to pick up some more air speed. Seconds later, the last two engines quit, their propellers wind milling noiselessly.

It was going to be a dreaded "dead stick" landing, and Westbrook tensed for it. "Forget about feathering, Tommy. Get on the wheel with me; we need to make it as smooth as possible." Passing through five hundred feet, the two pilots joined together pulling the large control wheels back slowly. Flaps were set to maximum down, fifty degrees. The Clipper landed hard and fast, shooting a spray of water thirty feet high. Anderson immediately shut off the engine magnetos and fuel lines, and after a short distance the Clipper came to a stop in the choppy waters of Rikers Channel. The fire boats extinguished their lights and the bridge crew could see that a gentle dawn was breaking. Both pilots slumped in their seats, letting the rush of adrenalin recede.

Littleton called the tower and asked the status of a tow to the ramp.

"Tugs on the way, sir. We're sure glad to see you and congratulations on the pick up. You guys are real heroes."

Littleton couldn't believe his ears. "Heroes? Us?"

"No," Westbrook said quietly. "We're not. We're lucky sons of bitches who did a good deed."

"Clipper, Company, over."

"Go, Company, this is Clipper," Sparks replied.

"Can you give us a status report on the English sailors? About how many will need hospitalization? Over." Sparks looked to Westbrook for guidance.

Westbrook was fighting the fatigue that had crept over him

after the Clipper had come to a stop.

"Tell them we don't know, Sparks. At least one has died, so they should assume all of the survivors--seventeen, I think--need serious medical attention."

Sparks relayed the message.

"OK, Clipper, we copy. There will be ambulances as needed. Can we get a preliminary report on damage control?"

"Don't know that either," Westbrook replied. "Soon as we do a walk through somebody will give you a call."

Suddenly, Sikes bore into the cockpit at blinding speed. He had a dead Havana cigar clenched between his teeth, his straw boater was pushed down over his ears. He was wearing a very rumpled blue, summer cord suit and black spectator shoes which badly needed a shine. "Curtis, you son of a bitch, you sure have attracted some attention. Reporters have been driving Trippe crazy. He's on his way to the Terminal now and wants to see you as soon as possible. Some fucking bureaucrat woke him early this morning saying there was going to have to be an investigation and you might lose your license. Trippe told him what to do with his pretty badge, but we ain't heard the last of it."

"Anything from the Krauts?" Westbrook asked, as he stood up, stiffly, to shake hands with Sikes.

"Not a word, but don't rule them bastards out."

"Charlie, that Nazi U-boat we saw was in deep trouble. Can we do anything to let the British Navy know about it? Wesley has the coordinates of where he was not more than four hours ago."

"Have Andrews feed us the numbers and we'll pass 'em on to the War Department. In case you don't remember, we ain't at war with the Germans, so let's remember Roosevelt's re-election pledge: none of our boys are going to war. OK?"

"Sure, Charlie. I'm...we're all dead tired. Let's get out of here and we'll talk about it later."

A red ocean tug and several ambulance boats were on their way to the Clipper.

Westbrook worked his way to the main cabin, leaving Littleton to secure the cockpit and oversee the deployment of the sea and anchor detail. Without power, Yankee Clipper had to be anchored as quickly as possible to avoid drifting.

The stench of bunker oil still permeated the Lounge, but it was satisfyingly clear to Westbrook that his stewards had done an admirable job of making the rescued sailors as comfortable as possible with the limited medical resources available.

Westbrook retreated to the aft luxury cabin, where the two Portuguese businessmen and Frau Beck had been moved after the landing at sea. Westbrook extended his hand to Frau Beck, who had obviously been in tears for the last few hours. It occurred to him then that he had promised the Ambassador that his wife would join him shortly after he was locked up. Westbrook had forgotten it.

"I'm terribly sorry, Frau Beck, but your husband got out of control. Shooting one of my crewmen was totally beyond anything a rational person would have done."

Westbrook got a cold, silent stare for his efforts. He realized she spoke no English, and noticed her face was etched with fear. The two Portuguese passengers were all smiles, and thanked Westbrook profusely, happy to be alive.

Westbrook spotted Stacey, who was preparing to go ashore. "Captain, thank you," Stacey said, tears in his eyes, clasping Westbrook's hands. He had managed to clean up a bit. "You've been a savior for a lot of us, and we thank you. 'Fraid I'm in for a bit of trouble, though."

"So am I, Commander. We do what we have to, don't we? I'm curious, though, Commander, how did you know to call 'Yankee Clipper' last night?"

Stacey smiled broadly, and said, "Right after the war started and the convoys were formed the Admiralty found out your firm's schedule for the North Atlantic in case of emergencies."

"Well, it sure worked this time. Maybe we'll meet after this damn war is over."

There was a loud knock on the port passenger entry door. Smiling, Westbrook patted Stacey on the shoulder and went to the door and unlatched it.

Two men in wide fedoras and almost identical matching summer worsted suits, were standing on the port sponson. Both men flashed badges that Westbrook couldn't read.

"F.B.I.," said one of the men, without expression. "Where's the Captain?"

"Speaking," Westbrook replied. "Please come in. My name is Curtis Westbrook."

"Captain, I'm Ed Hodges and this is my partner, Stan Beale. We're both special agents of the New York office, and we understand one of your crewmen was shot by a German diplomat last night. Any help you can give us will be very much appreciated. We're here to take the man into custody." Both of the agents were looking around the inside of the Clipper. Westbrook was amused. He suspected that the contrast between the Clipper's elegant interior appointments and the scruffy British ship-wreck survivors still milling around inside was quite an anomaly for the agents.

Beale started to pull a package of cigarettes from his coat pocket, thought better of it and let it slip back. He raised his fist to his mouth, stymieing a deep cough.

Westbrook could see the bulge of a holstered pistol under each of the agent's coat. Massaging the nape of his neck, he said, "Gentlemen, I'm sure you can appreciate this has been a hell of a long night, and we're all very anxious to get ashore."

Reaching into his coat pocket, Hodges produced an arrest warrant and handed it to Westbrook without saying a word. Westbrook studied the document, noticing it had been signed by a federal magistrate less than two hours ago. Looking up, he said with a slight frown, "All right, gentlemen, follow me."

Westbrook led the agents to the crew's quarters. As he began unlocking the door, he noticed Hodges pulling out a .45 caliber automatic.

As they entered the quarters Westbrook saw that Beck was sleeping, his head lolling from side to side. The door creaked slightly as Westbrook shut it. Awakened by the sound, Beck shot up as far he could, screaming in terror.

"Mr. Beck," Hodges said softly, "we're here to help you. We're from the F.B.I., and unfortunately, we have to take you into custody because of the events that happened last evening. You should call your Embassy as soon as it opens." The agents then hand-cuffed Beck and led him to the forward Lounge and then into a speed boat where his wife was waiting.

Westbrook knew that Sikes was worried about possible damage the Clipper had sustained during its trip across the Atlantic. He found him on the port sponson, unscrewing the cap of one of the main fuel tanks.

"Might as well light the damn thing," Sikes said as he pulled his dead cigar from his teeth. "For all the gasoline you don't have on this airplane, it really wouldn't matter. Shit, when I'm through with it, I could probably throw it into the gas tank lighted and nothing would happen." Sikes turned to Westbrook. "Like I said, Mr. Trippe is real anxious to see you. I imagine his limo's bringing him out to the airport even as we speak."

"That's fine, Charlie, but I'm staying here until everything is secured and we've been towed to the moorings."

"Wouldn't ask you not to, but Mr. Trippe may decide to saunter on out here pretty soon."

Westbrook was standing in the open port entry door when Juan Trippe and another man boarded the Clipper from another Pan American motor launch. Trippe, a powerfully built gray eyed man with a shock of brown hair and an iron will, was wearing a summer-wool blue pin stripe suit and black wing tipped shoes. Ignoring the no smoking regulation while on the water, Trippe was puffing his ever present pipe. The other man was blond, porcine looking and wearing a tan suit which appeared to be about two sizes too small. Westbrook thought he looked very uncomfortable.

"Well, Curtis, I'm certainly glad to see you after your adventure over the Atlantic. I'm anxious to hear all about it, but first a little business." Pointing to the man with him, he said, "This is Hal Carp of the CAA's New York office. He asked to come along with me, so what could I say? After all, he helps regulate the business."

"Captain Westbrook," Carp said with obvious pleasure, "I must regretfully inform you that your license to fly as an airline pilot in command is suspended until further notice. You are eligible to fly under category two, non-pilot in command, but nothing more until the Department of Commerce has conducted a full investigation and a formal hearing through the Civil

Aeronautics Authority."

Rubbing the stubble of his beard, Westbrook stared at Carp. He decided to say nothing. Westbrook was known for his subtle humor, and even though he was dead tired he found amusement in the situation, notwithstanding the potential enormity of it in terms of his career. He thought the fat little bureaucrat was at the zenith of his career at this moment, and he needed to enjoy it. An old English saying his uncle had taught him came to mind: "Petty authority vested in an ignoramus will inevitably turn him into a swine." He smiled. Carp even looked the part.

Speaking slowly and softly, Westbrook said, "Thank you, Mr. Carp for taking the trouble to come out here personally. Anything else? Mr. Trippe and I have a busy morning ahead of us." He had made his point. He still worked for the chief executive officer of Pan American.

Carp gave Westbrook a summons for the hearing and left, returning to shore in the Pan Am launch that had brought him out.

After a pause, Trippe put his arm around Westbrook's shoulder, gave him a partial hug, and said, "Well done, Curtis. I'm afraid if it had been me I would have thrown that fat turd overboard. I guess we'd better get right down to business. The CAA wants to hold a revocation hearing on your license in forty-eight hours. But you're going to be an all-American hero in less than twelve. My biggest problem, Curtis, is that you didn't keep us informed of what was going on. Almost like you were admitting that what you were doing was wrong and you knew it. That's very hard to explain away."

Wearily sitting down on the arm rest of a chair, the palms of his hands open and extended, Westbrook responded, "First of all, we tried to raise the Company as soon as we got the distress call from the <u>Pegasus</u>, but the weather conditions were too bad. We even climbed to over six thousand feet to try and reach New York, but couldn't. I'll be the first to tell you that we didn't try real hard because we were too busy, and after we landed and saw the German submarine, I ordered radio silence until we got back into the air.

"If you think I was grand standing, then do what you have to do, but please don't try to second guess me anymore."

His face flush, Trippe angrily snatched his pipe from his mouth. "Curtis, nobody talks to ..."

Trippe was interrupted by Sparks on the PA System. "Mr. Trippe, please come to the Control Cabin. One of President Roosevelt's aides is on the phone. The President wants to speak with you!"

After Sikes' initial telephone call at 0500 telling him of the Clipper's rescue of the British sailors, Trippe called the White House and told the duty operator, who immediately woke the President. Roosevelt ordered his personal secretary to issue a press release to the Washington press corps at 0730.

"You'd better come, Curtis. This could be real interesting."

Sparks excitedly handed Trippe the earphones from his radio set and Trippe reached out for the microphone.

"Hello, Juan Trippe here. Uh, why yes, good morning, Mr. President. Yes, I'm on the Clipper right now.... ran low on fuel on the landing so we're being towed in. He's here with me now. Would you like to speak with him? Yes, very good. Please hold on one second and I'll switch him over to you.

Trippe grinned broadly as he handed the radio head set to Westbrook.

"Good morning, Mr. President. Curtis Westbrook speaking."

"Good morning, Captain. I just wanted you to know how proud we all are of your heroism last night. Prime Minister Churchill sent me a cable, which I'm going to pass on to you, saying how grateful the people of England and its Commonwealth are for your heroism and valor. The same is, of course, extended to all of your fellow crewmen.

"We're awarding you the Distinguished Flying Cross for your valor. If our schedules work out, I'd like to pin it on you myself down here in Washington. Good luck, Captain. Good bye."

Trippe was grinning like Westbrook had never seen him. Westbrook knew that Roosevelt and Trippe were close friends. The President had been very instrumental in making Pan American a "chosen instrument" of American foreign policy all around the world by promoting its route system to nearly every corner of the globe.

"I booked you into the University Club. My car will take you there. If you're up to it, though, I suggest we start your campaign for exoneration as soon as we get ashore. There will be alot of reporters waiting there. Good press for the Company, which, by the way, will foot the bill for your lawyer." The two men shook hands and Trippe went below to wait in the cabin until the Clipper was at its moorings.

Looking from the cockpit window, Westbrook could see that Trippe had been right: the dock was swarming with reporters. He knew Trippe had become so successful because of his attention to the details, large and small. The man never misses a trick. He gave a heavy sigh, and started gathering his things to go ashore.

The Portuguese passengers had deplaned after the British sailors were taken ashore. Their stories could only have whet the appetite for the stories yet to come, for an America that was desperately looking for its next hero.

CHAPTER 3
LISBON

Major Hans Auchlin's assignment to Lisbon in early 1940 as Germany's senior military officer raised some eyebrows among the more seasoned dignitaries in both Lisbon and Berlin. His orders were personally signed by Adolph Hitler, and while Hitler dreamed of Portugal as an Axis ally, the assignment of Auchlin, a mere major, was seen as an insult to the Portuguese.

Now in his late thirties, Auchlin had the sleek good looks of a silent film star, with premature silver hair and a pencil thin black mustache. Auchlin dressed in custom made suits from Berlin's best tailors, paid for from a modest inheritance from his father. In spite of his medium frame, Auchlin grew physically powerful, which helped him during the late twenties and early thirties when the Nazis were still just street thugs spreading violence in the streets of Germany.

Due to his raw strength and his ruthlessness toward the enemies of the Reich, Auchlin caught Hitler's eye early on, and when the Nazis came to power Hitler offered him a commission in the regular Army, which irritated many professional Army officers in the Wermacht.

Although he had the means to obtain one and his family encouraged him to do so, Auchlin never got a formal education. Nevertheless, he was shrewd and clever, and adapted to his environment very well. He was also a man who hid his emotions beneath a Germanic frigidity.

Under special orders from Hitler, Auchlin was assigned temporary duty to Josef Dietrich, commander of Hitler's SS bodyguard regiment, to participate in the Night of The Long Knives when SS troops rounded up and executed senior SA Brown Shirts in June, 1934.

Auchlin's first arrest came at 1730 on June 30, in the suburbs of Munich, when he knocked on the door of an old friend's house, now a high ranking officer in the SA.

"Hans. Hans Auchlin. It's so good to see you. Come in!"

"There's no time for civilities, Ernest. You're under arrest.

Orders of the Fuhrer! Come with me." Auchlin brandished his unholstered Luger at the friend. By this time, Ernest's wife appeared, and seeing Auchlin and his pistol, began crying hysterically.

With a twisted smile, Auchlin waved his pistol at the woman, saying, "Frau Kaltenbruner, if you don't stop whining I'll shoot you."

The woman stopped, burying her face in her hands. Auchlin grabbed the stunned Kaltenbruner by the arm and roughly dragged him to an unmarked police car, and shoved him into the back seat where a waiting SS agent hand cuffed him. Auchlin got into the driver's seat.

"I don't understand, Hans, what's this all about?" protested Kaltenbruner.

Without saying a word, Auchlin turned in his seat and smashed his pistol in Kaltenbruner's face, grunting from the force of his own blow. Blood gushed from the nose of the hapless prisoner as he fell forward, unconscious. Auchlin noticed the SS agent wince when the blow landed.

"This one's mine when the time comes," said a smiling Auchlin to Dietrich, as he dragged the still unconscious Kaltenbruner to a cell in Stadelheim Prison in Munich.

It wasn't always convenient to arrest the targeted SA officers. The next evening Auchlin and his colleague, dressed in black SS uniforms, acting on a tip from an informer, went to a centuries old tavern in downtown Munich. Auchlin smelled stale beer, urine and the odor of unwashed bodies as they entered. There, they found four SA men, all dressed in their brown uniforms, seated around a large oak table in the center of the tavern, carousing and singing Army fighting songs.

Auchlin approached the table, banged his pistol butt on the table, and said in a loud voice, "Stop! You're all under arrest. Orders of the Fuhrer!"

Silence fell around the table. Disbelieving eyes looked at Auchlin. Then, one of the SA men, slightly intoxicated, laughingly yelled, "It's a joke! A fucking joke!"

Auchlin shot him between the eyes. The three remaining SA men quickly stood up, their hands over their heads. Auchlin could see that none of them appeared to be armed. He marched them out of the tavern, around the corner into one of the blackest alleys in Munich. Forcing them to kneel, he fired a bullet at close range into the back of each man's neck, saying, "The price of disloyalty to the Fuhrer is death." Auchlin knew none of the men or whether they had, in fact, been disloyal to the Fuhrer. Nor did he care.

Returning to Waldheim Prison, Auchlin and his colleague reported to Dietrich that all four men were armed and resisted arrest. The matter ended there.

Later that night, the round-up completed, Dietrich selected "six good shots." Auchlin was among them.

The six senior SA officers, including Kaltenbruner, were herded into the prison court yard and lined up against a wall which was bathed by a spot light so bright the condemned men could see nothing. Auchlin noticed with satisfaction that Kaltenbruner's face was swollen and black with bruises. His nose bore a zig zag of stitches where it had been hastily repaired by a prison medic.

One of Auchlin's fellow executioners read the death warrants in a loud voice.

"Hans, my friend, what on earth's happening? We're completely innocent," cried Kaltenbruner. The reply was a click of heels and a coldly worded "You have been condemned to death by the Fuhrer. Heil Hitler!" Then the shooting began. It was all over in less than a minute. Auchlin walked to where Kaltenbruner lay, and fired a shot into the back of his skull. Laughingly, he bid his old friend goodby, scolding him for picking the wrong side.

After a series of routine Army assignments, Auchlin was named Deputy Commandant of Dachau concentration camp in the summer of 1939. Built in 1935, Dachau was originally a place where Hitler sent his political enemies, regardless of their race, color or creed. By the time Auchlin arrived it had become the home of the undesirable, especially the Jews and the gypsies.

The Commandant of Dachau was a tired old lieutenant colonel, passed over for promotion many times. He was only months away from his pension. Heinrich Himmler, the small, rotund chicken farmer-turned-Reichsfuhrer of the SS and Chief of the Gestapo ordered Auchlin to "tighten things up at Dachau."

The second day on the job Auchlin was sitting at his desk in a modestly furnished office in the camp's administration building, studying the plan of the day when a young guard dragged in a Jewish prisoner.

Auchlin was annoyed. Looking up, and frowning, he said, "Yes, what is it corporal?" Then he looked contemptuously toward the bedraggled prisoner.

"This man was caught stealing a loaf of bread from the bakery just moments ago, sir."

"Don't call this thing a 'man,' corporal. It's a bag of shit. Do you understand?"

The ferocity of Auchlin's voice intimidated the young soldier. "Yes, sir. I understand," he said meekly.

Picking up his newly-issued riding crop from the top of his desk, Auchlin stood up, tugged at his jacket, and walked over to the large window of his office. The window gave him a commanding view of the prison grounds and its surroundings.

"Come here, corporal," Auchlin said, gesturing with his riding crop.

His prisoner in tow, the corporal joined Auchlin at the window.

Pointing his riding crop to his left, he said, "Do you see that telephone pole over there? The one on the left, just outside the main gate?"

The corporal studied the landscape for a moment, then said, "Yes, sir I see it."

"Good. String this prisoner up by his wrists, hands behind his back, on the pole, at least ten feet off the ground."

"Yes sir. For how many hours, sir?"

An odd look came over Auchlin's face. "Hours? What do mean 'hours'?" he asked in a muted, sarcastic voice.

Turning to the prisoner and jabbing the end of his crop hard into his throat, Auchlin said in a low voice, "You have stolen your last piece of bread, at least in this world."

Auchlin was pleased an hour later when he saw that the prisoner was hanging by his wrists as he had ordered. Auchlin timed it: it took the prisoner two days and three hours to die.

Over the next several weeks Auchlin ordered six more prisoners strung up. By now the inmates lived mortal fear of Auchlin, and even the guards were intimidated. But Auchlin was happy. He was "tightening things up," as Himmler had ordered.

Auchlin felt that most of the guards and even the officers at Dachau were dullards, biding their time in the Army, hoping they would not be sent to the front.

One evening two months after Auchlin arrived at Dachau a new face appeared in the officers' mess for the evening meal. Sitting down next to Auchlin, he introduced himself. Extending his hand, he said, "Mengele, Herr Major. Josef Mengele."

Auchlin studied the bird-like man. He had dark eyes and black, unkempt hair. Auchlin estimated he was in his late twenties, and noticed he wore the rank of a first lieutenant on his collar.

"Yes, lieutenant. And what brings you to this garden spot of the world?"

"I'm the new camp doctor. Sent here to see after the sick, among other things."

Auchlin was curious. "And what might 'the other things' be?" he asked.

Smiling, Mengele put a finger to his lips, looked around the room and said, "Shhh. Later, Major. Let me buy you an after dinner drink."

After dinner the two men adjourned to the officers' club, which was really no more than a small room adjacent to the dining hall. The room was poorly lit, and besides the dour bartender they were alone. Mengele bought two brandies and brought them to where Auchlin was seated at a table in a corner of the room. Mengele sat down, proffered a brandy to Auchlin and unbuttoned the collar of his tunic.

"At university," Mengele began, "I took joint courses in medicine and philosophy. As I began my doctorate I developed a theory that, in reality, people are in many ways like animals. Some have pedigrees, others do not. Anatomically, I have begun to develop proof of this fact, but have not had sufficient, ah, how shall I say it? 'Subjects,' 'guinea pigs.' What have you."

Auchlin listened, mesmerized, as Mengele described his conversations with Himmler about his theories, and even a brief meeting with Hitler on the subject.

Mengele studied the backs of his hands for a few seconds, took a small sip of brandy, and said, "The Fuhrer was very enthusiastic about the subject. He instructed Himmler to cut orders for me to come here and, very discreetly, pursue my theories. Yesterday as I was preparing to leave Berlin, Himmler called and told me to take you into my fullest confidence. He said no one is more loyal to the Reich than you."

Auchlin could not believe his own good fortune. At last, the vermin could be eliminated-the Jews, the gypsies. He drew in his emotions. Everything would have to done very carefully and quietly. He was sure things would go much more slowly than we would wish them to.

"Do the subjects always die?" Auchlin asked.

"Not always, but most of the time. It's up to me, really." Mengele smiled at the question.

The next morning Mengele, dressed in a white coat, a stethoscope hanging around his neck, and carrying a clip board, began an informal inspection of the prison yard and barracks. He made extensive notes as he made his rounds. Auchlin accompanied him.

On Auchlin's orders a small, unused warehouse just outside the barbed wire fence enclosing the prison yard was hastily converted into a rudimentary operating theater. The necessary medical equipment had already been delivered in unmarked crates.

After the fifth day of rounds, Mengele made his way to Auchlin's office, poured himself a cup of coffee, and sat down in the chair facing Auchlin's desk. Making a slight slurping noise as he sipped his hot coffee, Mengele said, "I think we're ready."

Finally unable to suppress his pent up feelings, Auchlin said, "I want to be a witness to these experiments."

Frowning as he looked up from his clip board, Mengele said, "As you wish, Major. These people are your charges. For better or worse."

At 2100, two hours after curfew that night, two trusties led an old man into the operating room, which now reeked of ether. Unresisting, the old man was stripped of his clothes and strapped to the operating table. He seemed to be in a fog. The trusties quietly slipped out of the room, closing the door behind them. Auchlin quickly locked the door from the inside.

Auchlin and Mengele were both dressed in white surgical gowns, the lower half of their faces covered by masks.

Mengele placed an ether soaked gauze over the man's face, holding it in place. Looking up, he said, "This man is 74 years old. He was once a very successful builder in Dusseldorf. He's been here for about eighteen months and seems to be senile dementia. We'll perform a frontal lobotomy on him. Maybe we'll learn something."

Auchlin was riveted as he watched Mengele, after taking the man's pulse, begin an incision in his scalp. Blood spurted everywhere. Mengele cursed softly under his breath.

Finally, the front left side of the man's brain was exposed. Mengele was whistling.

After fifteen minutes of probing Mengele stood up, pulled down his mask, and said, "Nothing unusual here. I don't think a lobotomy's the thing. At least not on the left side."

Auchlin leaned over the man, studying his brain. "What now, Doctor?" he asked.

Mengele shrugged his shoulders, and said, "Up to you, Major. I can sew him and he might live, or I can leave him alone and he'll die of shock after the anesthesia wears off."

Auchlin opted for the latter. Maybe the man was not a despised Jew, but he was an enemy of the State or he wouldn't be here.

The next night, at the same time, the trusties led a young gypsy woman into the operating theater. She was screaming hysterically at the top of her voice as the trusties tried to disrobe her. Auchlin started to help them, but thought better of it. Mengele quickly grabbed her around the neck, placing the anesthesia gauze over her nose. She was still struggling when the trusties finally strapped her to the table, nude.

Mengele said nothing as he placed his gloved hand in the woman's vagina, feeling the area. After a few moments, he withdrew his hand and reached for a long, slender stick with a large cotton swab, a brownish substance on the end.

At Mengele's request, Auchlin held the woman's legs as far apart as they could go, while Mengele probed the swab deep into her womb. The sensuality of the whole thing made Auchlin's penis stiffen. Because of some unpleasant events in his early childhood, Auchlin hated women and was aroused when a woman was completely subjugated like this one. He almost told Mengele he was going to rape her when the doctor was through with her, but again thought better of it.

Finally, Mengele finished his probing and Auchlin reluctantly released the woman's legs. He was in a cold sweat, and couldn't remember seeing a more beautiful mound.

"Part of my theories hinge on the hypothesis that the gypsies of middle Europe, such as this woman, are born with inferior strains which inhibit their abilities to be useful, productive citizens. I've taken some tissue from this woman which I will send to a laboratory for further study. She'll be fine, unless you have some other plans, Major." Mengele was smiling, almost as though he could read Auchlin's mind. Mengele had made Auchlin feel uncomfortable. Even so, he paused for several moments giving serious consideration to ravishing the woman. His problem was that he really didn't know Mengele that well, or how far he could be trusted.

"I have no other plans, Doctor," Auchlin said curtly, and not without regret.

Auchlin enjoyed the nightly experiments with Mengele until December, 1939, when he was suddenly summoned to the Chancellery in Berlin by Hitler. Hitler warmly greeted his old friend and told him he was being appointed the senior German military officer to Portugal and would be immediately posted to Lisbon. Over lunch, in the Fuhrer's lavishly appointed private dining room, Hitler told Auchlin what his expectations were for Portugal.

"I want Portugal to join as an ally before the end of 1940. Accomplish that, my friend, and your next duty post is yours to choose. It also goes without saying you will be promoted to full colonel."

Auchlin had never seen Hitler looking better. His face radiated a healthy glow, which Auchlin attributed to the military successes Germany had enjoyed and was continuing to enjoy on the Continent of Europe.

Returning to Dachau for the last time, Auchlin had mixed feelings. He was elated to going to Lisbon, although not without some reservations about the Portuguese people themselves. He had heard they were a lazy, worthless people, much the way Mengele had described the gypsies. He resolved to be patient as he worked the German will on the Portuguese.

While it was true, Auchlin tried to deny he would miss the evening experiments performed by Mengele. The helpless, nude women had given him sexual release he had never found with a whore. Since he despised them so much, he had no women friends and had never tried to make them.

Provided with an ample budget and his own funds, Auchlin took up residency in the Presidential Suite of the luxurious Palacio Hotel in the ocean resort area of Estoril, just thirty minutes to the south and west of Lisbon. All necessary state-of-the art equipment to communicate with Berlin and other German facilities in Europe was installed. Auchlin was very much a loner in his work habits, but he recruited one commissioned officer, Lieutenant Werner Ludke, from the German Embassy staff in Lisbon, and two non-coms from one of his old units in Germany, to perform the undercover activities the Embassy could not risk.

At dusk during one chilly evening in April, six weeks after his arrival in Lisbon, Auchlin slipped into the bar of the elegant Aviz Hotel. He had spent his first six weeks learning his way around the city.

The Aviz bar was a favorite hangout where the Allies gathered to share their gossip and rumors.

"Boa tarde, Senhor," said the bartender, "Como esta?"

"Ja, danke," Auchlin replied. "A German beer, faca favor."

The portly, smiling bartender quickly produced a Lowenbrau, slightly cooler than room temperature. Auchlin was obviously pleased.

"So few places in Lisbon offer German beer." A voice to his right startled him. "My name is Gasparo--Inspector Gasparo,

Major Auchlin. I hope you are being received cordially here in Lisbon." It was almost as though Gasparo had been waiting for him. Auchlin turned to his right, their eyes meeting. Gasparo, resting his elbows on the shiny mahogany bar, was wearing his poorly fitted brown suit, a white handkerchief prominently protruding from the outside breast pocket.

"By the way," a smiling Gasparo said, "we must try the Cervejaria da Trinidade some evening. It's a lovely old tavern that specializes in German beer. Been in the city for hundreds of years."

"So, tell me, what exactly are you 'inspector' of, Gasparo. Police? Fire? Dog pound?"

The smile left Gasparo's face. He cleared his throat, and said "Police, Major. You will understand, I'm sure, that I'm a policeman, first and foremost, but I want to welcome you and offer my assistance in any way I can. It's no secret in police circles that your appointment to Lisbon was made by Herr Hitler himself. While others may view this as quite an honor, I must confess, Major, I personally find it a bit peculiar." He paused a moment to let this sink in. "But then, we live in peculiar times, don't we?" Gasparo lit a Fatima and tapped his fingers on his glass for another port.

Auchlin studied Gasparo with a deep frown. It was the Inspector who he found to be peculiar. "Why do you think my appointment is 'peculiar,' Inspector?" He paused, then said, "On second thought, I don't really care." He drained the last of his beer, and glancing at his watch, said, "Ah, well, thank you for your time, Inspector. I didn't realize how late it is. Perhaps we can meet again soon. Good night."

As Auchlin left the Aviz, a chilling rain was falling. He felt somewhat unsettled. The head of the Lisbon police knew who he was. But why should he care? He'd done nothing wrong, and had no plans to do so. Nevertheless, he felt an involuntary shiver from the cold, pulled up the collar of his raincoat, and hailed a taxi.

CHAPTER 4
NEW YORK

After speaking with a throng of reporters for thirty minutes, Westbrook went inside the Terminal and to Pan American's operations office and closed out the flight plan for Flight 9032. Then he walked through the "Employees Only" door to the executive parking lot where Juan Trippe's limousine was waiting for him. After checking in at the University Club, he headed for his room. It was on a corner, so he opened the windows on both sides, hoping for some cross ventilation on what was already becoming one of those hot, sultry summer days that only mid-town Manhattan can conjure up. Then he gave the Club's switchboard operator the telephone number for Joanna Davis' penthouse. Joanna's maid Hattie answered, pleased that he had called. "Miss Joanna has been so worried about you, Capt'n. I hope I can tell her you're all right." Assuring her that he was, he said he would call back at five-thirty when Joanna got home.

Westbrook and Joanna led hectic lives. He flew the Atlantic on a regular basis. She commuted between Hollywood and New York trying to decide which direction she wanted her acting career to take: Hollywood and the movies or Broadway and the stage. It seemed as though they would never find the opportunity to be together for any length of time. As soon as he landed the Clipper safely in Rikers Channel, though, Westbrook made a vow that nothing was going to keep them apart. Phineas Holloran's sudden murder had at least taught him one positive thing: there are no guarantees in this life. He was too young and stupid to have been able to figure that out in the Great War, but he was thankful to have been able to figure it out now, especially with Joanna in his life. Westbrook sat down on his bed, and telephoned Holloran's widow in Boston and told her as much as he had learned in Lisbon. The next thing he heard was the telephone ringing at five forty-five. It was Joanna.

"Curtis, are you OK? I've been calling Pan Am all day from the theater. I guess I didn't have the good sense to call Hattie to see if you'd called, we were so damn busy. Are we still on for dinner? I can't wait to see you!"

Groggy, but refreshed, Westbrook said, "Of course we are. I passed out late morning; suppose I pick you up in an hour and we go to the Oak Room, or we could eat here in the Club, whichever you prefer." Westbrook hoped she'd opt for the privacy of the Club.

"The Club sounds great. It's the only place in New York that has wonderful oysters this time of year. I'll have Jeffrey drive me over. No point in you're making the extra trip."

Westbrook smiled as he hung up. He knew how much Joanna loved the seventh-floor dining room of the University Club, with its high, beautiful ceiling embossed with elegantly carved coats of arms representing a number of universities and colleges. Most important, they both knew the Club's dining room wasn't crowded during the week in the summer time, and they would have private time together.

Westbrook sat on the edge of the bed, buried his face in his hands as he tried to sort out the mess he figured he'd made for himself. Concluding the only thing he was sure of at the moment was that he was going to propose to Joanna tonight and wouldn't take no for an answer, he stood up, slipped off his undershorts and turned on the shower. Cold at first, gradually turning warmer, the water refreshed him. After showering, his towel wrapped around him, Westbrook sat down at the small mahogany desk in his room and pulled the Manhattan Telephone Directory from the bottom drawer.

In spite of Juan Trippe's generous offer, he decided to call an Annapolis classmate who had gone to law school and now worked with white collar criminal defendants. The lawyer was Westbrook's first choice to represent him in the license revocation hearing.

Joseph Daugherty, working late, was delighted to hear from Westbrook. "Curtis, it's been a hundred years. It's great to hear from you."

Westbrook outlined the nature of his problem, saying, "That's the bare bones, Joe. It's six now. If you could have somebody stop by the Club an hour from now I'll make notes of everything I can think of and leave them at the front desk in an envelope with your name on it. Assuming, of course, that you can represent me."

"Hold on a sec, Curtis."

Westbrook heard Daugherty talking to another person, apparently in his office.

"OK. Sorry, Curtis. I just wanted to make sure somebody was available to come by the Club. Would've come myself if there wasn't," he laughed. "Sure, we'd be glad to represent you. I can tell you without checking that the firm doesn't have any conflicts representing a client against the United States Government." Westbrook was greatly relieved, and the two men agreed to meet for lunch in the Oyster Bar on the second floor of the Club at 1230 the next day.

The airmen who flew with Westbrook greatly admired the patient thoughtfulness with which he approached all facets of airline flying. Pulling a piece of stationery and a pen from the center drawer of the desk, and using that same thoughtfulness, Westbrook began a letter to Daugherty, detailing as fully as he could, the events of last night and this morning on Flight 9032. Occasionally he would pause momentarily, his brow furrowed in thought as he tapped the pen lightly on the stationery. Having finished the letter, he glanced at his watch, surprised to see it was nearly seven o'clock. He dressed hurriedly, and went downstairs to the lobby where he found the runner from Daugherty's firm just inquiring at the front desk about the letter from Captain Westbrook.

After delivering the letter, and mindful of the strict Club rule prohibiting unescorted women from roaming about the premises, he decided to wait in the Lobby until Joanna arrived. Patting the pocket of his blazer, he felt the box with the ring in it. He smiled and sat down on a sofa near the entrance.

Promptly at seven-thirty, Joanna's chauffeured sedan delivered her to the front door of the University Club, One West Fifty-fourth Street.

She looked stunning in a green silk dress that matched her eyes.

His spirits soaring, Westbrook greeted her with a quick kiss and guided her to the elevator which took them to the seventh floor dining room.

Seated at a table near the piano, they placed their drink orders. "Mr. Trippe insisted yesterday that I stay here as his guest," Westbrook said with a laugh. "I didn't have the heart to tell him I've been a member since '25."

"Tell me what's going on," she said sadly, looking straight at him. Westbrook thought he noticed tears in her eyes.

His brow furrowed, Westbrook said, "What's going on is that some hard asses in the Department of Commerce think I should lose my license to fly and maybe go to jail for provoking a Nazi submarine. But I'd do it again in a heart beat." Westbrook's voice rattled with a vaguely concealed anger, and he pounded his fist on the table silently.

He paused when the waiter re-appeared with their drinks, and after giving him dinner orders, resumed. "Joanna, the one resolution I've made as a result of all this is that I'm not going to leave you any more. We're going to get married, and if I have to sit on my butt in Hollywood while you make movies or sell pencils on Fifth Avenue, so be it." He slipped the box from his pocket, opened it on his lap so she couldn't see it and lifted the ring out. Taking her left hand in his, he silently slipped the ring on her finger.

Joanna looked at it in stunned silence. "This makes it official," Westbrook said in a voice trembling with emotion.

Joanna glanced away as two platters of chilled oysters on the half shell were brought to the table with embellishments-- Tabasco, horseradish, oyster crackers, lemon wedges and cocktail sauce.

Then, as she held her hand up to look at the ring, Westbrook noticed a splash of blue light sparkle from it.

Tears streaming down her cheeks, Joanna dabbed her eyes with her napkin, smiled and said, "Oh, darling, I can honestly say this is the happiest moment of my life. Not just because of the ring. It's so beautiful! Thank you! But, it means I can spend the rest of my life with you. I'd be very happy living here in New York with you, just doing Broadway. We could stay here and go to Elmira when the weather's nice. I don't care as long as I'm with you." She reached across the table, drew his hand to her and kissed it lovingly.

His mind drifted back to one Saturday in October, 1939, when, at the urging of his fellow Pan Am pilots, he had gone to Elmira, New York to see what soaring was all about. Just as he arrived at the airfield in the early afternoon he noticed a large crowd of onlookers, mostly men, looking skyward. Then he saw a large Schweizer sport-glider on its final approach. As the glider rolled to a stop a trickle of applause turned into a loud ovation as the pilot disembarked. Joanna Davis had just won another badge in her quest for the Lilienthal Medal, the highest competition award a glider pilot can achieve. She was quickly swallowed up by the admiring crowd.

During his thirty minute familiarization flight his instructor told Westbrook all about Joanna and her passion for soaring.

"Best damn pilot here," the instructor said. As they touched down the instructor commented to Westbrook that he'd be a natural at soaring. After deplaning the normally reserved Westbrook, who admired everything he'd heard about her, couldn't resist walking over to Joanna, who was alone, loading her parachute and other flying paraphernalia into the trunk of her car. Her back was to him.

"Uh, Miss Davis, my name is Westbrook. Curtis Westbrook. I..."

Joanna turned with a start, frowning. "I'm sorry. You scared me. My mind was someplace else," she said. "What did you say your name was?"

Westbrook felt like a dolt. He realized he could have at least waited until she had seen him to say something. Shifting his weight and fidgeting with his key ring, he said, "Curtis Westbrook. Terribly sorry I startled you. I just finished my first glider flight and my instructor said you were the best glider pilot around. Besides, I've admired your movies and just wanted to introduce myself." He'd gotten it off his chest and felt better, but he knew he'd handled himself poorly.

"Was Charlie Pruitt your instructor?"

"Why, yes he was." Westbrook was surprised by the question.

"Mr. Westbrook, I hate to tell you this, but Charlie Pruitt is as full of shit as a Christmas turkey. He's proposed to me six times, and can't take an unqualified 'no' for an answer. Frankly, he drives me nuts."

Westbrook was dumbfounded and knew he looked it.

The two looked at each other for a few seconds, then Joanna, brushed a blonde curl from her forehead, smiled and said, "But that's not what you had in mind, was it?"

Relieved, Westbrook said "Well, no. Not exactly. Maybe I should start over," he laughed. "I was hoping you'd have dinner with me on the way back to Manhattan."

Joanna frowned, glanced at her watch, and said, "It would be lot's of fun, but I'm auditioning for a new play early in the morning and I need to get back early."

Westbrook persisted. "Miss Davis, Joanna, I give you my solemn promise I won't propose to you once, let alone six times, and you can leave anytime you want."

Joanna studied him for a few moments, then said with a smile, "OK, but it'll have to be fast. Follow me and we'll stop at an old inn just this side of Binghamton. Great food."

Sitting in front of a roaring fire they lingered for two hours over dinner. Initially, their love for flying was the common denominator of their relationship, but it soon turned to much more than that. The unanswered question was when and where they'd be married, still open as his focus returned.

Still admiring the ring, she turned very serious. "What'll you do if your license is taken away?"

Westbrook's knuckles whitened as he clinched his fists. He stared at the table top for several seconds as though it might provide some answers. "It'll be tough. And very, very unfair. If we'd had a planeload of little grannies from Des Moines, I probably wouldn't have landed. But the Germans are such bastards. I know from the last war that they can be savages. According to the Pegasus' Captain, the wolf pack, or some of them, surfaced and actually machine-gunned survivors in the water! Most of those men, maybe two-thirds of them, were civilians--family men!

"So we came through, saved lives and, yes, we did cause some inconvenience, but so what? When the injured sailors were being put into ambulance boats one of them, burned so badly I couldn't make out his features looked at me and said: 'You're a bloody saint. As long as I live, I owe you.'"

Smiling sadly, Joanna said, "You're tired, Curtis. Let's finish dinner, and I'll let you get some sleep."

Westbrook smiled and said, "I've booked a room on the third floor and you're staying to play the loving wife of Curtis Westbrook."

Joanna persisted. "I'm serious. What will you do if your license is suspended? I know I sound like a harpy, but I'm very worried about you."

Westbrook shifted his weight and folded his hands and placed them in his lap, leaning forward as he did so. With a sigh, he said, "I really don't know. I'm hoping some offers will come in, but it's too early. I really haven't had a chance to give it much thought. Colonel Doolittle's doing some interesting things on instrument flying. Maybe I'll call him." He started rubbing his chin as he warmed to the subject. "The Navy's doing some high level research on sea plane design. Maybe those two years I spent at M.I.T. getting a masters in aeronautical engineering after the war and working with Doolittle during the '25 Schneider Cup Race in Baltimore will come in handy. At least I don't need my airline transport rating for these types of things." He may have overstated the opportunities, but he was anguished over his efforts to set Joanna at ease, and just saying it cheered him up.

Dinner was served, perfectly broiled chops accompanied with mint jelly and vegetables. They ate in silence for a few moments before Joanna said, "I'm due in California as soon as the play finishes up. Shooting will take about six months, maybe seven. Can we get married then? Maybe Honolulu?"

"Too damn long. How about Hong Kong next month?"

"How can we get to Hong Kong?"

"Assuming I still have a job, I can bid the trip on the China Clipper and get you a pass. We get married in the old Peninsula Hotel, take the bridal suite, and live happily ever after."

The candle on the table was burning low. The piano player had finished playing "South of the Border" for the fifth time and was packing up to leave, but both Joanna and Westbrook knew there was some unfinished business at hand. "Love that song," she said, softly singing a few bars.

"Would you like to walk up to the Waldorf? Get some fresh air and have a Rusty Nail?" he asked.

"No. What I'd really like is to have you take me to bed right now."

Without speaking, they took the elevator down to the lobby. As she went outside to dismiss her driver, Westbrook, for the hundredth time, walked over to the bronze plaque to pay his respects to the Club's dead from the Great War.

When Joanna returned, they stepped back into the elevator alone. As the door closed, Westbrook took her in his arms and started caressing her breasts, feeling her nipples harden through the soft silk.

Exiting on the third floor, they walked toward his room in a tight, awkward embrace.

"I don't know if I can wait," Joanna said as the door shut.

A cool breeze was blowing the curtains gently into the room as Westbrook turned down the freshly made bed. Then he turned and slipped his hand down the back of her dress, gently unhooked her bra, and moved his hand around to her firm breasts. He wondered why she bothered to wear one.

"Oh, darling! Hurry!" She unbuckled his belt.

Finally slipping off her step-ins and inhaling her delicious scent, he caressed her body as they fell onto the bed in a coupling embrace.

Their abstinence, fostered by hectic schedules, had been too much. It gave way to a passionate release and a total silence, pierced only by their heavy breathing and the traffic noises from Fifth Avenue.

* * * * *

Westbrook's license revocation hearing was scheduled to take place at Pan American's headquarters in the new Marine Air Terminal at New York's LaGuardia Airport.

The Terminal opened in the spring of 1940 and served as the home base for Pan American's Clipper operations over the North Atlantic.

Construction of the Terminal had been commissioned by

President Roosevelt through one of his WPA New Deal programs. The President selected William Delano--no relation--a noted New York architect, as Project Chief. It was three stories high, built like a wedding cake in decreasing concentric circles with the control tower nestled on top.

While Delano was more devoted to the functional aspects of the Terminal, he nevertheless was sensitive to the historical importance of the building, deliberately and carefully weaving a theme of Art Deco throughout. Nowhere was this more evident than in the main passenger rotunda on the first level. The internationally famous artist James Brooks painted a mural that wrapped around the entire wall of the rotunda. Entitled <u>Flight</u>, the painting depicted the allegorical and physical aspects of man's quest for flight.

On the second and third floors there was a complex of offices, off limits to the public, where Pan American conducted its business of flying the Atlantic.

Westbrook's hearing room was set up in a large second floor conference room, normally used by Pan Am's personnel department for employee meetings. A spectator gallery with metal folding chairs was set up at the rear of the room. The first four of the six rows of chairs were roped off for the press. In front of the room, two counsel tables and chairs were arranged, along with a large desk and lectern for the hearing examiner.

Crisp and tailored in his Captain's uniform, Westbrook was the first to appear in the room for the preliminary conference which would set the ground rules for the formal hearing scheduled to begin the following day. It had been just over twenty-four hours since he landed the Clipper in Rikers Channel.

Ten minutes later Joseph Daugherty entered the room. Daugherty had been one of the more innovative midshipmen in the class of 1917, but his abrasive personality made it difficult for him to form friendships. Despite this, his law practice had taken off in the last ten years.

"Good morning, Curtis," said Daugherty, extending his hand. "You look great." He glanced at his watch, and said, "The Examiner should be here any second, so, real quick, some of my folks did some research last night and told me they think the

Government's case is without merit. They said your letter was really helpful. There should be a memorandum waiting for me when I get back to the office, so I'll call you soon as I've looked it over. This morning is just housekeeping stuff for the hearing." Daugherty smiled, patted Westbrook on the shoulder, and pointed to a chair at defense counsel's table at the front of the room.

The Commerce Department thought otherwise about their charges. Its complaint first charged Westbrook with wantonly and recklessly endangering lives of the passengers and crew of the Yankee Clipper, and the second charge alleged he intentionally violated the Neutrality Act of the United States.

The first charge, if proven to the satisfaction of the Civil Aeronautics Authority, would result in the revocation or suspension of Westbrook's airman's certificate, meaning he could no longer fly as pilot in command of a commercial airliner, or worse, never fly again at all. If the second allegation was proven, he could be remanded for grand jury proceedings from which, if indicted and convicted, he might spend up to twenty years in prison.

The CAA Examiner hearing the case was Marvin Kaminsky, a respected New York lawyer specializing in administrative law who, after being diagnosed with Parkinson's Disease, opted for the lighter burden of handling federal administrative hearings on occasional assignment. He was a Jew with close family members in Poland, the main reason Daugherty thought Westbrook's case was open and shut.

After counsel for both sides entered their appearances with the court reporter, Kaminsky began reading the charges against Westbrook.

"Mr. Examiner," began Daugherty, rising from his chair, "we waive the reading of the charges against Captain Westbrook, but take exception to all of the allegations and plead not guilty. I might add that my client is, regardless of how you care to characterize it, an American hero. He made certain calculated risks in his endeavors while in command of the Yankee Clipper, but he saved seventeen British sailors on the high seas. The President of the United States has publicly praised Captain

Westbrook. I respectfully move you adjourn these proceedings as being contrary to the best interests of the United States."

Kaminsky banged his gavel loudly on the hearing table. "Thank you very much, Mr. Daugherty, but we are not entertaining oral argument on this matter now. At my request, Miss Sylvia Meyers is coming up from Washington this evening, so we will postpone the commencement of the formal proceedings until day after tomorrow. I apologize to the parties for any inconvenience."

Daugherty shot out of his seat. "What in the name of Heaven is Sylvia Meyers doing in these proceedings, sir?"

Kaminsky said sternly, "Mr. Daugherty, I must ask you to refrain from these unwarranted outbursts in my hearing room. Miss Meyers is one of the most respected lawyers in the United States on the subjects of maritime and admiralty laws. She will appear only as a friend of the court, and will not be subject to either cross or direct examination by counsel for either side; she will respond only to questions from me. To the extent you feel dissatisfied with statements she makes, you may state your reasons in the course of writing your brief. Understood?"

"Yes, Mr. Examiner," Daugherty said, shaking his head in disbelief.

"Any questions, Mr. Furgeson?" Kaminsky asked counsel for the Civil Aeronautics Authority.

"No, Mr. Examiner," Furgeson said, smiling.

"I'm sorry Curtis, really sorry," Daugherty said as he and Westbrook headed for Daugherty's car, hot from sitting in the sun. "This thing seems to have gotten out of hand. Maybe I'm paranoid, but something smells rotten. Really rotten. I find it hard to believe that anybody with a serious bone in their body thinks you're guilty." He shrugged his shoulders and said, "But who the hell knows these days?"

CHAPTER 5
LISBON

Dr. Mario Branquinho was the Coroner of Lisbon, a pathologist of some renown. He was obsessed with deaths by violence. He was therefore fascinated with the murder of Phineas Holloran, and had taken several tissue specimens from the body, as well as some unusual, almost infinitesimal metal filings from the fatal groin wound. He had carefully placed the filings in a small sterile envelope and stored them in his personal safe. Holloran's remains were kept for evidence in the Lisbon Morgue, much to the anguish of his grieving family in Boston.

Inspector Gasparo was invited by Branquino to visit the morgue. He knew the doctor by reputation, but not otherwise. He was curious why the coroner wanted to see him, but he hoped he wouldn't have to view the bloated, mangled corpse again. In spite of his many years in the homicide business, he never quite got used to it.

It was late afternoon on the Wednesday following the murder. Branquino, wearing a white surgeon's gown, welcomed the Inspector into the morgue, a large slab building with high ceilings.

As soon as he entered the building, Gasparo turned pale. The stench of decomposing flesh assaulted his nostrils. He pulled his handkerchief from his jacket and covered his nose. He gagged for several seconds.

"You'll get quite used to it, Inspector," Branquino said, eyeing Gasparo's evident discomfort with some disdain. "Our refrigeration equipment doesn't quite do the job in the summer time. We do use a lot of ice, but some decomposition is inevitable in this heat."

"Oh, yes, I understand," Gasparo said, gasping and still covering his nose with his handkerchief. He wondered if this was the hundredth or two hundredth time he had been there in his career. He wondered, too, why he had never met the coroner.

"Inspector, I know you quite by reputation, I don't remember meeting you personally."

"We may not have, Doctor. Tell me, what do you have for me?"

"Well, when the American's corpse was found, it had been in the water for several hours, but before that the blood from the wound coagulated, forming a sort of protective covering that prevented the filings from being washed away."

"What do you mean filings?"

"It seems that the murderer actually sharpened the murder weapon moments before it was used to kill the victim. This murder was one in which the perpetrator went to great lengths to satisfy himself and torment his victim. A sadist, if you will, who coldly planned and executed the murder. The source of the filings might give you a clue as to the kind of murder weapon used."

Gasparo was a bit dumbfounded, but his curiosity was piqued. Perhaps here was a new dimension to the case. Branquino leading the way, the two men moved from the entrance of the morgue to its high-ceiling holding room where corpses were stacked like cord wood on marble slabs. An antiquated refrigeration machine struggled in the background to keep the room cool. Fortunately, Branquino did not offer to show Gasparo Holloran's body.

"Doctor, you may be on to something. I must have your absolute assurance that you will discuss this case with me and only me. No one, and I mean no one, in my office or any other department of the Policia, has authority to talk to you about this matter. Do you understand?" Gasparo placed his handkerchief back in his pocket, then raised his hand, fully extended, as though emphasizing the importance of what he had just said.

"Of course, Inspector. It's our little secret." Branquino smiled wanly, as though he found the whole thing amusing.

"Doctor--may I call you Mario?" Gasparo asked, smiling, his head turned to one side. Branquino pursed his lips and nodded his assent. "Good. There is something about this case that has intrigued me from the first, Mario. Again, this is for your ears only, but I have a suspicion that the murder of Captain Holloran was committed by a foreigner, a German to be exact. Does anything you've discovered lead you to think that?"

Branquinho frowned as he pondered Gasparo's question. "At this point, no. However, it's possible that a metallurgist could analyze the material and at least come up with the origin of the steel from which the murder weapon was made. I know of no one here in Lisbon, but there are several in London. It is a rather laborious process, as I understand it, and costly. At the same time, such a test might prove nothing. Would you like me to make some inquiries, Inspector?"

"Please do. Your kind assistance is most valuable and informative, and I look forward to working very closely with you." The two men shook hands before parting.

Gasparo welcomed the light summer breeze, clearing the stench from his nostrils, as he stepped out from the morgue. He felt much had been accomplished during the meeting. He thought Branquino a bit peculiar, but given the doctor's vocation that didn't surprise him. Gasparo asked himself several questions as he slowly strolled for several minutes. He kept wondering why, in his own mind, Auchlin was a suspect in the first place. Branquino's theory about the filings was interesting, but as the doctor himself had said, learning the origin of the metal from which the murder weapon was manufactured might prove nothing at all. He crossed the Rua da Prata, one of several streets in the heart of old Lisbon paved with black and white checkered mosaics, and found a bar to his liking. Taking a stool and ordering a beer, Gasparo lit a Fatima. He let his mind drift as he drank the beer. Deciding it was time to come to grips with his poorly defined theories and unanswered questions, he ordered another beer and moved to a small booth. He took out a soiled piece of notebook paper and a pencil from his coat pocket. He wrote down a rather simple check-list. The list posed several questions which would be useful in evaluating Auchlin's guilt or innocence: Why was he sent to Lisbon in the first place? He is in no sense of the word a diplomat--he's too brutish for that. Nothing we know about him suggests a distinguished military record. Was he even in the Great War? Probably too young. It all must revolve around his relationship with Hitler.

He remembered expressing his cynicism about Auchlin's appointment to Auchlin himself the first night they met.

Still, serious doubts about his theory nagged him. He had conducted a thorough investigation and still had nothing, yet he was convinced the murder was not done by locals. Every known suspect, every informer and gang leader in Portugal, had been questioned about the killing, and they all had solid alibis. Gasparo had solved many crimes over the years on the basis of his own hunches. He relied on them. But now, he knew, it was time for some good basic sleuthing.

The next morning he called his trusted lieutenant, Deputy Inspector Jose Morgado, into his office and briefed him on his visit to the morgue. Morgado was a young energetic policeman who had proven to be one of the most competent and effective officers on the force and was always eager for additional work. Gasparo usually obliged him with the most difficult assignments available, and had immediately assigned him to the Holloran case on a full-time basis.

Gasparo motioned Morgado to sit down.

"Do you have the file, Jose?"

"Yes, Inspector."

"Anything jump out at you?"

"The one thing that jumped out at me, Inspector, is the lack of details concerning Auchlin's whereabouts for at least a year before coming to Lisbon. Normally, our immigration people require proof of prior work records up until the time the visa is granted, but this was not the case with Senhor Auchlin. Another peculiar aspect of the file--as you already know--is that Auchlin's orders were personally signed by Hitler. In my opinion, this signifies nothing."

"That's where we disagree," said Gasparo, who had been reclining in his office chair, eyes closed, filtering everything his young colleague had to say. He had known for some time Hitler had signed Auchlin's papers, but continued to wonder why. Suddenly, it dawned on him.

He sat straight up, smiled at Morgado, and said, "Auchlin must be a problem child of the Third Reich. Orders signed by Hitler personally to post him to an out-of-the-way job where there is little chance for distinction. Yet, we have no information on what the man's been up to for the last year or so. Prison?

Committing crimes in the name of the Third Reich? These are the things we need to learn."

"If we do come to the conclusion that Auchlin is our man, will you arrest him? What would that do to relationships between us and Germany?"

Gasparo was surprised by the question, then he realized that Morgado was testing him. He smiled to himself over the mettle of the young policeman.

"No, of course I won't arrest him, Jose. You will."

"I will? Ah yes, Inspector, I <u>will</u>." He smiled, obviously pleased.

"Call our embassy in Berlin. They may know more than we give them credit for. Use a secret code, of course. Most important, find all information possible on our friend. Is there anything else, Morgado?"

"Yes. We have confirmed that Holloran had no known friends <u>or</u> enemies in Lisbon, and indeed, according to his fellow crewmen, stayed very much to himself while here. Also, this was only the second or third time he had been here. I think we can safely conclude that the victim did not know his murderers, although he certainly spent some very unpleasant time in their company."

"Well, my young friend, do you have any hunches of your own?"

"No, Inspector, I don't, but I must tell you that I like your hunch better all the time."

Two days later Gasparo was called upon by one of his men, Detective Sergeant Luis Sanguino, a loyal, but plodding, detective.

Gasparo recalled that on his first encounter with armed criminals Sanguino had frozen during a high speed chase of two bank robbery suspects. The suspects jumped from their car and began firing sub-machine guns at the two policemen.

Gasparo shot both suspects with a long-barreled .10 gauge shotgun before the trembling Sanguino ever unholstered his pistol.

"Thanks for your cover!" Gasparo exclaimed. "You may get a medal for this!"

Gasparo had seen men turn into permanent cowards if there was not some approbation of their conduct. He knew Sanguino would go that route without the proper psychological manipulation.

His tactics had worked with Sanguino. He had become one of the most loyal, if not ambitious, officers on the force and had an undying gratitude to Gasparo, who didn't mention Sanguino's conduct in his reports of the incident. There were no medals because the Commissioner found nothing extraordinary in either man's conduct but in truth, Sanguino's life had been saved. It was a proud day for Gasparo, too. The son of a local fisherman, he was promoted to Inspector for his meritorious work in killing the criminals.

"Ah, Inspector, I have procrastinated too long, but there have been the summer holidays."

"I understand. What's on your mind?"

"Well, shortly before I went on holiday, I was coming off shift and ran into the German military attache'. I felt he had planned to meet me and knew my habits."

"Are you talking about Major Auchlin?"

"Yes, Auchlin is the one."

Gasparo raised his hand to silence him and stepped into the hall to summon Morgado. Returning to his office, he drew close to Sanguino, and shaking his finger just under Sanguino's nose, his lips tight, Gasparo said, "You are sworn to absolute secrecy, Luis. Make no mistake about it, a leak from you will cost you your job and may cost you your life. Do you understand?" Gasparo poked his finger into Sanguino's chest to emphasize his point.

Sanguino swallowed hard and nodded in agreement. Morgado slipped quietly into Gasparo's office and sat down.

"We are talking about more than murder, which is terrible enough, but possibly matters of state," said Gasparo, pacing back and forth in his small office, hands clutched behind his back.

"All right, now, Luis, from the beginning. Tell us everything you know about this man Auchlin, including everything he's ever said to you."

Sanguino sat still for a moment, his head bowed and his eyes tightly closed, then he told the story of what appeared a chance encounter.

"He speaks reasonably good Portuguese," Sanguino said, "so it was easy to talk. I was off-duty and since it was the beginning of the summer, I perhaps had a few more whiskeys than I should have, but I was fine. Auchlin spent a lot of time telling me about the glories of the new order in Europe and what a shame it would be if Portugal failed to join forces with Germany. He asked me what I thought the chances of that happening were. As you know Inspector, I am not a political person, so I told him I thought we would likely try to remain neutral.

"He then asked some very specific questions about you. Were you sympathetic to the Germans? Were you corruptible? When I told him I would lay down my life for you, he suddenly turned very cold and made an abrupt departure. At the end, he had become a pest."

"Unfortunately for you he may become an even larger pest."

Gasparo made the decision to bring Sanguino into his and Morgado's confidence.

"In honesty, Luis, did you complain enough about the government and Minister Salazar to have been perhaps a bit treasonous?"

Sanguino looked shocked.

"You're among friends, at least for now, " Gasparo said, teasingly.

"Well, maybe," Sanguino said meekly.

"Good," said Gasparo. "Now we can begin."

Gasparo and Morgado spent the next thirty minutes describing the Holloran case. When they were finished, Gasparo said, "Now, we have said and however convincingly we may have said it, we would be laughed out of magistrate's court if we tried to arrest this man. This is where I think you may be able to help us."

"Of course, Inspector, what can I do?"

Gasparo thought Sanguino looked dubious, but decided to press on. "Get to know this man as well as you can. Find out if he hates Americans--it is probably something he would reveal early on. Cater to his weaknesses, of which there must be many.

Most of all, find out if he committed the crime. If he did, he will undoubtedly brag about it, at least indirectly if you secure his trust.

"But the murder, Inspector, how will I know?"

"You will know, Luis, you will know. It may be at a time when things are dangerous for you personally, but that will be the acid test. I will be your contact within the Department, so please coordinate your schedules with me."

Gasparo knew Sanguino had become a strong number two man on any assignment, but he wondered if he had the ability, the theatrics, to ingratiate himself with a foreigner who was a murder suspect. Gasparo decided to gamble. He felt he had no other choice.

"What do you think, Jose?" Gasparo asked after Sanguino had left.

"I think Luis will do a good job, but we must be able to come to his aid at a moment's notice. He won't be able to deal with the brutality of a man like Auchlin. Luis is brave, but he is not a man of this world."

"Oh, I agree, but that is part of the reason I think he'll succeed."

Four days later, Sanguino reported to Gasparo that he'd made contact with Auchlin. The German acted indifferent to pursuing the earlier acquaintanceship until Sanguino told him that he had been assigned to work on the Holloran case. This had the immediate effect of making Auchlin much friendlier. Sanguino also reported he'd told Auchlin the police suspected Holloran had gotten involved in one of the gangs in Lisbon trying to smuggle drugs and had perhaps reneged on a promise to smuggle a load of contraband back to America.

"Brilliant!" Gasparo told Sanguino. "If Auchlin tries to nose around with that crowd, he'll likely end up like our poor friend Captain Holloran."

The same day, a diplomatic pouch addressed to Captain Morgado arrived from the Portuguese Embassy in Berlin. After digesting it carefully, Morgado called Gasparo, who was still in his office, although it was well after normal working hours.

"Inspector, we have Auchlin's dossier from our Embassy in

Berlin."

Gasparo walked down the hall to Morgado's office, sat down and lit a Fatima. "Splendid. Things seem to be coming together for us. What do you have?"

"Unfortunately, not much. About the only thing new is the fact that just prior to coming here, Major Auchlin was Deputy Commanan- dant of a prison camp called Dachau, which is near Munich. He was only there six months before being posted here. No reason given as to why his tour was cut short. Who knows, maybe that <u>was</u> a normal tour.

"No surprise, he joined the Nazi Party early on. That's about all there is."

Gasparo leaned forward, and crushed his cigarette in an ashtray on Morgado's desk. Sighing in frustration, he said, "For what it's worth, pass this information on to Luis and tell him to exercise extreme caution. Also, we should put a tail on Auchlin. Whenever he leaves his hotel have him followed. My hunches still tell me he's our man. I want him for murder, and we'll put all the resources we can spare to get him."

CHAPTER 6
NEW YORK

Daugherty sat down across from Westbrook and said, "Beck is a defector." Westbrook stared at Daugherty in wide-eyed disbelief, his jaw slack as though he was in a trance. For a moment he was totally speechless. The two men had just met for lunch in the walnut paneled Oyster Bar on the second floor of the University Club. "Defected!" Westbrook roared, restraining himself from jumping to his feet. "Why in the hell didn't the German sub do something about it?"

"Well, I gather the German Navy is not particularly fond of Hitler's thugs, especially the Gestapo," Daugherty said, smiling. He took off his horn rimmed glasses and rubbed them with his napkin. "It's unlikely that the German submarine commander had a clue about Beck."

Westbrook looked directly at Daugherty. Shaking his head, he said, "I don't get it, Joe. Why all the turmoil in the cabin? He nearly killed my back-up navigator, and was ranting and raving about the glories of the Third Reich. Hell, I thought I was going to have to kill the little bastard."

"He was scared--and paranoid. He believed you were landing to turn him--and his wife--over to that submarine. He saw the sub before you locked him up. Now he's actually a big fan of yours. Says you're the bravest man he's ever met. All this comes from my friends at the U.S. Attorney's Office.

"He was defecting because he thought he was about to be sent back to Berlin to be fired, maybe even thrown in jail. Seems his wife was a big time madam in the early days of the Reich and got to know a lot of Nazi officials--and a lot about them. While she never made threats, I understand she could have tarnished the Third Reich's reputation, and Hitler knew it. Anyway, Herr Beck will probably replace you on the front pages pretty soon. The Feds are stalling on Germany's request for repatriation. My guess is that he and the frau will get asylum." Daugherty motioned to the bar tender for another beer.

"Is there any point in his testifying?" Westbrook asked.

"Not really. He admits he was quite drunk by the time you guys met up with the <u>Pegasus</u>. The enigma is Littleton. Thinking back, has there ever been any personal or professional animosity between the two of you--however petty?"

Westbrook frowned and pursed his lips while reflecting on his answer. The mirrored bar near their table was bustling as well dressed business men passed through the buffet line helping themselves to a wide assortment of lunch meats, cheeses and cold shell fish.

After taking a sip of his iced tea, Westbrook said "Tom's a good pilot. Not outstanding, just a good pilot. Flies captain to South America several times a year, mostly on the older Martin flying boats. I'm sure he's frustrated by the seniority system, like we all are from time to time, but that's the way it goes. Every time he's flown with me--and it'd been a hell of a long time before this last flight--he was in the right seat. I'm younger, but I was hired first. He's been a fairly solid performer, but I have some serious reservations about his courage factor after this last trip. How do things look right now?"

"As far as I'm concerned, things look great," Daugherty said. "We have written statements from all the crew, except Littleton, and they think you did the right thing. Also on the positive side, you made a solid effort to try and contact the Company to get permission to land. It's fortunate that you weren't successful. Had you succeeded and been denied but went ahead anyway, you'd probably be unemployed right now.

"Given Mr. Trippe's public support for what you did, and the President's obvious delight, I'd say things should go pretty smooth. The Bureau's lawyer isn't getting enough time for much discovery either--he's only coming to New York tomorrow evening. So far he hasn't requested any files from the Company."

Pending the outcome of the administrative hearing, Pan Am had, as required by law, suspended Westbrook with pay from duty. Trippe was annoyed by the technicality but there were laws that were bigger than him.

After going through the buffet, Daugherty and Westbrook spent forty-five minutes discussing the hearing over lunch, and Daugherty began explaining Civil Aeronautics Authority administrative proceedings: how they differed from court proceedings, with hearsay evidence often admitted and lawyers given more leeway in asking leading questions of their own witnesses than would be allowed in a normal court proceeding.

"Sylvia Meyers is an anomaly in this case. She's a fire breathing Communist, but as Kaminsky said, she is one hell of an expert on admiralty law. She's about thirty five, good looking, and smokes Cuban cigars. She's been a part of the feminist movement for years. Good friend of Diana Trilling, although Trilling thinks she overdoes the feminist bit." Daugherty paused, his face screwing up as though he'd just eaten a sour persimmon. "God, Meyers told President Roosevelt to his face he should fill the next vacancy on the Supreme Court with a woman. Can you believe that shit?"

Daugherty drained the last of his beer, and continued, "Meyers practices with a small Washington firm and teaches part time at George Washington Law School. One of the top students in her class at Columbia Law School. But let me tell you, she thinks Stalin is the Second Coming of Jesus, so <u>never</u> touch the subject if you have occasion to talk to her. The funny thing is that this is all fairly recent--last six or nine months. It's like she went to some revival meeting and saw the light. She used to be very conservative. Devout Jew, all that, but when she changed-- wow! Whatever else, she's smart as a shit-house-rat."

Sylvia Meyers' father was a second generation Russian Jew whose father had been moderately successful in the Garment District of New York, Meyers had worked his way through New York University Law School. Good grades, but no takers. The Wall Street law firms said he didn't have the academic credentials; Ivy League law schools only. The fact is, Wall Street firms didn't hire Jews in the early part of the century. After being told repeatedly that he wasn't qualified, Meyers opened his own small practice. He specialized in immigration law and by the time his only child, Sylvia, headed toward Baltimore with a full academic scholarship to Goucher College, he was prospering. Her father beamed with pride when she got the scholarship to Columbia Law School. Graduating at the top of her class, Order of the Coif, Sylvia clerked for a federal judge in the Southern

District of New York. As it happened, the judge had an unusually heavy load of admiralty cases at the time Sylvia arrived. She quickly found her niche in that specialized area, and after her clerkship was up, she returned to the Washington area and joined an internationally recognized firm that specialized in admiralty law. Throughout college and law school Sylvia became an outspoken liberal, particularly interested in women's rights. She shared Diana Trilling's belief in a life of "significant contention"--arguing culture and politics in a deep, broad and serious way. Although extremely attractive, she seemed to make a point of dressing indifferently--sweaters too big, no make up or attention to colors or ensemble. She was a respected voice in the liberal movement of her time. Never strident, she made her point through hard work and was always conciliatory.

Daugherty looked at his watch. "All right, Curtis, old boy, that's about it. Gotta run. But there's one more thing--Joanna."

"Is that a question or a statement of law?" Westbrook asked pointedly in an unfriendly tone.

"Seriously, you two were an item for some time and then something went astray. What's going on now? Personal question, I know, but bear with me. Background information if we need it."

Westbrook had forgotten how irritating Daugherty could be. He stared straight into Daugherty's eyes, a scowl on his face. "As an old friend, I'm delighted to talk to you about Joanna, but you're here on the meter. So unless you can give me a very good reason for asking the question, it's none of your business."

"Fair enough, Curtis, but some silly ass reporter might try to make something of it, obscure the issues unintentionally and complicate your lives unnecessarily. You've been married before, so it's your call. I'm just trying to cover all the bases."

"Fair enough. Helen may or may not know about Joanna." Westbrook relaxed and stared vacantly out the window. "Doesn't matter. Haven't heard from her in over nine years."

The mention of his former wife brought Westbrook some painful memories.

Through a mutual friend he had met Helen Peters, a reporter for the <u>Miami Herald</u>, in 1928. A petite redhead, Peters, originally from Philadelphia, loved Miami and fell in love with Westbrook, and he with her. They were married in 1929. She continued to work for the _Herald_ while Westbrook pioneered Pan Am's expansion into South America--principally Buenos Aires and Rio. It was, even to Westbrook, hairy flying. Long stretches over dense jungles. Landings on rivers and lakes infested with alligators and dense undergrowth. The worst part, though, was navigation. Everything was dead reckoning and lights were a rare luxury.

It lasted just over a year. In late 1930 Westbrook was transferred to New York, Pan Am's new headquarters, for the initiation of its service to the Orient.

Helen got a job with the _Post_, but it didn't last long. She hated New York and it showed. She complained incessantly to Westbrook, and anybody else that would listen, about the weather, the crowds, the noise and the filth. After futile efforts to get on with another paper Helen gave up and spent her days in their apartment doing very little except eating sweets and gaining weight.

As Pan Am's expansion to the Orient became intense, Westbrook was in New York less and less. Helen became demanding and derisive, claiming Westbrook had adopted a nomadic lifestyle just to avoid her. While it wasn't technically true, he admitted to himself that it suited him fine.

Helen began drinking hard and was asleep or incoherent when Westbrook returned home at any time of the day. He encouraged her to get help, but it did no good.

After a particular grueling trip to Hong Kong where his Martin Clipper was plagued with engine problems from the start, causing extended layovers for repairs in both directions, Westbrook returned to the apartment to find Helen had moved out, leaving a terse note saying she was moving back to Philadelphia and wanted a divorce.

Full of self-recrimination, Westbrook rushed to Philadelphia. Helen refused to see him and everything was communicated through her father, who was uncooperative. Westbrook finally relented and consented to the divorce, relieved there were no children. A bachelor for nearly ten years before he met Joanna,

Westbrook cherished his relationship with her more than anything, and prayed he wouldn't fail again.

Westbrook looked down at the table and then at Daugherty. "Anything else we need to discuss?" he asked, anxious to drop the subject.

"Don't think so. Just hope I haven't pissed you off, Curtis." The two men shook hands, and Daugherty promised to pick him up at the Club for the drive to LaGuardia in the morning.

When Westbrook returned to his room, he found a message to call Trippe as soon as possible.

"Curtis Westbrook returning your call."

Trippe's voice was very cheerful. "Ah yes, Curtis, a very good day to you. I have some great news. The President just called. Prime Minister Churchill called him to tell him the King of England has awarded you the Knight Grand Cross of the British Empire for your rescue of <u>Pegasus</u> survivors. Congratulations! On another subject, plan on flying to Washington with me for the DFC ceremony at the White House next week."

* * * * *

The morning of the hearing Daugherty picked Westbrook up at the front entrance of the University Club twenty minutes early and the two discussed the case as they drove to LaGuardia. At Daugherty's request, Westbrook was dressed in his navy blue Pan Am captain's uniform.

"Going to be a steamer," Daugherty said as they entered the traffic across the Triborough Bridge. "Sorry about the uniform, but I really think it's a good idea for the man in authority to look like he's just that."

Westbrook nodded. The heat of the day was beginning to make him uncomfortable. Before leaving the Club he had folded his uniform jacket neatly and placed it on the back seat of Daugherty's car, but he still felt the heat building up in the car by the moment.

"Remember, don't ever try to guess at the questions. If you don't know the answer, be candid and say so. Too many people try to be master of all things when they're testifying."

"Why would I give an answer to a question I didn't know?"

Westbrook asked, a quizzical look on his face.

"Everybody who has ever testified in a case asks that question before the hearing or trial, and then they try to do it anyway," Daugherty said with a chuckle.

Westbrook caught a glimpse of the Yankee Clipper being serviced at the Marine Air Terminal. Her next flight back to Lisbon was scheduled in two days. He wondered whether he would be allowed to fly her again.

In the hearing room Kaminsky's clerk advised the gentlemen that they should feel free to take off their coats. Westbrook left his on.

Turning around in his chair after several minutes, Westbrook saw that most of the spectators in the back of the room were reporters. That suited him fine; he needed all the publicity he could get and he knew Daugherty intended to use this forum as the source for it. He also noticed Littleton entering through the side door, dressed casually, but with a worried look on his face. Littleton did not look at him, and went directly to Bureau Counsel's table, sat down and huddled with Ferguson.

Examiner Kaminsky entered the hearing room along with Sylvia Meyers. As he sat down, Kaminsky rustled some papers in an accordion file he placed in front of him. A few of the cameras clicked, the flashes sounding like small arms fire. Kaminsky immediately admonished the journalists that there would be no further picture taking during the hearing.

Westbrook noticed that Sylvia Meyers was as Daugherty had described her--attractive, medium-height with black hair fashioned in a page boy. She was wearing a black turtle-neck sweater and tan slacks. She looked at him, smiled, and sat down in the front row of the spectator gallery. Westbrook thought he detected a hint of sadness in her smile.

Kaminsky wasted no time. "If all counsel are present, kindly enter your appearances with the court reporter. If there are any preliminary matters that should be brought to my attention at this time, please do so."

As on cue, Daugherty stood up and said, "Mr. Examiner, I'm Joseph Daugherty, counsel for the respondent. I'd like to make a brief preliminary statement for the record which I think will save this proceeding and you from making a big mistake."

Kaminsky dourly asked, "Bureau Counsel, do you have any objections to a very <u>brief</u> statement, by Captain Westbrook's counsel?"

Ferguson rose to his feet, and said, "No objection, Mr. Examiner," then sat back down.

"Very well, Mr. Daugherty, you may make your statement. Keep it short. I want to finish these proceedings by the close of business today. Obviously, it's going to get increasingly hot in this room and it would serve us well to be out of here as quickly as possible. Proceed, Mr. Daugherty."

Pleased, Daugherty stood and turned to the spectators smiling, then turned back to Kaminsky. "Thank you very much, Mr. Examiner. I would first like to bring to the attention of this hearing a fact which I don't believe is publicly known. Two days ago President Roosevelt advised Captain Westbrook that he plans to personally award him the Distinguished Flying Cross for his efforts in rescuing the British sailors, the circumstances of which are the subject of this hearing. Second, and even more unusual, is the news that King George of England has awarded Captain Westbrook the Knight Grand Cross, the highest award the King can bestow on a non-citizen of the United Kingdom." Daugherty paused to let his last statement sink in. Then, after sipping water from a glass on the defense table, he resumed. "I call this to the attention of these proceedings, Mr. Examiner, because of the significance they have regarding Captain Westbrook's stature. He's a genuine American hero, or at least about to be." He punctuated his last remark by turning to the spectators and flashing a "V" for victory sign with his right hand, then sat down with a satisfied smile. There was a ripple of applause from the spectators which Kaminsky ignored.

Hearing the confusion of scrambling reporters trying to be first to the telephones outside gave Westbrook the assurance he knew Daugherty wanted.

Looking bored, Kaminsky asked, "Mr. Ferguson, would you like to comment on Mr. Daugherty's statement?"

Ferguson rose to his feet, cleared his throat, and said, "Mr. Examiner, due to Mr. Daugherty's statement I'd like to ask for a recess of ten minutes to consult with my superiors in Washington."

Kaminsky begrudgingly granted the request and left the hearing room through the back door. Sylvia Meyers moved to the defense table to say hello to Daugherty.

"It's been a long time, Sylvia, how are you?" asked Daugherty flatly, extending his hand while remaining seated.

"Fine, Joseph. I just wanted to meet your client and pay my respects."

She sat on the edge of the table, took Westbrook's hand and squeezed it. Her hand was ice cold. "How nice to meet you, Captain," she said, smiling. "It's good to meet a man who's not afraid to act on his convictions. I hope we meet again very soon. Good luck. With Joseph representing you, I'm sure you'll do very well." She stood up and over her shoulder said, "Particularly against government lawyers." She smiled at Daugherty and returned to her seat, brushing a lock of her coal- black hair from her forehead.

Kaminsky returned to the hearing room, Ferguson preceded him. "Well, Mr. Ferguson, what's the verdict from Washington?" Kaminsky asked.

Ferguson stood, looked at Westbrook sheepishly, then looked down at his handwritten notes, saying, "Mr. Examiner, I spoke with the Chairman of the Authority and the general counsel, and I regret to report, Mr. Examiner, that the Bureau must proceed. The Chairman feels, and the general counsel agrees, that this matter could set a precedent for other pilots if it were ignored or dismissed. Given the unsettled situation in Europe, we would be ignoring our statutory obligations." He paused, coughed into his hand and said, "I say this in the face of the fact that we concede that Captain Westbrook is perceived as a hero by many people, not only in this country, but others as well."

Ferguson sat down and Daugherty shot to his feet, bristling, but Kaminsky held out an admonishing hand. "Hold it right there, Mr. Daugherty, you gambled and lost. This hearing will come to order. Mr. Reporter, kindly note for the record that the chair calls as a special witness, Miss Sylvia Meyers."

Kaminsky asked Meyers a number of questions about her education and practice, focusing on her background in teaching and consulting on international law on the high seas.

Westbrook could see that Daugherty was having trouble restraining himself by the way he leaned over, pounding his fist silently on the top of the table. Westbrook was puzzled by Daugherty's actions, and began to wonder if there wasn't something seriously amiss going on here.

"Now, Miss Meyers, you are generally familiar with the facts in this case, are you not?" Kaminsky asked.

"Yes I am, Mr. Examiner."

"Good, then would you, for the record, kindly describe them."

Meyers then gave an essentially correct description of the events at sea involving the Yankee Clipper, _Pegasus_ and the German submarine. She'd clearly done her homework.

"Based on the facts you have just described do you have an expert opinion as to whether Captain Westbrook violated any international laws of the sea?"

"Yes I do."

"And what is that opinion?"

"It is my professional opinion that Captain Westbrook, by putting the lives of his passengers and crew at risk in landing at the scene of recent hostilities, violated several principles of international law as it regards to the conduct of a captain in charge of a vessel--or as in this case, an airplane--in international waters. I'd be happy to elaborate on these issues, if you like." Sylvia looked at Westbrook, a faint smile on her face.

"Thank you. That won't be necessary. You may step down," Kaminsky said.

It was too much for Daugherty. He stood up, removed his spectacles and began, obsessively angry, wiping them. His voice was barely more than a hushed whisper. "Mr. Examiner, with all due respect for your earlier caveat concerning Miss Meyers' testimony, I must insist on having the opportunity to impeach the testimony. It's no secret that Miss Meyers swears allegiance to the U.S.S.R., which has a friendship treaty with Nazi Germany. She has said as much herself on prior public occasions. I must insist that my client have the opportunity to have her cross examined." He threw up his hands in despair, saying, "None of this can effectively be handled on brief."

"You are very eloquent, Mr. Daugherty, but my earlier caveat stands. Mr. Ferguson, are you ready?"

"Yes, Mr. Examiner. The Bureau calls Captain Thomas Littleton."

Littleton, stood up, wiped the palms of his hands on his slacks, and, glancing at Westbrook, took the witness chair and was administered the oath by the court reporter. He sat erect, his hands clenched.

"On the night in question, did you object to Captain Westbrook's decision to land in the open sea in the effort to rescue sailors from the ship, Pegasus, previously torpedoed by a German submarine?"

"Yes sir, I did."

"Did you openly question that decision? Did you actually state your objections to Captain Westbrook about the action he proposed to take?"

"Yes sir."

"And what response, if any, did you get from Captain Westbrook?"

Littleton was silent for a moment, scowling and pursing his lips to recall the answer.

"I honestly don't recall the Captain's response; he never threatened me or anything like that, and in all fairness, we were very busy on the bridge preparing for the landing."

"Do you or your fellow Clipper pilots routinely make landings at night in open seas?"

"No, we do not."

"Is there a reason for that, Captain?"

"Well, I would say it's largely a function of our schedules. We normally land, whether at an intermediate refucling spot, or at our final destination, between early and late afternoon. Sometimes we land at night during scheduled operations, but then we have landing aids such as harbor lighting."

"But isn't it true that landing on the open sea at night is inherently less safe than during the day?"

"To some degree it's less safe, and the same is true for landings at night on land."

"Why is that?"

"Impaired vision due to the darkness and reduced depth perception."

"Did any of the other crew members complain to Captain Westbrook about his decision to land?"

"No."

"The German submarine had already been spotted on the surface by the time the Clipper was in its landing approach, had it not?"

"Yes."

"Captain, one last question, if you had been in command of the Yankee Clipper, would you have made the same decision that Captain Westbrook made?"

"No, sir, I would not."

Ferguson, smiling, and looking well satisfied, said, "Your witness, Mr. Daugherty."

Daugherty huddled briefly with Westbrook, asking a few last minute questions. Then, he walked over to the witness chair and got as close to Littleton as he could. He scowled as he said, "The truth is, sir, you were not in command of the Clipper on the night in question, were you?"

"No, sir."

"Right. And the truth is you panicked on the bridge of the Clipper that night, didn't you?"

Ferguson immediately rose to his feet and said, "Mr. Examiner, please, I object. Captain Littleton's state of mind, actual or perceived, during the events we are considering here is not an issue. This line of questioning should not be allowed."

"What's your point, Mr. Daugherty?" Kaminsky asked.

"My point, Mr. Examiner," he said, waving his hand at Littleton, "is that if Captain Littleton is permitted by the wisdom of 20/20 hindsight to testify that he would not have followed the same course of action as Captain Westbrook, we should be able to explore events that actually took place on the night in question, including the possibility that Captain Littleton panicked." Daugherty looked straight at Littleton, his voice increasing in tempo, and said, "And as a result of Captain Littleton's panic, the Clipper was in even more jeopardy that it otherwise would have been."

Kaminsky, scratched his head, and in a disgusted tone said, "I'll allow the question. Objection overruled, Mr. Ferguson."

"Please answer the question, Captain Littleton," Daugherty said in a low voice, smiling.

Westbrook could tell Littleton was very uncomfortable. He was shifting constantly in his chair, rubbing the palms of his hands together.

"Did I panic? Well, uh, no I don't think so. I was upset. But, no, I didn't panic."

"Well, sir, did you not only disavow the actions taken by your commanding officer, but state that you might have to relieve him during a critical phase of the landing approach?"

"Yes, I did say something to that effect."

"But you never attempted to carry out that threat, did you?" Daugherty was glowering at Littleton.

"No, I didn't."

"And the reason you didn't carry out the threat was because one of the officers on the bridge of the Clipper placed his service revolver at your neck and threatened to shoot you, didn't he?"

"Yes," Littleton said tersely.

"Captain Littleton, you testified earlier that none of the other crewmen of the Yankee Clipper objected to Captain Westbrook's plan to try and make an open sea rescue of the British sailors, is that not true?"

"That's correct."

"Yes, and isn't it equally true that these other crewmen actually gave Captain Westbrook their open, vocal support?"

"Yes, that's true." Littleton was shifting from side to side in his chair, a pained look on his face.

"That's all I have, Mr. Examiner."

"Call your next witness, Mr. Ferguson," Kaminsky said.

"We have no further witnesses, Mr. Examiner."

Kaminsky's gray eye brows arched in disbelief. "What do you mean no other witnesses? You have the burden of proof here, sir. Surely you intend to call other crew members, passengers--somebody, to corroborate Captain Littleton's testimony."

"It is the opinion of Bureau Counsel that such additional witnesses would be repetitive and cumulative, and that the testimony of Captain Littleton, given his extensive experience in over-water flight operations, creates a prima facie case.

"We would also add that the testimony of Miss Meyers supports the prima facie case, inasmuch as she testified as an expert that Captain Westbrook's conduct was a violation of international law."

"Well, Mr. Daugherty, what do you make of all this?" Kaminsky asked. "No more hero speeches, please," he added, raising his hand in admonition.

"With all due respect, Mr. Examiner, this hearing has confirmed our worst fears; it shouldn't have been convened in the first place, and I take this opportunity to move for dismissal."

Kaminsky pondered for a moment and said, "I'll take the whole matter under advisement. We'll recess for two hours, until two-thirty."

Westbrook stood up, and Sylvia Meyers approached him. "Captain Westbrook, I'd like to buy your lunch in the Main Terminal." She looked away, then said, "I am not a German sympathizer."

Westbrook smiled broadly and said, "Thank you, Miss Meyers, but I'll be lunching with my lawyer. But thank you."

"Then another time--the next time you come to Washington. Better yet, make it dinner."

"We'll see."

Westbrook and Daugherty ate in silence. Very little was left to be said. Westbrook felt he was at the center of a great dichotomy. Here in New York he was accused of illegal conduct, but in Washington the President was waiting to decorate him for the same conduct.

Toying with his food and resisting the temptation to light a cigarette, something he hadn't done in almost five years, Westbrook thought about his immediate future. He was to meet the President and receive his DFC next week. And Roosevelt's secretary had asked him to stay over for at least another day to discuss some unspecified matters relating to aviation.

As they walked back to the Marine Air Terminal, Daugherty said he still felt confident that Kaminsky would throw the case against Westbrook out, but things had been so bizarre during the course of the hearing, nothing was certain.

"Looks like the press is back in full force," said a subdued Daugherty as the two men entered the hearing room. Sylvia Meyers approached Westbrook and said, "I have to leave now to return to Washington, but I hope you'll call me next week. Here's my telephone number. I miss very little that goes on in Washington, and I know the President has a meeting scheduled with you on Wednesday. I'll be very interested in hearing from you afterwards." She smiled at Westbrook as she turned to leave.

"Trouble with a capital T," Daugherty said, catching the tail end of the conversation. "She's a damn nut."

Kaminsky returned to the hearing room promptly at 1430. He had shed his sports jacket and was carrying a stuffed accordion file under his left arm. He asked Daugherty if he had any witnesses besides Captain Westbrook.

"No, Mr. Examiner, Captain Westbrook is our only witness, and I would now like to call him to the stand. Obviously, we would also like the opportunity to file a brief challenging Miss Meyers' conclusions of law."

"Denied on both counts. All right, Mr. Reporter, please enter the following order as the determination of the Hearing Examiner in this docket matter: Having heard the testimony of two witnesses, one who appeared in the capacity of friend of the court, and the other produced by counsel for the Civil Aeronautics Authority, this hearing has determined that Captain Westbrook, while acting heroically and with commendation, did nevertheless raise the danger of injury and loss of life to his passengers and crewmen by his actions in landing in the open sea. With the conflict in Europe, and particularly on the high seas, there must be some deterrent from this matter occurring again. Therefore, it is determined that Captain Westbrook's airman's certificate be, and the same hereby is, suspended for the period of ten days, effective immediately. It is also determined that Captain Westbrook did not have the requisite intent to violate the Neutrality Act of the United States, and any such claims relating to such violations are terminated insofar as these proceedings are concerned. So ordered."

Daugherty shot to his feet, livid with rage. "Wait just a fucking minute, Mr. Kaminsky, if you don't mind. There's not a small issue here of due process. My client has the right to be heard in this matter and...."

Westbrook tugged at Daugherty's sleeve indicating he'd had enough.

"You were saying, Mr. Daugherty?" Kaminsky said staring coldly at the lawyer.

Daugherty sat down in silence.

Once again Westbrook made the front page of <u>The New York Times</u>, but this time it was in the shadow of the radical Sylvia Meyers, who made the headlines. Her incriminating testimony against America's new hero shocked the nation.

CHAPTER 7
WASHINGTON

Westbrook and Trippe sat in the spartan passenger cabin of a new silver Douglas DC-3 from the Douglas Aircraft plant in California. They were taxiing out to Runway 13 at LaGuardia for the unscheduled flight to Washington.

"Ever fly one of these?" Trippe asked.

"I flew the right seat with Charlie Sikes on a ferry flight to Miami, but that's it. Nice airplane, but it doesn't compare to the Clipper."

"Nothing does. Damn Clipper costs five times as much as this bird, though." Trippe busily packed his pipe bowl with Edgeworth tobacco and lit up as soon as the "No Smoking" sign was turned off climbing through 1500 feet. They were served orange juice and coffee by a young steward, obviously awed by being in the exalted company of the Chairman of the Board and senior pilot of the airline.

"So, what did you think about the decision?" Westbrook asked.

"Lousy, just lousy. That guy Kaminsky should have his head handed to him on a platter. What did you think?"

"Well, I'd do it over in a second. If there was a point to be made, it was lost on me. I'd give long odds that any Clipper captain would get into that situation again. Essentially, it's a slap on the wrist and I can live with it."

"I agree. And we'd stand behind you-or anyone-again."

Trippe greatly admired Westbrook, although they were not especially close. Trippe dropped out of Yale in 1917, enlisted in the Navy, and served in the Naval Reserve Flying Corps. He was designated a Naval Aviator and received a commission in mid-1918, too late to go to Europe where the war was winding down. After finishing a tour at Rockaway Naval Air Station, he returned to Yale to finish his studies.

Trippe was firmly convinced that the United States would be in the war within a year's time or so, and he was glad Roosevelt had invited him to attend Westbrook's award ceremony. He

93

wanted to offer the President his Clippers' services when the war did come.

On the way to the Capital, Westbrook said to Trippe, "I never get tired of this city. I used to come here every first class weekend I could take from the Academy. Spent most of my time at the Smithsonian looking at the precious few airplanes they had back in those days. I had some great times."

The early days at Annapolis were anything but great times for Westbrook. Entering with the class of 1917 right out of his rural high school--no written exam was required for entering midshipmen so long as they had the appointment and passed the physical--he soon fell far behind in the fast moving math and science classes. By the Christmas break he was failing algebra and chemistry. Not having the money to travel back to Tallahassee for Christmas leave, he stayed in Bancroft Hall with the study materials for plebes having a difficult time or failing one or more subjects. Westbrook studied the materials, euphemistically called "The Plebe Christmas Package," uninterrupted for ten straight days. As a result, he scored high enough on the semester exams to pass all of his courses. After that, he managed well enough with his studies to graduate slightly above the middle of the class. He would always remember plebe Christmas as his moment of lonely triumph.

"I bet you did at that. Tell me something, Curtis. Do you think we're going to end up in the war?"

Westbrook looked out the window, as he recalled the First World War and the rampant German aggression. "I don't see how we can avoid it. Hitler's running amok in Europe. Sooner or later, he'll have long-range bombers that can reach the east coast of the States. Seaplanes, probably. Land-based bombers would be one-way suicide missions. I read in The Times that the Germans are claiming they've effectively eliminated the Royal Air Force's fighters. If that's true, then some kind of invasion landing on the east coast of England can't be too far behind."

"I agree," said Trippe. "The worst of it is with modern weapons there's going to be an awful lot of bloodshed this time around. Civilians will take the brunt. Hell, they already have-- Poland, Holland, France..." Trippe's voice drifted off. In a few moments he said, "Changing the subject, I've got to go back to New York right after lunch, but I understand you're going to stay in town until at least tomorrow. Call Charlie Sikes when you're ready to go back. He can pick you up in this plane. It's not going into scheduled service for another week."

As they pulled into the circular drive of the White House Westbrook saw a familiar figure standing under the White House portico.

"Why, that's Di Gates!" he exclaimed.

The car stopped under the portico and Westbrook stepped out onto the driveway. "You old son of a gun," said Artemus Gates, a cheerful, large ruddy man still looking like the college football star he once was. He warmly embraced Westbrook. "Can't stop playing hero, can you?"

Westbrook introduced Gates to Trippe. "Whatever else he is, he's a hell of a pilot."

Gates had been among the elite Ivy Leaguers who had become Naval Aviators in the Naval Reserve Force in World War I. Ironically, he had landed his seaplane in the open sea to rescue several British sailors from a sunken British warship under heavy German fire. Gates had been recommended for the Congressional Medal of Honor, but it was never awarded for reasons now lost to history.

After the war, Gates had enjoyed a successful business career until late in Roosevelt's second term, when he was appointed Deputy Secretary of the Navy for Air.

Gates led them into the White House and directly to the Oval Office. The President was seated behind a large mahogany desk that had belonged to his famous distant cousin, Teddy.

Westbrook was surprised how much older than his fifty-eight years Roosevelt looked. His face was rather gray and his hands were gnarled with purplish veins. But he was buoyant with enthusiasm, and Westbrook noticed his barrel chest, hardened with muscle from his years of having to use his upper torso instead of his legs to move about. His black Scottie, Fala, was curled up asleep on a hooked rug in front of the small fire place.

"Three Naval Aviators at once is a little much to handle," Roosevelt said warmly, shaking hands with Westbrook and

Trippe.

"These two fellows were combat heros, Mr. President, I didn't do too much," Trippe said modestly.

"You passed the course, Juan, that's what really matters," Roosevelt replied, holding a wooden match to his cigarette, held by his ebony cigarette holder.

"All right, gentlemen, we have a lot to talk about. Di has to get back in about an hour, but I'd like you two fellows to stay for lunch." Adjusting his spectacles, Roosevelt took a parchment sheet from inside a leather writing folder and said in a cheerful voice, "Captain Westbrook, it gives me great pleasure to award you the Distinguished Flying Cross for the bravery and courage you displayed on the night of June 12th, Nineteen Hundred and Forty."

The President then read part of the citation from the parchment paper, citing the "highest skills of airmanship and bravery" exercised by Westbrook in his "daring open sea rescue of Allied sailors."

"It's a very great pleasure, indeed, Captain," continued the President, reaching into a right hand drawer and handing a small box to Westbrook. Inside was a serrated bronze cross emblazoned with a propeller hanging from a brightly colored red, white and blue ribbon.

"I'd pin it on you if you were in uniform. Let's see, you are a lieutenant commander in the Naval Reserve right now, aren't you?" Westbrook nodded, then Roosevelt added in a mysterious tone, "Well, we may want to do something about that very soon."

Roosevelt had a light coughing spell, after which, undeterred, he put another cigarette into his long, slender holder and lit it.

"The cartoonists have more damn fun with this little holder than anything I've ever seen," he said, talking it between his teeth and exhaling puffs of smoke at the same time. It bobbed up and down as he spoke, punctuating his words.

"Thank you for the award, Mr. President. I'll cherish it, particularly because it gave me the opportunity to meet you personally," Westbrook said.

"Well, I'd like to think you would have done the same thing

if those had been German boys in the drink, but I won't ask the question, at least right now," Roosevelt said teasingly.

Shortly after the German invasion of Poland and the beginning of World War II in Europe, in a speech to the American people, Roosevelt said, "This nation will remain a neutral nation, but I cannot ask that every American remain neutral in thought as well." There was no hiding where the President's sympathies lay.

Roosevelt turned to Trippe. "Juan, what do you think about the war? Can we afford to let Britain go down to defeat?"

"No, Mr. President, we cannot. In my opinion, we should be in the war sooner rather than later."

"H'mm. And you, Commander, what do you think?"

"I agree with Mr. Trippe, Mr. President. There's a cancer eating Europe, and it does so in the name of racial supremacy, it's called fascism, a very dangerous notion. It must be eradicated once and for all."

"I wish I had the luxury of office to do just that, but there are enough people in this country who'd turn me out of office if I were to propose or declare that the United States was at war with Germany, or do <u>anything</u> but steer a neutral course at the present time."

"Mr. President," Trippe said, "Pan American has orders for nine more Boeing Clippers with deliveries through '43. If you have a need, they're available."

"Why, that's a grand gesture, Juan. Let me study on it, but it sure has the ring of the things I want to talk to Captain Westbrook about in the next day or so."

Roosevelt pulled his chain fob from his vest and glanced at the time. "Artemus, looks like you're back to the grindstone while we have lunch."

Gates took his leave, shaking hands with Westbrook and said, "I'm sure we'll be working together very soon on some important matters. Congratulations on the DFC!"

At the President's request, Westbrook opened the french doors to the terrace of the Rose Garden and Roosevelt wheeled himself out.

Westbrook paused and looked at his Distinguished Flying

Cross one more time. Smiling to himself, he slipped it into the outside jacket pocket of his suit.

Outside, two Filipinos, Navy stewards, busied themselves with setting the table. There was a pleasant light breeze blowing as they sat and were served tall glasses of lemonade and plates of cold poached salmon. The President was clearly preoccupied, and it showed in his eyes. Vacant, staring in the distance.

"And you, Mr. President," Westbrook asked, "how do you think England will fare in this face-off with the Germans?"

Roosevelt put his fork on his plate and dabbed his mouth with his napkin. "If it continues to be a war of attrition, England will lose. Our intelligence people tell me that if Nazi U-boats continue their toll of Allied shipping at the current rate for another six, even four, weeks, the British Isles will virtually be blockaded from the rest of the world. Compound that with dwindling British aircraft and loss of pilots. It's bad. Don't let anyone varnish that over for you. Churchill's cables are grim. Very grim.

"On the other hand, if Hitler does something really stupid, like attack Russia, then it's a whole new ball game. Obviously, I can't say anything in public, but we have some fairly high level German contacts in Berlin who've hinted that war with Russia has been discussed by Hitler with his senior officers more than once."

"Excuse me, Mr. President," Trippe said, "but you mentioned the possible isolation of Great Britain a few minutes ago. Our Clippers can fly eastbound non-stop to Southampton. What if we converted a few to freighters? It would take at least ninety days, but they might do the job."

"Too long, Juan, too long." Roosevelt paused, shifting his weight in his wheel chair. Then smiling he said, "But there's food for thought there. We're more than likely going to have some mighty dangerous diplomatic missions over the next several weeks and months. That's why I see some real possibilities for the Clippers.

"This all ties into what I wanted to pursue with Captain Westbrook."

After lunch, pleading the need to return to New York, Trippe excused himself as planned. He shook Roosevelt's hand and said to Westbrook, "Remember, call when you're ready to come back to New York."

Alone in the Rose Garden with Westbrook, Roosevelt pushed his wheel chair away from the table, belched loudly, and lit a cigarette.

"Afraid when one's in my condition, Captain, there tends to be a lot of gas. Funny thing, I'm told by a reliable source that Hitler's flatulent--farts all the time."

Westbrook, who had just started on a hot cup of coffee, choked.

Roosevelt leaned towards Westbrook and cupped his right hand to his mouth, as though sharing a naughty secret. "Not a word, Curtis, not a word. It's our joke, which I think we should keep for posterity. Now that we're sharing secrets, I think I'll call you by your first name."

Both men laughed, agreeing solemnly that Hitler's flatulence should not, at least for the time being, be made public to the American people.

Roosevelt turned abruptly serious. The interlude had restored some color to his face.

"As you probably know, in September of last year, right after hostilities broke out in Europe, I ordered the Navy to establish the Neutrality Patrol to guard our sea approaches from the United States to the West Indies. We have the old, venerable PBY Catalinas flying from Greenland to the northern coast of South America. Trouble is, they're slow and have limited range, with almost no strategic capabilities.

"There are newer versions in production, but this airplane is not the answer. What I want to ask you is what you think about the possibility of using seaplanes or amphibian airplanes for strategic bombing of enemy territory--land-based targets as well as ships? You've written rather extensively on the subject in the past, and I'll be interested in hearing your current views on the subject."

Shortly after Westbrook joined Pan American, the internecine warfare in the U. S. Navy over the use of the aircraft carrier reached its crescendo. The so-called "battleship admirals"--the old guard who stridently held the view that sea power meant supremacy and the airplane was, at best, useful only for auxiliary things such as scouting--were losing to the visionaries who saw the future of the carrier. Westbrook followed the debate closely and began writing articles on the strategic use of the sea plane, two of which had been published in the prestigious U. S. Naval Institute Proceedings. Writing came natural to him, with long-layovers in far away places and long spells alone in the crew's cabin while a back-up pilot was spelling him at the controls.

Westbrook considered his response carefully. "It's a difficult question, Mr. President. In order to make seaplanes work as long-range strategic aircraft, they'd have to have either a port, which would be preferred, or some kind of a home at sea--a seaplane tender--which infers naval superiority in their areas of operations. My hunch is that it would be difficult to structure and design an airplane that would be both a good strategic, offensive bomber, and a seaplane at the same time. I'd really like to be wrong, though."

"Maybe you are. The Martin Company is working on a prototype seaplane which it's calling the PBM Mariner. This airplane is bigger, faster, and has a much longer range than the PBY, to say nothing of a substantially increased pay load. I've arranged for you to meet with some of the fellows down there in Baltimore tomorrow morning at nine o'clock; chief engineer and chief pilot, maybe some others. I want your honest appraisal. Martin wants a big contract from the Navy, and I'm willing to support it in Congress if some objective expert like you tells me it's worth supporting. But if it has shortcomings which I'm not hearing about, tell me.

"One last thing, Curtis, then Will can take you to your hotel. I may have sounded ungrateful when I passed over Juan's offer of the Clippers. Truth is, I've been thinking about this for a long time. As the war expands on the Continent, and particularly in Britain, we're going to need long-range planes to perform diplomatic and, probably, clandestine flights. As far as I know, the Clippers are the only thing we have that fits the bill.

Roosevelt leaned towards Westbrook, and said in a low

whisper, "I've been advised by the Attorney General to use military crews, at least the pilot-in-command, if there is the remotest possibility of being captured by the Germans. The AG feels that otherwise the Germans could use the pretext that the civilians are spies, not entitled to treatment as prisoners of war and possibly executed. Sounds farfetched to me, but I'm not going to argue the point. If I decide to move forward, would you be willing to return to active duty and help organize a unit to fly the Clippers, as well as fly some trips yourself? You'll be promoted to full commander and billeted either here or in New York, if you prefer."

Westbrook was surprised. "I'm flattered, Mr. President, but why me? There must be a number of current active duty Navy pilots who could do the job better."

"Not true. The active duty pilots don't have experience flying the Clipper. That's crucial--where she can land, where she can't, all sorts of things that only experience behind the wheel can provide. There's something else too, Curtis. Courage. I've read the citation for your Navy Cross in 1918, and I know what you did just two weeks ago." The President paused to light a cigarette and then looked Westbrook straight in the eye. Westbrook remembered the day as if it were yesterday.

On August 12, 1918 they took off before dawn from the U.S. Naval Air Station in Porto Corsini, Italy. The flight consisted of one Macchi-8 bomber, a single seat seaplane capable of delivering a modest bomb load, accompanied by four M-5 seaplane fighters for cover, including one piloted by Ensign Westbrook. The target was the Austrian naval base at Pola on the Adriatic Sea, due east of Porto Corsini.

As the five Allied aircraft began their run over Pola, they were met by five Albatross fighters of the Austrian Air Force. There was brief dog-fight, and one of the M-5s was shot down, crash landing close to the shore. Westbrook's wing man noticed that the pilot of the crashed M-5 had survived and was trying to avoid strafing fighters and two Austrian naval boats firing at him enroute to the crash scene. While his wing man maneuvered for an attempted rescue of the downed pilot, Westbrook turned into the four remaining Albatrosses. In a tight turn he saw the first one attempting to fire on his wing man as he landed on the water. Hit in the engine, the enemy fighter exploded. Seeing their boats closing on the downed airman, the remaining Albatrosses headed for home.

Westbrook immediately turned toward the gun boats, less than a mile from the crash scene. Descending to mast level, he began weaving in an S pattern as he closed on the bows of the two converging targets. He fired a burst at the lead boat which veered sharply to the left, its helmsman mortally wounded. Turning 180 degrees to make a pass at the remaining boat, Westbrook's guns jammed. Then he noticed that his wingman was on his take off run, the downed pilot safely aboard. Westbrook flew over the gun boat to distract it one more time. He was met with a hail of gun fire which ripped holes in the fabric of his M-5, but he was able to return to Porto Corsini unscathed. The rescue had been successful and champagne flowed at the officers' club that night. The Commander in Chief, Naval Forces Europe, pinned the Navy Cross on his tunic two months later, less than a month before the Armistice was signed.

"Think about it overnight. We can talk tomorrow afternoon when you get back from the Martin plant. Come around four, for cocktails. I think and feel a lot better after I've had a nice cold martini."

"Have you made up your mind about taking Mr. Trippe up on his offer?" Westbrook asked.

"Yes, I have, and I've also made up my mind that I'm going to make it very difficult for you to back out of my offer."

Roosevelt took both of Westbrook's hands in his own, and with his trademark smile, bid him good afternoon.

* * * * *

After checking in at the Mayflower, Westbrook strolled to the lobby newsstand and bought a copy of The Wall Street Journal and The Washington Post. He had enjoyed The Post since Annapolis, delivered to his room in Bancroft Hall early in the morning before reveille by some hapless plebe.

Once in his room, Westbrook called Joanna. No answer. Then he remembered Joanna had afternoon rehearsal and it was Hattie's day off.

He tried to relax with his papers, but he was too preoccupied. His-slap-on-the wrist suspension would be over next week, but he was not going get any time at the airline for the rest of the month. He needed time to sort a lot of things out. He was very interested in the possibility of going back on active duty if it could help the Allied cause, and still let him fly the Clipper.

The phone rang, giving Westbrook a start.

"Captain Westbrook, Sylvia Meyers. You've been in Washington almost half a day and you haven't called me yet. I trust we're still on for dinner."

"Good afternoon. You didn't give me your phone number last week," he lied, trying to forestall any involvement with Meyers.

"Sorry. Thought I did. Will you please have dinner with me tonight? Time's running out and I need to talk to you. It'll be painless for you." Her voice was somehow unsure.

"What can I say?" Westbrook said.

Meyers' voice suddenly broke with emotion. "Look, I feel like I owe you one for that stupid railroad job you went through in New York. I need to talk to you. There's a lot more to it than you imagine. I need to see you.

"Please, I'll have you back in your hotel in two hours. All I want to do is have dinner with you, damn it, and tell you some things you should know."

Westbrook was silent for a moment, then said, "OK, Miss Meyers--Sylvia--when and where?"

Sylvia's voice reflected her relief. "I'll meet you in the lobby of at the Shoreham at 6:30. We'll eat there. My treat."

The phone clicked dead in Westbrook's ear.

He tried Joanna again. Still no answer.

He looked at the time, and saw he had two hours. He showered and tried to take a short nap, to no avail.

When his phone rang twenty minutes later, he was in a foul mood. He hoped it was Sylvia Meyers calling to cancel dinner.

"Curtis, I haven't heard from you. What's going on?"

It was Joanna. Her voice immediately cheered him.

"Not much right now. Tried to call you a few times when I got to the hotel this afternoon, but I guess you were going

103

through the afternoon drill."

"I was, and it's exhausting, but I love it. Tell me all about your visit with the President."

Carefully choosing his words, he described the meeting and lunch with the President. He said nothing about the President's request that he return to active duty. That could wait until they were together. Alone.

He told her about his dinner date with Sylvia Meyers, trying not to sound defensive. "She mentioned a 'railroad job in New York.' Daugherty said at least a dozen times that it was a 'kangaroo court.'"

Joanna's voice was frosty. "She tried to do you in."

"I want to see what makes this woman tick. She testified against me at the suspension hearing and now she's been pleading with me to have dinner. She was articulate as hell at the hearing, but it sounds like a guilty conscious wants to confess. There's more here than meets the eye. She's afraid, and not the fire-brand Daugherty portrayed."

Joanna was irked, but reasonable. "At least you told me about it instead of letting me read about it in the papers. But call me....oops, I've got rehearsal tonight, damn it."

They made plans for dinner on Friday and rang off. Once again, Westbrook cursed his curiosity, but what if there had been a set-up? And why?

* * * * *

He found Sylvia waiting in the large lobby of the Shoreham, crowded with lawyers and their wives checking in for the annual meeting of the American Bar Association. She was clearly agitated. She extended her hand to Westbrook and led him toward the dining room. "Nice to see you, Curtis. I hope I didn't create an awkward situation for you, but I'm dying to at least begin setting matters straight after that debacle in New York."

The maitre d' treated her like on old friend. As soon as they were seated Sylvia lit a Cuban cigarillo. It had the aroma of a mild, expensive cigar.

"Obviously, I can't say very much in a public place like this, but..."

Suddenly, a large swarthy man with a black watch cap pulled

down nearly to his eyes approached Sylvia from behind. Westbrook watched him lunge toward her with much more agility than a man of his size would suggest.

"Fucking commie whore!" the man shouted as he grabbed her neck in a vise-like grip, dragging her from her chair. Her high heels made staccato noises as she tried to maintain her balance.

Startled, and in great pain, Sylvia tried to scream but couldn't. Her face went white as she gurgled a peculiar sound. She clawed desperately with both hands at his choking arm. She was dying.

Westbrook leapt to his feet to assist her. The man dropped his right arm and pulled out a snub-nosed .38-caliber pistol and fired. The shot went wild, hitting a large crystal chandelier and lodging in the ceiling, creating pandemonium in the dining room. Frightened guests scrambled for the exits.

As her attacker dragged Sylvia toward the fire exit two men appeared through the doorway. One slugged Sylvia's attacker behind his right ear with a lead filled blackjack, causing him to fall to the floor. The sound of splintering jaw bone and skull sounded like the dull thud of a large naval shell.

The rescuer quickly scooped up the dead man's pistol and the other man put Sylvia's wrap around her shoulders. Neither said a word, but were clearly intent on getting her away as quickly as possible.

Westbrook stood by the table, stunned.

Sylvia, barely able to stand, and grimacing with pain, said in a hoarse whisper, "I'm sorry. I can explain this--someday." Then she turned, and the two men led her towards the corner fire exit.

Hotel security guards and Metro police officers converged on the scene, leaving Westbrook to do the explaining for something he had no clue about.

CHAPTER 8
WASHINGTON AND BALTIMORE

Westbrook spent the next day at the Glenn L. Martin aircraft manufacturing facility, but couldn't get the events of the last evening out of his mind. It seemed as if it had all taken place in slow motion, accentuated by the tinkling of falling shards of chandelier and the sound of the blackjack breaking bone.

Although he had wanted to, Westbrook didn't call Sylvia. He wondered what was at work in Sylvia's life, and how badly hurt she was. There had been no mention of the incident in the morning Post, and nothing was said about it on the morning radio news.

Westbrook was given the grand tour of the Martin plant, a huge complex of brick, concrete and four glass buildings which extended for several acres along the shores of Chesapeake Bay. He received a detailed, top secret briefing on the Martin PBM flying boat, including a visit to the assembly plant, a thorough cockpit check out and a high-speed taxi demonstration in the Chesapeake.

The evolution of the aircraft had not been entirely satisfactory to the Navy. It did not carry the payload or meet the range requirements that had been sold to the Navy. The payload problem had been partially solved by reducing the armor plate on the fuselage, but range was still a problem. Newer, more powerful and fuel efficient engines were still six months away. With the first production aircraft scheduled to be delivered in a little more than thirty days to Patrol Squadron Fifty-five, the Martin employees were understandably lobbying strongly for their airplane, and at the same time working hard to correct its problems.

Westbrook was impressed with the idea, but it clearly did not fit in the role of a strategic bomber that the President had hoped for. It didn't have enough firepower to successfully defend itself, and the range deficiency made it a marginal strategic aircraft. Nevertheless, the PBM was conceptually important, and he would give the President a solid vote on the airplane for its intended mission--anti-shipping and anti-submarine warfare--but not beyond that.

* * * * *

Roosevelt looked solemn and preoccupied when Westbrook was ushered into the Oval Office just after 1600. He was sitting with his hands folded in his lap in almost the same spot behind his desk as he had been yesterday. They were alone when they exchanged greetings.

To the President's left was a silver tea caddy on a trolley with hors d'oeuvres, a pitcher of cold martinis, and several bottles of other liquors and mixers. Leaning over to his left, towards the caddy Roosevelt said, "Martini, Curtis?"

"No thanks, Mr. President. A splash of the Johnny Walker on the rocks would be fine."

"Good. I'll Fix it." After putting some ice in a glass and pouring some scotch, Roosevelt leaned forward, handing the drink to Westbrook. "Quite a little session you had at the Shoreham last night," Roosevelt said, smiling and sounding a little sheepish.

Before Westbrook could respond, the President, raising his hand, continued, "She's one of ours. Sylvia Meyers is one of ours."

Westbrook looked at Roosevelt. Nothing made sense. "Mr. President, I'm sorry, but I'm so far behind the power curve here, you're going to have to help me."

Roosevelt sighed, his shoulders sagging. "As contrived as it may sound to you, some things have happened very recently which don't make a lot of common sense but <u>do</u> require positive action, and very soon.

"I'm telling you this off the record only because J. Edgar Hoover urged me to do so in the interest of time. He's gambling you'll abide by the terms of the top secret clearance you received during the war, and which was never revoked according to the F.B.I. and War Department files.

"Sylvia Meyers is one of the bravest people ever to serve the United States Government. I say that without fear of exaggeration. For some time, she has been posing as a very sympathetic--and fanatic--Communist who acts like she thinks

108

Stalin is a god. In fact, she is a devout Jew who has made enormous personal sacrifices of her own, including those of personal security, to infiltrate what appears to be the growing support of Communism in this country. She's now in mortal danger, and swift action must be taken. Unfortunately, there is a small lunatic fringe which is well funded; its charter is to kill prominent left-wingers. It started shortly after the Spanish Civil War ended, and the F.B.I. is having difficulty smoking out its leaders. Worst of all, Berlin was recently told she's a double agent trying to get as much info she can on Russo-German relations and feeding it back to the F.B.I. I can't go much further into specific details, but she is being groomed for what should be a significant role should we get into the war--if she hasn't been compromised--and that's a big if at this point. Remember I alluded yesterday to the fact that there is increasing evidence the Germans may turn on their ally Russia and invade her? We want to be ready, even if we're not in the war." Roosevelt paused, lit a cigarette and sipped his martini.

"Three days ago we received word from the French Underground, via Mr. Churchill, that a man named Jacques LaDieux, a leading Communist in France who'd spearheaded the Resistance until his capture by the Germans, has been liberated from prison in France, and is being smuggled out of France to Lisbon. DeGaulle insists that LaDieux go to London to show that the solidarity of the Free French is the only way the French Underground can survive, whatever their political beliefs may be. LaDieux is an ardent Communist with only a common hatred of the Germans linking him to DeGaulle. The matter is complicated by the opposition of the Vichy French, who will, along with the Nazis, do anything to ensure the meeting in London never takes place. We see the meeting as an opportunity for America." Roosevelt paused again, gestured to Westbrook to help himself to another drink. Nodding his head, Westbrook declined. Westbrook sensed from the President's raspy voice that he was growing weary. Trying to fit the pieces together, Westbrook felt the President was being a little vague. Intentionally or not, he couldn't tell.

"Unfortunately, Mr. LaDieux," Roosevelt continued, "who I

gather is a clever man, has insisted that Sylvia Meyers either be in London or meet him in Lisbon when he gets there. He wants to show DeGaulle his strength and influence over the American Communist Party, which he knows will pour big bucks into the Resistance Movement if he is perceived as an equal to DeGaulle. DeGaulle desperately needs a show of support, even with someone who represents everything he abhors. Without it he's likely to be viewed as no more than a weak voice in the wilderness, a coward who fled his country and signifies nothing."

Roosevelt paused, took off his glasses, closed his eyes, and began rubbing the bridge of this nose. "I may be rambling, Curtis, so ask any questions that come to mind." Roosevelt turned in his chair and looked straight at Westbrook, saying in a firm, authoritative voice, "I want you to come back on active duty. I'll take your generous chairman up on his offer of a Clipper, and we'll start making history. You will fly to Lisbon on what'll appear to be a routine flight. There, you pick up Mr. LaDieux. Miss Meyers will be with you, and then you'll fly the airplane to London. Not Southampton, but London. I'm told your landing on the Thames will be difficult and tricky, but it has to be done for security. Questions?"

As if coming off a wild roller coaster ride, Westbrook raised his hands defensively, and said, "Excuse me Mr. President, but with all due respect, I'm hearing a lot of loose ends that aren't being tied up in any way. I'm flattered to be asked for something as special as this, but I don't feel like I know the half of it."

"You don't, but you will. The main thing to do now is get set for this flight to Lisbon, which will take place within the next two weeks, so that LaDieux won't have to wait around long. The Germans will be hot on his tail and have agents in both places to kill him on sight. Given what happened last night, I'm increasingly concerned about Sylvia's well-being, too. The thug who tried to kill her was a professional assassin, and we don't know yet which of several extremist groups might be responsible, although I'm reasonably confident it's the one I mentioned a few moments ago. However, it also might be the Nazis. We just don't know."

There was silence between the two men as Westbrook sorted his thoughts. The President lit a cigarette, and rearranged his legs to stimulate their limited circulation.

"Of course, I'll be honored, Mr. President."

Roosevelt poured himself another martini, offering the bottle of scotch to Westbrook, who declined.

"Ah, well, cheers." Roosevelt held his glass up in a toast.

Roosevelt confided in Westbrook that Sylvia, a tenacious lawyer, had been spotted by OSS operatives who came to the conclusion that she would be the perfect cover to lobby for Soviet causes in the United States.

The plan had worked only too well. Meyers had become a target of ever-increasing viciousness, for groups as diverse as the America Firsters, firebrands determined to keep America out of the war, and the American Nazi Party. It became imperative that she be protected by the F.B.I. twenty-four hours a day.

She had done a good job with the role, but the price was becoming higher. Her law practice had suffered; clients simply weren't comfortable with a radical lawyer who had been a devout Jew and was now an atheist zealot. Her lecture schedule at Georgetown Law Center had been drastically curtailed.

"Bill Donovan's boys at the OSS searched all around for ways for Sylvia to get extensive public exposure," said Roosevelt. "When it became obvious that you were on the way to becoming a new American hero, facing possible sanctions from your own government, the OSS fellows pointed out that the public hearing provided the perfect forum for Sylvia. She'd receive world wide notoriety, enhancing her credibility with the Communists, but also further endangering her life, particularly because of the new German suspicions about her."

"What about Kaminsky?" asked Westbrook, as he finished his watered down drink, incredulous over what he was hearing from the President of the United States.

"Kaminsky was brought into the scheme first, and the matter was then presented to Sylvia as a <u>fait accompli</u>. She had no choice.

"Now, on the other hand," said Roosevelt smiling, "neither Ferguson or Daugherty had a clue. The whole thing was put together in a matter of hours, and was so damn convincing it exceeded our wildest expectations.

"I'm truly sorry for the misery and uncertainty you must have gone through. Don't think for a minute it didn't make us all feel bad. Miss Meyers called me after the hearing and told me in no uncertain terms she would never do anything like it again--for anybody.

"When you and Juan joined me for lunch yesterday everything came into focus--send a Clipper to Lisbon with Sylvia, pick up LaDieux and fly on to London. So simple it almost escaped me altogether." Roosevelt drained his martini glass, obviously pleased.

"After you left yesterday I phoned Churchill and told him my idea. He was ecstatic. His intelligence advisors nixed a landing at Southampton. LaDieux is a condemned man and the German agents in the U.K would find a way to ambush him in the countryside. So, my boy, you'll have to find a way to land in London." He patted Westbrook on the knee and wished him well. Nobody told him whether, in fact, there was <u>any place</u> on the Thames that a Clipper <u>could</u> land.

* * * * *

Westbrook was immediately issued orders recalling him to active duty. He was promoted to full commander and assigned to Naval Air Station, Floyd Bennett Field, New York. For all practical purposes, however, he continued to work out of the Marine Air Terminal at LaGuardia.

Westbrook was given the immediate assignment of developing a plan to land the Clipper on the Thames in close proximity to a yet- undetermined meeting place. Any landing would be difficult, given the many bridges and the amount of river traffic. Several experienced captains recruited by Westbrook wagered it couldn't be done at all.

True to his word, Juan Trippe leased the Yankee Clipper for a period of one year to the Navy's Bureau of Aeronautics on a nominal basis.

CHAPTER 9
LISBON

It was 0300 and Luis Sanguino called to report that a hysterical young woman had been found in a dark alley in the Alfama district. Gasparo was livid. "Excremento! Salazar's niece? How stupid can these Germans be." He began fumbling in the darkness for his Fatimas and matches. Alfama was no place for <u>anybody</u> after dark, let alone an aristocratic young woman. Nude from the waist up, her face was beaten and bloody. She just happened to be the favorite niece of the First Minister Antonio de Oliveira Salazar, who ran the country with an iron-fist. Salazar had his own secret police force, accountable to no one but him, who were feared by the populace of Portugal at every social and economical level. No one was immune from their inquiry--or their brutality.

Her assailant, a German Army officer in mufti, had been found unconscious near the victim, his shirt covered with her blood and his own vomit.

Gasparo's initial thought, for which he later asked Heavenly forgiveness, was that this whole episode would complicate his investigation of the Holloran murder. He had little doubt that the assailant worked for Auchlin, but he would wait until later in the morning to confirm this. Sitting on the side of the bed, he lit a cigarette. The sulphur match popped like miniature fire works in the dark.

Sanguino told him that the officer was passed out in a cell and the hysterical victim had described him. She would confirm his identity as soon as she was released from the hospital.

After they hung up, Gasparo made the call he dreaded most-- to the First Minister.

Antonio Salazar did not like to be awakened early in the morning by anyone, including the Chief Inspector of Lisbon, but when he learned why he exploded.

In a menacing voice void of mercy, Salazar said, "Gasparo, do not, under any circumstances set this man free! If you do, he will disappear and his headless body will be delivered to the

German Embassy by me personally. You'll lose your job and your pension. Everything!"

Gasparo knew the Minister's threats weren't idle, so he swore he would not release the accused, even if requested to do so on grounds of diplomatic immunity by Hitler himself.

Salazar rang off, the Minister's voice still ringing in Gasparo's ears.

After tossing and turning for a few hours, Gasparo rose, shaved, took a quick bath and lit another cigarette while dressing. He had recently developed a slight hacking cough which annoyed him more than it worried him.

After his usual breakfast he went back to the bedroom and kissed his wife gently on the cheek as she snored lightly.

Snapping on his shoulder holster, he patted his small Beretta. He seldom wore his gun to work, since he could check one out at the station, but putting on his own gun that day made him feel safer.

He knew Salazar's secret police would be watching both doors of the station. He wouldn't see them, but they would be there all the same. He got out of his car and walked into the building, eyes straight ahead. They're there. I can almost smell them.

"Bom dia, Inspector," said Carlos Carbanaro, who had just come on duty as the precinct watch officer. Carbanaro was a large sedentary man who was the court jester of Police headquarters, always given to playing practical jokes, as well as being the recipient of a few himself.

"Bom dia, Carlos. I understand we have a rather unusual guest this morning."

"'Peculiar' is the right word. He's been sleeping like the dead since he was brought in. Groaned a few times, but that's it."

"Any identification?"

"None. Apparently, a thief came along and stole his coat. His wallet and money were in it. Easy pickings. The victim told the patrolman who found them that she'd met him at a German-Portuguese friendship reception at the German Embassy earlier in the evening. He told her he worked out of the Palacio Hotel in Estoril on intelligence matters and was an officer in the German

Army, a member of an elite unit, the name of which she didn't remember."

Gasparo grimaced. The name of the hotel confirmed the fact the prisoner worked for Auchlin. He poured a cup of coffee and lit a cigarette.

The Inspector went to his office and rang Morgado.

"Jose? Gasparo. I hate to bother you on your day off, but two heads are better than one. Please come in as quickly as possible."

"I would've been disappointed if you hadn't rung, Inspector. I'm on my way."

Gasparo hung up and went to Carbanaro's desk near the front door of the station. "All right, my friend, introduce me to your guest."

They went into the reeking cell block. It was stifling hot in the new heat of another early September day. Gasparo had always said that any aspiring criminal should spend a summer day in the Lisbon jail before deciding to embark on such a career.

The German was lying on a small, soiled cot chained to the wall of the cell, his head thrown back, and his mouth open. Only the heaving of his chest indicated he was alive. The odor of vomit was overwhelming.

"Pretty bad shape, I'd say, from the looks of him."

"He's retched a few times. We haven't tried to wake him before instructions from you or Senhor Morgado."

"Well, let him sleep until I've discussed the matter with Jose. What's the latest on the victim?"

"Her uncle dispatched a special medical team to the hospital, and they report she's doing as well as can be expected. She's young--only twenty. None of her wounds are serious."

"Ah, yes, but she'll be scarred for life. What manner of beasts are these Germans?" He could tell by looking at the prisoner that he had to be over thirty. Is this what they're doing all over Europe?

Gasparo's phone was ringing when he returned to his office. This time there were no introductions.

"What's the status of the German pig who raped my niece?" Salazar yelled so loud Gasparo had to take the telephone away from his ear.

"He's still unconscious, Minister, but I expect to revive him momentarily and have a full confession by the end of the day."

"You are prepared to apply torture, are you not?"

"Yes, your Excellency," he lied, gesturing for Morgado, who had just arrived, to sit down.

"Have you notified the swine's commanding officer yet?"

Gasparo told him he would pursue the matter personally and immediately. It was still not quite 0800 and Gasparo wanted some time to consider his options before calling Auchlin. He hoped the prisoner would confess or at least tie Auchlin somehow into Holloran's murder.

"You'd better," Salazar snapped. He hung up.

Gasparo sighed and sat down at his desk, brushing dead cigarette ashes from his lapel. "This will not be a pleasant day," he said to Morgado. "I've spoken with the Minister twice, and he would have us execute this man now. In fact, if we don't, he may try it himself.

"My heart is heavy, Jose. If this man works for Auchlin it may complicate matters. I'm convinced that he will not leave Portugal alive, so unless you feel differently, I'll convey this fact to Auchlin."

"Let's interrogate him first," Morgado said. "Perhaps he can tell us some things about Auchlin that will help us solve our Holloran case. After all, the prisoner isn't going anywhere soon-- unless straight to Hell, courtesy of the First Minister. In any case, we need to make it clear to him what peril he's in."

This prompted a smile. "As usual, my young friend, you are full of good ideas."

Before entering the cell, Gasparo unholstered his pistol and handed it to Morgado, who locked the large steel door behind the Inspector as he entered the cell. The German was asleep, so Gasparo shook his shoulders vigorously. The man opened his eyes slowly, looking in unfocused disbelief. He groaned loudly.

"What is your name?" Gasparo asked. "Do you speak Portuguese or English?"

"English...I speak...some English," the German said weakly.

"Good. So do we. Let us begin. Do you know why you are

here?"

The German's head lolled from side to side.

"Yes, I think so. The girl...I had too much to drink. She...I tore her blouse. She ran off, I think. I must have passed out."

"In truth, you raped her before you passed out, did you not?"

"No. I was--I couldn't--it wouldn't..."

"Are you saying you were impotent, couldn't get an erection?" Gasparo asked.

"Too much to drink."

The prisoner sat up and buried his head in his hands. Gasparo brought the conversation to a head.

"Nevertheless, you're charged with the crime of rape, as well as assault, with the intent to do serious bodily harm. By the way, do you know who the young lady is?"

The German shook his head and said, "I don't remember."

"What a pity," Morgado said through the cell bars. "She happens to be a very dear relative of the First Minister. He has asked us to have you disappear, perhaps in the sewer system in small pieces upon which the rats can feast. If we release you, you'll be dead within a half hour."

"Water--could I please have some water?"

"Soon." Gasparo said, looking at his watch. He knew he only had a limited amount of time before Salazar would act on his own in dealing with the prisoner. "Your papers were missing when you were brought to the station. What is your name?"

"Ludke, Werner Ludke."

Gasparo was not surprised. Auchlin had told him of his high regard for his lieutenant.

"Ah, yes, you work for my good friend Major Auchlin. He has said complimentary things about you."

Gasparo's disclosure had the intended effect: Ludke froze in sheer terror.

"Please don`t tell Major Auchlin about this!"

"Your problems are much more serious than Major Auchlin. We'll let you sleep some more. I'll visit with you this afternoon. Remember, you are in danger of your life if you leave this place, as terrible as you may think it is."

"Incredible, Inspector, incredible," Morgado said admiringly when they were out of earshot.

"He'll tell us everything about Auchlin or he will tell us nothing," Gasparo said. "He's so scared it made him sick that Auchlin mentioned his name to a stranger like me. We'll see. And very soon." He thought for a moment and then added, "For the time being, say nothing to Luis. The less he knows, the better we'll be able to control what he tells Auchlin."

Late Friday afternoon Gasparo still had not kept his promise to visit Ludke again, and to his great relief Salazar had not called back either.

"He is very sick," Carbanaro updated the Inspector on the prisoner. "It's more than a hangover--it's more like he is hallucinations: bad dreams, nausea. It`s hard to tell."

"Have you sent for a doctor yet?" Morgado asked.

"No. He keeps asking to speak privately with Inspector Gasparo. He's adamant."

"Oh, how so?" Gasparo asked.

"It's something about his dreams. I don't really know."

Gasparo smelled blood. Ludke might answer a number of questions, including who murdered Holloran.

"Have him cleaned up and brought here. No hand cuffs or other restraints. Just remind him that there are people right outside this building who know who he is, where he is, and who will kill him on sight if he tries to leave this building."

Twenty minutes later, Ludke was escorted into Gasparo's office. He still looked like a man who had a rendezvous with death.

Smiling, Gasparo said, "Police work in the Third Reich is no doubt more rewarding than it is here in Lisbon. Please forgive me for such austere offices." Gasparo waved his hand toward a chair.

Ludke greedily accepted a cigarette.

"I must talk, Inspector. I fear I'm going mad."

"Please proceed," Gasparo said, still smiling. Morgado quietly entered the Inspector's office and sat down.

"What guarantees can you give me, Inspector? Can I be given asylum? Can you arrange that I will never be troubled by Auchlin?" His hands were trembling so badly Morgado had to light his cigarette.

"You ask too many questions, my friend," Gasparo said, again looking at his watch. "The short answer is that you're a lot of trouble to me. It would be most expedient to turn you over to the First Minister's secret police right now. If, however, you are able to shed some light on a matter of the utmost concern to us, you might be a free man soon. Please, let's get on with it, or I must be on to other things."

"What is this matter?" Ludke asked softly, inhaling cigarette smoke deeply.

"Holloran, Phineas Holloran, the American pilot who was murdered by your superior, probably with your knowledge, and possibly your assistance."

Gasparo stopped, letting this sink in.

"Do you deny this?" he asked quietly.

Ludke's cigarette fell out of his mouth onto the floor. He could barely pick it up. "How do you know, Inspector, how do you know?"

Gasparo studied Ludke with narrowed eyes, saying nothing.

Morgado smiled. "We know, Herr Ludke, we know. What we don't know is the extent of your personal involvement. That will determine the rest."

Ludke threw his head back, covering his eyes with his hands. "I saw it all! I still have horrible nightmares about the whole thing. I couldn't believe it!" He began shaking like a man with palsy.

"It would appear then that we may have a basis for discussion," Gasparo said evenly, leaning forward towards the shaking prisoner. "You help us get Auchlin, and you are a free man. But if you betray us, I turn you over to the secret police. Do you understand?" Gasparo would worry later about how he would deliver on his promise; he knew a deal with Salazar would be out of the question.

Ludke nodded silently.

"Good. Then I want you to begin at the beginning. If you lie, you go immediately to Salazar's men. Tell us everything. Proceed."

Ludke told them how pleased he had been to have been

119

selected as Auchlin's deputy. Before that, he had been attached to the Embassy, working for Count Beck, handling routine military matters. "I was very excited about working for a personal friend of the Fuhrer's. Besides, the work at the Embassy was dull." Ludke paused, staring vacantly ahead, as though regretting his decision to leave the Embassy. "At first, I enjoyed the new job but later I grew afraid of him. Major Auchlin told me all about his 'exciting times' at Dachau. He seemed to talk about it all the time. Stringing up prisoners. Watching medical experiments performed by the Camp doctor, particularly on women." Ludke closed his eyes and asked for another cigarette.

"Major Auchlin became agitated when he learned that the American seaplanes flew to Lisbon twice weekly. He was convinced they were flying supplies to the Allies through the underground. Claiming orders from Berlin, which I never saw, Major Auchlin decided to make an example of the Americans."

Ludke claimed he had nothing to do with the killing. "Until the very last minute I thought he was only trying to scare the American. On orders from Major Auchlin, I and an enlisted man attached to our unit detained Holloran on June eighth."

Gasparo held up his hand and said, "Stop for just a minute. Are you willing to put this whole testimony under oath, Senhor Ludke?" Sworn testimony would ensure the arrest warrant from a magistrate.

"Yes, yes. Of course. Anything!"

"Good. Jose, call the nearest court reporter. We need to make a record of this."

Within a few minutes, a reporter appeared, prepared to take the sworn testimony of Ludke.

After being sworn in, Ludke was questioned further by Gasparo.

"You are a citizen of the German Reich, are you not? Do you give this testimony freely and without reservation? If so, please continue." His voice was now mellow and soothing.

"Ja, this is all true, just as you describe it." Gasparo looked hard at Ludke. He wanted Ludke to know that his own life hinged on his testimony and remaining in the Inspector's good graces.

"He told me it would be a situation where we could embarrass the Americans about the amount of contraband they were smuggling to the Allies. I was specifically ordered to stand by until Berlin ordered certain things to happen."

"Perhaps you could elaborate," Gasparo said. "Use your own words to describe the events that led up to the murder of the American."

If Ludke was lying, Gasparo wanted to find out right away.

Ludke repeated the story with consistency. He had been ordered to kidnap Holloran on the grounds that he was engaging in activities hostile to Germany.

Ludke proceeded to describe his kidnapping of Holloran. He had been accompanied by one of his sergeant majors, an old prize fighter who had found his calling in the Army of the Third Reich.

Ludke and his accomplice had gained access to Holloran's room by claiming to be hotel maintenance men making early inspections of the steam radiators. They then knocked him unconscious and put him in the trunk of Auchlin's car. By arrangement with one of the bell captain's at the Palacio Hotel, Holloran was taken to Auchlin's suite.

"I tried to extract from the American the exact nature of the contraband that was onboard the plane, as ordered."

"What did Captain Holloran say about this?" Gasparo asked.

"He acted as if he didn't know what I was talking about. Later, Major Auchlin told me it was all a ruse so he could kill an American. I did not know, I did not know!" Ludke sobbed.

"How many times did you strike the American?"

"Several times," Ludke mumbled. Gasparo could see beads of perspiration forming on Ludke's brow.

"How long did this go on?"

"About four hours."

"Then what happened?"

"Major Auchlin appeared."

"What was the condition of your prisoner when Auchlin came to the scene?"

"He was conscious and, I think, clear-headed."

"Now, Herr Ludke," Gasparo said, "tell us what happened

after Auchlin's arrival. Take your time."

Ludke shuddered and began a painstakingly slow description of Holloran's murder.

He was confused, he said, by Auchlin's anger that Holloran wasn't gagged, since he'd been ordered by Auchlin to extract a confession. He described how Auchlin tortured Holloran and how Holloran tried to fight back, which resulted in a severe beating by Auchlin. He told them that Auchlin left the room abruptly, ordering Holloran gagged, even though he was by then unconscious. By the time he had regained consciousness, Ludke had stuffed a small towel in his mouth and secured it with a piece of thick cord.

Auchlin returned carrying a small medical kit.

Auchlin removed a pair of surgical gloves and carefully rolled up his shirt sleeves.

"He seemed different then, calmer. He was humming softly."

Ludke paused and pleaded for water. Morgado poured from a porcelain vacuum thermos on Gasparo's desk.

"The Major suddenly stopped humming. He said to Holloran something like, 'You are going to die in a few moments Captain Holloran.'"

"I thought it was still a joke, Inspector. Who would believe this?"

Auchlin withdrew a shining stainless steel scalpel, turning it over thoughtfully in his hands.

"Auchlin jerked the American's head back." Ludke paused and looked down at the floor. "About this time Holloran had soiled himself."

Auchlin made an incision in Holloran's throat, from ear to ear.

"It seemed nothing at first, just some light bleeding. I began to feel relieved that perhaps the terrible charade was over, but it was not."

Auchlin faced the prisoner, as though to admire his handiwork. Then, as though he had changed his mind, he approached the American, spread his legs, and buried the scalpel in his groin, then made a jerking upward movement and withdrew the scalpel.

"Blood was everywhere. The American began twitching. Auchlin stood behind him and placed his hand over his heart. 'Come Werner, feel his heart dying. It's like the fluttering of a small bird.' I didn't do as he asked. It took several minutes before the American died. Auchlin told me he had asked a prison doctor at Dachau how to prolong death by bleeding. The doctor told him the femoral artery in the thigh. It normally pumps blood to the lower part of the body, but will pump the body empty if severed."

Gasparo cleared his throat and said icily, "Is this something that occurs frequently within the officer ranks of the German Army?"

"Nein!" Ludke exclaimed. "Nein!"

When they were alone, Morgado shut the office door and turned to Gasparo. "What do we do now, Inspector? Arrest Auchlin?"

Gasparo, drained from his session with Ludke, leaned back in his chair, considering. "I have to let this settle a little before we take any action. Auchlin will be distressed when he learns of Ludke's arrest. He may try to leave the country, get back to Germany. Ludke's confession goes no further than this room, especially not to Sanguino. For now we must focus on Senhor Ludke's immediate future--if he has one."

CHAPTER 10
LISBON

Count Beck's successor as German Ambassador to Portugal, Heinrich Steiner, looked over the police sheets listing arrests the prior evening, confirming the First Minister's call of less than an hour ago.

"Get me this imbecile Auchlin immediately," he ordered one of his aides. "I want him here in fifteen minutes." He had met Auchlin only once, at the Embassy reception held soon after he was installed as Ambassador, and he had taken an instant dislike to him. Although Auchlin reported to Wermacht Headquarters in Berlin, Steiner was senior enough to command his presence.

Unlike Beck, Steiner was an ardent Nazi. A strict disciplinarian with his employees and family, Steiner was known to be fair, even sympathetic. He had been a mid-level foreign service officer when the Nazis came to power in 1933 and soon caught the eye of von Ribbentrop, who posted him to Lisbon after Beck defected. His unofficial orders were to secure Portugal into the Axis alliance. And while he had not yet met Salazar, he had enjoyed several pleasant phone conversations with him. Until today.

The police sheets had just made his life very complicated.

He was pacing the floor of the Embassy drawing room, running his hand continuously over his pate, when Auchlin arrived.

Wasting no time Steiner said, "Well, Herr Major, you look like a man without a worry this morning. Could that be because you're not on top of your job?"

Auchlin was surprised at this. He had no idea why he had been summoned to the Embassy.

Steiner handed him the yellow sheets showing the arrest of Werner Ludke for the assault on and rape of the niece of the First Minister of Portugal.

The blood drained from Auchlin's face. He leaned as unobtrusively as he could against a small mahogany table, in the cold grip of terror. He felt like he'd been hit in the solar plexus.

"This fool works for you, doesn't he?"

"Yes, Excellency." His eye began twitching rapidly. "But I had no idea; this comes as a total surprise."

Nothing made sense; a friendly phone call from Sanguino, followed by a frosty lunch with Gasparo, and now this. What came foremost to his mind was how to get away, go somewhere else and start over. But on second thought, maybe all was not lost. This might be the perfect way to get rid of Ludke once and for all. The problem was that Ludke could plea bargain, implicating him. Should he contact the Fuhrer? He needed to get away and think things through, alone.

"Excellency, I'm at a total loss for words, but we must do whatever is necessary to get to the bottom of this. If Ludke is guilty he should be dealt harshly. We cannot permit such conduct in neutral countries."

"You know the Chief Inspector of the Lisbon Police, don't you?"

"Yes. Quite well."

Pleased, Steiner folded his arms across his chest, smiled and said, "Good. I want you to go and see him today. Say it's at my request and tell him he has the full cooperation of the German government in handling this matter as expeditiously as possible. The First Minister made it clear to me he wants to deal with his niece's attacker himself, which I'm sure would not be pleasant, but if that's what it takes to buy peace with the Portuguese, so be it."

Steiner was about to dismiss Auchlin when there was a low knock at the door. Annoyed, Steiner opened it and an aide handed him a message, freshly decoded. He read it twice, then folded it into his breast pocket.

He motioned for Auchlin to sit. He then sat beside him and leaned forward pointedly, with a friendly smile. All of a sudden he needed Auchlin--or at least the connections in Lisbon he thought Auchlin had.

"The times are becoming increasingly difficult--and interesting--here in Lisbon. We may have some work to do together. Ribbentrop has just wired me that a Jew named LaDieux, a prominent French Communist organizer of the

French Underground who recently escaped from prison while under the death sentence, has been smuggled out of France into North Africa. Apparently he is on his way here to seek exile in England. Ribbentrop wants him taken--preferably alive--and sent to Germany for a public trial and hanging."

Auchlin was having difficulty thinking clearly, but he knew he was being reprieved, at least for now. He ran a fast check list. Gasparo was probably too honest, but there was Sanguino. Sanguino had shown some admiration for the German cause earlier.

"I'm quite prepared to deal with this," Auchlin said. "Excellency, do you mind if I smoke?" Steiner shrugged his shoulders, and Auchlin lit a cigarette.

"While we may not have the open support of the officials, I know people who will help us gladly, particularly if there is compensation," Auchlin said. He was regaining his footing as he spoke.

"I'm sure we'll receive more specific details soon, but I'd like you to see your Inspector friend as soon as possible," Steiner said.

They exchanged salutes, and Auchlin departed. He frowned into the noonday sun as he exited the Embassy. He wondered why the Inspector didn't call him about Ludke. Then he realized that if he could control the LaDieux operation personally he could become a hero. Ludke would then be inconsequential.

Once back at his hotel he sent a coded message to Himmler asking for full particulars on LaDieux. Then he called Sanguino.

CHAPTER 11
NEW YORK

Momentum built rapidly after Westbrook's meeting with the President. He was placed in overall command of the non-scheduled Clipper operations for Pan American, which was given the code name "Eagles Away." As a U.S. Navy Commander he reported directly to Artemus Gates in Washington. Requests from the Allies for secret Clipper operations would be carefully screened by the two men and submitted to the President for final approval.

A select few of the best Clipper crews were recruited for assigned missions. Each crewman had to qualify for top secret clearance, which the F.B.I. expedited. At a series of early briefings, the voluntary nature of the undertaking was emphasized and the recruits warned of the risks involved, including possible capture and execution.

A small area of the Pan Am archives in the Marine Air Terminal was converted to a soundproof meeting room where daily briefings could be held when missions were being planned. Westbrook dubbed it the "ready room." Dress was casual.

Westbrook spent a humid afternoon with Charlie Sikes checking out in the DC-3 at LaGuardia Airport so he'd be able to fly it alone to Washington on short notice. Westbrook hadn't flown a powered land based plane in years, and he tended to over-control the aircraft, particularly on landings. The Clipper needed that sort of manhandling, but the DC-3 was much lighter to the touch.

After the second landing, another hard one, Sikes turned in the co-pilot's seat and said, "Curtis, my boy, I ain't sure you're going to get the hang of this bird any time soon."

Westbrook, frustrated and angry with himself, turned into the wind and applied full power. "This'll be the one, Charlie,"

he said with a forced smile. Level at 1,000 feet, Westbrook, after clearance from the tower, turned down wind and lined the DC-3 up for another approach. Abeam the runway numbers, he reduced power, put the flaps halfway down and began a shallow bank to the left. After a 180 degree turn, he rolled out level, lowered the landing gear, reduced the flaps to the full down position and reduced power again. He noticed Sikes fidgeting uncomfortably in his seat as the aircraft approached the runway. As he crossed the runway threshold, Westbrook flared slightly, closing the throttles as he did so. The DC-3 touched down, its main wheels squeaking slightly.

"Beauty!" exclaimed Sikes. " Damn, couldn't do better myself."

"Maybe I ought to start flying these things to Miami," said Westbrook, only half kidding. If he did, he figured he'd have almost twice as much time in New York. But he knew it was out of the question for now.

After two more good landings in a row, Sikes pronounced Westbrook safe to fly alone.

"I really enjoyed it, Charlie," Westbrook said as he gave Sikes a friendly pat on the shoulder while taxiing back to the hangar. "Thanks for bearing with me."

Meanwhile, the news about LaDieux was not encouraging. There had been complications in getting him through North Africa. Some Vichy French, thought to be loyal to the Resistance, had betrayed him and there was a bloodbath in a small desert town ninety miles south of Casablanca. La Dieux was slightly wounded, but the ambush created panic among his native escorts, and they insisted on hiding out in the desert until the furor had died down. Intelligence from Lisbon was spotty, seldom prompt, and rarely reliable. The Lisbon operatives supporting the Allies were, however, able to confirm that the Germans had been uncharacteristically disorganized in dispatching agents to capture LaDieux.

Since a typical Clipper layover was about forty-eight hours, LaDieux's handlers would have to get him to Lisbon as soon as possible after the Clipper arrived in order to avoid suspicions. A short delay in departure could be explained as a mechanical problem requiring that parts be flown in. To linger too long, however, would create unwanted speculation among the curious and the dangerous.

The tentative departure date had been moved back to

Thursday, September 12th. The Clipper would operate as a regularly scheduled revenue flight, leaving New York late afternoon and arriving in Lisbon mid-afternoon the following day.

The date wasn't lost on Westbrook: Friday the 13th.

They would then leave for London around 0730 on Sunday morning, arriving about 1400 and hopefully departing that same afternoon for the return to Lisbon.

However, two problems existed. The first related to how much time LaDieux needed for his talk with DeGaulle. This was not a major problem, so long as the Clipper was able to take off before dark. But, that raised the specter of a night landing in Lisbon which, given the treachery of the Tagus River, no pilot, including Westbrook, looked forward to.

The OSS was insisting that the Clipper not shut down its engines in London. They'd let Meyers and La Dieux off at the landing site on the Thames and take off immediately in order to avoid being detected by the Germans.

This led to the second problem: the stepped-up bombing of London and its suburbs was a grave risk to the Clipper. The massive carpet bombing of London that had decimated the docks and barges in the Thames was a matter of great concern. The Germans were not discriminating in selecting their targets.

Having been invited to do so at any time, Westbrook called the President from a secure office in the Pan American Operations Department after checking out in the DC-3.

"Good afternoon, Curtis. Good to hear from you."

"Good afternoon, Mr. President. Thank you. I want to speak to you briefly about Eagles Away. I know there's been some lobbying for us not to stay in London once our passengers disembark. Obviously, that would mean two landings and take offs on the Thames. In my opinion, one successful landing on the Thames is going to be all we should ask for. Even if we come under attack after we land the worst thing is that we'll lose the Clipper. I'll make sure the crew goes ashore and gets as far out of harm's way as we can. We're just tempting the gods too much to risk a second landing, even without the Germans."

There was a long pause. "I think you're absolutely right,

131

Curtis. With this fellow Wilkie running such a hard campaign against me I sometimes find it difficult to detach my politics from my objectivity about certain things, so I might have favored another course which at least gives the appearance of less risk. But, you're right." Westbrook could hear Roosevelt chuckling.

"Besides, Curtis you're also the captain, and if you change your mind that's your prerogative too."

CHAPTER 12
LISBON

Auchlin was becoming increasingly paranoid as events cascaded. He saw Steiner as one who would meddle with his own contacts in Berlin--even with the Fuhrer. As an Army officer, he felt he was beyond the bidding of such aristocratic toads.

Auchlin tucked his scalpel, sheathed in a fine leather scabbard, into a pocket in the lining of his left sleeve. Then he strapped on his shoulder holster. The P.38 was even bulkier with the silencer on, but when he put the jacket on both weapons were concealed well enough. Looking into the mirror and seeing the puffiness around his eyes, he realized how tired he was. If things didn't take a turn for the better soon he would have to leave Lisbon and start over, but he had no idea where he'd go.

Since tomorrow was a bank holiday in Germany, he told his superiors in Berlin that his office would be closed and that he was going away overnight and could not be reached. He booked a room in a shabby pension in the Barrio District, near the waterfront, a discovery from his early days of learning his way around Lisbon.

It was dusk and a fairly heavy rain was falling when Auchlin got into the back seat of a waiting cab. Once again his thoughts turned to Sanguino. This man is either a clown or he's playing very clever tricks with me, he thought, expecting the worst and even relishing the excitement he felt. He felt the undeniable urge to kill again. He patted the P.38 through his rain coat.

Satisfied he could control Sanguino, he turned to the capture of LaDieux. He dreamed of capturing the filthy little Jew himself. Even though the Gestapo had made it clear that LaDieux was to be sent back to Berlin alive, Auchlin had his own agenda. And yet he knew that the only way he could take LaDieux was with the cooperation of the Embassy, the only source of information available on his movements. While Auchlin had a sophisticated set of communication equipment in his hotel, he knew von Ribbentrop and Himmler would have other channels at work in such a high-profile operation. Himmler had not responded to his earlier coded message, but Auchlin had hardly expected one.

Sanguino stood in the rain in front of La Bella's restaurant, so excited at meeting Auchlin he hardly noticed how drenched he was. He had bragged to his wife that he was having dinner with a Nazi big wig to whom, under orders from the Inspector himself, he would feed disinformation about the activities in the department. Impressed, his wife had insisted on ironing his best shirt and pressing the black serge pants to his only suit for the occasion. Now he was late and in his hurry he had left his service revolver in his bureau.

After paying his driver, Auchlin exited from the taxi in front of the restaurant, and quickly got under the umbrella Sanguino held out to him.

"It's good to see you, my friend. It's been awhile," said a smiling Auchlin as he extended his hand to Sanguino.

"Yes, it has. Thank's for inviting me this evening."

After the two men had been seated, Auchlin suppressed his thirst for a large whiskey and ordered a lager instead. He was pleased when Sanguino ordered a double whiskey. Auchlin quickly lit a cigarette. After meeting with Steiner, he had begun smoking again after having quit for two years.

"Prost, then, to you and yours." Auchlin raised his glass and motioned to the waitress for another whiskey for Sanguino. Auchlin remembered from their first meeting that Sanguino liked his drink, which could only make him freer with his opinions.

"So, Sergeant Sanguino, tell me about the Holloran case. Has it been solved? Are there any major leads? I've not seen the Inspector in some time." Auchlin relaxed, leaning back in his chair, looking straight at Sanguino, trying to assess his reaction. Clearing his throat, Sanguino said, "I have the impression there has been a major break in the case, but maybe I'm mistaken."

Auchlin studied Sanguino carefully. He could usually tell when he was being lied to, but he wasn't sure in this case. Sanguino was a fool. As dangerous as it could prove to be, he decided to have some sport.

Sanguino finished his whiskey and appeared to relax a bit.

"You think I killed the American, don't you?"

"Senhor, por favor." He raised his hands in protest, a puzzled look on his face. The waitress brought him his third drink, and he took a deep swallow. "How can you say such a thing? Would I be here tonight if that were the case? I'm a simple policeman. It's not my place to have such beliefs, one way or the other."

Auchlin suddenly smelled it. Gasparo was using Sanguino to bait him, and the fool didn't even know it. He lit another cigarette and finished his lager. He almost ordered a whiskey but thought better of it: there was much ahead of him before the evening was over.

Auchlin noticed Sanguino hastily putting away most of his meal, which appeared to be undercooked greasy cod. Sanguino pushed his plate away. Auchlin saw that his face had turned pasty looking, and he was swallowing hard, as if trying to avoid nausea.

"Major, I must beg your indulgence. I feel ill. The fish was poorly prepared, I'm afraid. Perhaps I should excuse myself and go home."

"Does the Inspector know we're having dinner tonight?"

"Of course not. My time off is my time, and nobody knows what I do with it, except perhaps my wife."

Auchlin formulated a plan. "Well, then, I must insist that one of my men drive you home. If you would come with me to my hotel, I'll arrange it."

Auchlin tried to seem genuinely concerned over Sanguino having to go home so early. Playing on Sanguino's pride, he said, "Surely you don't want your wife to see you sick, and with just perhaps a little too much to drink. It's still so early." Sanguino agreed.

Auchlin made no effort to turn on the lights in his suite, but went straight to the kitchenette, dropped a large sleeping potion into a highball glass, added a stiff brandy and brought it back to Sanguino.

"Drink this, Luis, and you'll feel much better."

Sanguino swallowed most of the brandy and within moments his knees gave way and he fell to the floor. Auchlin propped him up and searched him; he was pleased to find his badge and hand cuffs, with the key in the lock.

When he awoke two and a half hours later, Sanguino's arms were bound. His head was splitting from the drug-and-whiskey hangover. A faint light filtered in from the kitchenette. There was a large towel tied tightly, like a large bib around his neck.

Auchlin was staring at him intently. Despite the dim light, Sanguino saw a shiny object in Auchlin's hand, and...rubber gloves? Mother of God, rubber gloves?

"The eyes, Luis, the eyes always tell the truth, and you are about to tell me the truth. The eyes are also the first sign of death in a dying man. They get hazy, lose focus and then nothing. Nothing. I will be watching your eyes very carefully." Auchlin crossed his arms and leaned back against the wall. "What has Ludke told your Inspector?" Auchlin's voice was soft and reassuring.

Sanguino asked Auchlin for water.

Auchlin tapped a glass of water and set it on the small end table about three feet away from Sanguino.

"Are you thirsty?" Auchlin asked. He watched the question sink in. "Answer my question--truthfully!--and you can drink to your heart's content. Now: what has the Inspector learned?"

"I don't know, Major. Please, I truly don't know."

Auchlin knocked the glass off the table, spilling the water over the fine Aubusson carpet.

Then, with surprising speed, he struck Sanguino in the mouth with his fist. A small pool of blood formed on the right side of his mouth. His lust was pounding so hard Auchlin wasn't sure he could stop, before he got the information. Blood trickled from Sanguino's mouth.

"You fool!" he snarled, his face contorted in rage. "You have played into my hands. The night is waning. If I have to gag you it is all over. Do you know what I'll do to you? You'll feel the pain every second. Again: tell me everything. What does the Inspector know?"

Sanguino's head dropped to his chest. He remained silent.

So! He knows nothing after all...

Auchlin felt very tired.

"All right, Luis, I'm going to spare your life. Not because I should, but because it would only complicate things if I killed you now."

Auchlin retrieved the glass he had thrown on the floor, went into the kitchenette, and prepared another brandy-and-drug-potion. He forced Sanguino to drink, and when he passed out, he stuffed a hand towel into his mouth. Then he went to bed, setting his alarm for 0400. He would take Sanguino downstairs to the garage, put him in the trunk of his car and drive into the countryside. There he would shoot him where it would be several days before the body was found.

When he awoke and went into the living room four hours later, Auchlin saw that Sanguino's head was rolled back, his vacant eyes staring at the ceiling in the early signs of rigor mortis. He had panicked during the night and, struggling for breath, hyperventilated and swallowed the towel. He had choked to death.

Auchlin drove the thirty miles to the seaplane terminal. Behind an old warehouse at the nearby Cais De Santa Apolonia Dock, he found a rough ten-pound concrete block. He went back to the car, pulled Sanguino's body from the trunk and was in the process of lashing the block to Sanguino's ankles when a voice hailed him.

"Bom dia, Senhor, que passe?"

At first the echoing between the warehouses confused Auchlin, but then he spotted a dock guard carrying only a nightstick. Auchlin pulled out his P.38, pushed off the safety and fired.

The guard screamed and started to run as the bullet grazed him.

Cursing, Auchlin quickly overtook him and jabbed the pistol into his left shoulder blade, the bullet sounding like it had pierced a ripe melon.

Auchlin finished with Sanguino and dragged him to the water's edge. He pushed his body off the dock where it promptly sank from sight in the Tagus.

Exhausted, even a little delirious, Auchlin started his drive into the city, planning. Later he would drive east, into Spain.

Auchlin went directly to his room at the pension. He slept all day with a smile on his face.

CHAPTER 13
NEW YORK

Sunday, September 8, 1940.

Westbrook was having an early breakfast at LaGuardia with Albert Collins, the OSS coordinator for the upcoming flight to Lisbon. They were alone in a far corner of the restaurant. Since he had spent a great deal of time working in Lisbon over the past several months, Collins briefed Westbrook on the current intelligence reports that could ensure the success of getting LaDieux to London safely.

Collins had become acquainted with Inspector Gasparo in Lisbon when Roosevelt had instructed the OSS to offer any possible assistance they could to the Lisbon police in the Holloran investigation. Gasparo had listened politely to Collins, but for the most part he was tight-lipped about his own suspicions and the progress being made in solving the crime.

Westbrook told Collins about his own brief meeting with Gasparo after the murder, expressing the belief that he was a decent police officer. Collins agreed.

"Perhaps the two of us can persuade the Inspector to help us get our guest safely across town to the seaplane terminal. That's where our real exposure is, as I see it," Westbrook said.

After they ordered, Westbrook gave Collins the background of the operation, emphasizing the logistics involved and the parameters of the Clipper's operational characteristics. He mentioned that all of the crew members would be armed, trained by the F.B.I.. And finally, Westbrook said he planned to contact Gasparo to set up a meeting as soon as they arrived in Lisbon. "I'm sure he'll think I'm calling about Phineas, and that's fine. At least we'll get an audience." When they finished breakfast Collins excused himself. "I'll be back in about fifteen minutes, Curtis. Have to make a couple of phone calls."

Westbrook lingered at the breakfast table with his second cup of coffee and a copy of the Sunday Times.

When they entered the ready room twenty minutes later, Westbrook saw a man sitting at the table pouring over some enlarged aerial maps. He appeared to be in his early forties with reddish hair and an RAF-style handlebar mustache. Collins smiled, and greeted him.

"Geoffrey! Good to see you!" he said warmly. "Let me introduce Commander Curtis Westbrook, U.S. Navy. He'll be captain of the Clipper."

"Commander, this is my good friend Geoffrey Tuck, now Lieutenant Commander, Fleet Air Arm. Before the war Geoffrey was a captain for Imperial Airways. Still is, I guess. He flew the Sunderland flying boats all over the world.

"Good to meet you, Commander," Tuck said, extending his hand to Westbrook. "I'm sure we'll get along, particularly if you hate the Germans as much as I do."

Westbrook detected a real loathing in Tuck's voice. "You got that right," he said dryly. "Welcome aboard."

The crew members had begun assembling in the ready room. Flight 9034 was scheduled for departure from New York to Lisbon on September 12, 1940.

A map of London was projected on a screen showing the Thames as it wound its way through London and its suburbs.

Collins turned to the group assembled and came right to the point, warning them that the Germans would try to re-capture LaDieux in Lisbon. And they would not hesitate to murder him.

"He is a symbol of French Resistance to the Germans, and his escape from a prison in Occupied France was a major embarrassment for them. They will not likely provoke the Portuguese government any further than they have to, but given the choice they'll kill or kidnap LaDieux without regard to the diplomatic damage."

Collins described the recent affair involving Ludke, and the friction it had created between the Portuguese and German governments. He speculated that while this might hamper the Germans' net work in Lisbon, he doubted it would create a lasting problem for them.

"I don't mean to alarm you, gentlemen, but you should be prepared for extraordinary measures. Stay together, carry sidearms; and, above all else, don't let strangers near the airplane, regardless of what they say. Either I or one of our agents will be onboard the plane at all times, so if there's any trouble don't try to be a hero. Let us handle it. That's what we're paid for.

"Miss Meyers, along with an OSS agent will stay on the aircraft overnight in Lisbon to minimize suspicions--neither one of their names will be on the passenger manifest. That's all I have, fellows, so let me turn the meeting over to Commander Tuck. He's going to brief us on various options for our landing approach in London."

Tuck's background certainly lent itself to his new assignment. When he graduated from the Royal Naval Academy at Dartmouth in 1922, the British Navy, unlike the U.S. Navy, had a full appreciation of the potential of the aircraft carrier. The Royal Navy had just finished sea trials with HMS <u>Argus</u>, the first effective carrier ever built. After his basic flight training Tuck was assigned to an advance training squadron where he learned to make carrier landings in a Sopwith fighter. Like Westbrook he had an affinity for seaplanes and soon found himself flying some of the Royal Navy's early flying boats, temperamental beasts strung together with fabric and wire. After his eight year tour was finished Tuck signed on with Imperial Airways as it began its flying boat expansion into Africa and overseas. However, there was a note in his file at the Admiralty that he was a qualified carrier pilot.

"Good morning," Tuck said, removing his suit coat as he stood up. "Didn't know it was going to be so hot in New York this late in the summer.

"First off, I think I speak for the entire Royal Navy in saying thanks for this effort to help the Allied cause. It'll be a special pleasure to work with you, and particularly with Commander Westbrook, who is held in the highest esteem by the Royal Navy for his rescue of the men of <u>Pegasus</u>. I promise to do everything in my power to make things as safe as possible for each of you."

He turned to the map of London. "Things are very grim in England right now, gentlemen. The Germans are bombing the bloody hell out of us, and they're starting to increase their raids on London. No discretion, just laying their eggs all over the place... civilians getting killed left and right."

Pointing to an area to the right of center and north of the Thames, Tuck said, "Here's the City, the old part of London and the Financial District. The Germans have hit us hard in this area, especially along the docks." Tuck moved his pointer slightly to the right and down from the City.

"Wapping is the center of the dock area, and the places around here are being hit the hardest. That's where the barges and ships are concentrated, although we're doing a fairly good job of dispersing them now. Oil storage facilities are there, too." Frowning, Tuck paused. "Air raids have been fierce here, too, so this is obviously not where we want the Clipper to land."

He paused again, craning his neck as he studied the map.

"My first idea, depending on the wind direction, is that we should try to land in this area."

Tuck's pointer scratched over the area around the Chelsea Embankment to the east of the Chelsea Bridge and well west of the City.

"Pretty much an east to west, or vice versa, landing here, with about two and one-half miles of space between the Chelsea and Vauxhaull Bridges.

"If we're favored with more north to south winds, or vice versa, we should probably try to land in this area."

He pointed to the portion of the Thames that ran between the Lambeth and Westminster Bridges.

"A tight fit, but right at Parliament, where your charges can be escorted quickly to Ten Downing Street. Only about a mile and a half of room here, though, and a tail wind would likely eliminate this spot."

Sitting on a front row seat, Westbrook, leaning forward towards the screen, his brow furrowed, studied the charts intensely, making notes in a small spiral ring notebook. Looking around briefly, he could see the other airmen in the room were equally attentive to Tuck's presentation.

"There should be a mobile radio station nearby to the landing place to give last minute advice regarding winds, river traffic, and possible German aircraft in the area.

"Until I took this on I didn't appreciate how many bloody bridges there are across the river. Anyway, those are the highlights and we will, of course, help Commander Westbrook make further decisions as we proceed."

Westbrook and Gates had agonized over whether the State Department should advise the Germans about the Clipper's flying a diplomatic mission to London. Pan Am had canceled regular service to Southampton right after the war started, so the Germans would know the Clipper's presence there was irregular. The hope was they would not consider this ominous or threatening since the Clipper was a civilian aircraft.

After the meeting ended, Westbrook took Tuck down to the moorings where the Clipper was being serviced for its regular Monday run to Lisbon. He showed Tuck the hatches on either side of the aft section of the Control Cabin which allowed flight engineers access to a crawlway to the engines, allowing minor engine repairs to be made during flight.

"Ride up here with us as much as you like," Westbrook said as they entered the bridge. "You'll get a feel for how temperamental she is on the water and how glorious in the air."

"Strikes me that security could be a problem, with all these nice nooks and crannies," Tuck said, poking his head into the port crawlway.

"You're absolutely right, and that's why we're going to post an armed guard outside the plane as long as we're on the water."

Ground crew activity had increased as they deplaned, and the din of voices and machinery noises had grown.

Tuck said he was planning to spend the next few days at the British Consulate in New York, but go to Washington later in the week for an eleventh-hour briefing at the embassy there.

"Keep us informed," Westbrook said, and they shook hands warmly.

CHAPTER 14
LISBON

Detective Sergeant Carbonara, his fat face beet red, and brow beaded in sweat, was wringing his hands. "He couldn't have done it himself; his hands are tied."

Gasparo shot him a look of contempt as they entered the cell block. "You are so observant, Sergeant. Perhaps I should take a peek at your wallet, no?"

Gasparo was furious. They were discussing Werner Ludke, whom Carbonara had found an hour earlier, hanging from a ceiling bar of his cell, quite dead, his hands bound behind his back. Gasparo shuddered when he saw the corpse, still dangling from the rafters of his cell. Ludke's face was ashen, suggesting that he had been strangled instead of having his neck broken instantaneously. Someone had wanted him to suffer. Carbonara called Gasparo immediately, but it had taken Gasparo an hour to get to the station.

"Inspector, I saw no one. Please, I wouldn't allow this to happen on my watch!"

In a way, Gasparo was relieved that one of his problems was solved. Salazar would not have let him rest until Ludke was disposed of. At the same time, he knew that the murder was an inside job. Someone must have paid Carbonara a small fortune to turn his back while Ludke was done in. Despite his disappointment in one of his trusted lieutenants, however, Gasparo was not prepared to pursue the issue at this time. He had more serious and delicate things on his mind. Carbonara could wait.

Gasparo had called Auchlin at the Palacio several times over the past 24 hours to report the Ludke arrest to him, but with no answer. He was anxious to get Auchlin's reaction. After sitting down at his desk and lighting a cigarette, he tried Auchlin again, but hung up after several rings. Probably on holiday, he thought.

These Germans love their holidays. Almost as much as they love parades. Salazar had suppressed any news stories about the rape of his niece by a German officer, so it was possible Auchlin did not even know about Ludke's arrest. But the Embassy surely knew, he thought, as he put through a call to Steiner. A secretary told him that the Ambassador was on the telephone to Berlin but would call him back as soon as possible. Gasparo left no message.

To compound matters, Luis Sanguino's wife had called, hysterical because her husband had not returned from his dinner with Major Auchlin the night before. Obviously, Gasparo didn't tell her his fears, but he cursed Sanguino for ignoring orders.

Steiner called him back almost immediately, apologizing for not being able to take the call. Gasparo was impressed.

"Thank you very much for returning my call, Excellency. I have a few questions, if you don't mind."

Steiner resigned himself. "Go ahead. We are terribly embarrassed about the behavior of Lieutenant Ludke and want to cooperate."

Gasparo chuckled to himself. "Well, Excellency, that problem has been resolved. Lieutenant Ludke was found dead in his cell earlier this morning. Hanged."

There was silence on the other end of the line. "The poor man must have committed suicide in shame for the dishonor to his country. I hope you will consider the case closed, and that we can move forward in friendship."

Gasparo assured Steiner that he agreed, adding, "May I ask you a frank question?"

"Please do," Steiner said, cautiously.

"Can you tell me where Major Auchlin is? Earlier he asked for some information about a recent crime here in Lisbon, which I now have. I can't seem to reach him."

"We don't know where he is either. It's possible there's foul play involved. We may have to ask your assistance. He missed a staff meeting here this morning, and as you must be aware, that's not customary for the Major." Steiner had no idea where Auchlin was and didn't really care.

Steiner was interrupted by another call from Berlin and had to ring off, with a promise to call the Inspector very soon.

Even so, Gasparo was fairly sure of his answer. Steiner had not concocted a story about Auchlin to throw him off the track.

If he had, he was a better actor than Gasparo gave him credit.

Gasparo, hearing a knock, looked up and saw Morgado standing in the doorway, a large manila envelope under his arm. "Ah, Jose," he said smiling. "Come in." Morgado sat down, placing the envelope on Gasparo's desk.

Ignoring the envelope, Gasparo leaned back in his chair, lit a cigarette, and said, "I was just thinking how uncomplicated life was until Ludke came into the picture. Do you believe he killed himself?"

Morgado quickly responded, "Not for a moment, Inspector. But, we have his sworn confession. Doesn't that mean we can arrest Auchlin?"

"Only if we can persuade the magistrate that it's true, sworn or not. I've been sitting here wondering where Auchlin is, what's he doing, and whether he's being helped out of the country this very minute. I find it depressing to think about, but I want you to issue an all points bulletin for his arrest, beginning with a sweep of the Palacio in Estoril. I'll find the magistrate. I've just been talking with the German Ambassador, and he said he has no idea where Auchlin is. I believe him." Gasparo paused, running his hand through his thick black hair, then he said, "I also believe there's something big going on around here. The Ambassador was on the phone to Berlin at least twice in the last twenty minutes. That's too damn much telephone traffic to waste on some poor fish like Ludke, or even a bigger one like Auchlin. By the way, what's in the envelope?"

On September 9, Steiner received a flurry of coded messages about the arrival in Lisbon of the ardent American Communist Sylvia Meyers. The purpose of her trip was not clear, but Berlin suspected it had something to do with the efforts to get Pierre LaDieux into Portugal. Based on feed-back from agents in the United States, Berlin was becoming increasingly suspicious that Meyers was engaging in activities inimical to the Russo-German Friendship Pact.

Steiner had been ordered to work with Major Auchlin in arresting LaDieux and detaining Ms. Meyers for questioning and possible detention and transfer to Germany.

With no confidence in Auchlin, Steiner immediately cabled Berlin asking for at least two agents to carry out the assignment. Steiner's request had been immediately referred to Hitler who instructed Himmler to select two men to assist the Major. Steiner breathed a sigh of relief at the news.

Two days later Steiner sat in the Embassy library with two agents from the SD, the special extermination unit organized and commanded by Reinhard Heydrich, Himmler's deputy. They had just arrived on the last Lufthansa flight of the day from Berlin. Steiner had just finished hosting a small party for several Portuguese cabinet members before his new guests arrived. Salazar had declined an invitation to the party, but he had telephoned Steiner to express his satisfaction at the way Ludke had been disposed of, knowing full well it was the work of his own assassins. Steiner was beginning to mend his fences.

The senior agent was Otto Stass--a dour, rumpled man in his late forties. He had delivered Steiner a letter from Himmler which expressed his personal concerns about Auchlin's effectiveness in handling LaDieux. Himmler felt the Ludke arrest had destroyed Auchlin's credibility in local circles. Even given the Fuhrer's feelings of loyalty to Auchlin, Himmler encouraged Steiner to let Stass direct the operation.

He was a good choice. In Warsaw Stass had rapidly rounded

up thousands of suspected anti-Nazis, from Communist politicians to Jewish businessmen with no effective resistance. One of the reasons for his success was that once in Warsaw he had immediately pressed persons into his service who knew the city well. Such information helped him succeed even before the dust of battle had settled.

"Auchlin's men have not done their homework," Stass spat.

"Apparently, Major Auchlin handles all the locals himself, and allows his subordinate very little freedom," said Stass' colleague, Johann Lusdorff. Terrifyingly ugly, Lusdorff was a young, bull-necked, giant Austrian with hooded eyes, who specialized in assassinations. Walking almost like an ape, he had amazing physical strength and stamina and enjoyed the pursuit of his quarry, always human, particularly if he ended the chase by breaking a neck or a spine with his bare hands. Well aware of orders to return LaDieux alive, Lusdorff hoped that the effete Jew would give him a legitimate excuse to kill him before the journey was over. Lusdorff cracked his huge knuckles incessantly, much to Steiner's great annoyance.

"Where is Auchlin anyway?" Steiner asked, irritated.

Steiner's aide answered quickly, "He was not invited to this meeting, Excellency, but I'll ring him now, if you like."

"He may still be our strongest hope," Stass said. "I'm not persuaded that a complete and reliable map of Lisbon actually exists."

Steiner motioned, and his aide left to call Auchlin.

The three men discussed alternative plans to kidnap LaDieux with the least embarrassment to the German government. Steiner advocated taking him once he was away from the airport. Stass argued that they didn't know the city well enough. "Whoever is behind this could out-maneuver and evade us easily. On the other hand this is one of the smallest capitals in Europe. Reliable maps have to exist somewhere."

Auchlin arrived from Estoril in thirty minutes. His tic was worsening and he squinted trying to make it seem less obvious, thus actually heightening the affliction. He was pre-occupied with the idea of moving out of the Palacio because he was worried that Gasparo was setting a trap.

Stass and Auchlin exchanged cool but correct greetings. They had known each other, although not well, for years. Lusdorff remained seated and nodded his head at Auchlin.

"I apologize for my delay, but I've been occupied with the Ludke affair. Not only was Werner my best aide, but there could be repercussions for all of us."

"Save your concerns over Ludke for another day," Steiner answered. "He hanged himself early this morning. Tell us of your progress with the police inspector."

Auchlin wavered between his shock at the news about Ludke and his anger at Steiner's presumptuousness. He went into great detail describing his dinner with Sanguino, who had been of immense value in networking the city. He claimed Gasparo was unavailable, and of course, failed to mention that the sergeant was now at the bottom of the Tagus. Auchlin knew he was fighting a losing battle. His failure to secure anything tangible for Germany during his nine months in Lisbon was catching up with him like a tidal wave. And now he was further distracted, concerned about what Ludke might have told the police before he died.

"There's no time for networking, Major," Stass snapped with distaste. "If you cannot supply us with a reliable informant who knows the city of Lisbon now, we'll have to make other arrangements."

Everyone in the room now knew that LaDieux would have to be taken at the airport, probably with bloodshed.

Stass said he favored the airport scheme. He felt they could succeed there more easily than in an alley-to-alley chase. The consequences were Steiner's problem anyway, one he was no doubt well paid to deal with.

Further questioning of Auchlin clarified the fact that he would be no help whatsoever in LaDieux's capture. He attributed his lack of information problems to the outcry that had arisen from the arrest of Ludke.

In the end it was decided that Stass and Lusdorff, neither with a known presence in Lisbon, would carry out LaDieux's kidnapping by themselves. It was cleaner, and had a better chance of keeping German-Portuguese relations intact.

CHAPTER 16
CASABLANCA

Pierre LaDieux was not sleeping well. His right arm ached from the graze wound he'd gotten when attacked by pro-German Moroccans. Although he had little personal fear, his physical constitution was frail. His sixty days in prison had weakened him to begin with and was exacerbated by the trek across North Africa. Now, with the final stage of his journey to freedom only hours away, he was anxious to be on with it.

Across the room, Raoul Cardin was not sleeping well either. An ardent Communist, Cardin was LaDieux's chief lieutenant in the Resistance and had masterminded his liberation from the Vichy jail. Cardin had been tossing and turning with worry for hours, thinking all the while about the journey he and his beloved comrade were embarked on. He smelled a trap. He knew how anxious the Germans were to get LaDieux back. The perfidy of the supposedly loyal Moroccans in the desert skirmish, which nearly cost both he and La Dieux their lives, should never have happened. In spite of the repeated assurances of their Allied operatives of the reliability and loyalty of the Moroccans, it had happened, creating doubts in Cardin's mind about how much the Allies really knew. To make matters worse, the agents who briefed LaDieux and Cardin in Casablanca had warned that getting safely out of Lisbon's Cintra Airport to the seaplane terminal would be very risky, and that troubled Cardin a great deal. That leg of the journey would be handled by persons of untested reliability.

His thoughts suddenly coalescing after hours of deliberation, he sat up, "I have it, I have it!" Dawn was just beginning to light the distant shore.

He got up and dressed quickly, then made his way cautiously into the shadowy streets of Casablanca. It was a very long shot, but it was worth it.

CHAPTER 17
NEW YORK

"Any significance to the fact we're flying out of here the day before Friday the 13th?" Westbrook's radio operator, asked as they sat in the Clipper fine-tuning the radio and navigational instruments for the flights ahead. Oceanic charts were stacked neatly on the table, and Westbrook began to fill out his flight plan.

"Just looking out for witches on broomsticks," Westbrook answered, looking up at the early fall sunlight washing throughout the cabin as the plane bobbed on the swells of Long Island Sound. The prospect of the upcoming flights excited him. Flying never got too old for him.

Nothing was being left to chance. Emergency procedures had been thoroughly drilled. Success could depend upon slim margins of error.

In anticipation of the possibilities of being anchored during an air raid, Westbrook ordered large American flags painted on the upper wings of the Yankee Clipper.

Although it was unobtrusive, security was heavy. Dressed as mechanics, armed F.B.I. agents were stationed outside the aircraft. A Coast Guard cutter, also with armed sailors, was anchored several hundred yards offshore.

Unfortunately, no such elaborate security procedures would be available for the arrival and departure from Lisbon.

Going over the passenger manifest for the hundredth time, Westbrook again saw nothing unusual. During the pre-boarding process F.B.I. agents would assist Customs in screening the manifest, particularly with passports and visas.

A ship-to-shore-telephone had been temporarily installed three days earlier and it rang as Westbrook was putting away the manifest. The crew was startled: nothing was supposed to be happening for another twenty-four hours.

"It's for you, Captain," Jenkins said, passing the handset to Westbrook.

A Pan American switchboard operator announced an

overseas radio call from Lisbon, Portugal. "The party says it's urgent and gives his name as Gasparo."

Westbrook tensed.

It was after 2200 in Lisbon.

He crisply exchanged greetings with Gasparo, asking what he could do for him.

"Captain, I must see you as soon as you arrive," Gasparo said through oceans of static. "It's a matter of life and death, or I would not disturb you. I know you're coming because the Diario de Noticias publishes shipping and Clipper arrivals with the names of the captains."

"Can you tell me what this is about?" Westbrook held his breath. Gasparo probably didn't know anything about the LaDieux assignment.

"It concerns your friend Holloran. That's all I can say, but it's important that I see you right away. Can I meet you when you land? We need your help."

Westbrook breathed a sigh of relief. "Yes, of course. Show your badge to the steward at the gangway, and come aboard. We can talk privately in the Clipper."

Because everybody in the cabin had known Holloran, Westbrook told them about his conversation with Gasparo, fueling speculation that the murder had been solved.

"Let's not be too sure," Westbrook said. "Sounds like the Inspector might be in some kind of jam."

* * * * *

Westbrook sank in deep thought as his taxi weaved its way toward the University Club. After pleading with her several times to go to Lisbon on the flight, Joanna had, to his amazement and great delight, acquiesced. She told her producer she was going abroad on doctor's orders for some rest. Westbrook was thrilled when she told him how much she wanted to go. Now, he was worried about having her aboard. He dismissed this as being over-protective and began going over the options for the Thames landing and how long he could keep the Clipper on the river. If LaDieux opted to return to Lisbon they'd be under intense security. Everyone involved, including Roosevelt, hoped he would stay in London with DeGaulle to present a united front for the Free French Government in exile. DeGaulle had by no means convinced Churchill that he had the raw talent and popularity to warrant a role in liberating France.

And then Sylvia Meyers came to mind. How will she handle herself if things get rough? he wondered. She'd done all right under the harsh circumstances in the Shoreham Hotel, and probably in a number of other circumstances he didn't know about. The President had said as much. He hoped she would remain competent to carry out her next role.

That night he dreamed fitfully: first that Joanna was trying to explain that something was dreadfully wrong. Next he was in the Clipper, which was glowing, as though on fire. There was an explosion and he could see Sylvia, lying dead in the Lounge, her face missing. The plane was spinning like a leaf, half of its right wing gone. He could hear passengers scream in panic, struggling against G forces as the ship fell to the ocean. Then, he thought he had the Clipper under control, but the control wheel came off in his hands.

When his alarm went off at 0630 he sat up with a start, drenched in sweat.

Sipping coffee, he noticed there was a slight haze over the city, mostly a pall of coal smoke. Typical summer crud that wouldn't affect take-off. The long-range weather forecast had predicted smooth flying eastbound to Lisbon, but it was predicted to become murky for Europe over the weekend; some conflicting Arctic air masses would be coming down from the North Sea to the United Kingdom and then over to the Continent, meaning either fog or crystal clear weather, depending on which air mass prevailed.

Westbrook had long since become stoic about the weather; there was nothing to be done about it one way or the other. Besides, on this trip there were decided advantages to having either good or bad weather, depending on the phase of the journey. More than anything, Westbrook wanted clear weather for his approach on the Thames. Without it, he'd be faced with aborting the whole thing. With busy German submarines and anti-shipping attacks around England these past few weeks he had ruled out an open sea landing. But returning to Lisbon with his mission unaccomplished would mean total failure.

When he got into the cab he glimpsed into the rear view mirror and saw he was wearing a deep scowl on his face. Settling back into the seat, he smiled to himself. Lighten up, old boy,-- this trip's a piece of cake with all the talent backing you up. Besides, you'll get some time with Joanna in Lisbon, you lucky son-of-bitch. That makes it all worth while.

CHAPTER 18
NEW YORK

There was a hubbub of activity in and around the boarding area of the Marine Air Terminal. Porters shouted as they pushed their luggage carts for loading on the Clipper, and every minute a loud public address system announced the latest information on departure in English, Portuguese and French. But, overshadowing everything, in majestic silence, was the Clipper, waiting patiently at her moorings. It was a perfect day for flying--a light wind on the water surface and only a scattering of clouds in the sky.

Westbrook had just returned from filing the flight plan and was standing just inside the boarding area when see saw Sylvia approaching. Plainly dressed, wearing a beret, carrying a small valise and without make-up, she was, he thought, quite handsome. He was pleased to see Collins, who was carrying her large suitcase as well as his own.

"Hello, Curtis." Sylvia extended her hand with a melancholy smile. It was cold and clammy.

"Hello, Sylvia. All I can say is that my lawyer was dead wrong about you. We're going to do everything we possibly can to make you comfortable. Welcome to the Yankee Clipper.

"Al, sure glad you're joining us." Collins nodded as they shook hands. He had his ticket envelope between his teeth as they hauled the suitcases up the gangway. The interior lighting was still off, except for the galley area where the caterers could load.

Apologizing for the lack of light, Westbrook told them they had to weigh every passenger and their luggage to keep the airplane in trim condition. "Not too much weight in the forward section, and not too much in the tail." He gave them a tour of the main deck, showing off such safety features as the location of the life rafts and emergency exits.

Finally, they went up the spiral stair case to the bridge, where Westbrook showed them first the cockpit with its panels of instruments, and then through the locked door to the crew's quarters immediately to the rear of the Control Cabin. He handed the key to Collins, opened the door and said, "It's a tight fit, but you can always take a stretch in the Control Cabin anytime you like."

Collins had an awkward time shouldering through the crew's tiny quarters door. Sylvia slipped in easily and seeing the neatly made up cots, was satisfied with the arrangements.

Excusing himself with a promise to check back before take off, Westbrook returned to the bridge to continue the pre-flight check.

The co-pilot for the flight was Powell Waters, a captain who had flown the New York to Southampton route before the outbreak of the war. Barely five feet-eight inches tall, he had to use a back cushion to get full rudder throw of the aircraft. Too young for the First World War, Waters had been swept up as a teenager in the barn storming euphoria of the early twenties, and was hired by Pan American in 1928. Westbrook had picked him to be his co-pilot for what he thought would be the first of many assignments as the war unfolded.

Waters and Wesley Andrews, the navigator, were reviewing the logarithmic tables for evening star sights. Waters had also begun plugging in the numbers for the Weight and Balance tables to insure the payload was correctly distributed.

"Gentlemen, our two guests are safely in their quarters," Westbrook announced as he picked up his copy of the flight plan. He sat silently for a few minutes plunged in thought, staring out the cockpit window at the Terminal area, where a trickle of passengers were checking in. Joanna should be arriving soon. He pulled out a clipping from the September 8 <u>Sunday Times</u> that had stunned Broadway:

Broadway was shocked on Friday when Joanna Davis, the star of Boy Meets Girl, scheduled to open to a sold-out performance next Friday, announced that she was going abroad for a short period to recover from exhaustion.

Close friends said she was headed for a spa in some neutral European country and would be returning in less than two weeks. There was no indication as to whether Miss Davis would resume the lead in the musical. In a press release issued by her agent, Miss Davis was quoted as saying, "I'm going to miss opening night with deep regrets, but my doctors have convinced me this is something I must do. My understudy, Karen Price, will excite everyone with her talent and enthusiasm for the role."

"Everything looking OK, Powell?" he finally asked.

"Top notch, Captain. The juice is on, and we're standing by to start engines. I ran into Commander Tuck in flight operations. He was able to pick up the BBC on our short wave earlier, so he'll likely have a current report on German air activity over London when he comes aboard." Powers struggled with his seat to adjust the rudder throw and still see over the cockpit dash.

Armed F.B.I. agents in mechanics' coveralls were positioned in and around the Clipper. As soon as the first boarding call was announced, a motor launch from the Port Authority slipped into the channel. Normally the launch would be looking for debris which might pose a hazard to the aircraft. Today, however, the armed F.B.I. agents on the launch were looking for hazards of a different variety.

Joanna was running very late and Westbrook was beginning to get nervous. Glancing at his watch as he left the cockpit, he began pacing just inside the boarding area, estimating he had eight minutes to finish the pre-flight check list. The flight crew could not start engines until the captain was on board.

A checkered taxi pulled up in front of the terminal. A diminutive nun dressed in a black flowing wool habit and wearing dark glasses disembarked from the taxi and struggled to retrieve a large Luis Vuitton suitcase from the trunk of the cab.

Westbrook walked over to her and picked up her suitcase. "I was worried something had happened," he said quietly.

Joanna was miserable. "If I didn't <u>know</u> you were worth it, I wouldn't be here. If lightning hits this outfit it's designed to burst into flames. All I've got on under this thing is a bra and panties and I'm roasting."

Westbrook escorted her to customs--she had a passport prepared by the F.B.I. identifying her only as "Sister Mary Joseph of Mt. Carmel, New York." The Customs official smiled and waved her through the gate, where Westbrook escorted her directly to the luxury suite at the rear of the aircraft. A curious steward stared at her as she walked down the aisle. Westbrook opened the door and handed her the key. She immediately disentangled herself from her habit. "It's a long trip before I'll see you in Lisbon,"

he said.

They thought they had no choice. After much debate about how to get Joanna abroad without being recognized, they'd settled on the nun's habit. Joanna had dyed her blonde hair black as well, and as she pulled off the wimple, Westbrook caught a fleeting resemblance to Sylvia Meyers.

He had to laugh at the inconsistencies of her disguise--the nun's outfit with Luis Vuitton suitcase and private quarters in the most expensive accommodations onboard. Westbrook had bet that everyone would be too occupied with their own business, and that thirty minutes after takeoff no one would remember there was a nun on board, let alone in the luxury suite. After a few days in Lisbon it wouldn't matter. The main thing was not to have her be seen leaving the U. S.

Westbrook slipped both his hands into her panties, cupping her buttocks and pressing her into him. "Don't be surprised if you see me before Lisbon," she said.

By the time Westbrook returned to the bridge, Waters was ready to start engines. Westbrook was relieved to be getting underway. The assignment had weighed heavily on his mind the past several days. He didn't want to embarrass or disappoint the President.

The last intelligence reports said that LaDieux and Cardin would arrive at Cintra Airport just after dusk on Saturday the 14th, a day later than originally planned. They were to be ferried by a British reconnaissance aircraft from Casablanca to Lisbon. The Germans were now known to be making an all out effort to capture LaDieux in Lisbon. OSS agents were watching Cintra Airport and the beaches as far west as Estoril for possible landing parties from German submarines. The delay at least had the advantage of giving Westbrook time to figure out what Gasparo's call was all about, and to persuade him to help in LaDieux's escape.

He ordered Waters to start the engines, and left the bridge

for the crew's quarters. It was a bit stuffy, but Westbrook noticed that Sylvia's delicate perfume masked everything, including her own cigar smoke. She actually seemed relaxed. He also observed a Thompson sub-machine gun, which Collins had field-stripped on his cot, and was in the process of cleaning and oiling. There were several clips of ammunition stacked neatly on the small table beside Collins' cot.

The whine of the electric engine starter startled Sylvia. "We're just cranking up the engines. We'll be taking off shortly," Westbrook said, smiling. "Al, do you have anything new to report or talk about before I get busy for the rest of the day and night?"

Collins paused, pursed his lips, and said, "Not now, Curtis."

"By the way, I want both of you to join me on the bridge after dinner tonight. There'll be plenty of stars and the moon is about three quarters full. Should be a great night for flying." Even the circumstances of the mission couldn't dampen his enthusiasm for flying.

"Has LaDieux gotten away from Casablanca?"

"Don't know yet, Sylvia. We might get some messages en route tonight, but I think for now no news is good news."

* * * * *

All engines had been started, and the final items of the departure check list were being completed when Westbrook returned to the bridge.

The Port Authority launch had found no debris that posed a threat to the Clipper for its take off run. Westbrook presumed that the F.B.I. agents had seen nothing suspicious either.

Westbrook slipped into his seat and studied the gauges on his side of the cockpit for a moment. Satisfied, he picked up his radio microphone, "New York tower, Pan Am 3094 ready for taxi." He adjusted the friction locks on the four throttles.

"Pan Am 3094, New York, cleared to taxi. Flight plan approved as filed. Call Departure Control on 111.4 prior to take off."

Westbrook acknowledged the clearance, adjusted his seat and fastened his lap belt. He made another visual check out of the cockpit, catching the aroma of the exhaust gas from the burning 95 octane aviation fuel, which brought back fresh memories of other adventures. Seeing a thumbs up from the head of the sea and anchor detail standing on the pier, he ordered cast off from the cockpit and slowly advanced the throttles. The Clipper was underway.

CHAPTER 19
LISBON

September 11, 1940.

Although he had returned to the Palacio, and gone right to bed after leaving the Embassy, Auchlin could not sleep. He got up at 0230, packed some essentials, slipped out the back way and found a cab which had just delivered some late revelers to the hotel. He had to knock several times to wake up the proprietor of the pension he had booked into; the proprietor finally answered the door with a sleepy, puzzled look, and handed Auchlin the key to his room without saying a word.

After a day of sound, dreamless sleep Auchlin felt better. He awoke late in the afternoon. As he shaved he thought about the loose ends in his life. He dismissed the idea of fleeing Lisbon on the Clipper as a fantasy. If the police were looking for him the Clipper would be one of the first places they'd be watching. Gasparo was well aware of his fascination with the large flying machines. Besides, what would he do in New York, anyway? Carefully wiping the blade of his straight edge razor with a hand towel, he considered seeking asylum at the Embassy until he could be smuggled back to Germany. He remembered, though, how anxious Steiner was in his willingness to hand Ludke over to Salazar. While he was not sure the same fate would await a personal friend of the Fuhrer's, he couldn't take the chance. Steiner was overly ambitious, and couldn't be trusted with any one else's destiny. He went down to the front desk and engaged the room for another week, and then walked out into the fresh air of a sunny day.

Wandering around lost in thought, Auchlin happened to enter the Alfama quarter, a remnant of Lisbon's past, with buildings dating back to medieval times. Houses are so close that neighbors can shake hands from their windows. In the morning, barefoot women, in black shawls, hawked trays of fresh fish along the dock areas, as their ancestors had for hundreds of years before them.

One of the stranger sights in the Alfama was the legions of

cats roaming everywhere, presumably controlling the rodent population. The black shawled women cooking breakfast on the brazier on their balconies could often be seen throwing the cats a sardine head or two.

Auchlin searched for a decent restaurant as he dodged around the narrow and crooked streets.

He still had fantasies of capturing LaDieux--or at least assisting in his capture--but he was out of touch with the unfolding events of the episode. Maybe he could do something about the Meyers woman, although he had to admit that his knowledge of that scheme was equally vague. Much as he was trying to avoid it, there was no alternative: Steiner was his salvation and he needed to talk with him soon. It would probably be his last hope of salvaging his career and reputation--indeed, perhaps his life. Auchlin was on the verge of despair.

Still looking for a restaurant, he passed a public phone booth on the Rua dos Remedios. He lit a cigarette. His face was contorted with fear as he gave the operator the number of the German Embassy and deposited four escudos. I know this is my last hope, he thought. His hand trembled as he held the receiver.

His voice cracking, he told the Embassy operator that he was calling with a personal message from the Fuhrer for the Ambassador. The operator sounded doubtful as she checked with Steiner's secretary. Auchlin was immediately put through to Steiner.

"Auchlin, where in the name of Heaven are you? LaDieux is due to arrive in just over twenty-four hours and we've just received orders from Berlin to capture Meyers. She's a double agent working for the Americans. We're depending on you and you suddenly disappear. What are you up to, Major? What's this nonsense about a personal message from the Fuhrer?"

Auchlin's hunger pangs went away. There was no mention of his status as a fugitive, and the anxious Ambassador was actually seeking his help.

Joseph Gasparo had decided not to seek the help of the German Embassy in tracking him down. Instead, as instructed, Morgado had issued an all points bulletin to the Lisbon Police Department for Auchlin's capture. Morgado and two deputies had missed him by only two hours at the Palacio, where the front desk clerk was surprised to learn he was gone. Since Auchlin did not have diplomatic immunity, all his possessions left behind in the suite and his Mercedes in the hotel garage were impounded by the Lisbon Police.

"Perhaps you should come to the Embassy, Hans. It will be safer," Steiner suggested.

Auchlin was surprised to hear the Ambassador call him by his first name. He paused momentarily and then said, "Excellency, is there a role for me in the LaDieux affair? I'd like to assist you however you think I could in capturing the Frenchman, and getting rid of the American woman."

"I've been given specific instructions through von-Ribbentrop to let Herr Stass direct the LaDieux operation. You can count on our support in capturing the Jewess, so long as you understand that if anything goes wrong we will have to disavow you completely. Now, let me have a telephone number where you can be reached."

Auchlin stalled. He had another phone call to make. "I'm currently moving about, talking to my contacts. I've moved out of the Palacio, and haven't found permanent quarters yet. I'll call you as soon as possible."

Auchlin concluded that nothing had been said to the Embassy about his involvement in Holloran's murder--unless it was a trap--which he quickly dismissed as being too remote a possibility. He'd be able to prove himself after all.

He lit another cigarette, picked up the telephone once again. His hand had stopped trembling, and he felt much more at ease. He now saw his worse case scenario as having to seek asylum in the Embassy. He gave the operator the number of the Lisbon Police Department and deposited another four escudos. Morgado took the call. "The Inspector is out at the moment, Senhor Auchlin, but can I help?" Morgado strained to hear some indicator where Auchlin was--the noise of a street car, a ship's horn--anything.

Auchlin weighed his words carefully. The Germans had equipment that could trace a telephone call if close enough to the source. Where the Portuguese this sophisticated?

He decided on a course of pleasantries. "Thank you, Senhor Morgado. I don't believe I've had the pleasure of meeting you, but I've heard many good things about you from the Inspector. I haven't heard from the Inspector in some time and was wondering if an arrest had been made in the murder of the American pilot? Can you tell me when the Inspector might return?"

Morgado ignored the first question. He was busy frantically rifling through the mountain of paper work on his desk looking for the last report on Auchlin's activities. "Sir, I'm afraid I can't tell you when the Inspector will return. He's on brief holiday. But I'm very glad you called. One of our colleagues, Luis Sanguino, hasn't been heard from in over two days. His wife thinks he was scheduled to have dinner with you two nights ago. Can you tell me anything about that?"

Auchlin knew he was being tested. In a very concerned voice, he said, "Why, yes, as a matter of fact, Luis and I did have dinner the night before last at La Bella's restaurant in the old Barrito District. He became very ill--his dinner apparently was not cooked well--and asked to leave, so I put him in a taxi and sent him home early. He's been missing since then?" Auchlin went to great pains to express his concerns.

"Yes, apparently since close to the time you left him." Morgado held his breath. "Please tell me where the Inspector can reach you. I'm sure he'll want to talk to you as soon as he returns."

The Sanguino complication clinched it. Auchlin shifted to the final phase of his plan. "Unfortunately, on advice from my medical advisor, I'm going to a sanitorium in Spain for several days, I'll call as soon as I return." Auchlin hoped this would cause Gasparo to thin his resources by posting men at the several highway checkpoints and La Cintra Airport.

The body of a warehouse guard, shot at close range with a high caliber pistol, had been found in a pool of blood on the rain-soaked docks. Gasparo had no choice but to assign every available officer to the murder scene. Several hours later this would all change when the search for Auchlin began in earnest.

After hanging up, Auchlin called the Embassy again and

arranged to be picked up at his pension. He checked out, canceling his future reservations, unsure when or if he would return. He explained that a sudden change in plans required his return to Berlin immediately.

During the ride to the Embassy, Auchlin instructed his driver to stop briefly at the seaplane facility where he rented a locker and stored his bag. As the trip continued toward the Embassy he began making a list of what he would need to do in preparation for the abduction of Sylvia Meyers. The thought of having her to himself, even briefly, washed warm waves of desire over him, a pleasure that was almost pain quickening between his thighs.

CHAPTER 20
LISBON

Observing the niceties of neutrality, the First Minister had sent identical messages to the British and the German Embassies. Upon petition from the King of England the Portuguese government, in a humanitarian gesture, has agreed to accept a war refugee from Vichy France. The messages did not reveal the name of the refugee or the reasons for the sanctuary, but emphasized that he would be allowed to stay in Portugal for no more than twenty-four hours after arrival.

Steiner, Stass and Lusdorff had been discussing the matter of La Dieux when Steiner's charge d'affaires handed him the Salazar message, the contents of which he immediately shared with the other two men.

Lusdorff began pacing. "The Portuguese are trying to thwart us. This complicates the whole thing. Damn!" He slammed his fist into his hand.

Steiner was more discerning. "Not at all," he said calmly. "This turn of events provides us with a golden opportunity to execute--excuse the pun--the plan with a much higher degree of certainty.

"I'll call Salazar, thank him for his notice, but express my grave concerns that Portugal has agreed to harbor a fugitive from a legitimate government. A mild but firm protest, if you will. Having done that, I'll bend over backwards to assure our cooperation, pointing out that it will be necessary for us to have specific arrival times and places for the refugee, so we can insure he is out of danger from German terrorists acting on their own. No doubt he'll provide the necessary information in recognition of our contriteness in the Ludke matter." Steiner paused, sat down behind his desk, and started tapping his fingers lightly on the desk top. He was smiling, pleased as he unfolded his plan. "Every member of my staff and Auchlin will have air tight alibis when you carry out your orders. Unfortunately, this leaves us no option but to eliminate LaDieux and any accomplices on the spot. I'm sure von- Ribbentrop will fully appreciate this

171

necessity. You'll have to be on your way out of the country as soon as it's over. No time to extradite the Jewess. If Auchlin can handle her, fine. If not, pity. In any case, we'll have to advance the arrival time of the submarine." The next problem was how to alert Auchlin. But how? While Meyers was not as important as LaDieux, Steiner wanted her because Berlin did.

Once again, Auchlin was the weak link in the chain. It was amazing that one of the Fuhrer's cronies could be so incompetent and so much trouble at the same time.

Steiner ordered the Embassy operator to put a call through to Salazar. When he finally reached Salazar, the First Minister heard him out and then thanked him for his concerns over the refugee's safety. He advised Steiner that Inspector Gasparo had been put in charge of security for the refugee's arrival, and he should feel free to call him immediately. Steiner was annoyed at having to deal with a policeman, but hoped Gasparo would be quick to respond to a senior German official.

Lusdorf and Stass were impressed with Steiner's cleverness. Indeed, he was impressed with the powers of his own duplicity.

* * * * *

War creates its own peculiar rules. Joseph Gasparo was sensitive about his naivete and had developed the habit of pondering motives when strangers asked him questions or requested favors. He was thus suspicious of the German Ambassador's questions concerning the plans for the unknown refugee. By now Gasparo guessed he was a fugitive from a German-occupied country and was being methodically hunted down by them. This much he read between the lines. He didn't know, however, that the Allies and their American friends were anxiously interested in the success of the refugee's mission. At this point the outcome didn't matter to Gasparo.

Gasparo sidestepped the Ambassador's request for details on the refugee's arrival. "Excellency, I'm a simple policeman. I've been told to observe the arrival and departure of the person in question and to provide protection from certain criminal elements, if such elements do in fact come into play."

Steiner said in an irritated voice, "I'm hanging up now to call Minister Salazar and tell him that the Inspector of the Lisbon

Police has refused to cooperate with the German Ambassador on a very ticklish matter." Gasparo could hear Steiner's phone slammed onto its cradle. Gasparo shrugged, hung up his phone and sat back in his chair. Lighting a cigarette, he began to wonder if the refugee was worth all of this trouble. He decided he probably wasn't.

Within twenty minutes Salazar was on the phone to Gasparo. The Minister wasted no time. "You are to give Ambassador Steiner sufficient information that he can keep his clowns at bay for twenty-four hours. Nothing more, but at least that."

"Minister, with respect, I find it curious that the English have not made the same request."

Salazar sounded exasperated. "First of all, Inspector, it was not an Englishman who raped my niece, but even more importantly, it's the English who have put us in this awkward situation with the Germans. They requested assistance for this person and they're conducting the operation. We owe the Germans something, and you are to give it to them."

Gasparo was still uneasy when he called Steiner back and promised him full details as soon as they were made available to him.

War and all of its intrigues were beginning to fascinate the Ambassador, even invigorate him. "It will be like shooting fish in a barrel," he told Stass and Lusdorff, gleefully. All they had to do was wait for the information to plot the final details. In the meantime, Stass persuaded the Ambassador to provide a stolen car, without identification, as soon as possible. The owner would be disposed of to avoid problems during the two or three days they needed it.

It all seemed so simple. Gasparo would provide the time of arrival, and there would be a car waiting at the airport. Automatic weapons, perhaps an explosion, and a quick trip to Estoril to await the submarine.

Very pleased with himself, Steiner called for a bottle of cold champagne from the basement wine cellar which had been thoughtfully constructed by the now-deceased former owner of the building.

CHAPTER 21
ACROSS THE ATLANTIC

After taking off from Rikers Channel at 1630 in a right climbing bank, Westbrook leveled off at 2,000 feet, his assigned altitude. He gently rolled out of the bank on a heading of 082 degrees magnetic for the Azores. The aircraft was cruising at 154 knots, with the cowl flaps open five degrees to draw cool outside air through the engines to optimize their temperatures for the best operating performance. Flying east, the Clipper was favored with tail winds of fifteen knots. While the pilots and the flight engineer would keep an eye on fuel consumption, the luxury of the tail wind would not require them to be as judicious as when flying westbound into the teeth of prevailing head winds. During the climb out, the passengers could clearly see a number of large sail boats assembling in Long Island Sound preparing for the last regatta of the season.

At lift off, the Clipper weighed 72,000 pounds, with twelve passengers and a good load of cargo, mostly food staples for the International Red Cross. The crew was relaxed and in good spirits. Each wore a holstered Smith & Wesson .38 revolver while in the Control Cabin.

About three hundred miles east of New York, Sparks Jenkins picked up radio traffic among several ships of a Canadian and English convoy headed towards England. They sounded terse and cryptic, but there were no indications they'd been spotted.

Unfastening his seat belt and reclining his chair back slightly, Westbrook wondered how he would respond this evening if he received a distress call similar to <u>Pegasus</u>. He concluded that he would not honor such a call under any circumstances. He would not compromise his mission for anyone.

It felt peculiar to be flying over an Atlantic where tragedy could strike at any moment, while the Clipper would still be above it all.

Two hours after take off, Westbrook put the plane on auto-pilot and gave Waters command. The sky was clear, and the onrushing night held the promise of a dazzling display of stars soon to paint the heavens.

At Westbrook's invitation, Sylvia and Collins joined the flight crew in the Control Cabin where they had more room to move about. Sylvia was introduced to the flight deck crew, while Collins had already met them at the first briefing. Wesley Andrews gave the two a tour of the cabin, ending at the astral bubble where he would be taking star sights through the night. "Sometimes we go the whole flight without seeing the stars," he said. "That's what creates the 'pucker factor.'" Andrews blushed when Sylvia asked what that meant.

"I believe it has to do with a sharp contraction of the anus brought on by nervousness," Collins volunteered. Sylvia's laugh relieved Andrews.

A steward entered with a tray of coffee cups and light aperitifs from the buffet in the dining room. Normally, Westbrook forbade any alcohol on the bridge during flight, but he offered an exception for Collins and Sylvia this evening. Both declined, but took coffee. No introductions were offered.

Commander Tuck joined them. Before take off he'd learned through the BBC that London had been bombed during the day, and expressed his concerns that it might be a prelude to something even heavier over the next few days. "Could really mess us up if they're bombing us in London." Westbrook thought he might on the verge of tears.

"Things going smoothly below?" he asked, hoping to change the subject.

Tuck brightened. "Oh, yes, Captain. Some beautiful woman showed up just as I was leaving. She's gorgeous. Could be a cinema star."

Westbrook was amused. He'd seen the other female passengers after leaving Joanna--an English dowager pushing ninety, two wives of American business men, both frumpy. Joanna had warned him she might show up for dinner, although she had wanted to remain incognito. The curious cat he thought, smiling to himself.

Joanna's curiosity <u>had</u> gotten the better of her, and her resolve to stay alone dissolved. She was dying to see Westbrook in his element. What the hell, she thought. My agent said I was going abroad, so why shouldn't I have a little fun and start enjoying it? She dressed in a light green, stylish cocktail dress. Admiring her engagement ring one more time as she slipped it on her finger, she left the suite.

As she entered the Lounge, she was disappointed that Westbrook hadn't arrived as cocktails were being served. She was impressed with the dining room's opulence. It could easily pass as a small, fashionable restaurant in New York or London.

Other than the routine traffic and meteorological messages, there had been no communications from either Lisbon or the States, so Westbrook took his leave from the flight deck crew. He went down to the Lounge to mingle with the passengers and eat with a group selected at random by the steward.

When he spotted Joanna, she was surrounded by four men drinking cocktails, all talking effusively at the same time. She sipped a martini, flashing her dazzling smile and pretending to know and understand what each was saying.

She saw Westbrook spearing a fresh shrimp from a platter on the buffet table, and with a promise to return, she walked over and pretended to introduce herself.

"Here I am, supposed to be the big cheese in this operation, and some Hollywood queen steals my thunder," he said, in a feigned angry voice.

"The people here are so nice."

Westbrook laughed. "These men want your lovely body as much as I do." He was only half kidding.

Their conversation was cut short when a short, owlish looking Englishman joined them to claim Joanna. "We should be considering dinner. Will you join me?"

"Oh, Lord Kittenberg this is Captain Westbrook. Lord Kittenberg represents a number of German banking interests throughout the world, and thinks Britain should sign a peace treaty with Germany," Joanna said smiling, knowing how this would annoy Westbrook.

"Yes, quite right, your boy Joe Kennedy knows what he's talking about, I'd say."

"How can one represent a country that's at war with your

own?" Westbrook asked politely. He was goading Kittenberg, but not as much as he would have if he wasn't who he was and where he was.

"There's always a way, you know." Westbrook's question had apparently worried the man. He squinted at a table on the other side of the Lounge and said, "I see two places over there. Shall we go, my dear?" He took Joanna by the arm and steered her away as she threw Westbrook a furtive look over her shoulder.

He greeted the guests assigned to the captain's table, then excused himself for a moment, inviting them to enjoy their appetizers.

He sought out the steward, who was carving a rack of lamb in the galley, and gave him instructions on announcing an after-dinner treat for the passengers. Next, he called the bridge.

"New York just advised us they will be sending a coded message for your eyes only in less than an hour. Want Sparks to find you?" Waters asked.

"No. I'll be back before then. Thanks."

Joining his fellow dinner mates, Westbrook sat down in the middle of a heated exchange between two American business men on the pros and cons of declaring war on Germany. When asked his opinion Westbrook took a diplomatic approach. "I was in the Great War, as we called it. I have serious reservations about Americans fighting in Europe again. At the same time, I believe Hitler must be stopped."

Further discussion was halted by an announcement over the PA system: "Ladies and gentlemen, we have a special treat tonight. Because of the smooth air and expected lack of weather problems, the Captain has asked me to hold a drawing. One of you will get to have dessert and coffee upstairs with the flight deck crew, as well as a tour of the Control Cabin and bridge." As if on cue, the Clipper hit a patch of cold air which caused it to shudder for a brief moment. The only casualties were a few bottles of wine and champagne which fell off a trolley.

Westbrook hurriedly finished eating as the stewards began passing out small blank cards to each of the passengers. As he excused himself from the table, a winner was called. Luckily, there was no demand for an audit of the drawing.

Westbrook paused at the next table and said to Joanna, "Congratulations, Miss Morgan. If you've finished dinner I'll be most pleased to escort you upstairs." Joanna looked surprised.

As she stood up, Kittenberg, clearly annoyed that she was leaving, took Joanna's hand, planted a wet kiss on it, and said, "I look forward to seeing you soon, Joan."

When they were out of sight Westbrook took Joanna's hand. "Looks like I've got serious competition. Dessert's not even served, and he's calling you Joan."

"That man is loathsome!" Joanna wasn't amused.

Westbrook introduced Miss Morgan to the flight deck crew and Sylvia and Collins, who were finishing their dinner at the navigator's table which Brighton had brought up earlier.

When Joanna sat down, Sylvia recognized her instantly. She welcomed her, pretending she didn't know who she really was. Joanna had been told very little about Sylvia Meyers and she, too, played her part. She knew just enough to be intrigued by this handsome, eccentric woman.

Westbrook sat down in his chair and Andrews handed him the latest navigation plot and weather report. As he was scanning them Collins leaned over into the cockpit and said, "Captain, may I have a word with you?"

"Sure. What's up?"

"I know it was innocent," Collins said in a whisper, "but I think you made a mistake in bringing that woman up here. You can never tell in this business."

Westbrook realized quickly that Collins didn't know any thing about her. His complaint was valid.

"I guess you're right. Hadn't thought about it in that light. I'll have her out of here in two minutes, and tell her you're airline employees riding on passes."

Sylvia and Joanna were sitting together talking like long lost friends. As he stood up, Westbrook could see some resemblances in the two women. Same color eyes, although Joanna's were greener. And their profiles revealed similarly shaped noses. What the hell does that have to do with the price of tea in China, Westbrook wondered. As they went down to the Lounge Joanna asked, "What was that all about?"

"Collins, the OSS fellow who's looking after Sylvia, is upset that I brought you upstairs. As far as he's concerned, you're an unknown security risk, and he's absolutely right since he doesn't know who you are. I'm not prepared to tell him anything right now; we'll straighten it out on the way back to New York." Westbrook kissed her lightly on the cheek. "Watch out for Lord-what's-his-name. I'll see you in the morning. Love you."

Night had fallen in the control Cabin. The bridge was dark, and the instrument dials glowed like fire-flies. The moon looked like it was racing the Clipper across the Atlantic. There was a crackle of radio traffic--routine weather data from a light ship, somewhere in the darkness below.

Westbrook strapped on his pistol and took the controls. A few moments later, Sparks said, "Message coming in, Captain." He decoded it and wrote it out in long hand and handed it to Westbrook, who took a deep breath. It simply read:

"From: Cargo Department, PA, La Guardia

To: Captain Curtis Westbrook

　　Package scheduled for arrival Lisbon International Airport Saturday, 14 Sept. ETA 1900 local time. Please make arrangements for pick up."

"It's what we've been waiting for," said a relieved Westbrook, showing the message to Collins.

"At least I'll sleep better," Collins said. "Good night, Captain."

About thirty minutes later, Westbrook noticed the rpm gauge on the number one engine--the outboard engine on the left wing--was oscillating, as though unable to make up its mind about where to position itself. Such a malfunction could eventually result in loss of power on the engine, or worse, a run-away propeller.

"Number one's acting up a bit, Dutch."

Only at the flight engineer's panel could the engine revolutions be synchronized separately for each engine.

"I've been watching it, Captain. It's gotten progressively worse--if it doesn't settle down soon I'm going to go have a look." After a few more minutes of tinkering Anderson was unable to fix the rpms from his flight panel, so he collected his large flashlight and a small tool kit and went to the hatch on the left side of the aircraft. A few minutes later Anderson returned, clearly not satisfied with what he had seen. "Got some wiring problems, and it looks like some of the plugs on number one might be pretty badly fouled," he said, wiping his oily hands on a rag. "Not enough time to fix it in Horta, but we should be able to fix it in Lisbon. Damn thing annoys me, though, because I gave the engines a full run-up this morning, before we even did the pre-flight check. Let's keep the mixture pretty rich on number one for now. I can get a better look when we land in daylight."

The four powerful 1500 horsepower Wright Cyclone engines which powered the Clipper had 36 spark plugs each, which often tested the mettle of the flight engineers, particularly when it came to the conservation of fuel.

Their landing in the harbor at Horta was smooth and uneventful. The Clipper was moored to a floating pier just off the beach. Westbrook and Andrews deplaned and walked to the metal shack which served as Pan Am's operation building. Memories of the June flight and the pounding rain flooded Westbrook as he went in.

Fuelers scrambled up to the top of the Clipper's wing and began feeding the reserve tanks for the final leg of the trip to Lisbon, some 800 miles away. The main tanks, located in the lower wing hydrostabilizers were being topped off as well.

Since it was barely dawn, most of the passengers chose to stay on board and continue their sleep while the Clipper was refueled. Joanna, however, was a early riser, and had deplaned to enjoy the fresh ocean air of the Azores as she strolled along the volcanic ash beach. In the distance she could see a number of small white houses with geometric chimneys, typical of local architecture. She watched a sleepy shepherd tending his flock in a pasture not far away when Lord Kittenberg startled her by putting his arm around her waist from behind. "You disappointed me last night, dear lady," he said in a menacing voice.

After her visit to the Control Cabin, Kittenberg had insinuated he would like her to invite him to spend the night, describing his wealth and plans to further his interests in

Germany. Joanna had told him as politely as she could that he made her skin crawl. And it wasn't just his political views.

Stepping away, she wrapped her arms around her shoulders. "Lord Kittenberg, there was nothing about me to disappoint you." Flashing her ring, she said "I'm happily engaged." She looked around and was relieved to see a number of crewmen gathered in easy hailing distance. "I would be much happier if you would leave me alone."

Kittenberg lingered, studying her intently, before he left to reboard the Clipper.

Joanna wandered further along the shore, relieved to be alone again. Spotting a sea shell, she stooped to examine it and as she stood up, she saw yet another man approaching.

"Morning, Ma'am. Geoffrey Tuck, Royal Navy. Saw that chap hovering around you, and thought I should keep an eye out. Lord Kittenberg's not very savory."

"So, you know him?" Joanna asked.

"Know of him might be a better way to put it. A Judas, that one. With Churchill in power I'm hoping we'll have a proper necktie party for him one day soon."

"Tell me more," Joanna said as she and Tuck turned back to the Clipper.

"I can't say, really. He works in the bowels of the banking business and he thinks Hitler is going to rule the world sooner or later. The way things look right now, he may be right, but there are those of us who think the Germans can't afford to invade England, at least not just now."

The stewards began closing the entry door and Joanna returned to her room. Tuck took a seat in the dining room, wondering where he'd seen Joan Morgan before.

Of all the sites Pan Am operated in and out of, Westbrook disliked the Tagus River the most. In fact, he hated it. While it provided a beautiful panorama of the city of Lisbon, and appeared tranquil on its surface, the river was frequently possessed of a demonic mind of its own. It could turn to menacing swells in moments, clear air could turn to fog in less time than a Clipper took making its final approach, and surface winds could change direction by fifteen degrees in a heartbeat. These natural factors, coupled with the teeming river commerce made it a very dangerous place for the unwary pilot.

It was for these reasons that Westbrook had developed procedures, which Sparks Jenkins was well-acquainted with, for establishing radio contact with Lisbon approach control and the Pan Am meteorological office in Lisbon forty minutes or so before landing.

The first weather report gave winds out of the northeast 048 degrees, a calm surface with moderate swells, and sea state less than one.

"Want to shoot this one, Powell?" Westbrook asked forty miles from touch-down.

"Love to, Captain." Waters adjusted his chair slightly upward and forward to improve his visibility over the nose of the Clipper. Placing his feet on the rudder pedals and taking the wheel in his hands, he announced that he had the controls.

Westbrook handled the flap settings and acted as backup on the throttles in case sudden reductions or application of power were required.

"OK, Captain Waters, we have final clearance. Heading 050 degrees, wind still out of the northeast, and the water conditions remain the same. Visibility is unlimited and we are number one to land," Jenkins reported.

Waters began a gentle bank to the right for the final course heading, called for fifteen degrees of flaps and pulled back on the throttles to set up an approach speed of ninety knots. He would land to the east, about eleven miles up river toward Lisbon's northern shore. Westbrook lowered the flaps to the requested setting and then made the final announcement to the passenger cabin.

Twenty miles from touch down, Waters called for forty degrees of flaps and began to slow the Clipper to its touchdown speed of eighty knots. The pre-landing check list was complete and Westbrook began a visual scan of the water up ahead, looking for river traffic or debris that might threaten their landing. "Water's clear so far," he said as the Clipper roared towards touchdown.

When the barometric altimeter read one hundred feet Waters began pulling the nose back and working the throttles to maintain eighty knots of air speed. As soon as he felt the hull touch the river, he pulled the throttles to full off. The Clipper ground slowly to a stop, its momentum halted by the water's friction.

Mooring or docking a large seaplane is an awkward procedure but thirty minutes after touchdown, the Clipper, with the assistance of the ground crew, was secure at its moorings at the Cabo Ruivo seaplane pier.

Westbrook went to the crew's cabin and knocked lightly. "Everything all right?" he asked Collins, who answered the door. "Yes. Fine, Captain. Any more news?"

" OK. After I go ashore and find out what the locals have in mind for security, I'll come back aboard and we'll have a skull session about it. No more news." Westbrook had tentatively decided not to use the usual flood lights installed along the pier. He reasoned that the dark was more hostile to would-be mischief makers. At least they'd have second thoughts about any high jinx around the aircraft. At the same time, he realized darkness offered more cover to the mischief makers. It was a close call, and he hadn't made up his mind yet.

Entering the Lounge, Westbrook observed the confusion of the end of a trans-oceanic crossing. Passengers--some with hangovers, some just tired--were collecting their personal belongings, filling out disembarkation cards, searching for passports and visas. Suddenly, the dream was over and reality settled in like a heavy fog.

Joanna loitered in her suite in the hopes that she'd have a few more moments with Westbrook before she went ashore. Westbrook duly let himself in and took her in his arms. "Long line out there. You might as well wait a few minutes."

She sighed. "Oh, how I want you."

They were interrupted by a paging call. "Must be important. I'll call you at the hotel soon as I get there."

Only as he was closing the door behind did he remember: Inspector Gasparo. Westbrook found him standing on the sponson in an animated discussion with a steward, badge in hand.

"My fault, Eddie." Westbrook said. "I should have told you we're expecting this gentleman."

The steward waved the Inspector aboard. Gasparo looked tired --much more so than when they met only several weeks ago.

"Is there some place we can visit alone?" Gasparo asked. "This is important."

Westbrook ushered him to the Control Cabin where the flight crew was just leaving. The two men were alone.

Gasparo gave Westbrook the full details on Hans Auchlin. "I know he is the man who murdered your friend. We have a complete confession from a German Army officer who was a witness. Not only did he kill Captain Holloran, but I'm certain he also killed one of my deputies. But he's gone underground. As recently as two days ago his Embassy claimed they have no idea where he is, and at the time I had no reason to believe they were not telling the truth."

Gasparo told Westbrook about the contents of the envelope Morgado had left on his desk. "We received a report from a metallurgy firm confirming that the weapon used to murder Captain Holloran was manufactured in Germany by a firm that had patents on the process of producing a special high-grade, metal alloy used to produce everything from scalpels to bayonets. After the war started last year the German War Ministry banned the further export of the alloy. Not conclusive proof, obviously, but it helps confirm my original suspicions about Auchlin.

"To compound matters, we have a so-called special guest arriving tomorrow night from Casablanca. This person has raised a substantial interest among the Germans, and I've been ordered to protect him at all costs."

Westbrook was alarmed. "Wait here a few moments, please. I'll be right back." He went to crew's quarters and briefed Collins on Gasparo's instructions about the "special guest." Sylvia listened attentively to what Westbrook had to say. He could tell by her concerned frown that she knew her moment of truth was at hand.

"It's no damn good, Curtis," Collins said, nodding his head negatively. "The Germans will kill him and the Portuguese will do nothing. Absolutely nothing. I know them too well."

Westbrook had been growing increasingly uneasy about Collins. "You owe it to our success to talk to the Inspector, Al. He's already said his government is going to provide security for LaDieux. That at least means a safe ride out here by locals who know their way around. Besides, they'll be armed."

Standing up from his bunk, his palms spread upward, Collins shrugged, and said, "OK, Curtis. It's your show, but I tell you right now we may be blowing our cover, our plans--everything."

"I get the feeling you think we're destined for failure, Al, and we can't afford that. Inspector Gasparo is a good man, he's been diligent in tracking down Holloran's killer, and I think he'll take the job of protecting LaDieux seriously--and of getting the Clipper back in the air again."

Gasparo slowly told Collins what he'd told Westbrook, re-counting Ludke's confession and Sanguino's disappearance, and going over his orders to protect a "special guest" who was being given brief sanctuary in Lisbon.

"OK, Curtis," a somber Collins said. "Tell him." He had remained silent throughout Gasparo's account.

Westbrook told Gasparo about the Clipper's assignment, and the Inspector looked stunned at this turn of events. He reached for a cigarette, thought better of it and put it back in his pocket. "I would never have dreamed the Americans would get involved in a game of cat and mouse in which the stakes were so high," he said, almost in a whisper.

Westbrook and Collins gave him a full briefing, reminding him constantly, to his own annoyance, that if there was a leak it would surely come from the Lisbon Police. Collins came alive while questioning Gasparo on a wide range of subjects, from alternative hiding places for LaDieux, to possible weak links in his own department.

Two hours later the three men had an understanding. Collins seemed to have his old enthusiasm back, comforted by Gasparo's straight forwardness and abilities.

As a parting gesture, Gasparo suggested they accompany

him to the LaDieux pickup, which would relieve him of involving any of his other officers. Westbrook readily agreed. It removed all the unanswered questions about whether the locals could be trusted to get LaDieux across town from one airport to the other.

Pan Am had hired four armed guards to provide security for the Clipper overnight. Each would stand four hour watches. When Collins and Sylvia went to bed, Collins would lock both cabin doors from the inside. Westbrook and Waters had the only two keys this side of the Atlantic that could open the doors from the outside.

At Westbrook's suggestion, Sylvia moved her belongings to the deluxe suite. The move gave her and Collins more privacy and leg room.

After giving Collins another thorough walk around the interior of the Clipper, highlighting all the exits, Westbrook told him of his decision to leave the Clipper and the surrounding area in darkness. Collins thought it was a good idea.

As he deplaned, Westbrook saw the catering service arrive with box dinners for Sylvia and Collins.

A beautiful sunset formed just above the horizon of the river as Westbrook entered the seaplane terminal and proceeded to the Pan American operations office in the building, situated right next to the now closed offices of Imperial Airways, Great Britain's commercial seaplane counterpart of Pan American. Spartan but clean, the office provided the "eyes and ears" of the world to the Clipper flight crews arriving and departing Lisbon. Greeting the sole agent in the terminal's Pan Am office, Westbrook began filling in the flight plan for the flight to London. The Clipper would undergo repairs and refurbishing all day Saturday the 14th, ready to be underway for London by 0700 on Sunday the 15th.

Westbrook and Tuck had planned a four hour skull session on the Clipper for Saturday, beginning at 1000. Westbrook needed to know the Thames and all of its eccentricities like the back of his hand by the time the Clipper departed Lisbon.

Finished with the first draft of the flight plan, he folded it and placed it in the inside pocket of his coat. He would finalize it with Waters and Andrews on Saturday, then file it that evening.

Next, he went to the teletype machine, where the latest weather was chattering in. Although the long range forecast still looked promising for the London flight, with high cloud ceilings and good visibility, the local weather for the next twenty-four hours was disturbing. The forecast called for a strong warm air mass to move in with heavy fog forming on the Tagus beginning at 2100 that night. The visibility on the water front was expected to fall to zero about an hour thereafter.

Slumped in the back seat of a taxi on the way to his hotel, Westbrook pondered the day's events. Collins seemed to have turned around, but he wondered why he'd been so morose in the first place. Picturing Collins poised with his sub-machine gun, he smiled. He was pleased with Gasparo, too. He appeared to be a first rate police officer, thorough and honest. And the knottiest problem--getting LaDieux from the airport to the seaplane facility--had apparently been solved. Things were going smoothly, and he was dog-tired.

At the front desk, he felt a light tap on his shoulder. It was Gasparo. "I'm glad I found you. Would you join me for a brief drink? I know you're tired after your long trip, so I won't take long."

Westbrook tipped the bell boy in advance to take his bag up to his room, excused himself to Gasparo and went to call Joanna, who answered on the first ring. She had settled into the Aviz after taking a taxi from the terminal. The customs officer had smiled as he waved her through using a second passport in the name of "Joan Morgan."

Explaining his unexpected visit from the Inspector, he suggested they spend the night in his room, just in case he got a telephone call during the night.

"OK, Inspector, what's on your mind?" Westbrook said as he joined Gasparo at a small table in a corner of the hotel bar.

Gasparo, dipping into a bowl of pistachio nuts, said "I have a terrible fear of this man Auchlin."

Westbrook watched Gasparo count out exactly fourteen nuts. "What can we do to stop him?"

Gasparo was silent. He opened each one of his nuts,

carefully placed the shells in a tiny corner of the ashtray, and aligned his nuts in front of him so that they all faced north. As he apparently thought about what they could do to stop Auchlin, he ate each nut slowly, as if each one were a filet of steak. Westbrook had to stop himself from scooping up the pile of pistachios and eating them himself. All at the same time.

"I'm comfortable with you, but somehow I think your Mr. Collins doesn't think too highly of me. I just wanted you to know I think we could face real problems when your Frenchman arrives tomorrow evening. From what I can tell Auchlin is not accountable to anyone in Lisbon, not even the German Ambassador. He's a pet of Hitler's, and that tells us a lot. My men have been trying to find him for two days, and Lisbon is not that big."

"Any recommendations?" Westbrook asked.

"I've thought of sealing off the airport as much as two hours before the scheduled arrival time, but it would take the cooperation of the Army. I don't have enough men to do it alone. So with you, Senhor Collins and myself--each armed--I think we are equal to the task."

"What about the Clipper, Inspector? Think anyone might try anything out there tonight? There's heavy fog rolling in around 2100."

Gasparo considered the question before answering. "I'll have one of my patrol cars drive by as often as possible and check on the guards."

Gasparo reached for the bill, but Westbrook got it first.

"My treat, Inspector. Here's to a successful twenty-four hours." The two men shook hands and left the bar.

Westbrook went to his room, found his luggage in order, and called Joanna.

"You must be bushed, darling. I had a nice nap after you called."

Westbrook looked out of the corner window of his room. He could see the lights of central Lisbon against the night. No sign of fog yet, but it would be much thicker on the waterfront.

"You're right, it's been a long day, but pack some things, and I'll come get you."

As soon as the door to Westbrook's room was locked they fell into an embrace, exchanging long lingering kisses.

Later, Joanna ordered a supper from the dining room--paying a small ransom to have it delivered--and they chatted happily into the night, looking forward to the new day and the future they expected to claim for themselves.

CHAPTER 22
LISBON

"I was evading the police," Auchlin told an irate Steiner. Auchlin was clearly a liability, but Steiner needed him to capture the American. Her abduction had been debated at the highest levels of the Nazi Party. The disappearance of America's foremost Communist spokeswoman would not go over well with Stalin, but when he was informed that Germany had irrefutable evidence that she was a double agent feeding secrets about Russia's war plans to the OSS, Stalin would be grateful. Hitler ordered her arrest and, if need be, her assassination. Preferably, she was to be returned to Germany for a show trial and execution by hanging--an example of how Germany and its allies deal with foreign spies. Steiner was determined to get LaDieux and all of its associated perils, including this Meyers woman, behind him as efficiently as possible. He had fences to mend with the Portuguese, hopefully influencing them to join the Axis.

"Stass and Lusdorff are finalizing their plan to take LaDieux the day after tomorrow. The Clipper arrives tomorrow afternoon. Do you think you could abduct the woman tomorrow night and hold her twenty-four hours until the submarine arrives?"

"What about bringing her here?"

"Out of the question! I've told you before that we can have no involvement in this, directly or indirectly. You're acting on your own, Auchlin. If you don't care to proceed, so be it. But I must tell you your record here is a sorry one, and you're obviously a fugitive from something. I therefore urge you to consider doing this my way, and I'll lay as much groundwork for you as I possibly can."

Auchlin was taken back by the ferocity of Steiner's tone, but he knew the Ambassador was right. "I recently let a room near the waterfront. I'm quite sure I can get another room there. If I could slip her a sleeping potion I could take advantage of her illness. A little payoff to the proprietor, perhaps, but that should pose no problem."

"We can arrange that. You'll no doubt need a car as well?"

"Yes, Excellency, thank you. Where will the woman be staying?" "We think she'll be on board the sea plane. One of our agents works for the caterers of the Pan American flights. He tells us that two meals have been ordered for Friday, to be delivered to the airplane after it arrives. Her name is not on the manifest, so we presume she's staying on the airplane incognito. There must be somebody else with her so you'll have to be careful. And there'll no doubt be guards of some kind posted on the outside of the craft and along the water front, so you'll have to deal with them as well. Anything else? Firearms?" Steiner was anxious for him to leave.

"No thank you, Excellency. With your permission, I would now like to dye my hair and get some rest."

In spite of Steiner's sternness, Auchlin was relieved that he was still considered a useful member of the team. As he unpacked, he found Sanguino's police badge. He had almost forgotten about it. Fortunate, he thought. This could be very handy.

A steward arrived at Auchlin's room carrying a tray of sausage and bread with a large pitcher of lager. There was also a vial of morphine and hypodermic needle, and a tube of black hair dye. He still had his trusty P.38 with silencer and several boxes of ammunition.

The next morning, he looked in the mirror to see a young black-haired man, clean shaven. Even Gasparo would not recognize me, he thought.

Part of the cavernous Embassy basement had been converted into a combination print shop and photography studio for the production of false identity papers for German agents operating throughout Europe. Master photographers worked along side forgers. Many of them were convicted criminals and were delighted to have their prison sentences commuted to a tour in Lisbon. Here they worked as free men with a salary, producing forgeries which were virtually impossible to detect.

"Age, Herr Major?" a young Army clerk asked.

He began going through a stack of newspapers, glancing up from time to time to study Auchlin's face.

"What's this all about, if I may ask?."

"Obituaries, Herr Major, obituaries. We match you as closely as possible with a recent deceased, in age and physical appearance if at all possible." The clerk held up the second section of the Frankfurt Allgemeine, obviously pleased with himself. "Ah, here we are. Helmut Deitrich, age 34, died in Frankfurt two weeks ago. Lived there all his life. He was a school teacher and left no family. Probably never had a passport. Perfect."

In two hours Auchlin had a new identity card, passport and visa. He also had a new work permit. He was a new man.

While Auchlin was having his documents made, a young foreign service officer made a call on an elderly Lisbon pensioner who had advertised an old Renault for sale. A deal was struck, in cash. He handed Auchlin the keys and told him where it was parked. "Drives like a charm," he added.

And so it was that both Helmut Deitrich and Hans Auchlin got a new lease on life. The Embassy even provided him with several thousand reichsmarks.

Although he had a little difficulty with the gears in the old Renault while fighting downtown Lisbon traffic, Auchlin made it down to the winding streets of the Rossario District. He checked in as Helmut Deitrich with the same proprietor who had checked Hans Auchlin out without a second glance, passing his first test. When he got to his room he quickly opened the lock box he had rented at the front desk. The box was made of lead and could be chained to the bed. Whistling under his breath as he worked the combination lock of the old box, Auchlin gave passing thought to disappearing. Helmut Deitrich could book passage anywhere in the world, but his loyalties to the Fuhrer ran too deep. Something these newcomers to the Order don't understand.

He had no idea what Sylvia Meyers looked like, but he intended to find out. He was undeterred by the assumption that she would stay inside the Clipper—in fact, he was excited about seeing the flying machine for himself. The Clipper was due to land in less than forty-five minutes. Hurriedly, he knelt beside his bed, opened the lead box and stashed his loaded P.38 pistol, ammunition, the vial and needle, his scalpel and surgical gloves, most of his money, and several sundry items, including

Sanguino's hand cuffs, inside. He put Sanguino's badge in his pocket. Then, he left the room to survey the waterfront.

Hope she's attractive, he thought. It will make much more sport. Auchlin had been celibate too long. Since Dachau there had been random whores here and there in Berlin and Lisbon, but no one had really stirred his loins.

Reaching the Docha da Marinha, the busy shipyard facility, he stopped and lit a cigarette, like any idle tourist. Several ocean liners were at anchor in the estuary of the Tagus. Suddenly, a police car passed him at high speed in the direction of the seaplane facility. Auchlin only got a glance, but thought he saw Inspector Gasparo sitting in the passenger seat. What the hell does this mean? Do the police know we want to abduct the Jewess? He debated alerting the Embassy, until he realized a police presence could indicate a leak at the Embassy itself.

The best course was to call Steiner directly as soon as he had Meyers in his custody, probably at his pension. She was an insurance policy of sorts.

Steiner's only instruction was vague: have her ready to be delivered to a submarine somewhere off the coast of Estoril. What if he missed the connection? Should he kill her then? Walking toward the sea plane facility, these questions were interrupted by the low droning noise of the engines of the Clipper, glistening in the early afternoon sun as it made its final approach for landing. Fascinated, Auchlin watched it land on the water and begin its taxi towards shore. He edged down the pier until he was about fifty yards from the floating dock. A police car was parked off to the side of the pier, an area, he remembered, normally reserved for taxis picking up arriving Clipper passengers. There were no sirens and the flashing light wasn't on, so he relaxed a little, although he was still alert and curious.

Then he saw him again. Auchlin moved in closer, confident in his disguise. It was Gasparo--smoking a cigarette and pacing nervously on the floating dock.

He wanted to stay, but his presence might arouse suspicions.

Auchlin turned for one last look as he left the docks. Gasparo was standing on the Clipper's port sponson apparently arguing with someone inside the aircraft.

In his room, Auchlin retrieved the lock box. He pulled the P.38 with silencer attached, two clips of ammunition and Sanguino's hand cuffs from the box, and spread them on the bed. Then, breaking the glass tip of the vial, he carefully withdrew all of the morphine into the hypodermic needle. All of this would certainly kill you, but we'll use it sparingly. Wondering what would become of the American woman once she was in Germany, he went to his wash stand, wrapped the vial in a towel and pounded it until the glass was reduced to powder which he flushed down the toilet. Would she disappear into oblivion, or would the Fuhrer decide to try her as a spy and have her executed to embarrass the United States? There was no way of knowing. She might even be thrown overboard from the submarine. Auchlin was amused that his country, once so careful in its relations with the United States, was now about to kidnap one of its citizens.

Auchlin put the rest of his paraphernalia back into the box and chained it again to the bed frame.

He went downstairs to the dingy lobby and rang for the concierge.

"Bom noche, Senhor Deitrich," the concierge said when Auchlin appeared at the registration desk. Auchlin had tipped him generously when he engaged the pension in anticipation of this very moment.

He explained that he would be returning very late--possibly with a friend. He shuffled with embarrassment, conveying to the man this was not something he did very often.

The concierge produced a large key ring from his belt and sorted through them until he found one he liked. He handed it over with a smile. "I understand these things, Senhor." It was the key to the front door of the pension.

Auchlin reached the seaplane facility and started down the pier where the Clipper was moored. It was almost dark. He was instantly challenged by a guard holding a sub-machine gun strapped across his chest. He told the guard that he had arrived on the Clipper this afternoon and had left some belongings on board, which he needed to claim. The guard brusquely told him the Clipper was locked, and he would have to return when the Pan Am offices opened in the morning. Auchlin was a bit disturbed that the first security point was a considerable distance from the airplane. Stealth would be vital.

Auchlin called the Embassy from a public telephone. He was given the pre-arranged code word "schnee" to confirm there were two persons aboard the Clipper. The caterer had done his job.

Auchlin walked the dock somewhat aimlessly for another forty- five minutes, wondering who the second person could be. Whoever it was would be armed and dangerous. He--or she-- would have to be taken out quickly. No time for games. It was peculiar that the Clipper was moored in complete darkness. On prior visits after dark the Clipper had been bathed in flood lights. He was anxious about Gasparo's involvement, but he'd gone too far now.

It was just past 2130 when Auchlin returned to his room. The front door was locked and he let himself in easily.

He made a list of everything he needed to take for the job. Remembering how dark the waterfront around the Clipper was even without fog, he added a flashlight on his checklist. Rummaging through his belongings, he realized he'd left his only flashlight in the suitcase that he'd stored yesterday at the seaplane facility, which was now closed. He had a tinge of panic as he finalized his list.

At 0200 Auchlin went into the bathroom to wash his face. Looking into the mirror as he tightened his tie, he saw a face filled with anxiety. There's still time to leave, Helmut, he said to the reflection, half smiling. He placed his scalpel in its special sleeve pocket and strapped on his shoulder holster. He felt better. After putting on his suit jacket he collected the remainder of his gear--Sanguino's badge and hand cuffs, the hypodermic needle with its tip covered by a small rubber ball to prevent spills, and two clips of ammunition--and placed them in the right hand pocket of his trench coat and draped it over his arm.

The thickness of the fog surprised him. He couldn't recall seeing anything like it. Would it be his ally or his enemy? He shivered in the cool damp and put on his trench coat. The silence of the early morning made everything seem more eerie. There was no sign of life as far as he could see, although that was barely ten yards in either direction.

In the car, he turned on the small ceiling light and took a last look at the diagram he had drawn of the route he intended to follow to and from the seaplane facility. He had planned an indirect route for his return, mainly to lose any followers. Satisfied, he turned on the fog lights and began slowly winding down the embankment. The fog was so thick the car lights reflected the night and at one point he felt the bump and grinding noise of going up on a curb.

Cursing, he parked and set the brake, carefully opened the door and got out. In spite of the chilly morning he was sweating profusely. The real test of his cunning was at hand, and he was unnerved. He worked his way around the hood but as he stepped onto the curb he struck his head on a lamp post. Wincing with pain, Auchlin heard the sound of a muted channel fog horn. He calculated he was within a quarter mile of the Clipper, but he was afraid to leave the car in case he couldn't find it again in the fog. He cut the engine, locked the door and started walking towards the terminal, hoping to identify land marks for his return. The car was invisible in less than ten yards, even with its parking lamps on.

He was searching for another reference when he heard the muffled noise of a car approaching. He rushed back to the Renault, quickly unlocked the door, switched off the parking lights, his heart racing. He dove back to the side of the car away from the street and waited while the other car approached from behind. It came almost abreast of the Renault and stopped. Auchlin pulled out his P.38 and unlocked the safety. His hands were shaking.

Then a spot of bright, white light flashed his way, dancing around in the fog. It was a spotlight, but couldn't cut through the fog to find him.

As quickly as it appeared the other car disappeared into the fog. He reholstered his pistol and got back in the car.

As he inched his way off the curb he was growing more certain that he was at last moving towards the seaplane facility.

Auchlin figured that even with some resistance the job

would take no more than an hour. If the woman was not easily subdued, he planned to kill her and take her passport as proof of his accomplishment. He would kill anyone else on board, if for no other reason than for all the aggravation they had caused him.

Auchlin drove another five hundred yards and stopped again. Squinting, he could just make out the red brake lights of a car ahead at what he was sure was the entrance to the seaplane facility. He cut off his own lights and slowly approached, but the brake lights on the car ahead went off, then disappeared. The police car--if that's what it was--had moved on.

It was over thirty minutes since Auchlin left his room and he was worried he was running out of time. Still, with all that fog it would be dark until mid-morning, he argued to himself.

Auchlin parked and began walking towards the Clipper. The swirling fog gave him flashes of vertigo, and he had to stop and regain his balance. Walking slowly, he bumped into another invisible street lamp, jarring his shoulder and sending a burning pain down his back.

If it was that difficult for him it was equally so for anybody else. At the right turn down to what he thought would be the pier, a bright light flashed in his face. "Who is it?" demanded a harsh voice at the other end of the light.

"Policia," Auchlin whispered, holding Sanguino's badge up to the light.

"But, you were just..."

Sensing the distraction, Auchlin moved swiftly. He flicked his scalpel towards the source of the light, burying it in the throat of the unseen guard. He died without so much as a gasp, his warm blood spurting down Auchlin's arm. Auchlin grabbed the flashlight and turned it off. His primary fear had been eliminated. He couldn't resist flashing the light momentarily downward to look at the guard's eyes staring vacantly up, his mouth twisted painfully. Next to the body was a sub-machine gun, which Auchlin retrieved.

In darkness again, he stood up and slung the gun over his shoulder, and waited a few moments for his night vision to return. There had to be at least one more guard--maybe two. He began moving down the pier, trying to restrain his relief.

He could only vaguely make out the shape of the Clipper, ominous on the fog-shrouded water. It looked like a temple of doom.

He took a deep breath and switched the flashlight on and off three times to attract the attention of the guard who must be nearby.

His guess was correct. Another guard emerged up the gangway. In his left hand he carried a flashlight, its beam directed at Auchlin's face, blinding him once again. He sensed the guard was nervous and might shoot on the slightest provocation.

"Polica, Lisboa Policia," he whispered loudly. The guard stopped when he was toe to toe with Auchlin, pressing the sub-machine gun to his chest. Auchlin could smell both alcohol and garlic on the man's breath. The guard looked at the badge and dropped the barrel of his gun to his side and the light away from Auchlin's face. Auchlin chatted until his night vision improved, but his Portuguese was not up to the task.

When the guard demanded further identification, Auchlin reached inside his coat and pulled out his P.38. The silencer made a "zip" noise as the bullet struck the guard in the shoulder, knocking him into the river. His sub-machine gun clattered to the pier.

The guard popped his head out of the water and screamed for his mother once, but the wound and shock were too much and he fell silent as he inhaled water and slowly drowned.

Auchlin froze where he was, listening for sounds. He felt protected by the thick fog for the first time. He fumbled with the sub-machine gun and turned the safety off. The door of the Clipper was securely locked. He worked the handle several times, worried he would attract attention from inside. The door didn't budge.

Auchlin paused to consider his dilemma, his whole body drenched in sweat. He was tempted to light a cigarette, but knew that could be a real folly. He decided he had no choice but to use his silenced pistol to shoot the lock away.

Propping his sub-machine gun against the hull of the Clipper, he stepped back from the sponson to the pier and fired sideways at the lock, hoping to avoid a ricochet. The lock blew away, and in seconds he was in the darkened Lounge of the Clipper, his sub-machine gun ready. He could hear himself breathing--and somebody else, too.

* * * * *

At first Westbrook didn't hear the telephone, but Joanna nudged him awake. It was 0440. Lying on his stomach, he found the receiver and picked it up.

The Inspector's voice was shaking: "Captain, there has been a tragedy on the Clipper."

Every nerve in Westbrook's body tensed.

"One of my cars will be arriving to pick you up within minutes. Deputy Inspector Morgado will meet you in the lobby."

"Damn! He didn't give me a clue," Westbrook said as he started dressing. He expected the worst--multiple deaths and massive destruction.

"What's up?" Joanna asked huskily.

"Something's happened on the Clipper. That was Gasparo." He kissed Joanna lightly and rushed to the elevator, nauseated.

Morgado was waiting. Although they hadn't met, he recognized Westbrook from Gasparo's description. He introduced himself and they grimly shook hands. A light drizzle began to fall, dissipating some of the fog that was still thick and a threat to safe driving. They got into Morgado's squad car: the motor was running and the blue and white beacon light was turning silently on top.

"There have been at least three murders, and someone has broken into the Clipper. That's all I really know. The Inspector called me at home just moments ago, and I've never heard him so upset. He thinks this man Auchlin is responsible and he's rarely wrong about his hunches."

They rode in silence the rest of the way to the terminal. The pier was lit by a blaze of spot lights, and policemen and plain-clothes detectives were swarming the area. At the top of the pier was the first of Auchlin's handiwork: a crumpled body covered with a blood stained sheet.

"His weapon is missing," a grim detective told Morgado. "Sub-machine gun."

Westbrook saw Morgado shudder as they continued on to the Clipper. Gasparo emerged from the fog like a wraith. "Please come with me. I have some very bad news for you, Captain. Your colleague, Mr. Collins, is dead and the lady is missing. I hope you'll tell me that there were some last minute changes in her plans, but from the looks of things it appears she's been abducted or disposed of elsewhere." Gasparo pointed to another sheet clad body lying on the pier. "He was the other security guard--shot before drowning in the river. My men found him floating by the pier."

"How did you find out about this, Inspector?" Westbrook asked. While he was worried about physical damage to the Clipper, it paled beside his concern for Sylvia and shock and sorrow over Collins. He shook his head in disbelief.

"I instructed one of the precinct patrol cars to make an hourly check with the security guard at the top of the pier, the one who had his throat slashed. The officers talked with him at about 0225. When they returned at 0350 they found him dead. They were slow in their rounds because of the fog.

Gasparo shrugged his shoulders, and said, "We've been reluctant to do much on the Clipper, except look around, until you arrived, but I think we should go aboard, with your permission, of course."

Westbrook considered the Clipper his home, a place where joyous and interesting things happen, not a place of murder.

The cabin door was still ajar. "The lock was shot away. Probably a silencer," Gasparo said, without emotion.

The interior of the aircraft was dark and the air was stale. "I'll turn on the auxiliary power, and we'll get some lights on," Westbrook offered.

Gasparo flashed his light on Collins, slumped back in a center seat of the Lounge. "There he is." Westbrook and Morgado turned away. The right half of Collins' face had been blown away to the skull, exposing his eye and teeth. Brain matter was spattered on the head rest of his seat. His sub-machine gun lay in the middle of the aisle and Gasparo picked it up by the trigger ring, smelled the end of the barrel and checked the clip and safety. "Must have been surprised. Safety's still on; he didn't

201

fire a shot."

Gasparo had Morgado summon the forensic medical personnel and other detectives to come aboard the Clipper and begin searching for clues.

A gray dawn was barely visible in the cockpit when Westbrook reached the Control Cabin. He began a feverish examination to determine the extent of any damage to the controls, instrumentation and other systems that could cripple the aircraft. Finding none on his first check, he turned on the auxiliary electricity and switched on the cabin lighting and then began a more systematic cross-check of the aircraft's systems. After fifteen minutes he was satisfied that there was no damage, but he didn't understand why. He sat down at the navigator's table and wrote a note instructing the ground crew to test the onboard fuel for contamination.

Whoever was responsible for the terrible things that had happened this morning didn't realize the Clipper was the critical element in making the LaDieux affair work. If he had known, why didn't he just plant a small bomb on the bridge and leave? It would have taken a month or maybe longer to repair the damage. Maybe they were just after Sylvia, and didn't even know about LaDieux.

As he went back to the luxury suite he recalled how pessimistic Collins had become during the flight, in contrast to his enthusiasm in the early planning stages. Did he sense what was going to happen? Westbrook wondered. Surely not. Collins had mentioned after landing that he had not slept well on the journey over, but was going to take some medication in order to stay awake last night. Obviously, it hadn't worked Westbrook reflected sadly.

Sylvia's perfume still lingered in her suite. One of Gasparo's detectives was dusting white powder on her large suit case, hoping for finger prints. An intense, frowning Gasparo was sifting carefully through lingerie which was strewn across the floor. Westbrook was startled to see the nun's habit Joanna had worn aboard the Clipper carefully folded on the unused cot. Anger welled as he imagined the horrible personal invasion Sylvia must have felt. He remembered helping with her baggage at LaGuardia. There had been two matching pieces, one small and one large. The small one was missing. Also missing was the hooded coat she wore at LaGuardia.

Gasparo expressed little doubt Sylvia had been taken from the aircraft, probably alive. "Why can't we find Auchlin?" he wondered aloud. He had ordered check points set-up at all departure points from the city: the airport, railroad and bus stations, and port facilities. He told Westbrook he was particularly worried about the railroads; there were numerous daily departures to both France and Spain.

"Assuming it's Auchlin, Inspector, wouldn't it have been easy enough for him to have a boat meet him right here or even rendezvous with a submarine?"

"Your point is well taken, but based on conversations with him, particularly one Morgado had several days ago, we have the feeling he's a maverick and probably wants to stay in Lisbon, at least for awhile. Why, we don't know. He was hand-picked by Hitler for this assignment. He may have rubbed some of the career officers in the German Army the wrong way and wants to make amends. The one thing we do know is that he is a ruthless killer. The slaughter here this morning confirms that, but it's not new. What confounds me more than anything is why I can't find this devil in my own city." Gasparo swore, jamming his fist into the air. "Of course, we have to assume he's altered his identity."

At Westbrook's request, Gasparo ordered the stair case to the Control Cabin sealed off, and a police officer stationed at the landing.

The two men sat down in the Lounge facing each other. Westbrook told Gasparo how puzzled he was that the Clipper itself was intact. "It would have been so easy. Nobody would have had to be killed, and we'd be powerless to do anything for weeks. Now we're faced with an assignment that doesn't involve the United States directly, except for transportation. Will LaDieux refuse to fly to London because an American he greatly admires has disappeared? Hell no! It will only increase his determination. He obviously likes his propaganda, so he knows that Sylvia Meyers would give the meeting international solidarity and drama it needs." Westbrook stood up and began pacing up and down the aisle. "Her disappearance is even more dramatic, so he'll have a heyday pointing his finger at the Nazis." His tone was one of increasing anger and frustration.

"The key issue is whether what happened here this morning is related to the arrival of Senhor LaDieux," Gasparo said. "I happen to think so, but we can't take it for granted."

Stifling a yawn, Westbrook agreed with the Inspector. He looked at his watch, and saw that it was time to call Commander Tuck and give him the details of the morning and scrub their 1000 meeting.

Driving back to the city Westbrook and Gasparo discussed LaDieux and the limited police manpower in Lisbon.

"When I first received this assignment I begged the First Minister to provide some Army troops to cover the airport for a few hours until the Frenchman is safely under our protection, but he refused. He said it would look like we don't trust the Germans any more. Between the two of us I don't think the Minister cares what happens to LaDieux. It could prove very difficult, but I still feel you and I have a chance of success. I don't like involving you but it may be our only hope and, frankly, I don't know what else to do. By the way, I brought that along for you." Gasparo nodded to the back seat. It was Collins' Thompson sub-machine gun.

"There's no turning back," Westbrook said forcefully. "Success is too important for both of our countries--and the Allies."

They agreed they'd have supper that evening and get to the airport before dark. Gasparo put the Thompson in the trunk of his squad car. Westbrook didn't relish explaining to hotel security why he was walking around with a sub-machine gun.

When he opened the door of his hotel room, Westbrook saw Joanna sitting on the sofa, absent mindedly biting a finger nail, as she tried to concentrate on the morning edition of the International Herald Tribune, with little success. A dog eared copy of the script for Boys and Girls lay beside her. She looked up in surprise when Westbrook opened the door. She hadn't been expecting him so soon. "Sorry, darling. I would've called you from the Clipper, but I had to tell you in person. Al Collins has been murdered, along with two security guards, at the seaplane terminal. Sylvia Meyers is missing, and the Inspector thinks she's been kidnapped." The tone of his voice was dull, touched with anger. Joanna's eyes filled with tears.

Westbrook hugged her closely and told her what police were doing to find Sylvia. "I know I look like a hobo, but I've got to get a little shut eye. Why don't you go ahead reading here? I'm not comfortable letting you roam the city since three people involved with what we're doing have already been murdered today. Inspector Gasparo will call me right away if anything pops up on Sylvia. Give me thirty minutes, then I'll clean up and we'll have lunch."

Twenty-five minutes later he awoke with a bolt, sitting up in bed. Something he remembered from the flight over.... He wrestled with it until it came to him. "Of course!" he thought. He remembered seeing Joanna and Sylvia together in the Control Cabin. "They look alike; they could almost be sisters."

"Curtis, what's the matter? I thought you wanted to sleep," said Joanna with a puzzled look on her face. She was still sitting on the sofa, reading.

Westbrook sat on the edge of the bed, put his face in his hands and thought for several seconds. Turning to Joanna with a serious look on his face, he said, "Hold on a sec, I need to clear the cobwebs." He went to the bathroom, splashed his face and then went back to the bedroom and sat down next to Joanna. He took her in his arms and said, "I've got the craziest idea. So crazy it scares me." Then he came directly to the point.

Joanna was stunned. She pulled back from him, her face a mask of astonishment. "Curtis, I don't...It's crazy," she stammered.

Westbrook smiled, looking almost relieved. "Of course, I understand, darling. The world's slipped its moorings. I almost didn't mention it. There's danger involved and you shouldn't be exposed to it. New subject."

"What do you mean, 'new subject,' damn it!" Westbrook had never seen her so angry. "You bowl me over and then drop it? Of course I'll do it, but I'm going to need a hell of a lot of help from you. It'll be the challenge of my life."

The two looked at each other for a few moments, then embraced and burst into a combination of laughter and tears. Joanna had just agreed to impersonate Sylvia Meyers.

CHAPTER 23
LISBON

Auchlin had spotted Collins with the first play of his flashlight, and Collins, snoring lightly, never knew what hit him. Sylvia hadn't heard the short sub-machine gun burst that had taken Collins' life, and was still sleeping when Auchlin lifted her up from her cot, using Sanguino's hand cuffs to secure her hands behind her. Auchlin thought she looked like someone having a nightmare, so he slapped her with his gloved hand to make sure she was awake. He wanted her to know her enemies had found her.

Auchlin produced the hypodermic and explained what it was, threatening to use the full, fatal dosage if she uttered a sound or tried to escape.

He packed a bag for her at random for the long ocean journey she was going on soon. Auchlin gagged her with a silk stocking and cupped her left breast through her pajama top. Aroused, he whispered heavily, "More later." He had to exercise restraint to keep from raping her then and there.

Instead, he grabbed her roughly, and forced her into the main cabin. When they reached Collins' corpse he stopped, grabbed her by hair and forced her to look at the grisly remains, at which point she vomited. Auchlin had to untie her gag to keep her from choking. Annoyed, he struck her in the face and her knees buckled beneath her. She began sobbing silently. "Jew bitch, get up and come with me or you can join your friend right now." He grabbed her again and pulled her up. He forced her into the seat next to Collins and fastened the seat belt across her lap.

Auchlin inched his way to the entry door and stepped down on to the port sponson. He listened carefully, since seeing anything was hopeless in the thick fog. A new air of power came over him. The worst that could happen would be that he'd have to kill Meyers before he could get her to the submarine, although a Lisbon Police car at the wrong place during the next thirty minutes could still ruin everything.

He re-entered the Clipper, and unlatched Sylvia from her

seat belt, pulled her up and guided her to the entry door.

He forced her to lie down on the floor of the back seat of the car and put her suitcase and the sub-machine gun in the front seat beside him. If he encountered the police now he would shoot them and then Sylvia. He figured "Helmut Dietrich" could still get away with little difficulty. He'd won the battle and was about to win the war.

As soon as they were inside his room, Auchlin pointed, and ordered, "Lie down on the bed, and be quiet." He was smiling.

Sylvia struggled to lie on the bed comfortably, her hands still cuffed behind her. Auchlin could see her face was glazed with fear and she was still sobbing.

Auchlin poured a heavy scotch, lit a cigarette, then, rubbing his hands, said, "My name is Helmut Dietrich. I have been retained to deliver you to a submarine belonging to a foreign navy. In so doing, I've been given two options. My choice as to which one." He took a long swallow of the scotch. Leering, he continued, "If you cooperate I will deliver you safely to the submarine. If you do not, I will dispose of you and forward your passport to my employer as proof of my accomplishment, all that is required. No questions will be asked" He snuffed out his cigarette and drained the glass of scotch.

"Either way, you'll decide your own fate. Have you no tongue? You haven't spoken yet."

"What do you expect me to say? You're setting all the rules. Would you please take off these hand cuffs? They hurt."

Auchlin obliged, ordering her to sit in a straight back chair while he bound her to the chair with the heavy cord he had used with Holloran and Sanguino. As he bound her, he ran his hands roughly across her breasts and thighs. Her femininity was inviting, but he needed sleep first. He was considering delaying his call to the Embassy until afternoon instead of mid-morning as Steiner had ordered. The submarine's schedule should be more firm by then, anyway, he rationalized. He was having difficulty containing his desire for the prisoner, as evidenced by his hardened penis while he relieved himself before going to bed.

CHAPTER 24
LISBON

While an exhausted Hans Auchlin slept soundly, Sylvia Meyers tried to compose herself. Without a plan all would be lost. She tried to reason with herself about why she was here. It was clear her captor was a German who hated Jews and enjoyed the terror he inspired, but was he a Nazi? The OSS had warned her the Nazis suspected she was feeding intelligence from her Russian sources. She had to do something to save herself.

After being abducted, she had been in the car a fairly long time, but Sylvia felt they weren't too far from the Clipper. Her mind wandered. Auchlin had made numerous turns. It was Saturday and LaDieux would be arriving in a few hours. Surely someone will find out I'm missing. Maybe they already have. Who'll find poor Al? Her thoughts turned to her physical discomforts: the tape across her mouth was becoming painful, and she smelled vomit. She badly needed to go to the bathroom. She decided it was time to put her priorities in order.

She surveyed the room. From the dingy light filtering in, she could see that Auchlin was not a good housekeeper. He had turned her chair to face the room, with a desk at her back. Now she worked her way around, managing to move the chair enough to see the top of the desk. There was some loose change, a wad of reichsmarks and a hair brush. In the dim light, the brush appeared as though blond or silver hair had accumulated in the bristles. She knew immediately he was in disguise.

Then she spotted it. Against the wall was the hypodermic he had threatened her with. She remembered Auchlin telling her there was enough morphine in the needle to kill an elephant.

Straining to face the room again, Sylvia saw Auchlin's holster draped on the post of the bed. The sub-machine gun was parked, muzzle up, in a corner. Although she had never fired a gun in her life, the time had come to learn quick.

Each of her hands were bound separately to the back of her chair. When she tested the bonds she found they almost cut off her circulation. But a large wad of the left sleeve of her pajama top had been tucked up under the cord. She began to softly see-saw her hand against the sleeve to loosen it from the cord. Ten minutes later Sylvia had made some progress, and after several minutes more she had nearly finished.

But, as though on cue, Auchlin sat up yawning. He had been watching her for several minutes, realizing she might be close to freeing herself. He got out of bed and walked over to her, taking in the loosened cord and the perspiration on her face. Without a word he struck her on the mouth with the back of his hand. She groaned as the blow knocked her head backward.

"Jew bitch! I know how to deal with you. I've been watching you the whole time." Auchlin struck her again, this time in her right eye with his fist. Sylvia began to whimper. It was too much. He untied her hands, and jerked her to her feet. He ripped her pajama top right down the middle, tearing off most of the buttons, and ripped it again so that it fell to the floor in tatters. Then he forced her to step out of the bottoms. Placing the chair in the center of the room, he sat down to look at her, ordering her to raise her hands and keep turning around until he told her to stop. As she did so, her eyes stayed fixed on the floor. The fly of his undershorts gaped with his erection. Auchlin got up and fondled her breasts, next he cupped both hands around her buttocks and pulled her to him. Grinding against her, he pried a finger into her anus. "Just a beginning. We have the next twelve hours." He pulled her hand to his erect penis. She quickly jerked it away, but that was all the stimulus he needed. He ejaculated into his shorts.

Auchlin stared at her for several moments. She began sobbing uncontrollably. Momentarily pacified, he ordered her to dress. She motioned desperately to the bathroom, and Auchlin nodded his permission, ordering her to leave the door open. He laughed to himself, proud of his foresight in securing the only pension in the building with its own bathroom. As she dressed, he cleaned himself up and called the Embassy. It was 0820.

"Excellency is in a meeting with two gentlemen from Berlin, Herr Major. May I have him return your call?" the operator said.

Despite his frustration Auchlin remained calm. "Danke, I'll call later. Please tell him I have the package we discussed and am awaiting delivery instructions. I'll try again in another half-hour." Steiner must be getting a last-minute briefing from Lusdorff and Stass, he thought.

Back in the room, Sylvia was fiddling with the buttons on her silk blouse that Auchlin had packed for her. Seeing the hypodermic needle on the table top, she edged toward it. Auchlin seemed preoccupied with some notes he was reading. She was reaching for the needle when he looked up. Auchlin sprang across the room, and wrapped both arms around her in a ferocious bear hug that pinned her arms to her sides. As he tightened his embrace Auchlin uttered a deep guttural groan. Sylvia was becoming light headed--she couldn't breathe and thought she was going to pass out. Peeling the tape from her mouth Auchlin said, "You obviously have a great affection for my needle. Are you addicted, perhaps?" Laughing at his own joke, he rolled up the sleeve of her blouse and inserted the needle in her forearm. She felt the sharp bite of the needle. "No. Please don't," she pleaded.

"Ah, just a little bit. You've been quite troublesome. Be glad I'm letting you live." He depressed the plunger and released a small amount of morphine into her arm. In moments she was unconscious in his arms. He hand-cuffed her to the bed post. She wore only a blouse and panties.

On his way back to the pension from buying groceries it occurred to Auchlin that he should pinpoint where his car was. He knew he had parked it close to the pension. After checking the few landmarks he had identified last night, he found it. A police car was just pulling out from behind his car as he spotted it. Alarmed, he ran back to his room, half expecting Gasparo to be waiting for him. But nothing had been touched. Sylvia was still unconscious although she seemed to have trouble breathing from the morphine.

He called the Embassy again. Steiner was waiting for his call, obviously in a good mood. "Congratulations, Major, I understand you've found the package we're seeking, correct?"

Gulping for air, he said, "Yes, Excellency. Everything is secure and I await further instructions as to its disposal."

"Passport?"

"Yes, of course."

"We`ll need pictures. Give me your address."

"Excellency, I...forgive me, but I don't understand."

"There has been a change of plans. The package will <u>not</u> be sent to Germany, so we'll need proof of its existence. Not that <u>I</u> doubt you, Major, but Berlin requires hard evidence. After the pictures you are to dispose of the package as quickly as possible. Do you understand?" Steiner was tired of dealing with the Fuhrer's lout, and it showed in his exasperated tone of voice.

"Of course. I understand fully. Room 24, Pensione Mariscos, 96 R. Covos. Excellency, I regret to tell you my car is apparently under police surveillance." He said more than he'd intended, but it sounded as if Steiner was abandoning him, and he was uneasy.

"Well, Major, these are difficult times, aren't they? I suggest you come straight to the Embassy after you dispose of the package. But <u>not</u> tonight. There are too many things happening here at the moment. Come tomorrow, around noon. Bring full details of the disposal procedures. Pictures of the corpse, if at all possible. Take a taxi, and we'll be on the lookout for you. Meanwhile, our photographer will be coming to see you and the package this afternoon."

* * * * *

Auchlin was startled by her loud, blood curdling scream. He watched as she opened her eyes, apparently awaking from a nightmare. Auchlin was quickly beside her, poised to strike her again before he thought better of it. "If you draw attention here, you're dead. Do you understand that?" He was actually smiling. She nodded her head. Through her sleepiness and tears she saw they were not alone. A small man was busily peering into a large camera box on a tripod with his back to the window as he and Auchlin exchanged comments. Daylight was fading rapidly and a hint of more fog was in the air.

Auchlin went to her, unlocked the hand cuffs, and said, "Get up, bitch. Time to smile for the camera." He forced her to her feet. Every joint in her body ached but Auchlin was agitated and she didn't want to set him off.

"I believe the sitting position would be the best, face full to the camera," said the strange little man.

"For your obituary. Sit down here." Auchlin said, pointing to the chair.

Sylvia sat down, Auchlin close beside her.

The photographer took five rapid shots, the flash filling the room with sulfuric smoke. He had Auchlin hold her open passport in front of her, just below the chin. Several more pictures were taken and then he folded up his equipment and left with her passport.

Auchlin hand-cuffed her back to the bed post and ate ravenously. He needed time to think.

He turned to Sylvia and said, "Plans have changed. I am to dispose of you within the next twelve hours." Breaking into a crooked grin, he said, "Think about the way you wish to die. I may let you choose." He could see she was frightened as she cowered on the bed. He lit a cigarette, and began pacing the floor. Strangulation would be quiet, but he wanted to draw it out. The morphine would be too easy. The old way would be best. The scalpel. She's been a burden to me, so why go easy on her?

Auchlin continued nervously pacing the floor, smoking cigarettes one after the other. The sun had started to go down and he desperately wanted to get some fresh air, but he had to wait until dark. Even in disguise he felt uneasy, especially since the car had been discovered. He fixed himself a another neat whiskey and drank it in one gulp. He started to pour another but thought better of it. Clear head, must keep a clear head. I'll have another later. Instead, he dressed, gagged Sylvia with several layers of tape, and tied her feet to the foot posts. "A little uncomfortable, perhaps? Don't worry. You don't have time to get used to it. If you make any effort to free yourself, I'll kill you the minute I return. I would give you some more morphine, but then you wouldn't enjoy the time you have left, would you?"

As he walked to the waterfront he gave in to the temptation to go by the seaplane terminal. It was barely daylight, and the Clipper was bathed in search lights. Police swarmed the pier, going in and out of the aircraft. He looked in vain for Gasparo, then walked on. The fresh air and sense of freedom cheered him even as the uncertainty of his future persisted. He had followed orders and achieved success, but for reasons he couldn't quite fathom, he still felt uneasy about Steiner. He knew the Ambassador had been a late comer to Hitler's confidence, and the job he held was a sensitive one. If he could persuade the Portuguese to join the Axis, he would be a hero. Auchlin chalked it up, in a half-hearted way, to the Ambassador's jealousy.

As soon as Auchlin left the room Sylvia began testing the bonds. He had not made the same mistake in tying her up. She tried in vain to loosen the cord that bound her left wrist. The hypodermic needle was on the table, closer than before, but it did her no good. She cursed missing her earlier opportunity by mere seconds. Out of ideas, and exhausted with her struggle and the morphine hangover, she at last drifted off.

After walking an hour, watching police cars patrolling the streets and the dock area, Auchlin began to think about supper. Inland the local cafes and restaurants were replacing the noises of the dock yards with music and the sound of laughter. Happy people, these Portuguese. Innocent.

Whistling to himself, Auchlin walked briskly back to the room with dinner for both he and Sylvia. His appetite was whetted by his anticipation of the next few hours. He even forgot Gasparo as he hurried back to Sylvia.

He could tell Sylvia was rattled from sleep by the door's slam. "Did you miss me? I've brought you dinner--even the condemned have a right to a last meal."

* * * * *

The detective seemed to be in a hurry. He asked the concierge several questions about Hans Auchlin, and the concierge confirmed that a man by that name had checked out the day before. He also confirmed that Auchlin bore a resemblance to the description the detective had given him.

"Any other German guests now?" the detective asked. The concierge put on his glasses, looked at his ledger and told the detective that there was a German guest named Helmut Dietrich, but he was clean shaven and had dark hair.

"Anything unusual about Mr. Dietrich? Any strange habits?"

"Well, there was something peculiar earlier today. I was checking out a late departing guest when I heard a loud scream-female scream. I believe it came from Mr. Dietrich's room, although I can't be sure. Moments before the scream a small man, perhaps a dwarf, in a black suit, carrying a black bag, climbed the stairs without checking in with me."

"Why do you think the scream might have come from Mr. Dietrich's room?"

"Because at the time he was the only guest on the second floor. I'm not aware of ever having heard noises from the third floor. Too far away, I think."

The bored looking detective closed his notebook, thanked the concierge and left.

CHAPTER 25
LISBON

The Westland Lysander began a banking descent into the Lisbon control zone shortly after dark on Saturday, September 14th, 1940. It was a large single-radial engine utility airplane, painted black with fixed landing gear. The roundels of the Royal Air Force were painted on its fuselage and on the top and bottom of the wing tips of its high wing. The slow-flying aircraft had taken off from the Casablanca Airport nearly three hours earlier. Its running lights were off.

An anomaly existed in the early days of the war which was no- where more evident than at Lisbon's Cintra Airport. The bellige-rents had an unwritten agreement not to shoot down each other's commercial flights in neutral countries. So at any given time, an observer at Cintra could see U. S. manufactured British Dakota transports parked side-by-side with gray Lufthansa Junkers and the colorful mail planes of Italy's Ala Littoria.

In 1940 Cintra was a poorly equipped airport and normally planes did not arrive or depart after sunset because of the lack of lighting around the field. This flight was an exception. The RAF had given its assurances that the pilot was skilled in night landings, having ferried a number of Allied spies in and out of Occupied France in the dark.

About twenty minutes before its scheduled arrival, Westbrook and Gasparo parked across the runway in a secluded area beside a dilapidated, long abandoned wooden hangar. Westbrook held Collins' fully loaded sub-machine gun, and had four extra clips in his trouser pockets. He also had his Smith & Wesson .38 Special revolver strapped in a holster on his right hip.

A high cirrus cloud cover obscured the stars; another heavy fog was expected to roll in before midnight.

They could hear the droning engine before the plane came in sight. Gasparo threw his cigarette onto the gravel and cracked the barrel of his shotgun to confirm that two .10 gauge scatter shot shells were in the breech. Westbrook clicked off the safety of the sub-machine gun. They both felt the tension.

The RAF pilot rapidly flashed his landing light three times and the tower controller responded with a double blinking green light, clearing him to land.

As the Lysander landed, Westbrook grabbed Gasparo and pointed to a dark object on the other side of the runway, midway up the field, moving out of a row of parked transient aircraft.

"It's a car, Inspector. No lights! Damn!"

"We have a big problem on our hands," Gasparo exclaimed. He pulled Westbrook into a crouch and they ran toward the field.

The car's high beam came on and the driver swerved, speeding directly towards the aircraft as it was completing its landing roll out.

The pilot, blinded by the headlights, violently jammed in full-right rudder trying to turn away from the oncoming vehicle while applying full brakes. The combination was disastrous. The Lysander veered sharply to the right and its nose went forward, hitting the tarmac. The turning propeller struck the runway, spraying sparks, and sheared off, breaking the fuel lines. The force of the braked turn collapsed the right landing gear and the aircraft struck the ground sharply with its right wing tip, which crumpled like paper. As the Lysander came to rest, a small, snake-like fire from the broken fuel lines began crawling slowly away from the engine compartment toward the fuselage.

For a moment nothing happened. Then the front doors of the car now parked just in front of the plane with its lights painting the wreckage, opened and two men jumped out of the front seat and ran to the burning aircraft. Westbrook paused and fired a burst at them. They were still out of range.

The giant Lusdorff, grimacing from the heat of the growing fire, hoisted himself up to the cabin door and threw a hand grenade into the passenger compartment, then dropped down to the runway and ran. There was a muffled explosion and screams.

Raoul Cardin, his clothes and hair afire, leaped from the Lysander's cabin and started spraying sub-machine gun fire wildly into the darkness. The screams from the cabin intensified as the fire spread through the plane.

Two of Cardin's bullets found their mark on Lusdorff. One shattered his left shoulder, the other smashed his right thigh. The giant Austrian fell to the tarmac, not far from the aircraft.

Cardin rolled about on the runway trying to put out the fire all over his body. Stass seized the moment and fired four shots into the struggling man. Before dying, Cardin fired a single burst at Stass managing to nick him in the arm.

The cabin of the Lysander was now silent.

By the time Westbrook and Gasparo reached the scene, it was almost over. The only sound heard over the crackle of the fire were Lusdorff's pleas to his companion.

Walking as close to him as he dared because of the heat, Stass fired a single shot through Lusdorff's forehead.

As Stass turned back to the car, he saw Gasparo and Westbrook pointing a shotgun and a sub-machine gun at him at just about point blank range.

"Drop your pistol and put your hands over your head," Gasparo ordered.

Stass hesitated, frozen with indecision. It was a fatal mistake.

Gasparo fired both barrels into the German, nearly cutting him in half. As though dancing, Stass groaned before falling, his entrails spilling onto the tarmac. Gasparo started toward Stass's corpse, but Westbrook grabbed him by the arm. "Don't, Inspector. The airplane is about to blow up. We need to move back."

They reached the far upwind end of the runway just as the Lysander exploded, sending a shower of flame and sparks skyward like a colossal Roman candle.

There was a secondary explosion from the Lysander's fuel tank that took out what was left of the aircraft, the Germans' car and the three corpses on the tarmac. By the time the Lisbon Fire Department arrived forty five minutes later there would be nothing but charred metal and bones, unrecognizable in any form.

"I knew. I knew," Gasparo whispered, sadly shaking his head. "The Germans are treacherous, but the Minister insisted I tell them of LaDieux's plans." He got out his handkerchief and blew his nose. They stared into the dimming fire.

LaDieux was gone. Sylvia Meyers was missing, most likely in the hands of the Nazis, or dead--probably at the bottom of the Tagus. With Sylvia missing, Joanna had been the one hope, but now the whole endeavor lost its meaning. Westbrook felt hollow, his hatred for the Germans worse than ever.

Westbrook turned to Gasparo. "I've got to get back to the Clipper. My crew could be in danger." His voice was raspy and subdued. Gasparo agreed, and they went back with heavy hearts to Gasparo's car, which, because of the pecuniary nature of the city, had no radio. They'd have to wait and wonder until they reached the Clipper.

Westbrook sat slumped in the front seat of Gasparo's car. While he was relieved Joanna wouldn't have to go through with the charade with LaDieux, he was angered at such wanton slaughter. He took little solace from the thought that further provocation by the Germans might be all Portugal needed--and the United States as well--to join the Allies in the war.

Westbrook saw no unusual activity at the seaplane terminal. The Clipper was bathed by flood lights, its silver hull sending dapples of light to the surface of the dark river. Its brightness, though, was dimming as the fog began rolling in like banks of dirty cotton. Only a few uniformed police guards stood guard as several marksmen with high powered rifles scoured the river. All other available police officers were at Cintra Airport.

"Any survivors?" Morgado asked glumly, as the Inspector and Westbrook joined him on the gangway. The police had received a telephone call from the La Cintra tower as soon as the fireworks started.

"No. Any news about the American woman?"

"None. It's like she disappeared into a hole."

"Those were Germans, Jose. We've been betrayed. I know they took Miss Meyers. They must think we're complete fools." Almost under his breath, he added, "Perhaps we are."

"Why don't we go aboard?" Westbrook suggested. "It's going to get real chilly out here."

Westbrook went to the Control Cabin and called the hotel for messages. The concierge told him that the American Embassy had called several times, and finally left a number with instructions to call as soon as he could.

Westbrook called immediately, and was informed of a encoded message from Assistant Secretary Gates. Did he want it delivered to the Clipper now? "Yes, yes please. As soon as possible. Thank you very much." Westbrook hung up. His stomach was in knots. Was it over? He glanced at his watch. Joanna was due in less than thirty minutes with a police escort. Westbrook had decided earlier she would be safer spending the night on the Clipper.

He rejoined Gasparo and Morgado in the Lounge when one of Gasparo's marksmen rushed aboard, carrying a high-powered telescopic rifle. "Inspector, Captain, come quickly! There's a noise over the river. Some kind of an engine, very close."

Racing for the pier, Morgado drew his Beretta automatic pistol and unlocked the safety.

"It's a light airplane," Westbrook said after listening for several seconds upon reaching the pier. Its small engine was sputtering, as though it was running out of fuel. "Might be in trouble, but I can't tell yet. One thing's sure, though, he's coming down. What the hell is he doing out there on a night like this, anyway?"

The fog had covered the river as it had the night before.

"Maybe you should move some of your sharpshooters to the water's edge and radio your patrol boats to be on the look out for a small aircraft," Westbrook said. "He should have red and green running lights on the wing tips." The engine noise had ceased.

"He's down somewhere on the water, or soon will be."

After a few moments a faint splash, muffled in the fog, was heard not far from the Clipper, but exactly where was anybody's guess.

Their sector of the Tagus was lit up by high-beam searchlights from two Lisbon Police patrol boats.

Shouts and curses were heard from the river.

Westbrook looked at his watch again. Joanna could arrive anytime and this--whatever it was--worried him.

One of the police boats emerged from the fog. Although it was difficult to see, one of the occupants was hand cuffed to each of the unused oar locks in the boat. He was a large man, and seemed to be complaining, but his French sounding accent was so thick no one understood him.

One of the police officers managed to get ashore. He retrieved his rifle and pointed it at the prisoner who was now blinded by the search lights. The remaining policeman in the boat carefully unlocked the captive's hand cuffs from the oar locks and re-cuffed his hands behind his back. After a struggle between the policeman in the heaving boat and the police on the pier, the prisoner was pulled safely to the pier.

"Keep him covered, and don't hesitate to shoot if he makes a move," Gasparo ordered, motioning the prisoner into a small area of the gangplank. He reasoned that if the prisoner attempted to escape, odds were he would fall into the water and be of no further trouble to them. Except for the occasional mourn of the buoy horn in the channel, the night once again fell silent.

As he turned to join the Inspector, Westbrook noticed a small green light trailing above the police boat, visible only intermittently. Studying it a moment, he said to nobody in particular, "That's the right wing tip of an aircraft." The police had been able to secure the plane to their boat when they picked up the prisoner, but had not shut down the airplane's battery. "Captain Westbrook, the helmsman told us there's a man still in there. The crew didn't move him because they think he's dead. We're going to try and bring him ashore now."

A car turned onto the pier, as Gasparo and Westbrook were talking, heading directly for the Clipper's gangway. It was probably Joanna, but Westbrook drew his .38 as a precaution anyway. He watched the car as it slowed to a stop. Two uniformed policemen, pistols drawn, got out, looked around and helped Joanna out. She rushed To Westbrook who looked at her sadly. "It's over. LaDieux's been killed." Without another word, he took her arm and escorted her on board, a policeman following behind, directly to the luxury suite. He told her briefly about the murders at the airport, and the crash on the Tagus. "It's probably coincidental that a small plane got lost in the fog and crash-landed near us, but we can't take any chances." Telling her to stay put, Westbrook deplaned to join Morgado, who had succeeded in finding out their prisoner was Corsican.

"Other than that, he won't talk, Captain," Morgado said, his frustration plainly visible. The word "captain" made the Corsican's face light up. "Captain Wesbrook?, Captain Wesbrook?" he said in halting English. Westbrook nodded.

The Corsican smiled and started jabbering to Morgado, who raised his hand to stop him so he could get the Inspector, though it didn't work. Morgado motioned to a nearby guard to watch the prisoner while he and Westbrook looked for Gasparo. "He mentioned the name 'LaDieux'," Morgado said as they walked down the pier. They found Gasparo checking over a small man lying on the pier so pale he could be dead.

"His pulse is weak, but steady," Gasparo said. "I think he has a bad concussion."

"From what the Corsican told Inspector Morgado it just may be we're onto something," Westbrook told him.

"When Captain Westbrook identified himself the Corsican opened up," Morgado said. "So fast I couldn't keep up. His Portuguese is poor, but I think he mentioned LaDieux."

Westbrook and Gasparo looked at each other. "Let's have a chat with the gentleman," Gasparo said, shrugging his shoulders. After getting Westbrook's permission to do so, he instructed his men to take the unconscious man aboard the Clipper.

Gasparo unlocked the Corsican's hand cuffs and guided him out of the glare of the search light. The Corsican rubbed his wrists vigorously and asked Gasparo for a cigarette by putting two fingers to his mouth and making a loud puffing noise. He began talking to Gasparo in broken Portuguese, occasionally gesturing at Westbrook.

Gasparo turned with a broad smile. "Amazing! He claims the other man in the aircraft with him is Pierre LaDieux, and that he has specific orders to deliver him to you personally. Can that be, Captain? We saw that inferno at La Cintrra Airport first hand."

Westbrook's mind was racing. He bit his lip, and calculated rapidly. "It's possible. Certainly, it's possible. Except for the big fellow who jumped out of the airplane we didn't see anybody else besides the two Germans. What we heard inside could have been from the pilot. It's entirely plausible. Somebody on the

Allied side smelled a rat, knew the Germans had LaDieux's timetable, and set up the decoy!"

Westbrook's hopes soared. A second chance was at hand. Oh, God, please let it be so.

It wasn't long before an unsteady LaDieux was led to the Clipper Lounge where Westbrook and Gasparo were drinking coffee with the Corsican.

LaDieux introduced himself. He looked pale and exhausted, but his English, although accented, was understandable.

"Has Raoul Cardin arrived yet?"

Westbrook walked over to LaDieux with his right hand extended. "Curtis Westbrook, Mr. LaDieux. I'll be flying you to London in the morning. This is Inspector Gasparo of the Lisbon Police." He invited the Frenchman to sit down and poured him a cup of coffee.

"Unfortunately," he said as he took his own seat and exchanged a glance with Gasparo, "we fear Mr. Cardin was killed at Cintra Airport, about two hours ago. Two Germans were waiting for the flight--we assume to kill you as well. Thank God somebody had the foresight to predict such a thing might happen."

LaDieux sagged in his chair. "How much more? Raoul..." His head dropped to his chest.

Westbrook reached over and gripped LaDieux's shoulder in sympathy.

"He's alive, Joanna! He's alive. My God, it's a miracle."

Westbrook was buoyant. He prowled along the walls of Joanna's suite, fingering the drapes and backs of chairs as his mind raced with the flight to London in the morning. The nun's habit, folded neatly on the chair where she had left it, tinged his anticipation: Joanna was now faced with assuming a new role, and a much more dangerous one than Sister Theresa. She looked the part already. Before leaving the hotel she had her already dyed black hair styled as much like Sylvia's as she could remember, a basic page boy cut.

"It's still not too late to back out, darling." He took her hands in both of his. Could a star, used as she was to dressers, managers and directors hovering, carry this off? He loved her, and loved her gameness, but what had he, really, asked her to do, and in the final analysis, for what end?

But Joanna wasn't thinking about the difficulties ahead.

"Curtis, I'm worried sick about Sylvia."

"Inspector Gasparo has every available man looking for her," he told her. "We have to get on with what we're here to do. Sylvia would want it that way too. I'm sure we can convince LaDieux to meet with DeGaulle without you, though. Like I said, it's not too late to change your mind."

"No," she said shortly. Her eyes were determined and her jaw set. "I feel good about doing this. I've seen _you_ in action: maybe it's time you got a lesson in what _I_ can do for a change." She laughed, gaily. She pulled one of Sylvia's cigarillos from her blazer and crossed her legs to emphasize her--Sylvia's slim calves. "How do I look?"

"I see what you mean about changing the look." His blue eyes twinkled with amusement and pride as he reached out to tug her collar. Pulled up, it helped hide Joanna's longer neck, and the pearls she had added to the suit pulled the eye further away from comparisons. "You look beautiful," he said more seriously. "My admiration grows with my love." He left with a kiss and a promise to return as soon as he could.

Westbrook found Gasparo administering smelling salts to LaDieux, who had passed out again. A courier from the American Embassy had just arrived and was under the close scrutiny of one of Gasparo's men. He carried an envelope marked "For Commander Westbrook's Eyes Only."

The message was from Di Gates:

"The President has authorized me to inform you that you are hereby vested with total discretion with regard to carrying out or scrubbing Operation Eagles Away.

Godspeed"

Westbrook nodded in satisfaction and shredded the note. Turning to Gasparo, he said, "What do you think, Inspector? Should we get a doctor out here?"

"I don't think so--one more set of raised eyebrows. If need be I can get one at any time, so maybe you should wait a while. I think he'll be fine."

LaDieux revived in several minutes and announced he was feeling better, although he needed sleep. One of the Lounge seats was converted into a bed and soon he was snoring softly.

Westbrook and Gasparo walked out of the Clipper together. "It's been an interesting day, Inspector."

Grinning wearily, Gasparo said, "You are the master of understatement, amigo." He scuffed the sandy ground with his foot. "I only wish we could find your American friend. My men are honey combing the area where the car was found and I won't rest until we find Auchlin." He coughed slightly in the cool night air as he wished Westbrook good evening and happy hunting.

CHAPTER 26
LISBON

Auchlin untied Sylvia from the bed so she could regain circulation. The only light in the room came from the bathroom, but it was exactly right for what he had in mind. He poured himself a whiskey. She used the bathroom, keeping the door open as he had ordered. When she returned the time had come.

He stood up and stripped. He grabbed Sylvia by the arm and started undressing her. She quickly understood it was useless to resist: with each sound she made he hurt her. He kneaded her breasts and pubis.

"Kill me, but please don't do this," she begged in a whisper. "Why not do both?" he laughed before ordering her to lie down on the bed. He mounted her then tried to force his way into her, but he could see his efforts caused considerable pain. Sylvia's face was a mask of suffering, and the tears flowed down her cheeks. He bit her breasts hard, running his tongue across her nipples and licked the blood he drew. When he lost all patience he pushed her legs up and entered her. After several thrusts he came, too soon and too hard as always seemed his way. He collapsed at her side, disgusted now by her bloody nakedness and his own feeble sexual prowess. He silently cursed the memory of his step-sister, hoping she was dead, as he turned back to Sylvia.

Auchlin tried to kiss Sylvia as he caressed her. Tired of her unresponsiveness, he got up and poured another drink. When he'd finished half of it, he realized he was giddy and slightly alarmed by it. He ordered Sylvia to sit in the chair. He wanted to get some sleep, have sex with her again, then operate on her: a thought he anticipated as much as sex. One more time and I'll use the cord. Holloran had never been this much fun. First, Auchlin, who was feeling increasingly tipsy, used the cord to truss Sylvia's arms at her sides in the straight back chair. Then, he used the last of his tape to gag her, after he had bound each of her feet to the legs of the chair. To think, he said to himself, amused, she'll never utter another word again in this life. He fell asleep with plans buzzing through his brain.

Sylvia knew she only had several more hours, and that Auchlin was actually looking forward to killing her.

Her chair was next to the table and she hoped the hypodermic was still near the edge; she had not actually seen it since being dosed that afternoon. Once again she would have to try to somehow free herself and find it in the dark. First, she tried to shuffle the chair closer to the table, but found that she couldn't. It was too heavy for the restricted movement of her legs and feet. As she tested her bonds, she was cheered that a slightly drunk Auchlin had used a less than scientific method of tying her up. Her arms seemed bound in a crazy-quilt fashion: could she find a knot? Feverishly working her fingers around her left wrist, she found a knot, which was tight, but there was no other option. She began to scratch it in a continuous circular motion, and in a few minutes it began to loosen, although cramping her fingers. She ignored the pain and continued to work through the occasional snore from Auchlin.

She was finally able to unravel the knot. Flexing her hand to loosen the cramps, she found she had successfully freed her left hand and arm to the elbow. She was ecstatic until she reached and found the needle was not as close as she thought.

Carefully and silently, she began running her hand lightly across the top of the table. Now, her worst fear was that she would bump into it and send the needle rolling to the floor. She felt nothing and started to panic. Then she found it, on the far side of the table. The needle almost pricked her hand--he hadn't put the rubber ball back on the tip. Carefully feeling for the plunger, she picked it up with her left hand and placed her hand on her lap. She could feel the cold on her thigh. She tried once again without success to shuffle the heavy chair towards the sleeping Auchlin. Now all she could do was fight sleep. And wait. Auchlin had to come to her.

CHAPTER 27

LISBON TO LONDON

Westbrook woke up in the crew's quarters at 0430 on Sunday, September 15. Joanna had spent her night in the luxury suite, guarded by a Lisbon policeman stationed inside the Clipper.

The night before Westbrook had made a thorough inspection of the Clipper's interior. The forward bulkhead, still riddled by machine gun bullets and soiled by blood and brain matter would be a constant grim reminder of Collins' murder. Satisfied with the aircraft's internal integrity, Westbrook reviewed the maintenance report.

We're ready to go. Now will the weather cooperate? Westbrook wondered as he climbed the staircase to the crew's cabin. It was unbelievable to him that he had been in Lisbon less than forty- eight hours. They'd been the roller coaster ride of his life. He peered out the cockpit window. It was still very dark; he could barely see the forward searchlight. The fog had not yet dissipated, in spite of the weatherman's prediction of blue skies by take-off time.

The flight crew members and George Benson, chief mechanic, arrived together in a hotel jitney. Tuck was with them, dressed in the navy blue uniform of the Fleet Air Arm.

Waters and Anderson headed for the Control Cabin to start the pre-flight. "Any sign of the missing lady, Captain?" Waters asked on his way up.

"We'll discuss it shortly. La Dieux arrived safely last night and is resting in the forward lounge." Westbrook said nothing of last night's fireworks, assuming the word had gotten around. Anyway, he'd re-lived it himself too many times.

Wesley Andrews hurried in from the operations office, where he had filed the flight plan, and picked up a copy of the latest weather report.

Tuck, Jenkins and Westbrook were deep in conversation about the flight when Andrews arrived. He was the first to notice. "By damn, Captain, that's a real live Naval officer's uniform suit you got on."

"President's orders, Wesley," Westbrook said, smiling as he flicked invisible lint from the sleeves of his navy blue uniform. "Is this scud on its way out?"

"Believe it or not it is, but maybe not soon enough. Supposed to be completely burned away by 0930. Gorgeous flying weather once we get out of here."

Westbrook was not altogether happy. If the forecast was accurate a visual flight-rules take-off would be delayed by about two hours. "OK. Subject to the pre-flight check, we'll start engines in thirty minutes and ease into the harbor. We might have to amend the flight plan for an instrument takeoff.

"Sparks, be a good man and check on Mr. LaDieux. He's had a tough time, and he's probably hungry by now. Also, have the flight deck crew report for a briefing in fifteen minutes."

Westbrook knocked lightly on Joanna's door. She opened it, looking radiant in a rose-colored silk suit. Her sadness was evident. "I'm glad you're here. Did the police find anything new on Sylvia?"

He had to tell her Gasparo hadn't contacted him, which meant there was no news, good or bad. He added reluctantly, "If her body is found, Gasparo will conceal the fact from everybody--the press and even Salazar--until we're back in Lisbon.

"We're planning to cast off in a few minutes, but first I'm going to make a full disclosure to the crew, for the record. They'll know you're Joanna Davis the actress, and my fiancee. I'll tell them your presence is accidental but lucky. Nothing will be said to LaDieux, so you'd better plan to introduce yourself to him right after take-off."

Westbrook came directly to the point with the crew, making it clear there was no hidden agenda, and that everything about to happen was coincidental. Joanna would impersonate Sylvia Meyers in order to accomplish what President Roosevelt wanted so badly.

Tuck whistled through his teeth. "Dicey isn't?" The others took the matter well. They knew Westbrook well enough not to be suspicious.

"So much for that, gentlemen. Please feel free to ask questions." There were none. "From my point of view, this operation won't be a total success unless Sylvia Meyers is safely returned to us. Inspector Gasparo is working hard on it, so maybe we'll have good news when we get back. One last thing. New York has scrubbed the scheduled return flight to the States. The Dixie Clipper is coming in tomorrow to take our place on Tuesday, so Lisbon to New York will be a ferry flight, and we'll have an extra day here. Let's hope we'll have a lot to celebrate. My deepest thanks to each of you for making this trip, even though you didn't have to. I'm proud of you, and we'll all be better men for what we're about to do."

The Clipper was still at its moorings when Joanna encountered LaDieux at the galley coffee urn. After introducing themselves, he expressed his delight at finally meeting her. The charade began. Having grown up on the Continent following her father from one diplomatic post to another, Joanna spoke French fluently, so they chatted for several minutes. Fortunately, he didn't engage in any serious discussion of American Communism or the role the Communists should take in the War. Perhaps he took it for granted. LaDieux's looks contradicted the archetype of the Resistance hero, because of his small build, but he presented himself forcefully.

At 0715, Westbrook restlessly sipped at his third mug of coffee. Although he knew it wouldn't expedite anything, he ordered the engines started. There was plenty of fuel for a round-trip to London, even if the Clipper had to take some diversionary action. One by one the four Wright Cyclone engines coughed before howling to life. Waters moved the cowl flaps to full-open, and reduced the engine speeds to idle. The fog was beginning to lift on the shore, but the middle of the river was still veiled. "We'll standby here for another ten minutes, and then we'll give it a try," Westbrook said.

He could sense tension building on the bridge. Waters was preoccupied, peering out the windscreen silently, and Jenkins was nervously whistling a tune off-key. It was understandable; he was not fond of flying instruments either, but if the forecast was right he knew he could climb out in a sharp right bank toward the ocean and break out on top of the fog quickly.

Five minutes after the engines had been started the Lisbon tower requested the captain's intentions.

"Tell them we're going to hold here another five minutes and if the visibility hasn't improved we'll amend for an IFR take-off," Westbrook told Jenkins.

"Tower says since we're the only traffic this morning we're cleared for departure on discretion; no amendment to the flight plan required. The channel boat just radioed the tower and said the fog is so thick they can't determine whether there's any debris in the take-off path or not."

Frowning, Westbrook thought for a moment. Tuck had told him that the lull between bomber raids on London usually occurred between about 1330 and 1445. He looked at his watch, and then gazed for a moment out the window. According to Andrews' forecast the fog probably wouldn't burn off for at least another two hours. If they waited, they'd arrive over London just as the afternoon raids began. There was presently no wind on the surface of the Tagus, so he could work the Clipper to the middle of the channel and take off due west, toward the ocean. "Call the tower and tell them we're ready to go, Powell." Westbrook felt he had no choice. It was a risk he had to take.

"Tower says to hold, Captain. Company just radioed saying they're sending a message for you. They want a response before we leave." Westbrook remained silent, looking out the forward cockpit window, disguising his irritation and impatience.

Ten minutes later the message was transmitted by Morse code. Jenkins quickly decoded it and handed it to Westbrook. Washington had received conflicting reports about LaDieux and Sylvia, and wanted confirmation that both were on board. If the response was affirmative, Westbrook was ordered to send a message, "Eagles Away," as soon as they were airborne. Otherwise, they should wire "Clipped Wings." The message could be sent in the clear since it had no tactical or strategic significance, except to Di Gates and the President.

Clearance received, Westbrook gave the orders to cast off. Both he and Waters peered intently into the fog, looking for debris and the channel markers that would tell them they were in the take off lane. Finally, Westbrook saw a marker buoy pass under the port wing. He brought the throttles to idle, then eased up on the number three and four engines, swinging the Clipper to the left until it was on a magnetic compass heading of 275 degrees. He then retarded the throttles to idle. The pilots couldn't see fifty feet ahead.

Taking a deep breath and adjusting his seat slightly, Westbrook advanced all four throttles to full power. "Here we go, fellows!"

The Clipper was sluggish at first, and Westbrook had to fight the rudders to hold his magnetic heading, but because of its light load the aircraft quickly gained momentum and became airborne. Passing through five-hundred feet and still on instruments, Westbrook initiated a sharp bank toward a northeasterly course for England. He calculated he was clear of the Portuguese coast and over the Atlantic when he reached seven hundred feet.

"Send 'Eagles Away'," he said, leveling out at two thousand feet on a course of 025 magnetic degrees. Jenkins gleefully pounded away on his Morse code key.

About 100 miles north of Lisbon the fog disappeared, surrendering to an early fall day with no cloud cover and unlimited visibility.

After turning the controls over to Waters, Westbrook joined Tuck, seated at the navigator's table. The British commander was engrossed in making meticulous notes on the enlarged aerial chart of London, specially prepared for this mission by the Royal Observatory.

Measurements of distances, in feet and meters, as well as miles and kilometers, were set out in index fashion in both the Chelsea and Lambeth Reaches of the Thames, the two alternate landing sites. Each had advantages and disadvantages, and Westbrook would face a last minute decision about which to choose.

The preferred Reach--Lambeth--offered the nearby mooring facility and a temporary communication facility in the Victoria Tower Gardens. It was next to the Houses of Parliament, and only a short drive to the Cabinet War Rooms in Whitehall, where the meeting was scheduled to take place.

The powerful disadvantage of this location was the fact that there was only slightly more than a three-quarter mile separation of the spans of the Lambeth and Westminster bridges. There was twice as much distance between the Chelsea and Vauxhall bridges at the other site, but Westbrook would face a long and possibly dangerous time taxiing to the mooring site. Assuming the winds were reasonably favorable, he had tentatively decided to shoot the approach for Lambeth. It would be a tight squeeze and he would have to land at the extreme end of the touch down site, or else run the risk of running into Westminster Bridge, the lower beams of which were not high enough to let the Clipper pass under. If things got too uncomfortable, he had plenty of fuel for a missed approach and another go around for Chelsea.

After about forty minutes of discussion and debate with Tuck, Westbrook felt thoroughly briefed on all the strategies they had considered. The final decision would be his. He left the Control Cabin for the Lounge to see how Joanna and LaDieux were getting along.

Joanna and LaDieux were seated on a lounge sofa facing each other. LaDieux nursed a mug of tea, staring intently out of the window. He had removed the bandage from his head, revealing a deep and angry wound. Westbrook thought he looked tired, even perhaps ill. Joanna was filing her nails, looking very much at home. They had been chatting amicably for more than an hour. As Westbrook had predicted, Joanna had beguiled LaDieux, who was extraordinarily pleased that Sylvia Meyers, an American, cared enough to make this dangerous show of solidarity between the American Communist Party with the French Resistance Movement.

"Good morning, Captain," she said formally. "Are we getting close to London?"

"About another hour. Are you feeling rested this morning, Mr. LaDieux?"

He smiled wanly. "Yes, merci. Mademoiselle Meyers is good company, and I'm delighted to finally meet her. This will be a great and momentous occasion for me and for the Resistance Movement. Will the English Prime Minister attend?"

Westbrook sat on the arm of the sofa next to Joanna. "I

understand he plans to, but if the raids are still going on he may not be able to. I should warn you both that the Germans have increased their attacks on London in recent days, so we may be dodging some German airplanes and bombs. We're clearly marked as an American aircraft, though, so I hope they'll leave us alone."

"What's to stop them from shooting us down, Captain?" La Dieux placed his cup on his tray, and opened his hands in despair. "They weren't reluctant to destroy a British plane on neutral territory in an effort to kill me. Why not this one?"

Westbrook paused to frame his response, a frown creasing his brow. "First of all, we don't think they know where you are. If they thought you were flying on the Clipper from Lisbon, they would have crippled the plane when they had the chance. Secondly, the U.S. is not at war with the Nazis and Hitler won't want to provoke us. I could be dead wrong, but I don't think so."

"Let's hope you're right. Too many have died." He blinked rapidly and looked down at his hands.

"Pierre says he hasn't made up his mind about staying in London, Captain."

LaDieux shrugged his shoulders and arched his eyebrows. "It all depends on the General."

"Well, that's fine. We'll stay on the water as long as we can, but we need to be back in Lisbon before nightfall." A night landing on the treacherous Tagus was not the way Westbrook wanted to end the day.

CHAPTER 28
LISBON

Sylvia was still awake as the first light began filtering through the yellow stained curtains.

The room had just gotten a little brighter, when there was a commotion and men barking orders downstairs. Auchlin heard it too, and sat straight up in the bed. He hurriedly reached for his pistol, hanging on the foot post. Kneeling, he unholstered it, took off the safety and pumped the slide, putting a bullet into the chamber. He looked at Sylvia with a scowl, as if to say whatever it was that was about to happen was her fault, and pointed the pistol at her. He was stopped from proceeding any further by a loud pounding on the flimsy wooden door.

"Policia!" shouted a voice from the other side. "Open up!" Still kneeling, Auchlin swung the pistol to his left, aimed it halfway up the door, and fired twice. A cry was heard as Auchlin jumped to his feet and rushed toward Sylvia. He could smell his own body, bathed in the sweat of fear, as he moved closer. When Auchlin leaned over to move her chair, she twisted her body to her right and thrust the needle upward, jamming it as deeply into his chest as her limited motion would allow. She depressed the plunger, but Auchlin staggered backwards, his eyes staring in wild disbelief, before she could finish. The needle wobbled in his chest. He fired wildly, narrowly missing her as he fell backwards to the floor. Moments later, the door was blasted into splinters as two detectives dashed into the room and dove for the floor, covering the room with their weapons. One of the detectives spotted Auchlin and leveled his gun at him with an order to sit up. When there was no response he approached him cautiously at gun point. He checked the dilated eyes and began taking his pulse. It was only then that he noticed the needle.

The other detective freed Sylvia and offered some soothing words, "I'm Deputy Inspector Morgado, Senhorita, of the Lisbon Police. You're all right now." As he gently removed the tape from Sylvia's mouth, she let out a painful sigh.

"He's still alive, Deputy Inspector, but his pulse is weak.

What was in this needle, Senhorita?" asked the other detective.

"Morphine. He said it was morphine." Her voice was dull.

Morgado draped his coat around Sylvia's shoulders, and helped her stand. Every muscle in her body ached. With Morgado's help, she began walking slowly around the room, wincing when she saw the dead policeman beyond the splintered door. She gave the two policemen a halting description of Auchlin's kidnapping and torture, dwelling vividly on how Auchlin first told her she was going on a long ocean journey. Yesterday, though, he had changed his story and said he was going to kill her.

"This man has the constitution of a bull," said the other detective, who was kneeling over Auchlin taking his pulse and looking for other vital signs. "I think he may be gaining consciousness."

Morgado, who had never laid eyes on Auchlin, was frowning as he examined the papers of one Helmut Dietrich from Frankfurt, Germany. He noticed a work visa which was good for three more weeks. Puzzled, he decided to search the room. First, he instructed his colleague to summon medical help.

Looking on the top of the bureau, Morgado found a pair of regulation Lisbon Police hand cuffs, and in the top drawer of the bureau a badge with Luis Sanguino's number on it. He immediately called Gasparo, who was still at headquarters, trying to sort out the confusion of the night before.

"Auchlin is blond haired with a thin silver mustache, Jose," answered Gasparo. "Or at least was. But I don't care if the man you're looking at is a black man with green hair. And I don't care what his papers say, however genuine they appear. If he had Miss Meyers and Luis' badge and hand cuffs he is Hans Auchlin. Is he dying?"

"Hard to tell. At first we thought so, but he seems to be coming around some."

"I'll be there shortly. Don't move anything until I get there.

Gasparo was deeply relieved. He had put his career on the line when he went to the magistrate's home at 0530 this morning to seek a search warrant for the pension. After returning from the Clipper he had found a report from one of his detectives describing the interview with the concierge of Auchlin's pension. In the first place, the magistrate, irritated over the early hour, saw nothing in Gasparo's petition that couldn't wait until business hours Monday, the next day. Secondly, he thought Gasparo's evidence was too sketchy to be taken seriously. Ludke's sworn deposition was dismissed out of hand: too self-serving--"The man was desperate; he would have said anything. Besides, we might look like we're trying to pick on the Germans because of the matter with Salazar's niece," he had told Gasparo. Despite Salazar's efforts to muzzle the press, it was now common knowledge that his niece had been raped by a German officer, later found hanged in his cell.

Gasparo conceded to himself that the evidence might look tenuous, but he knew better. Hans Auchlin out of the pension one day and another German in the next? A woman screaming in the early afternoon, surely being tortured? No, it had been clear to Gasparo. The pension was not well known to foreigners and the likelihood of two different Germans letting a room in as many days was the clincher for Gasparo when he read the report. The run-down neighborhood of the pension would never be let by a typical German visitor--unless he was trying to avoid detection. After it became clear Gasparo wouldn't leave without his warrant, the magistrate gave in. Early Mass was just an hour away and he wanted another thirty minutes sleep.

Auchlin was semi-conscious, but he knew he was in serious trouble. He was having difficulty breathing and he could feel the painful irregularity of his heart. Though his mind was confused, he knew what happened. I've been killed by a Jew. A female Jew! Hate shot through his mind like a deadly venom. He desperately wanted to live. To take revenge.

Medical technicians were working feverishly over Auchlin when Gasparo arrived.

"Ah, yes this is indeed the good major," said Gasparo with a narrow smile as he stood over Auchlin, looking directly down at him.

Auchlin tried to raise his head, a glint of recognition in his eyes. Then, flecks of spittle formed at his mouth and soon he was foaming like a mad dog and he began convulsing. After one last groan he died. "I'm glad," Sylvia said in a low voice.

CHAPTER 29
LONDON

The Clipper was flying at two thousand feet, approximately ninety miles south of the English coast when swirling, angry, clouds of smoke, dark as ink, welled up in front of the cockpit window. The clouds plumed to heights of several thousand feet before they started dissipating.

"Bastards!" exclaimed an obviously agitated Tuck, who stood inside the entrance to the bridge looking at the land rushing toward them. He was jiggling up and down in place. It was 1240 and the Germans had just completed a massive raid on London, their first of the day and the heaviest to date. In addition to hitting the City of London itself and the Financial District, the bombs had struck oil storage facilities along the docks near Wapping, which now burned out of control.

"I don't like this, Captain. I've seen smoke like this last for half a day. Spooky. It's like midnight in the afternoon."

"The winds should tell us everything when we get there, Geoffrey," Westbrook said impatiently. Tuck's chatter was annoying him. "Any radio contact yet, Sparks?"

Between the American OSS and British MI-5, a portable, low frequency short-range radio transmitter had been set up at Victoria Tower Gardens, as close to the Thames as possible, to communicate with the Clipper. Two civilian air traffic frequencies in the lower spectrum had been assigned to the Clipper in hopes of avoiding the clatter of military communications during combat, interference which could pose serious problems during the Clipper's approach.

"Bit of crackle is all so far, Captain. We're a little far out yet, but I should have something in a few minutes."

As an evacuation precaution in case of a crash landing, Westbrook had Joanna and LaDieux take seats at the navigator's table in the Control Cabin. If it was necessary to ditch, all hands would be available to escape from the same station and assist each other in the process.

About fifty miles south of the coast Sparks was able to raise the Victoria Towers Garden. "Winds are out of the southwest at about five knots, Captain. Still some German bombers in the area, but all their fighters have retired. Coastal anti-aircraft in the south, as well as London, are on stand-down. Both landing sites have good visibility, and we're cleared at our discretion."

The news of the wind was good and bad. The direction accounted for why the smoke was blowing away from the landing area, but it also meant a downwind landing, decidedly unfavorable given the close margins of error.

Waters descended to 500 feet as he crossed the coast line and the western Dover Cliffs. Early afternoon thermals, created by the convergence of the cold water and warm shore line, bounced them up and down a few times. Evidence of the German attack was visible inland: smoking bomb craters and burning buildings dotted the countryside. Tuck cheered when he spotted the remains of a Bf-110 bomber which had crashed in an almost nose down position. "Nobody got out of that alive! Good show!"

As the London skyline rose before them, Westbrook returned to the controls while Tuck got his bearings, ready to assist as the landmarks hoved into view. Thirty miles from the city, Westbrook sighted the Thames and descended to 150 feet, reducing speed to 80 knots and tightening the throttles' friction locks. He wanted no slippage of the power settings. At Westbrook's request, Waters began the pre-landing check list.

"It's a bit snakelike from here on, Captain," Tuck said, pointing to the course of the Thames.

Passing over the Albert bridge, Tuck said, "Next one is Chelsea and then Vauxhall and Lambeth."

Westbrook eased the Clipper down to 100 feet where he began picking up thermals from the Thames. They were not extremely strong, but required that both he and Waters do some wrestling with the control wheel and rudders.

"OK, let's try the Lambeth approach." Westbrook started a left climbing bank to set up his final approach. He flew an extended down wind leg, trying to get a good reading on the winds by watching the Clipper's drift as it flew down the river. After several minutes he began a slow, shallow 180 degree turn back up the river.

The Lambeth Bridge stood seventy five feet over the river at its highest point, and Westbrook knew he couldn't be much higher when he passed over it and still land safely.

When the landing check list was completed they fell into strained silence. Two minutes from the Lambeth Bridge, Westbrook reduced power once again and descended to eighty feet. Sparks received the final barometric reading from the ground station, and reset the altimeters. Westbrook could only pray the reading was accurate, because he had to rely on it. As the bridge loomed closer it seemed from the cockpit that they were going to fly directly into it. Less than a half mile from the bridge, Westbrook eased back on the control wheel, and called for full flaps. As they extended, the Clipper ballooned slightly, barely missing the top of the bridge. Sparks Jenkins would swear later that he heard the bottom of the Clipper's hull scraping the suspension beams.

Past the bridge, Westbrook closed all four throttles to the full off position and the Clipper settled towards the water, bouncing off the thermals. At fifty feet there was a vicious cross-wind from the right, and Westbrook immediately dropped the right wing and applied full left rudder. As he struggled, the Clipper kept drifting left, edging close to the embankment. Finally, the aircraft landed with a sharp cracking noise, its right wing dipping close to the water. A huge fountain sprayed up from the river, covering the windscreen with water.

The two inboard engines were immediately shut down and the Clipper decelerated to a stop almost abeam the temporary mooring facilities. There were sighs of relief from everyone except LaDieux, who was airsick, clutching a paper bag Joanna had found.

"Good job, Curtis! I wouldn't have believed it if I hadn't been here. Greatest piece of flying I've ever seen," Tuck said excitedly. He pulled out a Havana cigar and bit the end off of it. Westbrook noticed Tuck's hands were shaking as he did so.

Westbrook slumped forward, drained. Relieved, he loosened his collar, stood up and asked Waters to handle the mooring operation. He left the bridge and stopped at Sparks' station to listen to the incoming radio traffic. "Germans still around here,

Captain, although the British feel the worst is over. They're sending a tug out to get us."

As soon as the Clipper was secured, Anderson opened the entry door to two Scotland Yard detectives waiting on a make-shift gang plank. The smell of burning oil crept into the main cabin, bringing back the night of the <u>Pegasus</u>. Otherwise, it was a cool early autumn day in London.

The detectives identified themselves as escorts for Mr. LaDieux and Miss Meyers.

LaDieux, Joanna and Westbrook joined the detectives.

"Looks like you've had a bad day here," Westbrook said.

One of the detectives smiled. "We have, sir, we have. But what the Germans dish out we'll repay twofold, you can bet your life on that."

As they left, an "all clear" siren sounded over a Royal Army band playing "La Marseillaise," in a shady corner of the Tower Gardens. Next to the band was a speaking platform, festooned with French Tri-Colors and Union Jack. Armed soldiers surrounded the platform. The siren stopped as the band struck up "God Save The King."

Joanna and Westbrook had not been able to talk privately, but they exchanged telling looks as they walked up the lawn. He tried not to have second thoughts about asking her to substitute for Sylvia, but it was difficult. At the same time, he was ecstatic at how much she was enjoying the play-acting, partly because of the challenge and partly because of her strong belief in making a contribution to the Allied cause.

An older detective met Westbrook as they reached the platform. "I'm Inspector Graves, Scotland Yard, Captain. I trust you had a pleasant flight? Now, Miss Meyers and Mr. LaDieux will be going off to meet General DeGaulle and Prime Minister Churchill, but first Mr. Churchill would like them to hold a press conference. Rankle Hitler as much as we can. Everything's set up. We've made arrangements for all of you at the Savoy, if you like. His Majesty's Government would be pleased."

Westbrook paused. Joanna loved London, or at least the pre-war city of theaters and clubs, as had he. But Joanna wasn't even Joanna--she was Sylvia Meyers, dedicated Communist and, so long as she was in London, the _cause celebre_ of the Allies. "Thanks very much, but the crew and I'll stay close to the Clipper. Besides, we had hoped to leave late this afternoon." Graves looked a bit surprised but said nothing. Instead, he led LaDieux and Joanna across to the platform where they were greeted by applause. The band swung into "The Stars and Stripes Forever" as Joanna and LaDieux waved to the crowd.

Westbrook regretted he had not been more adamant with LaDieux about leaving that day, but it was beside the point now, and the press conference wasn't going to help matters. Besides, he decided, his own concerns about a night landing in Lisbon shouldn't be much of a factor on a day as important as this one. Calm down, he told himself. You've made night landings before, and this won't be the last.

The rally for Ladieux and Meyers was a rousing success. Reporters and news photographers from around the free world were there to report the unprecedented showing of unity among the unlikely coalition of allies; including even the neutral U.S.. After an hour LaDieux and Joanna were whisked away to the Cabinet War Rooms where DeGaulle and Churchill were waiting for them. The press was told that a release, agreed to by all parties, would be issued after the meeting.

Joanna acquitted herself well during the press conference. She displayed poise and charm, and her performance so pleased LaDieux that he would later plead with her to stay and help raise money for the Resistance. (The Axis press, led by the _Deutsche Allgemeine Zeitung_, sarcastically denounced the meeting as the work of the gangster Roosevelt and his half-Jewish lackey, Churchill. DeGaulle was scornfully referred to as the "cowardly fugitive" whose only support came from the French criminal elements.) Everywhere else in Europe, however, the publicity created new hopes that America would soon enter the war and help liberate the darkened corridors of occupied Europe.

Tuck had gone to the Admiralty as soon as the press conference was over. Although it was Sunday, the old castle-like building at Whitehall was filled with people tracking shipping interests and troop movements. The Officer of the Day was an acquaintance of Tuck's, and he promptly got him permission to return to Lisbon on the Clipper.

Tuck looked like he was in a grim mood when he returned to the Clipper.

"You look upset Geoffrey," said Westbrook softly, remembering the time when he thought Tuck was near tears during the flight over.

Tuck bit his quivering lip, his eyes brimming with tears. He could hardly speak.

"Friend of mine at the Admiralty told me the Germans...," Tuck paused a moment, unable to continue. Tears were running down his cheeks.

Tuck blew his nose, and said, "Sorry, Captain. An unarmed Imperial Airways Sunderland flying boat used by the Royal Navy for anti-submarine patrols, was shot down by Germans over the Indian Ocean two days earlier. All the crew were lost. They were all friends...," his voice trailed off. After a few moments, he said in a voice trembling with rage, "If I ever get the chance I'll murder every German that crosses my path. In cold blood, mind you."

Westbrook put his hand on Tuck's shoulder. "You have to let go, Geoffrey. Otherwise, you'll find yourself living and reliving it. It's going to happen again, and it won't be any easier. Fight the good fight and that'll be your revenge."

Concerned about possible structural damage from the landing Westbrook ordered an inspection of the starboard side. He declined to refuel from a lighter in the Thames. The less they weighed the better the chances for a successful takeoff. Besides, no sense taking a chance on fuel that might be contaminated. Waters calculated they had enough fuel for Lisbon and a twenty minute reserve.

Shortly after the press conference broke up, a Navy lieutenant commander sought out Westbrook. He handed him a sealed envelope.

"Afternoon, Commander. Ambassador Kennedy asked me to deliver this to you with his best wishes."

Westbrook took out a folded message which read:

"The actions of you and your crew, and the gallant efforts of Mr. LaDieux and Miss Meyers, have impressed

the world. While it is still early morning as I write this,
you must know the tremendous personal pride I have in
all of you. Best wishes for a safe return.
                                        Sincerely,
                                        F.D.R."

Westbrook wondered about the possible ramifications once it was learned that Joanna had posed as Sylvia Meyers. He shrugged his shoulders. What's done's done.

Onboard the Clipper he was relieved to learn there had been no damage to the structural integrity. The waiting game resumed.

Westbrook ate a box lunch with Anderson, Waters and Tuck, sharing the message from Roosevelt.

At 1545 there was still no sign of the two celebrities. Westbrook resigned himself to a night landing. What he couldn't do, though, was execute a take-off in the dark from the Thames. The prospect of waiting until dawn was unsettling.

Tuck must have been reading his mind. "What do you reckon is taking so long?" he asked, now composed.

"Don't know. Just hope it's progress. Let's get the pre-flighting underway down to starting engines. I'll go check the weather."

The latest report showed no cloud cover over the Atlantic to Lisbon and a new moon rising. Winds still prevailed from the southwest, so the Clipper could expect head winds all the way of five to eight knots. The sea was relatively calm. Good flying conditions.

The shadows were lengthening over Parliament and the river when Joanna returned alone. She was euphoric: DeGaulle had persuaded LaDieux to stay in London. The flight crew, busy preparing for takeoff, were anxious to hear about the meeting. "I'll tell you guys all about it as soon as we take off. Captain Westbrook has that serious look about him, so I know better than to distract you now. Seriously, though, it was spectacular. You would have thought General DeGaulle and Pierre were long lost brothers. It went very smoothly, and some good things will come of it. I'm confident of that."

CHAPTER 30
LONDON TO LISBON

Westbrook and crew had an uneventful take off to the west, leveling off at two thousand feet before putting the Clipper on auto-pilot. They chased the sun, which would keep it light just a little longer.

Joanna, Tuck and the crew were relaxed and basking in their accomplishments. Joanna began rattling off her tales of DeGaulle and Churchill: "The Prime Minister is a real bear, but more teddy than grizzly. DeGaulle was stiff and terribly humorless, but he appreciated the significance of Pierre's visit. It will give him more clout in France than he's had before." Her face fell when she was interrupted by radio static on the international distress channel.

"Pan American Yankee Clipper, this is Fighter Command, Biggin Hill radio, do you read? Over."

Westbrook scrambled back to the bridge as Sparks picked up the microphone, and said, "Biggin Hill, Yankee Clipper, we read you. Over."

The voice of the English controller was filled with fatigue. "Right, Yankee Clipper. Our RDF picked up some fast- moving bandits over the Channel which appear to be headed in your direction. They were too far south and east for us to get a number. Don't mean to alarm you, but the Germans may be up to mischief. We've got four Spits headed your way, just in case. Keep a sharp lookout, and stay on this channel."

Westbrook started looking for cloud cover. There was none as far away as the horizon. "Geoffrey, station yourself in the astral bubble and keep an eye peeled," he ordered. The bubble was the only place they could see from the top and to the rear.

Just enough light remained to spot moving objects.

After several minutes Tuck reported over the intercom, "I see something coming in at six o'clock high, Curtis."

Darkness closed in, but Westbrook knew it did them no good because their four engines' exhaust flames were collectively as bright as the North Star. When he turned to the navigator's table to check on her, he saw Joanna still sitting there, head bowed. He was furious with himself for suggesting that she do something this dangerous.

Then, he was startled by a flash of light on his left. The profile of a German fighter loomed as close as he could without having his tail sheared off by the Clipper's propellers. The pilot flashed morse code by a hand-held lamp.

"He's ordering us to land," Westbrook said to Tuck, who had just returned to the bridge. "Says he'll shoot us down in five minutes if we don't comply."

"Bastards!" he answered. "Don't do it, Westbrook. The RAF'll be here soon enough. Besides, those bloody Jerries don't have enough fuel to stick around."

It had been nearly ten minutes since Sparks had given the RAF flight their coordinates. There had been radio silence since.

Westbrook weighed his options. His choices were biased in favor of whatever gave Joanna the best chance of getting out alive. If they want us to land that's not the end of the story. Machine gun us in the water? Too dark for that if we shut the engines down. Besides, it was easy enough to do that right now. More sport, too. Submarine? The last thought made his blood run cold, but what else could it be? He had a fleeting image of grimy Germans raping Joanna in their darkened U-boat. He decided to buy time, relying on Tuck's observation about the German fuel problem. "Geoffrey's right. They're going to have to turn back soon. We'll stall for a few minutes. Powell, start the check list, just in case."

Westbrook saw the Spitfires as they approached from the north. It looked like they surprised the Germans, but they overshot both the German planes and the Clipper, and were now in high-g turns back to the fray. One German plane had been caught by lucky shots from an English pilot as he finished clearing his guns. Westbrook could see the German aircraft as it flamed into the sea.

The remaining German Me 109s wasted no time. They each made a run on the Clipper, guns blazing. As the last German aircraft finished his run and began his turn home, Westbrook caught sight of several huge phosphorous parachute flares descending slowly towards the Atlantic. He knew they were markers for the submarine.

As the RAF aircraft departed the area to give chase to the Germans, the bridge crew of the Clipper could hear an RAF pilot radioing the Air-Sea rescue service that the Clipper was on fire and apparently going down. After a brief pause, the RAF pilot could be heard giving Air-Sea the coordinates of the Clipper's location.

After the initial burst from the Germans, the Clipper's two inboard engines burst into flames.

The attack by the Me-109s caused heavy damage to the Clipper. The second burst hit the astral bubble, shattering it just after Tuck had left. The third burst raked the wings and fuselage, damaging the aileron controls in the starboard wing so that the plane fell off sharply to the right, shuddering as it rapidly lost altitude. Shrapnel shattered the right side of the windscreen and Waters was sprayed with glass fragments, causing superficial though vivid and painful lacerations. He could barely see with the wind blowing his own blood into his eyes, and he moaned and wiped his eyes as though trying to scratch sand away. Maps, charts and debris blew around throughout the cockpit.

Westbrook grappled with the control wheel to keep them from crashing. The fuselage was vibrating so hard he feared the aircraft might break up.

Finally level at 300 feet, Westbrook continued struggling to stay airborne, hoping for at least a controlled crash.

"We've got to stay away from those damn flares," Westbrook said, strain heavy in his voice. "Those bastards have marked our position."

The burning engines had been feathered as soon as they caught fire and the fire in the port engine seemed to be contained, but the starboard engine fire was out of control, making it seem like daylight in the cockpit. Anderson picked up a portable fire extinguisher and eased himself into the right wing crawlway.

Westbrook successfully maneuvered the Clipper several hundred yards beyond the flares, but landing seemed inevitable. There was no way to predict the extent of the damage to the control surfaces, and the Clipper might stop flying on its own if the damage kept spreading. It continued to vibrate violently. His night vision had been momentarily destroyed by the light of the flares and the burning engine. He was struggling to regain his depth perception.

Now flying the Clipper alone, Westbrook pushed the flap lever to full down and turned on the landing lights. In the last few seconds of the approach the Clipper stalled, and pancaked into the water hard, shaking up everyone onboard. Sea water splashed up over the right wing, helping to dampen the still burning engine fire, but Anderson, still in the crawlway, was pitched forward and hit his head on the engine fire wall, knocking him unconscious. His efforts had helped, but the fire was not out and began to spread again, despite the sea water.

Joanna picked herself up and found the first aid kit to minister what assistance she could to Waters. Except for the radios and internal lighting Westbrook shut everything down as Tuck inched into the wing crawlway to check on Anderson.

Sparks raised an English shore station on the international distress channel and was advised an ocean going tug and destroyer escort had been dispatched, but were at least two hours away.

"Ask if we can get some more fighter protection, tell them about the flare drops. The Germans must have some follow-up in mind, probably a submarine!" Westbrook yelled as he and Joanna moved Waters to the floor of the Control Cabin. Westbrook looked at Joanna, and winced. The thought of her being a German prisoner was more than he could handle. The facts seemed hard to deny. The Germans probably thought LaDieux was onboard and they were determined to get him, even at the risk of provoking the United States. For some reason this made him feel better, but he knew they had a battle on their hands.

Everyone worked feverishly. Sparks set up an omni-directional intermittent SOS on the short range radio in the hope that another friendly surface vessel might be closer than those just dispatched. The signal was an invitation to any German submarine also, but that was considered a <u>fait accompli</u> anyway.

Westbrook rechecked the engineer's and pilots' panels to ensure that their power drainage was as low as possible.

"Brits report negative on the additional fighter protection, Captain," reported Sparks. "Says the RAF needs the night to make repairs for tomorrow."

Westbrook shook his head in disgust. Who the hell they think we're doing this for?

Tuck came in supporting a shaky Anderson, both coughing and filthy from the smoke. "Fire's still smoldering in the wing. Looks like it may be trying to spread," Tuck said.

"Engine's pretty tore up, Captain. Nothing we can do about it until we get to a full repair facility, so far as I can tell. Sure wouldn't hurt to have George look at it, though."

Westbrook dispatched Benson to the starboard wing to finish off the fire and assess the damage.

"Right, Captain, but you need to know we've got a small leak below the water line just forward of section four, Captain, and the bow compartment is taking on water. Won't sink us anytime soon, but there'll be hell to pay if we don't takeoff in the next hour or so. Our center of gravity will be too screwed up to lift off."

Westbrook unbattened the hatch between the pilots' seats and went down the short ladder to the anchor compartment. He opened the outside hatch and began rigging a bilge pump. It would drain the airplane's meager electricity, but he had no choice. Once it was ready for operation, Westbrook plugged the leak as best he could and started the pump. After a few moments, the water was going out faster than it was trickling in.

He sat back on his heels in gratification and looked around. He could see nothing but the stars overhead and an occasional iridescent wave. It was silent except for waves lapping against the Clipper.

He climbed back up to the bridge so he could see if the last of the fire was out. Progress, he thought to himself. We're making progress.

Now there was little to do but wait.

Everyone gathered in the Control Cabin. "My guess is they want us alive, so they'll have to get a boarding party from the submarine over here." On that premise, Westbrook issued instructions for repelling the Germans, and everyone disbursed to their assigned station.

Sparks saw it first. Peering about fifty yards off the starboard bow, he spotted a large raft gliding through the water. It was still too far away to tell how many people were on board, but he thought he saw several figures hunched down in the raft. Scrambling, he secured the forward bow hatch, leaving just enough room for the bilge pump to continue operating.

He climbed the ladder and ran to the Lounge where Westbrook and Tuck were shoring up both entry doors.

"There coming, Captain. Just spotted them about fifty yards off the port bow. Large raft, but I can't tell how many there are."

Hearing Spark's report, Westbrook took the stairs two at the time, went to the bridge and whispered, "Seen anything yet? Sparks spotted..." Just then Westbrook spotted a motorized rubber boat with four figures in black wet suits on board. Automatic weapons, covered in water-proof skins, were strapped across their chests.

Clutching the sub-machine gun, Westbrook toyed with the idea of opening fire through the broken windscreen, but thought better of it. He held some slim hope that there was room for negotiations. Anyhow, even if they could stop these Germans their comrades, who were surely nearby, would no doubt make short shift of everybody on the Clipper.

In the Lounge the men began shifting the previously erected barricade of seats, metal pantry shelves and boxes from the cargo hold from the right to the left door. Westbrook turned up the cabin lights as high as auxiliary power allowed to destroy the Germans' night vision when they entered. He knew the barricade would only be a temporary block, but it could buy them time.

"See anything more up there?" he asked the bridge on the crew intercom.

"No," Waters answered. "They worked their way around to the left just a few minutes ago and then disappeared."

Westbrook was tempted to ask for Joanna, but bit his lip and rang off instead. "They should be here any minute."

His hunch was right. The Germans were going for the left

door.

For minutes, the silence was overpowering. Then there was a muffled noise outside the cabin door, as though somebody was lightly pounding on it. "They're going to blow the bloody thing!" Tuck said.

The explosives blew the cabin door inward. Westbrook saw a German step inside the cabin. He looked around, then lobbed a concussion grenade into the forward part of the Lounge, and retreated to the sponson, shouting, "The interior is fully lighted! It may be a trap!"

The concussion grenade went off, stunning Westbrook, who had been behind the second row of seats forward of the door. He dropped the sub-machine gun and fell to his knees. If these guys wanted to do us in that would have been a fragmentation grenade, he thought through a dull haze. Groggily, he picked up the sub-machine gun and aimed it at the entrance.

"Hallo," the German said haltingly after several minutes, waving a white scarf just inside the cabin door. "We are soldiers of the Third Reich. We would like fifteen minutes of armistice to discuss our demands. I'm the commanding officer, and I'll come aboard unarmed, while the others wait in the boat. No shots will be fired while the armistice is in effect."

Westbrook felt a change in momentum. Ordering his men to stay in position, Westbrook answered, "All right. Fifteen minutes. I should tell you we're armed and there are more of us than you. Any false move, and you'll be shot."

The German stepped into the cabin with his hands over his head. He blinked in the unaccustomed light and appeared startled to see Westbrook, pointing the Thompson at his chest. "Dieters, Captain. Oberleutnant Dieters. I thought we had an agreement. No weapons."

"Not quite correct, lieutenant. <u>You</u> said no shots would be fired and that <u>you</u> would come onboard unarmed. Your air force fighters shot us down, you've blown a part of my plane away, and now you want to talk protocol. Get on with it or I <u>will</u> shoot you!"

"Very well, Captain. We are under orders to take you and your countrymen, as well as the Frenchman LaDieux, back to

Germany. I assure you that no harm will come to anyone if you follow instructions."

"What about the Clipper? Just let it drift in the Atlantic?"

There was a long pause. Dieters lowered his hands and rubbed his palms together nervously. "Regrettably, it must be destroyed."

Westbrook looked at his watch. "You've got less than ten minutes and you're making less sense all the time." Westbrook sensed that Dieters was confused and uncertain about what to do next. Probably didn't expect the resistance to be this firm.

After several moments of silence, Dieters shifted his weight, looked around the inside of the cabin and said, "Perhaps we can strike a bargain. LaDieux is a fugitive from justice. It's not right that Americans harbor him. Turn him over to us and we'll depart. Our airplane is about two hundred meters from here. We can go quickly."

Westbrook couldn't believe it. Airplane! This is incredible. There's no sub after all! He had a split second to make a decision but his spirits were soaring. Dieters and three men in the rubber boat, probably freezing their asses right now, were the attack force. If the Germans found out LaDieux wasn't on board, would they go back empty handed? He doubted it. Taking a step closer to Dieters and pointing the Thompson directly at his chest, Westbrook said, "Regrettably, my orders are to take Mr. LaDieux to Lisbon, so it sure looks like we're at some kind of an impasse here. Let me suggest you and your men surrender peaceably. Leave your weapons here and go back to your airplane and we'll call it even. You're outnumbered, and we're not going to give in to any of your demands. If you attack you're just leading your men to their own deaths."

Westbrook could see that Tuck, who was standing directly behind Dieters, was becoming increasingly agitated by the presence of the German officer. Tuck's face wore a scowl, and he seemed to seethe every time Dieters said something, as if it was too much for him to bear. Westbrook remembered Tuck saying something about killing Germans "in cold blood" every time he could while telling about his dead colleagues in the unarmed Sunderland flying boat. He had a narrow smile on his face, but

Westbrook knew he was serious.

Dieters forced a smile. "We cannot agree to your request, Captain. We have enough plastique affixed to your airplane to create an explosion that will be seen for miles. Think about it. I see my time is up. Auf Wiedersehen, Captain."

As Dieters turned to leave, Tuck pulled his Webley service revolver from his belt, and fired at Dieters. The bullet struck Dieters in the chest, dangerously close to his heart. He spun around, hitting the barricade, creating a loud clanging noise as he fell to the floor. "I've been shot!" he shouted in German.

"Damnit, Geoffrey, we didn't need that!" Westbrook exclaimed angrily, jumping to the other side of the cabin in the expectation of another grenade. The cabin lights began dimming, as the auxiliary power ran low.

Using the turmoil and dimming lights as cover, Anderson and Jenkins repositioned themselves behind chairs on either side of the entry door so they could put Germans trying to enter in a cross fire.

Suddenly, the cabin lights went out. Westbrook planned to shoot from right to left as he inched his way past Dieters, counting on Jenkins and Anderson to cover him. The German was begging him for help. "Just as soon as your men surrender, Lieutenant," Westbrook replied in a less than assuring way.

He fired a short burst from the sub-machine gun as close to the side of the Clipper as he dared. There was a sound of a body hitting the water, then the rapid tattoo of a Sten-gun firing in the automatic position just outside the cabin door. A slug hit Westbrook in the left shoulder, knocking him to the floor of the cabin. He dropped the sub-machine gun in the darkness and his flashlight tumbled away. Now, there are only two left. We should be able to deal with them. Light headed and disoriented, he worked his way to his feet with his right hand and pulled his .38 out of its holster.

Another concussion grenade arched through the doorway, only managing to stun Dieters, but then, two men firing Sten-guns darted into the cabin. The darkness had given the advantage back to the Germans.

Both Westbrook and Tuck fired but missed their targets.

Only the sound of Dieters' labored breathing could be heard until the two Germans began spraying the cabin with more gunfire. Jenkins was hit in the back, and seriously wounded.

As he tried to reposition himself, Westbrook saw the muzzle flash from one of the Sten-guns and fired toward it. There was a cry of pain.

Westbrook had one last idea. He needed some time and luck, but it was probably the only chance left. His shoulder wound was bleeding badly and he worried he'd pass out soon if he didn't get it stopped. Laboriously, he worked his way up the staircase to the Control Cabin, using the stair railing to pull himself up each step. The Germans were unfamiliar with the interior of the Clipper and probably didn't know the stairway existed. He found what he wanted in the back of the navigator's chair and made his way back down. He took a deep breath and shouted the word "Very!" and fired an emergency VERY flare into the ceiling. He took a terrible risk, including that of setting a fire, but there was no time left for this game of attrition.

The flare momentarily blinded everyone, but as it fell Westbrook saw the only non-wounded German standing between the front row of seats gaping with surprise. When he realized what had happened he wheeled on Westbrook and fired, then turned on Jenkins with a short burst and killed him before Anderson and Tuck could open fire. It was Anderson who took him out with a single bullet in the head.

"Lights," Westbrook directed faintly. He'd been hit in the back of the neck with shrapnel. "We need lights."

Anderson turned his flashlight to the front of the cabin. The soldier who had been wounded by Westbrook opened fire at it, hitting Anderson in the throat. The flashlight rolled under the seat behind him. A repeated clicking of a trigger told Westbrook the German was out of ammunition. He slowly walked toward the soldier with the empty gun, who was on his knees, trying to reload. Pointing his pistol at the kneeling soldier, Westbrook said, "Lieutenant Dieters, if you can hear me, order your man to surrender or we're going to throw each of you into the ocean feet first. All of you will be dead and you'll be the first to go."

Dieters moaned. "Ubergen! Ubergen! We surrender. Help

us!"

The thuds of two guns on the cabin floor was reassuring for the Americans, but they remained wary.

"Any more weapons?" Westbrook asked.

"No."

"Plastique?"

"In the boat. Only in the boat."

"Radio?"

"In the boat."

Westbrook picked up the PA intercom. "It`s over, Powell, but we've got three dead and three wounded. A pistol flare started a fire in the ceiling. It may be burning out, but bring down what's left of the fire extinguisher. Also, bring down some flashlights and the first aid kit. We'll need to start an engine to get the power going. I want Joanna to stay on the bridge until we get the prisoners secure. Please leave her your pistol." Realizing he was starting to faint, Westbrook dropped the phone, and sat down in the front row of the cabin, then tried to get up, but without success. He had passed out when Waters arrived.

CHAPTER 31
THE ATLANTIC OCEAN

When Westbrook awoke early the next morning, hazy light filled the cabin from the blown door of the entry way. A heavy fog clung to the sea. He yawned and rubbed his eyes. A man he didn't recognize was leaning over him and applying a new bandage to his left shoulder. He felt the steady dull ache of his shoulder. A blood soaked bandaged lay in the seat next to him.

"Good morning, Captain Westbrook. I'm Dr. Peters, a surgeon in the Royal Navy. Shoulder's going to be fine, but it'll smart rather badly for the next day or so, I'm afraid. Bullet went straight through. No permanent damage. Would you like a coffee or something?" There was a heavy medicinal smell of ether and iodine emanating from Peters.

Groggily, Westbrook said, "What's going on?"

Drawing himself up cautiously, he saw Joanna next to him, sleeping in a fully reclined seat. Tuck handed him a steaming mug and a stale croissant. He looked pale, his face still grimy from the engine fire. "It's good to see you almost up and about, Curtis. Guess I've got some explaining and apologizing..."

"No. No second guessing. But for the love of Heaven what happened after I passed out?" He tried moving sideways, but winced in pain and decided it was not a good idea.

Tuck described the final scenario. Both Jenkins and Anderson were dead--their remains had been transferred to the destroyer escort for refrigeration pending shipment back to the States. Westbrook bowed his head, deeply saddened at the news of his fellow crew members' deaths. One of the German soldiers, wounded earlier, was also dead by the time the lights came back on, after number one engine was started. The German leader, Dieters, was alive when the shooting stopped, but died before the Royal Navy arrived. The third German, wounded slightly, was locked in the crew's cabin until the British arrived. No sign was found of the German shot in the raft.

Tuck went on to describe how, about an hour later, a tug boat and a destroyer escort came along side. They surprised the

261

German seaplane pilot, who was then taken prisoner along with the other German survivor. "The Heinkel, or whatever the hell they call it, is tied astern of the destroyer escort as a nice prize for the Royal Navy, and with your permission we'd like to rig the tug so the Clipper can be towed to England for repairs."

"Out of the question," Westbrook shot back. He thought the Clipper would be too vulnerable as a target for German bombers if it was tied up along the English coast. "Can we fly the damn thing out of here? Is George Benson OK?"

"He's fine. He's been busy all morning checking and making repairs, humming all the while. Must be a good sign."

"Good. Then, I'll want a damage report as quickly as possible, and as soon as I can make an inspection we'll decide what to do. Anybody from the destroyer escort on board that I can talk with to get the lay of the land on the Germans?"

"Thought you'd never ask," said a familiar voice in the dim background of the cabin.

"Commander Stacey? Is that you?" Westbrook propped himself up on his good elbow.

"One and the same, Captain. One good turn deserves another, I'd say."

Smiling, Stacey said "Seems like a hundred years ago, doesn't it?"

Stacey told Westbrook that after the sinking of the Pegasus, the Admiralty planned to court-martial him, but because of the events stemming from the Clipper's landing and rescue, a reluctant Board of Enquiry issued a letter of reprimand instead. "Never make admiral, but I can stay in at least until the end of the war. Even got another command."

Their talk woke Joanna. She stretched and squeezed Westbrook's hand. "So glad you're OK." She leaned over and kissed him on the cheek.

With Stacey's help Westbrook got to his feet. "Are we sitting ducks out here?"

"Don't think so," Stacey answered. "We're pretty far south for the fighters, we hit the Germans pretty good yesterday, so they're probably licking their wounds today or else their bombers will find out it's a mistake to bother us. Fighter Command has stationed as many fighters as it can spare to provide an umbrella for us around the clock until we're out of here. On a personal note, though, I wish you'd come back to England with us."

Learning of the fighter protection buoyed Westbrook's spirits. "Thanks, we'll see. I guess I'd better check around and see what kind of shape this baby is really in."

The interior was in shambles. The heat of the Very flare had scorched and melted much of the kapok and spun glass wool sound-proofing in the ceiling, although it had fortunately died without spreading. The air was foul, however, from the stench of the burned materials. Bullet holes were everywhere, along with deep blood stains on the carpet.

Westbrook caught up with Chief Mechanic Benson. "What's the verdict, George? Before you answer you should know I'm determined to fly this lady out of here if it's at all possible."

Benson, who had been checking a small leak, stood up and said, "Not as bad as it looks, Captain. The big leak in the bow compartment looks OK, thanks to you. It needs further work but it'll be fine until we can get back to Lisbon. I'll need to bail some water before take off, but that's no big deal. All the engines are operable except number three. With the light load and the sea looking like a mill pond right now we should be able to make it. It'll be windy in the cabin without the door, but I suppose everybody could ride upstairs. I don't know, Captain, it's your call, but you`ll get no complaints from me if you decide to do it."

"Great!" Westbrook clapped him on the shoulder and went upstairs to the Control Cabin. Dr. Peters had just finished placing small bandages on Waters' cuts. Although there were some slight scratches on his eyes, his vision wasn't seriously impaired.

"Everything in the cockpit checks out fine, Captain," Waters said. "Hope you're planning to give it a try."

Pouring himself a cup of coffee from a thermos Joanna had brought upstairs, Westbrook scanned the panels. "Mr. Benson and Captain Waters say they'll ride with me. Anybody else?" The other two made it unanimous.

"Geoffrey, you could ride back to England on the destroyer escort with Commander Stacey. No need for you to fly all the way to Lisbon and then come right back."

"I was afraid you'd think of that. Unfortunately, I'm in love with this airplane and besides, I get seasick on those smaller boats. If it's all the same to you I'd like to carry on here. The Admiralty's already approved it."

"That's settled then. Powell, I'll assist you as much as I can, but this left arm isn't going to let me handle the takeoff or landing by myself." He rubbed his right hand over the prominent black stubble on his face. "I'm going to shave and say goodby to Commander Stacey. In the meantime, start the pre-flight check list. I'll be back as soon as I can."

When the British destroyer escort found the Clipper it was drifting southward. The crew of the Seraphim were able to jury-rig lines from a powered life boat to secure the Clipper through its nose mounted cleats and stop its drift. The lifeboat was used to commute between the two vessels.

Stacey had several dispatches for Westbrook. The Royal Navy--through its dispersed fleet--had advised the U.S.Navy of the Clipper's location and predicament. The U.S. Navy, in turn, had notified Washington and Pan American in New York.

Westbrook eased himself into a cabin seat to read the cables. The first was a long one from Sikes. It began by praising his airmanship on the Thames, and described Pan Am's great pride in the entire crew. Sikes then gave his arguments for why the Clipper should be towed to England. Good old Charlie must be reading my mind. But Sikes was ignoring the threat of German air attacks while the Clipper was in repair. Maybe Charlie's right and I'm paranoid, thought Westbrook.

Another cable was a copy of a letter delivered to the German Ambassador in Washington expressing the outrage of the United States for the attack on a neutral, unarmed aircraft over international waters. It ended with the intention to retaliate if such an incident were repeated. The message was signed by President Roosevelt.

Finally, there was a short congratulatory note from Di Gates. "Don`t be surprised if you get your second Navy Cross this time."

Wincing as he stood up, Westbrook said, "Commander, we're going to try it. How long will it take you to cast us off and get clear?" The sound of the number one engine turning over at idle could be heard, and the smell of gasoline exhaust wafted through the wide open entry door.

"Oh, not too long. I'd say twenty minutes or so."

"Fine. Let's start. I'd appreciate your radioing our flight plan to London and Lisbon." He handed Stacey a short, hand-written plan on a crumpled piece of passenger stationery. "Not too much to say," Westbrook said. "We're going to be limping along at about two-thirds our normal cruising speed, but we don't have that far to go."

Stacey saluted, and they shook hands with promises of getting together after the war. As Stacey deplaned Westbrook returned to the bridge. Never took the time to shave, he thought, laughing to himself. The three good engines had been started, and Benson had put up some tightly drawn transparent cheese cloth on the right side of the windscreen to limit the full impact of the slip stream in Waters' face.

As Westbrook was completing the adjustment of the cowl flaps the Seraphim hove into view, the bridge lamp blinking an "All clear and Godspeed." The Heinkel float plane was being towed from the stern of the ship.

As soon as the wake from Seraphim subsided, Westbrook told Waters to swing into the wind, start a high speed taxi and check the rudders as the Clipper's speed accelerated.

Waters carefully applied power, turning slightly to the left to head into the wind. He had to use heavy left rudder to compensate for the asymmetrical thrust resulting from the dead engine on the right wing. As they gained speed, Westbrook carefully checked the instruments and listened for unusual sounds. There were slight vibrations from the starboard wing, but nothing as severe as last night. The controls were fully operative. When the aircraft reached takeoff speed Westbrook said, "OK, let's do it. She's ready to fly." With Westbrook's help, Waters eased back on the control wheel. The Clipper climbed the step and broke free. Everyone cheered.

As the Clipper climbed through one thousand feet Westbrook spotted two aircraft closing from the one o'clock position. Tensing, he warned, "Two airplanes closing on us from the right. Keep a sharp lookout."

The two aircraft came within two miles of the Clipper and suddenly climbed sharply, each doing a victory roll in the opposite direction. Westbrook saw the elliptical wings and knew they were RAF Spitfires. "Thanks, guys," he said softly.

CHAPTER 32
LISBON

The Yankee Clipper was over Lisbon at approximately 1630 on Monday, September 16th. The aircraft gradually descended and made a smooth landing about three miles off shore. A tug boat had to tow the crippled aircraft to its moorings, a laborious process which took over an hour.

As the Clipper approached the pier, Westbrook could see the ground personnel of Pan American and the flight crew of the Dixie Clipper, which had arrived as a scheduled flight from New York an hour earlier, standing near the mooring site. Just out of sight, Sylvia Meyers and Inspector Gasparo waited together in the parking area.

When the Clipper was finally secured, Westbrook pled the need for a bath and a shave and left Waters in command to oversee the Clipper's final landing check list. He deplaned first, helping Joanna negotiate the step down to the gangplank as best he could.

Sylvia rushed up and embraced Joanna. She started to hug Westbrook, but was stopped by the blood on his shirt. Westbrook said, "Don't worry about me," embracing her with his good arm. "Everything's fine, but how about you? How did you get that ugly welt under your eye?"

She broke down in tears. "I'll have to tell you later. I'm so happy you and Joanna are all right." Sylvia dabbed her eyes and hugged Joanna again.

The Pan American Station Manager shook hands with Westbrook. "Congratulations, Captain. We are all very proud of you. I'm very sorry to tell you but the Aviz is full for the next several days, so we've booked you into the Hotel Avenida Palace in Restauradores Square. It's old, but quite nice. We hope you don't mind."

"Sure, that's fine," Westbrook said as he turned to Gasparo and embraced him.

At Gasparo's request, the Company had radioed the Clipper earlier, advising the crew that Sylvia was safe and Holloran's suspected killer was dead. "At last, amigo. At last," Gasparo said, smiling wider then Westbrook could remember. He thought Gasparo had shed ten years since they had been at La Cintra Airport.

At the Avenida Palace Hotel, Westbrook learned that there was a spare engine available in Lisbon, so the Clipper's down time was estimated to be no more than five working days. Further, he was ordered to stay in Lisbon to command the flight home, his medical condition permitting. He laughed when he was informed that the Company now wanted the trip home to be operated as a revenue flight.

Westbrook more than welcomed the time off to rest and--finally--have time alone with Joanna. Sylvia had booked the Thursday flight out but snafus with her replacement passport caused her to miss it, so she'd be going home with Westbrook and Joanna.

Reams of cables arrived. Joanna had one from President Roosevelt advising her that she was being awarded the Distinguished Service Medal for her outstanding service to her country. Sylvia had a similar cable, citing her "conspicuous bravery" in the face of hostile forces. Westbrook was being recommended for his second Navy Cross. The President planned to have a formal ceremony at the White House. With an eye on the upcoming election, Roosevelt wanted to have the ceremony before the voters went to the polls. Public support for what they had all done continued to grow.

"We've got to celebrate," Westbrook told Joanna over dinner in the hotel.

Nodding her agreement, she said, "I'll speak to the concierge and put something together for tomorrow night."

It was a joyous celebration, when Joanna, Sylvia, Tuck and Westbrook met for dinner at the Tavares Rico. The restaurant had the ambience of a fine old palace. Gasparo was there too, the guest of Pan American Airways Systems.

Champagne flowed throughout dinner. Tuck stood up and proposed toasts to the "two most courageous women" in the world. Then, Tuck said solemnly, "If I live to be a hundred I know I shall never see the likes of the bravery and courage of this man. A skilled airman, to be sure. But, most important, a great and wonderful friend. Godspeed to you and Joanna always."

Patrons of the normally sedate restaurant turned their heads, curious about a loud standing ovation coming from a table for five.

After the toasts Westbrook glanced at Joanna. Her smile told him it was time to leave. Still standing, he excused them from the group, bidding each a fond farewell.

Walking hand in hand down the avenue towards the hotel, the two didn't speak for several minutes, each lost in their own thoughts of the unrequited love they shared.

"Funny thing," Westbrook said as they turned the corner onto Restauradores Square. "Inspector Gasparo asked me if I had any regrets about all that's happened. For some reason I recalled a quote from Colonel Roosevelt my father repeated so often it's seared in my brain like it was yesterday:

'Far better is it to dare mighty things, to win glorious triumphs, even though checkered by failure, than to take rank with those poor spirits who neither enjoy much nor suffer much because they live in the gray twilight that knows not victory nor defeat.'

ABOUT THE AUTHOR

Sid Davis is a graduate of the U.S. Naval Academy and a former Naval Aviator. He is a multi-rated commercial pilot and has a passion for flying. <u>MURDER IN LISBON</u> was meticulously researched. Davis was given a copy of the operating manual for the Clipper by the Boeing Company, which helped enhance the flying scenes in the book. Davis is a lawyer and lives with his wife in Naples, Florida.